D1475664

The Merrow *of* Lake Michigan

CLAIRE O. FAHEY

Madison Ready Publishing

Pleasanton, CA

MRP
Madison Ready Publishing
www.madisonready.com
8300 Black Avenue #93
Pleasanton, CA 94566
madisonready@hotmail.com

ISBN: 978-0-9914329-0-5

Printed in the U.S.A.

Cover design by Derek Murphy at creativeindie.com
Cover photo by Jamie Link at jamielinkphotography.com
Interior design by 52 Novels at 52novels.com

For John Ready who always wanted to write a novel, and Mary Frances who championed my effort to do so.

History, real solemn history, I cannot be interested in .... The quarrels of popes and kings, with wars and pestilences in every page; the men all so good for nothing, and hardly any women at all.

—*Jane Austen*

What is past is prologue.

—*William Shakespeare*

Chapter One
Before the Fall

December 23, 1992

She was aware of two things. The holes were small and there was very little blood. That had to be a good sign. Someone yelled—was still yelling—about a gun.

Three holes, *but so small*. She pressed against them, thinking it would help, her eyes locked on Martin.

"Joey, I can't breathe." His words fast and ragged, spoken with none of his usual confidence. His clutch on her arm was tight, desperate.

"Easy. Stay with me," she whispered, lips just touching his ear, masking her fright with proximity. How bad could it be?

Very bad. All three hit his chest.

"Hear the sirens?" Joey cradled him, hoping to warm him. "Help is coming. Stay with me." Blood passed between her fingers, and cooled fast in the winter air.

Please God. Not now. Not yet.

Martin pushed against the snow, trying to move, pulling in air, every breath wretched and futile. "Pix, help me. I can't breathe."

He had fallen by a lamp post and she slipped behind him, tugging at his shoulders as he struggled with his feet. She managed to prop him against the base. The blood on her fingers left red slashes on the snow.

"Try to relax." False serenity strained her husky voice as she crouched beside him. Her hands found the holes again and covered them. "Please, please, please."

They locked eyes and his grip on her arm returned, tighter now. She knew he was fighting. He didn't want to let go. "That's it, stay with me," she repeated. "We still have to build that little tool bench for Michael tonight."

His breath uneven, Martin smiled, and the intensity of his grip eased. It was a good sign, Joey thought, as if he was directing his energy inward, to keep his heart beating for his family.

"Maybe not tonight," he said. An unsteady hand reached for her cheek.

"Okay then," she confirmed, tears running freely. "We celebrate Christmas later, after you're better. Michael's barely two, he won't even notice." Nervous fingers passed through her hair as selfish thoughts clouded her features. She wanted five minutes back. Another chance. Not fair, but still she ached for it. Joey raised her head, searching for the ambulance.

Please, God, just five stupid minutes.

Only five minutes ago, they left the restaurant and trudged arm in arm toward Michigan Avenue, eyes open for an empty cab. Fresh snow muted the nightfall, and kept the full dark at bay. Random Christmas lights played on patches of the white blanket, transforming the humble neighborhood into something fine. It was one of Joey's favorite things about winter in Chicago.

They approached a house with a party in full swing. Whitney Houston blared from inside the crowded space. Revelers spilled from the front door onto the porch. Martin joined the chorus and sang "I'm Every Woman" in an affected soprano, one hand on his hip. She laughed at the sashay that replaced his usual gait, watched the shadow of his breath move in time with the music. A car drove slowly down the street looking, Joey presumed, for a place to park.

Martin raised his arms and spun around just as loud, cracking noises cut through the song. The first came as he faced the street, no rhythmic connection to the music. Joey thought the CD was scratched. When he turned back around, Martin was no longer smiling.

Not even five minutes.

Just one. Maybe thirty seconds. Even ten. Enough time to pull him away. Get him out of range. Get him back from where they were now. Joey fought the urge to scream, so unfair to unleash it. Martin didn't need that from her. Didn't need—

"If you can't," He struggled for breath. "I'll help ... somehow."

Clutching his chest, she managed a frustrated laugh, invoked the closeness of nicknames, anything to feel normal. "Mac, I can build the tool bench. I just want you there with me."

"Anniversary," he whispered, "I'll ...."

The hint of a smile lit his face and Martin's hand slipped from her cheek.

October 21, 1993

Joey Fagan stared at the clothing strewn across her bed, a collision of color and texture, a pile of indecision amassed for an unwanted trip. Her mother had insisted she take this vacation, ten days in Kauai to celebrate their fifth anniversary. Martin's last Christmas gift.

"Honey, it's what he would want for you. Have you seen Fuzz?"

Joey retrieved a baby blanket from the dryer and walked to Michael's room. Her son played on a plush forested area rug with two plastic dinosaurs. Judging by the ferocity of his sound effects, they were engaged in mortal combat.

"Hey, little man!" She knelt beside him. "Ready to go to Gran's?"

Michael nodded and gave her a Martin-like smile. Normally toddler pudgy, he showed a little more bone than usual today, revealing a good deal more of his father. She scooped him up and hugged him all the way to the car, kissing his head as they walked.

"Miss you already, Pumpkin. Take care of Gran for me."

Susan Lawrence kissed Joey's cheek and gripped her shoulders. "Try to enjoy this trip. If your grandmother was still alive she'd tell you to get out there and *find yourself.*"

"Mom, if Beck were still alive, she'd have taken the tickets and gone in my place."

Both women laughed as her mother slid into the driver's seat and said, "Now don't worry about a thing. Michael is safe with us."

"I know." Joey stepped away from the car, blowing kisses to Michael. "It's the only reason I agreed to go."

As they drove away, she looked at the sky. The afternoon sun warmed a perfect fall day. The breeze held a fragment of the faded summer, promising a good run. A quick one would be nice. Then she could face the thought of this unwanted vacation.

Vacation ... packing ....

With a sigh, she walked back to the house. Back in the bedroom she picked up a t-shirt and leaned against the wall, staring at the mess on the bed. Who was she kidding? She didn't want to go anywhere or do anything.

Concentrate, Joey. Focus on what you can do.

That's what Martin would have said. She ran a hand through her close-cropped hair. He was right. After ten months she needed to accept her loss and move on, but acceptance eluded her and movement took effort. She woke every day feeling as if she'd been abandoned outside the city, oddly distanced from her own life. Thanks to the persistence of a few close friends she still did the occasional night out, but her heart wasn't in it. Martin's death had hollowed her out, left her with barely enough resolve to make it through the day.

But, there was Michael. He needed her. And for her son's sake, her mother was right. She needed to regain her footing. The boy was not yet three, and in an odd way he was lucky. He didn't understand how much had been taken from him. Her responsibility now was to keep Martin alive for Michael, to show him what an amazing man his father had been. Would she ever be able to do his memory justice?

Not in her present state of mind.

Joey threw the t-shirt onto the pile and strode to the closet, shedding clothes as she went. A quick seven miles and she would feel much better about leaving town.

After donning a pair of black tights and her favorite running bra, she slipped into Martin's old green sweater and a black skull cap. The tights were slack, and hung loose on her gaunt frame. One hand smoothed out the extra fabric as she reached for her socks.

Warm for October, but late afternoon and getting cooler. Joey bounded out the door, stopped to stretch and tie her house key into the knot of her shoelaces. She turned the first corner and set a quick pace. The breeze bordered on crisp, but once her body warmed up the cool air would keep her comfortable. She could run forever in this weather.

Joey first met Martin on a day like this. She was new to Michael Reese Hospital, working in program administration. He was a third-year resident, sandy-haired, attractive, and very involved in the expansion of their outreach programs. As a result, he spent a lot of time in her building and he made quite an impression.

Despite the demands of his profession, Martin always wore an easy smile. He struck her as a guy who found joy in unexpected places. Like most women in the office, Joey had certainly noticed him but never spoken to him. His visits were infrequent. Catching a glimpse of him was like discovering a bouquet of bright flowers on someone else's desk. Even though they weren't meant for her, the sight still lifted her mood.

The day they finally met, Joey was headed to the copy room, arms loaded with file folders for a new maternity program. She backed into the door, turned, bumped right into his chest, and everything went flying.

"Easy there, Pixie," he said lightly, catching a folder.

Joanna 'Joey' Lawrence was 5' 3" and small framed, but had never thought of herself as diminutive.

"Ah come on, Mac!" she said, eyes locked on the tangle of paper. "No nicknames. I'm a professional here." She raised her head at the sound of his laughter. It was him.

That guy.

His vivid blue eyes hinted at mischief, so much brighter than a bunch of flowers. Joey's heart beat a little faster.

"I'm *so* sorry," he grinned, overemphasizing his regret as he knelt to help her. "I'm sure you're a *consummate* professional." He leaned close and whispered. "No offense intended."

Still stunned, Joey stared at him, mouth slightly open.

"So, what is your name?"

She melted and grinned. "Actually, it is Pixie. Pixie Sticks. But I don't get out of the can too often." She gestured to the mess on the floor. "I wreak too much havoc."

His laugh was as mischievous as his eyes. "Well, Pix, allow me to introduce myself. Mac Daddy at your service."

Joey ran at an energetic pace, her breath steady. She passed the new construction along Navy Pier, reached the end of the great rectangle and then turned, running alongside Lake Michigan, headed for the corner that would take her west again, back to shore. A strong breeze blew in from the lake, a welcome sensation to her flushed frame. The afternoon sun was low but full in the sky, and soon she would be running right into it. She wished briefly she had worn sunglasses, then brushed the notion aside. Her thoughts returned to Martin.

God, I miss you, Mac.

Joey slowed, her mind in lockstep with her pace, recounting her loss. The police had called it a gang-related shooting. They were simply in the wrong place at the wrong time. It was so frustrating, dealing with *the ifs*. If only they'd stayed at the restaurant for one more drink. If only Martin hadn't been dancing, his arms might have been lower, protecting his chest. If only they had walked faster, or slower. *If only, if only, if only.* God, it was maddening! In her anger she ran faster, eyes down as she turned the corner, anxious to get back home and try—as she always did—to leave this last, awful memory behind.

Joey didn't see the load of lumber that extended beyond the bed of the truck, but she caught the full force of it in the left side of her chest. The world flashed a hideous white. When her vision cleared everything, including the pain, was excruciatingly vivid. Spun violently by the force of the blow, she went reeling backward.

There was still too much momentum in her step when her calf hit the dock rope. Joey stumbled back, but there was nothing behind her to break her fall. She saw the top of the pier recede and cringed, knowing the cold lake waited for her below.

Chapter Two
To Be or Not

Joey blasted into the water as if shot there by a cannon. The icy lake bit into every inch of her skin, stunning her into stillness. Frigid and silent, the water isolated her, offering a remote view of her life. One disjointed fragment of her mind studied this new environment and she held off kicking to the surface. She pictured Martin in his last minutes, eyes wide, hand tight on her arm. Had he felt a distance then, separating them? Was it anything like the distance she felt from everything now? Down here, in the cold and the quiet, she had no one to cling to. Joey closed her eyes.

As the chill stole over her, the pain in her ribs dissipated and the constant ache of Martin's loss began to fade. She let go any thought of getting air, felt an odd connection to the glacial space, and relaxed into this unlikely source of solitude.

Death had been swift. That's what they told her. All the well-intended, meaningless words said back in December echoed through her head. *He's in a better place now … didn't feel a thing in the end … he's at peace….*

Peace.

What an oddly inviting word.

It occurred to her that she was approaching her own peaceful place for the first time since Martin's death. The sense of calm beckoned like an old friend, inviting her to come closer, settle in and stay a while. Joey didn't need to work to make her way toward it. Somehow the calm reached her, stole over her, and compelled her to let her troubles go.

Just rest.

Quite unexpectedly, her shoulder bumped something. The sensation jarred her, and Joey opened her eyes. One look and her tranquility vanished. Her senses returned, sharp again, like the pain in her side. Suspended beside her was a boy, not much older than Michael, and in the shadowed water he reminded her very much of her son.

No!

This was wrong. She couldn't begin to imagine the pain of losing Michael, yet she realized that only seconds before she had very nearly abandoned him. She shook her head, finally grasping the danger of her thoughts. This little boy needed air. Hell, she needed air. Joey suddenly, desperately, needed to get this child out of the lake and home to his mother.

And she needed to go home to Michael.

Grabbing the boy around the waist, she pulled him close and kicked toward the surface with every ounce of strength she could muster. He wasn't a burden, but her own body betrayed her. Pain clawed at her chest, and the chilly water now felt like drying cement, impeding movement. She wasn't even sure she was going up. Fighting panic, she looked around. Yes! A hint of the sun remained above the water. Joey concentrated on kicking. Her legs, still strong from the run, responded, propelling her toward the light.

She broke the surface, gasping for air, and yanked the boy's head out of the water as she looked for a way up the pier. The brisk lake wind lashed at her cheeks. "Help me!" she called out, her voice too low to attract attention. The effort was excruciating. Bracing herself, she forced a deeper breath and tried again.

"SOMEBODY! HELP! ME!"

That was all she had. The water was her enemy now, bitter cold, a menace to her ragged senses. Her grasp on the child held firm, and she forced herself to keep kicking, determined to keep him above the surface.

From the pier, she heard voices.

"Over there, Car!" A baritone voice fought panic. "He has William!"

Up on the pier, she saw two men highlighted by the setting sun. A tall, broad-shouldered man wearing a long overcoat stood motionless. His wiry companion scrambled down a ladder attached to the piling. Joey kicked her way toward him. He leaned out over the water, grabbed the child, climbed the steps, and passed him to the tall man. He descended again and reached for her, calling out in an Irish accent.

"Yer hand, mate! Gi' me yer hand!"

Joey unleashed a terrific howl as he pulled her toward the ladder. His hand closed over hers on the bottom rung. "Hold steady," he said. "I'll help ya up top."

There were only a few steps, but the climb brought new levels of agony. Tears came and Joey didn't fight them. The young Irishman was already on the pier, one hand reaching for her. With a brutal pull, he hoisted her up beside him. She lay where she landed, eyes closed, too overwhelmed to move.

"Car, quick. Find a barrel!" The voice boomed like a timpani.

A barrel? What about an ambulance?

Joey opened her eyes. A few feet away, the tall man knelt over the boy, muttering softly. He clutched the child and released him, searching his ashen face, shaking his little shoulders, smoothing his hair, doing everything he could think of—and none of it useful. Joey watched, reliving a horrible feeling of helplessness. He was losing someone he loved and he had no idea what to do.

ABC.

The lifesaving class she'd taken in college slammed to the forefront of her mind. Airway. Breathing. Circulation.

"What did you say?" The tall man stared at her, still panicked but puzzled.

"ABC!" She didn't realize she'd spoken aloud, but now she responded with force. The boy needed mouth-to-mouth, and if she remembered the procedure correctly, she might be able to save him. She shifted to her knees and crawled to the two of them, fighting to stay calm.

"Get out of the way," she said, reaching for the boy. Joey grabbed him from behind, thinking she should start with the Heimlich maneuver. The man looked horrified and leaned forward, as if to take the child back.

"No!" she shouted, and with one good heave she thrust her fist into the base of his ribcage. Water trickled from the child's mouth. She forced his lungs again. A little more water.

The man settled back, watching, and she cast him a quick glance. His face registered fearful shock, but his dark eyes revealed a hint of trust. She shifted her focus back to the boy. Chanting the first three letters of the alphabet, Joey laid him flat on his back and took a long, deep breath. Pain seared across the left side of her chest. She stopped for an instant. A lungful of air was too much for a child. Filling only her cheeks, Joey bent down, pinched his nose, opened his mouth and blew.

Nothing.

She tried again.

"Come on, kid. Breathe!" She repeated the motion.

Still nothing.

"Shit! Shit! Shit! Come on!"

Instinctively, she pulled him up for another Heimlich, with no result. She tried again. "Did you see anything?" she asked.

The tall man said nothing.

"Water!" she screamed. "Did you see any?"

"No."

"Okay. Let's go again." Joey laid him back down and forced more air into his lungs.

"Do you know how to find a pulse?" she asked between blows.

"Yes, I do."

The man reacted quickly, fingers probing the boy's neck. She waited forever, anxious and unmoving, her eyes penetrating his, searching there for any sign of this little life. The man matched her stare, looking as if he expected to find the pulse beating in the depths of her own. They remained so, eyes locked, anxiously seeking the same answer.

Joey broke her gaze first. "Anything?" she whispered.

"No."

"God damn it!" She leaned over the boy. "No. This is not going to happen."

Crossing one hand over the other, Joey began CPR, counting aloud, pumping the boy's chest in time with her numbers. "One, one thousand. Two, one thousand. Three, one thousand. Four, one thousand. Five, one thousand."

After her first pass, she panicked. Was it three pumps or five? Hoping desperately that more was better, she stayed with five. After each count she paused and forced another breath. She kept on, pumping and forcing breath, her husky voice repeating the count. After several passes she looked at the man, who stared at her, open-mouthed and incredulous.

Fighting back tears, her voice fraught with desperation, Joey asked, "Check the pulse again. Please?" Death seemed very, very present, and, as with Martin, there was little she could do to prevent it.

Again and again she worked his little body. Force the breath. Pump the chest. In desperation, she abandoned the full-cheek method and simply filled her lungs, pouring breath into his. Pumping. Breathing. Pumping again. "One, one thousand. Two, one thousand. Three—"

All of a sudden the child convulsed. A gurgling sound came from his throat and he coughed. There was water, more coughing. Finally a great gasp of air and then an audible cry.

He was back.

Joey sat on her heels, exhausted. She watched the boy raise a small hand to the man's cheek. He pressed it tight and took charge. Removing his coat, he wrapped it around the child, gathered him in his arms and rocked him back and forth, reassuring him in rich, soothing tones.

Feeling completely drained, but very much alive, Joey collapsed on the dock, staring up at a darkening sky. From the look of it, rain was headed this way. She closed her eyes, thinking vaguely that rain wasn't in the forecast. But rain brings life, and life—in this instant—meant everything. The boy was breathing. He would survive. She had done something incredibly right. It was exhausting but blissful, and she hadn't experienced bliss in a very long time. She closed her eyes with a weary sigh.

"… bring him with us … need to discuss …"

"… give him some a m'dry clothes …"

It sounded as if the young Irish man was back. She heard snatches of discussion, but paid little attention. The stillness she'd found was exquisite. She could easily sleep here in the cold evening air. Forget Hawaii. This pier felt just fine. She drifted, imagining how nice it would be to wake up right here and feel the morning sun.

The voices came closer. Someone shook her, reawakening the pain in her side.

"Come on then, up with ya. Doc wants a word back at the house."

Joey forced her eyes open. This … Car? Was that his name? He was lean, and much younger than the other guy. Was the tall man the boy's father? He must be, given his anguish. From behind her came his low tone. He spoke softly, but the sound was rich and full, and not without a sense of command.

"What's your name, son?"

"Son?" she whispered. Was he kidding?

The deep voice ignored her reply. "My name is Peter Hastings. We need to get my boy home quickly, and I'd like to properly express my gratitude. I can offer you dry clothes and a warm meal, then Car will see you home to your family."

Dry clothes. The words passed through her along with a brush of lake wind and Joey realized her sweatshirt was soaking wet. She shivered. Dry clothes would be nice.

"Joey. It's Joey. But—"

Without another word, Hastings lifted her to her feet, and passed her to Car, who pushed her toward some kind of platform. Hastings had already climbed atop it. He took her by both hands and pulled her up. She screamed as pain slashed at her chest. Her legs threatened to give way and she fumbled for a seat.

"Are you injured?"

With great effort, Joey regarded him. Eyes filled with compassion, Peter Hastings didn't look nearly as intimidating as he sounded. At the moment his expression was very kind, though the stress of what they'd experienced was still etched deep in the lines of his face. The evening breeze sent a lock of dark hair across his forehead, softening his features. His eyes looked warm and familiar, a little like Martin's. They were brown rather than blue, but large and incapable of hiding emotion. His concern touched her.

"I think my rib ... the lumber ...."

He sat down beside her.

"You scraped the ladder? Well, perhaps I can be of some assistance. I'm a physician. I'll see to you once I've taken care of William." Peter jumped to the ground. "Take us home, Car. The rain can't be far off."

Car climbed in beside her. "Sorry 'bout yer ribs, mate. I must've banged ya against the ladder."

Lightning streaked across the charcoal sky and Joey glanced at the Irishman. Well, almost a man. Car looked barely twenty, and he seemed unruffled by the calamity. He was lean and lanky, and his face still held the traces of the trust of adolescence. He had a very pleasant energy about him, she decided. Car shook his arms and the vehicle started with a lurch, punctuating the ache in her side. There was an odd rhythmic clatter that gained speed as they moved. Joey looked forward.

Horses?

Before she could voice her surprise, they rounded a corner and she slid across the bench. Frigid air rushed through her wet clothes and she began to shake. Car pulled her back to the center of the bench, a fistful of Martin's sweater in his hand.

"Hang on to the railin'. I'll have us home in two ticks. "

Desperate to stop shaking, Joey complied. She grabbed the dark metal bar in front of her and lowered her head to her knees in an attempt to block the air. Car kept a reassuring hand on her back as they traveled an incredibly bumpy road. Lightning flashed, and Joey held tight to the rail, seeking oblivion amid the cold and the constant pain.

Chapter Three
Small Changes

Between the cold air and the constant motion, the carriage ride seemed endless. In an effort to block the wind, Joey slid down into the small space between the bench and the footboard. She clung to the young man's leg, but every bump in the road jolted her tender ribs.

"Take this," Car said, covering her with his coat.

The carriage finally slowed, and as they passed under a stand of sycamore trees Joey glimpsed a congenial two-story home with double bay windows and a generous front porch. It was centered in a large yard and framed by a white picket fence. They turned into the driveway and stopped in between the house and another building of equal stature. Hastings bellowed orders from the seat behind her.

"Car, take him to the parlor and bring him some dry clothes. Mrs. Milford and I will settle William and then I'll see to our guest."

The gathering storm echoed his orders as it advanced across the sky. Joey shifted to her knees and held fast to the bench, watching the doctor carry his child up the porch steps. The front door opened and a thickset woman appeared. As

Hastings spoke to her she glanced at the carriage, eyes hard, lipless mouth set in a straight line. Joey reached for Car.

"Can you give me a hand?"

"Sure, man, sure." He took her hand, guiding her to the ground. "This way … Joey, was it now?"

"Yes, thanks."

Car wrapped an arm around her waist and led her to the front door. Spots clouded her vision, but Joey managed to stay on her feet. They reached a front hall where a kerosene lamp hung from a hook, casting shadowed light beyond the entrance. Car closed the door, and in the eerie quiet of the house Joey felt like an ice cube, dumped without warning from a freezer to a glass. The absence of wind and motion held an uncanny resemblance to the isolation of the lake. The memory turned her legs to rubber.

"Easy now," Car said, supporting her. "What ya need's a good fire and some dry clothes. Take the chill right off a ya."

Dry clothes held great appeal, and the notion of a fire was nice, though she would have preferred a hot shower. Nevertheless, she would bathe when she got home, and she wasn't about to get back in that buggy until she was dry.

Carriage.

Was this Peter guy Amish? Wrestling with the question took more effort than she expected. Joey felt as if she was moving at half-speed and not quite thinking straight.

Dry clothes. That would help her regain a sense of normalcy. She glanced at Car, who chattered pleasantly beside her.

"That was some trick ya pulled, Joey. I never seen anything like it, not from a corner pup. I thought Will was a goner, sure as I'm standin' here."

He led her into a large living room. Well-populated bookshelves, accented with decorative miniatures, covered one wall. Centered at the far end was an enormous fireplace. A pair of high-backed chairs faced the fire, and a footstool sat on one side of the hearth. There wasn't a television in sight. Joey thought it looked quaint.

"Somebody likes Pottery Barn," she mused.

"Good thing we missed the rain," Car chattered over her. "Have a seat, warm yer bones." He lifted his coat from her shoulders. "I'll mind the horses, and be back with some clothes." He frowned, appraising her.

"My stuff'll be big on ya, but," he paused, eyeing Martin's huge sweater, "I doubt ya trouble much over the fit." With a wink he was off.

Joey didn't dare touch the chairs, drenched as she was in lake water. She removed a blanket from the back of one and headed for the footstool. Heat from the fire licked at her damp clothes. Once on the stool, she covered herself, and leaned against the stone wall, too tired to think. A shiny object on the table caught her eye. A tiny, pillow-shaped box adorned with silver filigree flashed in the firelight. She reached over, picked it up, and found the initials "WH" inscribed on the front. Engraved on the back, with equal flourish, were the letters "USG".

Joey's feet were freezing. She replaced the silver box, slipped out of her socks and shoes and set them behind the firewood. Then she removed her skullcap and ran a hand through her damp hair. One vague thought resurfaced. These people must be Amish. She could think of no other explanation for the carriage, and the dated feel of this room lent weight to her theory. Edging her toes closer to the fire, she rested her head against the wall, feeling numb. The cold stone on her temple contrasted nicely with the warm fire at her feet. Joey closed her eyes and barely heard Car when he returned.

"Here now. These ought ta do," he said, squatting in front of her. "Y'can keep 'em, ya know. Looks like ya mightn't have much." He set a bundle of clothes on the chair and reached for her. "Come on, now. Let's have that old jumper."

"Jumper?" Joey leaned toward him and the blanket slid from her shoulder.

"Yer overshirt. It's soakin' wet, man. Off with it." Car tugged at Martin's sweater.

"Ouch! Easy," she protested. "I've got it."

Joey braced herself, slid her right hand underneath the hem, and slipped her left arm carefully out of the sleeve. She lifted it over her head, exposing her running bra and the ragged side of her chest.

"Jesus, Mary and Joseph!" Car said, averting his eyes.

"Is it that bad?" Joey couldn't see the bruise.

Outside, lightning flashed titanium white, robbing the room of its color. On its heels, a sharp crack of thunder broke directly overhead and rain poured from the sky. Car lifted the fallen blanket with eyes downcast and covered her. Joey watched as he finally braved a look, his face a study in bewilderment.

"What is it? What's the matter?" She frowned and started to lower the blanket.

Car intercepted, holding it at a discreet level. "It's just that … em … well, what with yer clothes and yer hair, I took ya for a boyo." He offered her a shy smile.

"You mean a boy? You thought I was a boy?" She paused, her ribs throbbing. "Sorry about that. Is there a bruise? It feels like shi—" Joey stopped herself. If these guys were Amish, then foul language was off limits, no matter how much it hurt. Regardless, the pain demanded an outlet. "It hurts like hell."

Car stood, his face crimson. "There is, indeed. She's a monster all right, lots a color already and still fillin' in. Be singin' t'ya for a while, I think." He bumped into the chair as he backed away. "Guess I better fetch the doc. Back in a tick."

"Em, Doc?" Car stood in the doorway of William's bedroom. "I've a bit of a surprise for ya."

Peter Hastings sat beside William, who lay in bed. Mrs. Milford, his housekeeper, stood on the other side, tucking the boy in.

"A surprise?"

Car grinned. "That boy," he nodded toward the staircase. "He's not a boy."

"What?" Peter and Mrs. Milford responded in unison.

"Painted me a new shade of red." A bolt of lightning accentuated Car's news. "But, she's a Colleen if ever I saw one. Bit of a spark in her speech, too."

"No." The old housekeeper turned, thick hands on wide hips. "This will not do. She cannot stay here. I'll wrap her a few scraps and we'll send her on her way." She shook her head. "Sneaking into this house, posing as a boy ... the unmitigated gall!"

Car leaned against the door frame, effectively blocking her path. "There was no sneakin' about it, and not a bit a nerve needed." He inclined his head toward Peter. "She had an invitation."

Peter sighed, eyes on the rain-beaten window. "Well, I had planned to offer him—her—your sofa tonight, Car, but I don't suppose that will do." He turned to his housekeeper. "Mrs. Milford, prepare the spare room. It seems we have company."

"For a street rat?" The housekeeper spat her words. "You cannot be serious. Mark my words. Send her away. She's probably a thief, or worse. Girls like that are nothing but—"

"—welcome to our hospitality," Peter finished for her. "William is alive, thanks to that girl. The least I can do is offer her food and shelter for the night. Now, prepare the room and draw a hot bath for her. She may be many things, but tonight she is our guest and we will treat her accordingly."

Mrs. Milford grumbled an assent as she left. Car joined Peter on the other side of the bed, and sheltered William's hand in his. The child stirred.

"Hey ya, boyo," Car said. "Next time ya decide ta go for a swim, tell me. I'll join ya."

"Oh Car," he whispered a scratchy reply. "Did you see her?"

Car shared his grin with Peter. "Oh I saw her, all right. So, why'd ya jump in?"

William swallowed with difficulty, eyes wide. "But, you said you saw her. She ... she was there, and it's been so long."

His voice showed signs of agitation. Peter touched Car's shoulder and gave a slight shake of his head.

"Who did you see, son?" Peter leaned close.

"I looked down and she was there. I had to go and get her."

"Who, son? This … Joey?"

William gave his father a puzzled look. "Who is Joey, Papa?"

"Why, she's the girl who rescued you from Lake Michigan. Who are you talking about?"

"Mama," he said, closing his eyes. "She was in the water. I had to get her back."

A heavy silence stole over the room. Peter checked William for signs of fever as a breathy whistle came from the other side of the bed.

"Jesus, Mary and Joseph, Doc. What d'ya make a that?"

Joey scanned the room, feeling numb and detached. At the far end stood an ornate wooden desk. A kerosene lamp was perched upon it, offering a soft view of the area. A loveseat faced the desk, its upholstery complementing the chairs by the fireplace. She stood, looking for a telephone, thinking vaguely she should call her mother. But a sharp stab of pain cut through her ribs and Joey sank to the stool. The phone call could wait. Hawaii, she sighed with relief, was definitely out. Outside, rain pounded white noise on the rooftop. The long wall opposite the bookshelves boasted a bank of picture windows, and the lightning revealed a picturesque yard.

The sound of approaching footsteps caught her attention. It was the woman this time, Mrs. Milford. As she advanced, her long, dark dress cast a gloom about the room. Her face was closed, her manner brisk, and authority echoed in her heavy step. Short and thick, but not exactly stout, she possessed the solid build of an older woman. Her hair, a battle between salt and pepper, was pulled into a slightly disheveled bun. She wasn't smiling.

"I understand, *young miss*, you are quite full of surprises," she said, ice in her greeting.

Joey stared hard at her, certain she detected insult in her tone. The old woman glanced away and continued stiffly.

"Given the severity of the weather, Dr. Hastings has decided to extend his invitation. You'll stay here tonight, and Car will take you home in the morning." Without waiting for a response, she grabbed Joey's arm, pulling her to her feet. "Up with you, girl. You need a bath."

Joey cried out. Mrs. Milford let go and Joey attempted to follow her. She leaned briefly against the bookshelves for support, her eyes level with a tiny bronze baby carriage. It was a cute little antique, with an umbrella top and spoke wheels. Mrs. Milford barked at her from the hall, and she left the parlor, clutching the banister as she climbed the stairs. She didn't dare ask this woman for help.

Once upstairs, they entered a small room. Joey looked around in confusion. There was no tub or toilet in sight. An armoire stood against one wall, a narrow cedar chest across from it. By the door was a chest of drawers. Mrs. Milford opened the armoire, lowered a large metal oval to the floor and began turning something at the back of the unit. She cast an impatient glance at Joey.

"Well, off with your clothes. I'll clean them … *tonight*."

Joey sat on the cedar chest, watching in wonder as Mrs. Milford worked the strange unit. She turned one final knob and water flowed from a spigot. A bathtub. She'd never seen anything like it. This place was odd and uncomfortably primitive, but Joey was quelled by the notion of a hot bath.

"Cool," she said softly. "Hey, do you have a phone I can use?"

"A what?"

"A phone." Joey mimed a handset. "You know, a telephone."

"Pah." The housekeeper rolled her eyes. "Where do you think you are? Potter Mansion?"

"Never mind." Joey sighed, looking away.

Mrs. Milford returned to her task, busy adding powder. Joey was pleased to see bubbles rising, but decided a toilet would be nice, too.

"Um, Mrs. Milford?" She shifted in her seat.

The older woman gave her a look of exasperated severity. "What is it, girl?"

"I'm sorry to interrupt, but I need to go to the restroom."

Mrs. Milford continued to stare at her, expression unchanged.

"Um … do you have?" She sighed and tried again. "I mean, I need to use the toilet."

Mrs. Milford rolled her eyes and huffed, "You're sitting on it."

"Really?" Joey stared at the bench beneath her.

"Stand up and lift the lid."

Joey did as she was told. Inside the bench were two compartments. One held a large porcelain bowl. The compartment behind it held a few cloth towels and another, smaller receptacle. Joey gave Mrs. Milford a look of utter confusion. The old woman turned off the bathwater and stomped across the room.

"Take care of your needs here," she said curtly, pointing to the large bowl, "and put the soiled cloth back there. Once you've finished with your toilet, clean yourself thoroughly. I'll see about some proper bed clothes. You'll find the soap against the wall of the Mosely. Make good use of it," she ordered. Then she left the room, muttering about lice.

"Man, what a museum!" Joey said, as she shed the blanket and slid the running tights to her feet. "And what the hell is a Mosely?" Bracing herself for another burst of pain, she removed her bra and dropped it on the floor. She made quick work of what felt like a very public indignity and climbed into the bathtub.

The water was perfect. Joey surrendered to its heat, submerging her head along with everything else. She found the soap sitting on a small shelf of the tub. Inscribed there was the word Mosely, evidently the tub manufacturer.

As she bathed she thought about Mrs. Milford. The woman certainly seemed put out by her presence. Maybe having to deal with an unexpected guest ruined her plans for a quiet night. That would frustrate anyone. Regardless, her tone was unsettling. Joey shrugged and continued bathing. Once finished, she sat still, knees near her chest, cheek resting on her arm. It felt good to be warm and clean. She was tired. Without a knock, Mrs. Milford returned to the bathroom with a bundle of clothes. She set them on the small dresser.

"Out of the tub," she said briskly.

"Here goes." Joey gripped the sides of the metal oval, ready for a new onslaught of pain. She eased herself from the bathtub, giving the woman a full view of her injured ribs. The housekeeper gasped, just as Car had earlier.

"Yeah, I've heard." Joey gave her a weak smile.

Mrs. Milford thrust a towel at her. "That," she declared, "is no scrape from a ladder. "What did you do? Cross your procurer? Was that it? He dumped you in the lake because you failed to please?"

"Excuse me?" Joey eyed the older woman.

Mrs. Milford ignored her. "We'll dispense with the nightgown, too difficult," she said, picking up an article of clothing, "just the bed jacket and some underpants." Without another word, Mrs. Milford helped her into a heavily-laced, button-down shirt. The underpants were capri-length pajama bottoms, also trimmed in an excess of lace. Once she was dressed Mrs. Milford ordered her back into the hall.

"You'll sleep here," she said, opening another door.

The mattress was much higher than her bed at home. As Joey stepped on a stool by the bed, Mrs. Milford barked out instructions. "Sit up. Lean forward." The old woman adjusted pillows and blankets. "I made beef soup for dinner," she said. "I'll bring you a bowl."

Her stomach lurched at the suggestion. "Thank you. Soup sounds great." Joey gave her a grateful smile, hoping to melt some of the woman's ice, but Mrs. Milford remained expressionless.

"Dr. Hastings will be with you in short order." Turning briskly, she left the room.

"I hope he's in a better mood than you are," Joey mumbled after her.

Chapter Four
Preliminary Examination

May I come in?" The rich baritone accompanied a muffled knock on the door.

Joey assented, and Peter Hastings entered the room holding a black bag in one hand and a tulip-shaped glass in the other. Like Martin, he was tall and broad-shouldered. His brown eyes revealed nothing at the moment, but Joey sensed they harbored quite a bit. Even though his sideburns were overdone, she had to admit he was pretty easy on the eye. Peter set his bag on the bedside table and handed her the glass.

"Drink this," he told her. "It will ease the pain."

Joey complied, making a face as she sputtered, "Whoa. What is it?"

"Brandy. It's medicinal." He nodded at the glass. "A little more, please."

"It'll knock me flat," she responded.

"It will dull the pain. Once more, please."

Satisfied with her intake, he retrieved the glass and turned to face her.

"Now, then," he said, "let's have a look at your injury, Miss …."

The depth of his voice struck Joey again. On the pier it sounded almost fierce, but now it was warm, like the trace of brandy that lingered in her throat.

"Fagan. Joey Fagan," she said, sitting forward, arms wrapped around her ribs. They seemed to need the support. Her breath was shallow and she worked to keep it that way. Dr. Hastings sat down beside her, touched her hand, and looked directly into her eyes.

"Miss Fagan," he said, "can you raise your arms without difficulty?"

She sucked in hard and released her hold. Hastings lifted the bed jacket with surprising tact and examined the bruised area. A cry escaped her when he touched her injury.

"Sorry," she said, gritting her teeth. "Really tender right there! Daamm ... man that hurts!"

"You have an immense bruise forming. Now I need to check for signs of breakage. This may be painful."

Moving carefully, Hastings placed both hands near her spine and began to feel his way forward, hands exploring both sides of her ribs, his touch methodical and deliberate, maintaining eye contact throughout.

"Any difficulty breathing?" He reached the center of the bruise.

"Yes," Joey hissed.

"Drink." Peter held out the brandy and she emptied the glass eagerly.

Once he finished, Joey pulled her arms back to her sides. The area throbbed anew, pounding like a second heartbeat, matching the force of the rain outside. Hastings produced a thin wooden tube flared at both ends like some kind of horn. He placed the large end on her chest.

"Oh," Joey said. "Is that a stethoscope? It looks like a little trumpet."

"You know your medical instruments," Peter said, eyeing her quizzically. "It's a Piorry. It belonged to my father. Now, take a deep breath." He placed his ear close to the opposite end and asked her to breathe several times, moving the instrument each time.

"Well," he said, "you haven't punctured a lung. The worst of it appears to be confined to a single rib. I think you bruised the bone, but I found no evidence of a break." His hand covered hers with a pat of reassurance. "Regardless, we'll bind your ribs to keep them secure and in a few days you should be fine."

Peter pulled a roll of cloth from his bag. "Raise your arms again, please."

He leaned close to her, placed the end of the cloth at the back of her spine and began to wind it around her ribcage. He was tall enough that, sitting as they were, Joey's head met his chest. The first few passes hurt like hell, and Joey wanted to brace her head against him. Instead she dug her fist into a pillow for support. Fighting the urge to swear, she inhaled deeply through her nose and took in the unexpected scent of leather, wood smoke and sweat. Joey inhaled again. She hadn't been this close to a man in months, and Hastings' natural musk was a pleasant surprise. Her eyes remained locked on his shirt.

"May I ask you something, Miss Fagan? What were you doing at the dock? And how did you come to be in the water?"

"Please, call me Joey." She shifted her arm to accommodate his work. "I was running. The pier is usually pretty empty, but today there was a lumber truck, just out of view. A huge piece of wood stuck out beyond the truck bed. I slammed right into it when I turned the corner." Joey flinched at the memory. "It threw me completely off balance and knocked half the breath out of me. Then I guess I just tumbled back into the lake."

"Lumber truck? Similar to a cart?"

Reliving the accident was unsettling; Joey barely noticed his question. "Truck, cart, take your pick. It was the lumber that did the damage."

She glanced at the fire which cast a warm glow about the room, offering solace from the storm outside. The afternoon run seemed like a distant memory. The day had been long.

Although talking wasn't difficult, combined with breathing, it was tiring. Joey barely heard his next question.

"What, exactly, were you running from?"

Her eyes returned to him. He had paused from his work, brows raised. He leaned back slightly as if to get a better view of her.

"I wasn't running from anything," she said. "I was just running. You know, jogging."

His puzzled expression pressed her further.

"Exercise," she offered. "As in—get the heart rate up? Release some endorphins? Exercise?"

Peter's gaze never wavered. Something in his expression called her out. He seemed to know there was more. She reconsidered the question, and pictured each recent mile in her head. She thought about what running held for her now and finally saw it for what it really was, her grieving ritual for Martin. She sighed, slipped a hand through her hair and lowered her head.

"Honestly, I think I'm just chasing the past." She picked at a thread on the quilt. "I … I lost someone recently." She paused, but continued in a rush. "I know I can't resurrect the past, but I hate losing sight of it. When I run, when it's just me and my thoughts, the best of it tends to play back in my head, and the memories … well, for the most part, they keep me going."

She looked up. He seemed to accept this answer, though he said nothing. Joey didn't really want to discuss Martin with a stranger, no matter how sympathetic he might be. Thinking of Michael, she remembered the boy in the water.

"Hey, how's your son?"

Peter stared at her, expression set, eyes narrowed. "William is going to be just fine, thank you," he bristled. He opened his mouth to speak again, but hesitated.

Joey, initially taken aback, saw he was grappling with something. She watched him, and a flutter of unease began to gnaw at her stomach. Finally, his features softened. He inclined his head.

"And I do mean it sincerely. Thank you." He paused again, wearing the same look of frustration. "But, how did you know ...? Where did you learn that procedure?"

Joey gave him a puzzled look. "What, CPR? That's like Lifesaving 101."

Peter's skeptical expression remained. He pressed further. "You kept repeating the letters ABC."

She smiled, feeling self-conscious. "That was the way I learned it. A. Airway. B. Breathing. C. Circulation. You do it in that order. Clear the airway. Breathe for them if necessary, and then find the pulse. If you can't, then pump the chest to get the heart going."

"Pump the chest?" Peter put a fist to his lips. "Hmm ... like Maass's compressions. Tell me," he said, his face a study in intensity, "have you ever performed the procedure before?"

Joey heard the edge in his voice. The word 'lawsuit' crossed her mind, but she answered him truthfully.

"No. That was a first for me." Thinking back, she had been unsure of herself throughout most of the ordeal. Her execution lacked finesse, and resuscitation seemed to take forever. Still, the boy survived. "It's been several years since I took the class," she admitted, "but it did come back to me, and it did work."

Joey was nervous. His stare never wavered, but Hastings said nothing. It occurred to her that, despite the outcome, she could still be facing a lawsuit. Then another thought struck her.

"You're a doctor," she countered, "you've never done CPR, or revived a drowning victim?"

"You refer to the procedure you performed on William?"

She nodded, thinking his phrasing odd.

Hastings bowed his head. "No. Victims of such misfortune meet their Maker long before they reach my office. And, despite the fact that it was my son who was—" His voice broke, and he glanced away. "I've read about parts of the procedure and once I grasped your intention it was ... fascinating to watch you work. Again, you have my gratitude."

Peter finished winding the cotton and secured it.

Joey let out an anxious breath. Not the answer she expected, but at least he didn't threaten legal action. She slipped into a smile. "No problem." Her ribs were snug against the cotton cloth, preventing painful breath. "Man, that's much better. Thank you." Stifling a yawn, she settled into the bedding, the patter of rain as soft as the pillows behind her head.

"I've taken the course twice, but never used it. Thank God it worked. I'm sure you'd have done the same for my son."

He regarded her with mild surprise. "You have a son?"

Before she could reply, the door opened and Mrs. Milford entered the room carrying a tray. Peter stood and accepted it from her.

"Thank you. I'll take it from here."

She cast a distrustful eye to Joey and offered Hastings an uneasy plea. "You will let me know if you need anything else."

"Yes, of course. That will be all, Mrs. Milford."

The housekeeper gave Joey a daggered glance. "Your clothes will be ready in the morning."

"Thank you," Joey said.

Peter set the tray on the bed. The soup smelled heavenly, beef and onion wafting through the air, and Joey sat up eager and hungry. She picked up the spoon and bowl, took a bite and a contented moan slipped from her. Despite her obvious lack of charm, Mrs. Milford was a good cook. Joey lost herself in the soup, finishing most of the bowl. Stifling a yawn, she set it back on the tray.

"About your clothing," Peter said. "Why do you go about posing as a boy? I'm sorry I didn't immediately realize you were—" He faltered. "But your manner of dress, coupled with your low voice and short hair misled me. Is it a matter of personal safety?"

"No." Joey dabbed her lips with the napkin and set it on the tray. "Those are my running clothes," she said with a twinge of frustration. "That's what I wear when I run."

"Ah, the running … I see…."

Joey watched him raise his fist to his lips. He looked as if he saw nothing at all.

"But," he pressed on, "why the short hair?"

"I like it this way." She ran a hand through her hair, feeling perturbed. Plenty of women had short hair. Her Amish theory was gaining ground. A man would have to be in a pretty secluded society to avoid short hair and running tights.

Peter seemed to sense her frustration. "I'm sorry, Miss Fagan. I seldom encounter women with short hair. He offered a contrite expression. "Please, tell me about your son."

Joey let it go.

"His name is Michael and he's an absolute angel. He'll be three at the end of the month." She remembered the weight of his head on her chest as she carried him to the car. "He's with my mother for the next two weeks. I should be in Ha—"

Joey paused, realizing she didn't care about missing her flight. She could reschedule, but why bother? There was no point in going without Martin. Her eyes darted to the window and she swallowed hard, anxious to keep those thoughts at bay. She braved a look at Peter and changed the subject.

"How old is William?"

The hint of a smile touched his face. "He'll turn five on the fifth of January."

"What's he into?" She shifted, lying on her good side, her arms folded under her head.

"In to?" Peter looked confused.

"What does he like to do?" she yawned, feeling the pleasant veil of the brandy steal over her. "Is he all sports and outdoors, or is he a LEGOs man?"

"I'm not familiar with your leg hose, but …."

Definitely Amish, Joey decided. Probably just wooden alphabet blocks in this house. She watched through heavy-lidded eyes as Peter considered her question.

"He probably spends too much time around the stables with Car. But he is diligent in his lessons, so I allow it. He has a passion for horses."

"Cool," she said softly. "Michael is a dinosaur man." Joey found it hard to keep her eyes open. She pictured her son surrounded by plastic, long-tailed creatures, immersed in their era. "Maybe we could work out a play date," she murmured.

The bed was warm, the rain almost hypnotic, and her limbs felt limp.

"A play date?"

"Mm Hmm." Surely Amish children were allowed to play.

Hastings changed the subject.

Well, Miss ... Joey," he paused. "That's an interesting name for a woman."

"Short for Joanna. Joey ... Joanna, I answer to both." Her lids fluttered open. "Peter, you've been very kind. Thank you." As she closed her eyes, random thoughts spun round her head. *Nice guy ... so grave.* Odd questions, needing answers. *CPR? Horses?* She tried to give voice to her curiosity, but fatigue prevailed and she uttered only a few incoherent sounds before she fell asleep.

Peter sat in silence, watching her drift off. She was a delicate little thing. Much too thin, he noted, nestled like a bird in the midst of the quilted bed. In the firelight her fine features contrasted sharply with her manner of speech. Earlier in the evening, given her boyish appearance and colorful language, he had assumed she was some streetwise boy, too young for a razor, and definitely incapable of reviving a drowning victim. And yet, she had done exactly that. A fist reached his lips as he recalled the scene.

It was difficult to guess her age, but knowing she had a child, he assumed she was in her early twenties. And now that he knew she was a woman, he wondered how he had ever thought otherwise, despite the odd clothing she wore when Car pulled her from the water. Her skin was milk white and her features were delicate, save for her large brown eyes—owl's eyes—hidden now beneath dark lashes. She was quite pretty, he decided, and her short brown hair complemented her small face.

Still, she struck him as odd. Her language and clothing belied her warmth and sincerity. He wondered about the nature of her upbringing. Despite her denial, he assumed she dressed as a boy for reasons of safety. That would explain the language as well.

She had kept her foul language in check since they returned home, but her turn of phrase was unfamiliar to him, not quite abrasive, but it held much more spit than polish. Odder still, she recognized a stethoscope. Perhaps, like Car, she was born without means, but worked for a physician's family, and had thus developed an ability to adapt to individual circumstance. She displayed a brand of coarse diplomacy that was rough around the edges, but honest in its way. She certainly didn't seem likely to sneak away in the night with the good silver.

She said she was supposed be somewhere, though she didn't mention a destination. It didn't matter tonight. Peter stood and collected his things.

"Well, Miss Joanna Fagan, get a good night's rest. In the morning we'll see you safely on your way."

Her soft breath served as her response.

Chapter Five
Morning Becomes Electric

Five miles from the Hastings house, Eugene Prendergast prayed for a sign in the last pew of a sparsely populated church. He glanced at a stained glass window, reliving Friday's offense.

They had laughed at him.

In his own office.

Oh, they made assurances and patted his back, but he heard them laughing as he left. For ten months, he waited patiently for news of his appointment. When no word came, he went to City Hall, entered what should have been his office and demanded his place as General Counsel.

They appeased him with promises.

And then laughed at him.

And who perpetrated this vile joke, this grave indignity, at his expense? Who, after all, promised him a position in the first place? The mayor, himself! It mattered little that they had never met. Prendergast knew his lofty correspondence was entry enough. His effort was proof of his worth.

Carter Harrison had promised work for all who helped elect him and Prendergast worked tirelessly, extolling the virtues of the onetime mayor. Eugene knew his intellect was best suited for the position of General Counsel. Harrison would surely overlook his lack of formal education in light of his loyal service and steadfast correspondence. He wrote Carter Harrison often, claiming his coveted position just before the election. Since winning, Mayor Harrison had not once called upon him or acknowledged his effort. The lying, duplicitous, unprincipled mayor! Well, Eugene Prendergast was not a man to be used and cast aside. This was no mere insult, but a grievous injustice and it must be addressed.

An image on the window caught his eye. It depicted an angry God casting Adam and Eve from the Garden of Eden. The wretched, stained-glass sinners cowered in His presence, their guilt intensified by the flickering votive candles. The engraving read, "Vengeance is mine, sayeth the Lord."

Prendergast blinked and read the words again, his jaw slack.

Cast the sinner out. Rid Eden of one so unworthy.

Panic welled within him. Could this be the sign? A monumental endeavor, this casting out. Could he perform so bold a service? As he bowed his head to pray for guidance a thought struck.

Did not lowly David slay mighty Goliath?

Yes.

Yes, he did.

Prendergast raised his eyes to heaven, considering the path taken by one of the Lord's most underestimated soldiers. He made the sign of the cross, moved to the stained-glass image and bowed low to his God. "I am thy servant, and as thy servant I will cast this sinner from your garden. This David will slay his evil Goliath. Thy will be done."

He raised his head to Heaven, reveling in the righteousness of his newfound mission. "Lord, as thine instrument, I will have my vengeance."

"She's nothing but a street urchin. I doubt she's ever lived indoors, let alone bathed in a tub."

Mrs. Milford stood in Peter's office, hands on hips, apron stretched tight across her thick stomach. "She had no idea what to make of the commode. I had to show her what to do."

"Mrs. Milford, please." Peter raised a cautionary hand. "Spare me the details of her personal hygiene. She saved William's life last night. We owe her our gratitude."

"Hogwash! Only God in Heaven can raise the dead, and after Lazarus he decided against it. William fainted, pure and simple. She fussed over him to frighten you and make herself out a saint. She made a normal occurrence seem much worse, and you believed her performance."

Peter let out a weary sigh and pinched the bridge of his nose. "You weren't there."

"Well, I was here, and last night I heard someone bumping around downstairs. I wouldn't be surprised if something's already gone missing."

"I don't think our guest was inclined to move about. She drank enough brandy to ensure a good night's sleep. Now, if you please, I have some work to do before breakfast."

"You mark my words. She's a common thief and a sewer rat." She reached the door, muttering, "The sooner she's gone the better."

As Mrs. Milford trundled away Peter mentally replayed yesterday's drama, struggling to make sense of the miracle Joanna Fagan had managed. He considered himself well read in emerging medical technique. The chest compression procedure had been performed and documented by a German physician, Friedrich Maass. It was a lively topic in medical circles, but not in conversational society, and therefore highly unlikely she'd simply heard about it.

Odder still was the thrusting procedure she used to force water from William's lungs. He had never encountered it in print or in conference. Miss Fagan mentioned taking a class, but he knew of no such course, and, had it existed, no woman would have been admitted. She must be a keen observer, somehow associated with medicine, perhaps a naval physician. In truth, Peter could not find satisfaction in any theory he considered. The entire episode was utterly confounding.

The near drowning of his son resurrected memories best forgotten. As a child, while his father was away at war, Peter watched his mother suffer and die from typhoid fever. Last night, before Miss Fagan intervened, Peter felt the same sense of helplessness. In the darkest seconds, fearing William was lost, he clung to his son as he had his mother, incapable of preventing the inevitable. Worse still, were his last hours with his wife. Peter took in a sharp breath and steered his thoughts to a happier recollection....

The first time he saw her, Victoria Sullivan stood by a window, head bent to task, cleaning the wound of an injured child. She raised her head as he approached. Her radiant face, bathed in sunlight, marked her at once an angel.

"Are you Dr. Hastings?"

Peter stared at her, transfixed by her silken voice. Her cheeks were flush, her brow moist. She had rolled up her sleeves and her dress was soiled by her work. Wisps of golden blonde hair accented her fine features. He nodded.

"Then you, sir," she said with a playful smile, "are my knight in shining armor, my new champion."

Peter felt as if the earth had shifted under his feet. Everything about Victoria–her voice, the soft wave of her hair, and her delicate movement all served to arouse him. She radiated an energy that seemed to charge the world around her. Thinking nothing would please him more than to serve her, he bowed low and replied, "At your service, my lady ...."

Other memories haunted Peter Hastings and he fought hard daily to keep them at bay. Although yesterday's excitement threatened to unleash them, it also raised many questions and he put all his effort into seeking answers. He could not explain Joanna Fagan's appearance in the lake, her knowledge of advanced medical technique, her dress, or her language. He did think she was of humble birth, but she didn't strike him as a criminal.

"Papa?"

William stood in the doorway, and Peter suppressed the urge to gather his boy in his arms. He shook his head. There was nothing to be gained by further coddling, it would only prolong unpleasant memory, and he did not want to encourage unhealthy thoughts. He nodded a greeting and beckoned him closer.

"May I go up to see Miss Fagan now?"

"It's nearly eight, William. I expect she'll be down soon. Best to wait here"

"But I'd like to thank her. Please, Papa? I'll wait in the hall."

Peter smiled. Perhaps a little indulgence was in order. "Quiet as a mouse?"

"As a baby mouse," William whispered.

"Off you go then."

Joey awoke to sunlight spilling across the quilt through an open window. As she stretched her ribs responded, reminding her in an angry flash of all that had happened yesterday. The succession of images jolted her, and she sat up quickly, recounting them: Hitting the wood and then the water, finding and resuscitating William, the carriage ride and the odd bath, Car's amiability, Mrs. Milford's frost, and the quiet candor of Peter Hastings. The whole thing seemed surreal. She rubbed sleep from her eyes wishing she could have called a cab the night before. As she took in the humbly furnished room, Joey felt a twinge of unease. She couldn't put a name to it, but there was something strange about this house. She felt out of place. It was definitely time to go home.

She climbed out of bed and discovered two sets of clothes on the bedside table. Her running bra and tights were neatly folded, but her skull cap, sweater and socks were missing. Joey shrugged. They were probably still behind the firewood with her shoes. Well, she would borrow what was offered, and wash her things when she got home. Alongside her clothes lay a white blouse, a long blue skirt, a slip of some kind and another pair of frilly, old-fashioned underpants. Everything struck her as too formal, but she was in no position to complain. She ignored the slip, frowned at the underwear and put on her tights instead.

As she pulled the skirt over her hips, something bumped against her leg. She reached into the pocket and pulled out a silver box. It looked exactly like the one she had seen last night, the same pillow shape and the same etched letters. It must be from the library. She slipped it back in her pocket, intent on returning it before she left.

For now, she needed to finish dressing. She buttoned the skirt which covered her feet, then removed her bed jacket and picked up the blouse. It was a high-collared celebration of ruffles, designed to button in the back. She peeked in the armoire, but found no alternative. Eyeing the blouse she heaved a sigh. Even uninjured, she would need assistance. She slipped her arms into the sleeves, clutched it from behind, and went in search of help.

Joey opened the door to find William Hastings standing with his back to the wall, wearing a jacket and an old-fashioned pair of dress shorts. She gave him a big smile and knelt beside him.

"Well hi, little mister," Joey said. "Want to go swimming?"

He gave his head a vigorous shake. She exhaled exaggerated relief.

"Me neither."

Joey tilted her head and tapped a finger against her lips. His eyes followed her movement. "I could sure use some help," she said. "Do you know anything about buttons?"

William nodded.

"Like how to fasten them?"

"Yes, ma'am," he whispered.

"Well, I have a whole bunch behind my back. Think you can help me?"

William nodded again and moved toward her. Joey sat on the floor and turned to make the task easier. His small hand touched her back.

"Did you get hurt in that water?" he asked.

"Oh! No, sweetie." Joey faced him. "I ran into some wood up on the dock."

"And then you found me in the water?" William looked very serious.

Joey laughed. "Well, first I fell in, and then I found you."

"I thought I saw someone in the lake." His small face darkened and he lowered his head.

She let go of the blouse, leaned close, lifted his chin and looked straight into his serious brown eyes. "You did. You saw me, and I saw you. I don't think I would have made it back to the surface on my own, so I think we sort of saved each other." She brushed her fingers through his fine, brown hair. "You know what else I think?"

"What?"

"I think we should never do that again."

"Never," William said solemnly.

Joey turned away and William began to button the blouse. What a serious little guy. And, boy did he take after his dad. William shared his father's dark features, and it was a sure bet he would eventually acquire Peter's deep voice. Once he secured the last button, she tucked in the blouse and faced him.

"Thank you." She extended her hand and after a moment's hesitation, he shook it.

"Hey, I hear you like horses. You know, I've never actually met a horse."

William's eyes brightened. "I … I could show you mine. I know two of them."

"Wow! Really?"

William's eager smile confirmed they were safely past yesterday's nightmare.

"Perhaps we should let Miss Fagan eat breakfast first. She'll meet you in the stable afterward."

Joey and William started in unison at the sound of Peter's commanding baritone. He stared at them from the landing of the staircase.

"Yes sir." William stood and headed down the stairs. Joey followed, taking in her surroundings as she descended. The walls upstairs were covered in pretty wallpaper, a scattering of small pastel flowers. The pattern seemed Victorian. The staircase was simple, but the handrail revealed delicate detail, and Joey thought it might be hand-carved. On the first floor, a hall tree stood by the front door. The wooden floor was smooth and well-polished. Everything was so quaint. It reminded Joey of visiting her grandparents' house when she was a child.

"Miss Fagan?" Peter was already on the first floor, watching her descend. "I normally attend services on Sunday morning. I thought perhaps you'd like to join me, and I'll take you home afterward."

"That would be fine, thank you."

Joey didn't attend church regularly and wasn't interested in going this morning, but she felt obligated, given his hospitality. She could manage breakfast and church, then home.

Home.

She would drive straight to her mother's and collect Michael. The thought of him came with a rush of urgency. If nothing else, yesterday's drama cleared the fog she'd lived in since Martin's death. Her encounter with William had burned through that mournful haze, affording her clarity for the first time in months. Today she ached for Michael. Soon she would shower him with kisses, recount every finger and toe, and build a LEGO fort strong enough to withstand a thousand dinosaurs. She couldn't wait to begin.

Peter ushered her into a picture perfect dining room. Against one wall stood a hutch the size of a cathedral organ.

An elaborate set of elegant china graced the shelves. On the table, breakfast dishes sparkled upon an immaculate linen table cloth. Beneath the table was an area rug, a mix of blues and creams that complemented the wallpaper.

"This is just like a B and B," she said.

Peter turned. "I beg your pardon."

"Your home is beautiful. I don't know much about antiques, but you've created quite a memorable space here."

"Thank you, Miss Fagan. This was my father's house. Some of the furniture was his. The finer pieces belonged to my wife. She … ah—" His voice faltered and he coughed. "She had a fine eye for aesthetics."

"Please, call me Joey, or Joanna if you prefer. Will Mrs. Hastings be joining us?"

"I'm afraid not. She … she passed away several months ago."

Peter's vulnerable tone took Joey by surprise. "I'm so sorry. Given what little I know of you and your son, I imagine she was something special."

Hastings averted his eyes. "Far more than I ever deserved," he whispered.

"I can relate to that," she said softly, remembering Martin.

Neither spoke. Just as the silence began to gain weight, Peter cleared his throat and gestured to the table.

"Shall we, Miss … Joanna?"

"Sure. That would be great." She looked around. "William isn't eating?"

"He ate with Car and Mrs. Milford. They attended early services."

They sat in awkward silence. The table was laid as if for a special occasion. Linen napkins supported an excess of silverware, and all the little extras were out: a butter dish, a cream pitcher, a sugar bowl, even the salt and pepper shakers matched. Suddenly breakfast seemed a little intimidating. Joey decided to follow Peter's lead. He had taken a piece of toast from a serving plate and was pouring coffee. She repeated his movements, unsure how to start a conversation, and grateful for the tick of a nearby clock. But, as soon as she'd noticed it she became too keenly aware of its pace. She turned to find a Seth Thomas clock centered on a mantle framing yet another fireplace. This home could easily pass for a working museum.

Joey glanced at Peter, thinking about her Amish theory. His house was certainly a postcard for the lifestyle. Joey knew there were settlements in rural Illinois and Indiana, but in Chicago? She reached for the cream pitcher hoping Amish services lasted no longer than any other denomination. A decisive step interrupted her thoughts, and Mrs. Milford entered the room carrying a serving dish that matched the rest of the china.

"Eggs are ready."

"Thank you." Joey offered her a smile. Mrs. Milford glowered at her and marched from the room. Peter, serving himself eggs, seemed not to notice. She thought perhaps the mention of his late wife robbed him of his ability to converse.

"Excuse me, Peter?" She reached for the serving spoon. "What's up with Mrs. Milford?"

He gave her the same puzzled look she'd seen last night. "Up with her?"

"She seems angry with me. Did I do something wrong?"

Peter smiled and shook his head. "My housekeeper doesn't take well to strangers. Pay her no mind."

Just then Car bounded into the room, all smiles and chatter. "Got the paper, Doc. Found a newsie not four blocks away." He tossed a newspaper onto the table and flashed Joey an easy smile.

"Well, yer lookin' a lot drier! How're ya feelin', Mate?" He grabbed a piece of toast and topped it with scrambled eggs.

"Much better, thanks," Joey smiled as Car bit into his toast. Light brown hair framed his face and highlighted his blue eyes. He radiated simple joy, and seemed to brighten this vaguely shadowed place. She was grateful for his presence.

"Thank you, Car." Peter opened the newspaper. "I believe you'll find William waiting for you in the stable."

"I'm off, then." He grinned at Joey and left the room.

Peter seemed preoccupied, hiding behind the front page of the newspaper. Joey felt a bit forgotten. She finished her eggs and sat quietly. She was grateful for the hospitality, but the atmosphere here was just too formal, too old-fashioned. She felt so out of place she was ready to walk home. Joey decided to wait for an opening, thank him, make some hurried excuse for skipping church and be on her way. Amish or not, surely she'd find a cab within a few blocks. She stared at the paper, thinking he would eventually have to lower it. Something strange on the page caught her eye. She looked again. The masthead read *The Chicago Daily Sun*. She'd never heard of that paper. She looked closer. Directly under the masthead was the date.

It read October 22, 1893.

Emitting a slight gasp, Joey rubbed her eyes and looked again.

The date remained unchanged.

She swallowed hard and glanced at the layout. The front page had no pictures, only several columns of text printed in what must be pica type. Joey held her breath. She looked at the perfect fireplace, the immaculate table, and the newspaper. She remembered the metal bathtub and the antique commode. She thought about how formally William had been dressed.

1893. There must be some mistake.

"Hmm," Peter mumbled from behind the paper. "If this amendment passes their legislature, the women of Colorado will be the first in the country given the right to vote."

"Right to vote?" She fought hard to stifle a cry. "You're kidding, right?"

He spoke from behind his newspaper. "How I wish I were. So unnecessary."

No.

The tick of the clock became ominous. Joey wanted to find the nearest phone and call her mother, but she didn't dare ask where to look. Not now. She was sure Peter didn't have one, but what if no one else did either? Breath was increasingly hard to come by. Joey tugged at the neck of her blouse. The need for fresh air was suddenly, insanely urgent.

"Peter, will you excuse me, please?"

"Of course." He moved to stand, but she was already out of the room.

She hurried out the front door and stepped onto the porch. The sun shined bright, but the air was cold, much colder than yesterday. The shock of it felt good. She went down the steps and headed to the front gate. The stone pathway felt like ice on her bare feet. She didn't care; she needed a jolt she could deal with.

Trying hard not to panic, Joey considered all the peculiarities she had encountered since yesterday. She turned back to get a better look at the house. The clatter of hooves from behind startled her. Out on the street a horse-drawn cart passed by. She listened, but heard no sound of traffic. Her eyes darted skyward, searching for airplanes but found only a few clouds.

No.

She reached the picket fence and peered down the street, hoping to see something modern, something recognizable. She saw only a few old-fashioned lamp posts.

"Gas Lamps?" A small cry escaped her.

What in the world?

Another horse-drawn carriage came into view, and the driver raised his cap in greeting. It was too much. Joey spun around and staggered to a stone bench in the corner of the yard. Sinking down, she gripped the cold stone with both hands, anxious to collect herself and put some order to her thoughts. Joey held tight to the bench, rocking back and forth.

1893?

It can't be.

People don't travel through time. That's science fiction.

There must be another explanation.

Maybe she had gone insane yesterday and these kind strangers just didn't notice. Maybe she was already locked away, and these people were hospital personnel, and she had mentally morphed them into something else to make her confined existence bearable. Joey wanted very much to scream. The binding around her ribs prevented deep breath, which she desperately needed now. She took in small, rapid gulps of air, gripping the bench and pushing her bare feet deep into the cold grass beneath her, unsure of her next move.

Concentrate, Joey. Focus on what you can do.

The memory of Martin's words calmed her.

She exhaled slowly, let go of the bench and spread her hands over her skirt—the long old-fashioned skirt. She took in her surroundings and mentally replayed all that had happened since she slammed into the lumber. Everything she had experienced was too real. The pain in her chest was undeniable, the gas lights on the street were visible, and the skirt in her hands was tangible. This was no insane asylum. Peter just had to be Amish. Maybe the whole neighborhood was Amish. That would explain the gas lamps. And that remark about the vote? She must have misunderstood.

But, what if she hadn't?

Joey rubbed at her temples. She needed more definitive proof. She needed to get out of this house and explore the city. Surely on their ride to church, she would catch sight of modernity.

But, what if she didn't?

If she didn't recognize her own city, then she was in serious trouble. If the unthinkable had really happened, if she really managed to land back in time, then she needed help. Odd as this Peter guy seemed, he was clearly a gentleman. Maybe he would be willing to help her.

But, what would she tell him?

If it really was 1893, should she try to talk to him about it? Joey shook her head. It couldn't be 1893. That was impossible. From the street came the sound of another horse drawn carriage. She dug her nails into her sides, fighting tears. If it were possible, what should she do?

If her worst fears proved true, then she was alone here and Peter Hastings was her only hope. Joey hung her head in her hands. Ten minutes ago she couldn't wait to get out of this place. Now she was afraid to find what lay beyond this quiet, antiquated neighborhood.

Clutching the sides of her skirt, she felt the little box in her pocket. She should get moving. Her dirty clothes were still in the parlor, hidden behind the firewood, and she needed to return this box to its rightful place.

Joey slipped back through the front door, entered the parlor, and checked the table by the fireplace. It was empty. That must be where the box had come from. She pulled it out, set it on the table and turned to collect her soiled things, but hesitated. If she retrieved them now, and time was somehow mixed up, they might question her modern clothing. Maybe not the sweater, but certainly the running shoes would incite questions. If she put them on now and anyone saw them ....

Get a grip, Joey. She shook her head. This had to be 1993, and Amish people may not own sneakers, but surely they'd seen them on others.

And if it wasn't?

Joey trembled. She didn't want to go near that thought.

Mrs. Milford's disdainful tone interrupted Peter's breakfast reverie.

"You'd best get her out of here before we lose anything else."

"What do you mean?"

Mrs. Milford crossed her arms. Smug omniscience marked her face. "Your father's match safe is missing."

Peter folded the paper and placed his napkin on the table. "Impossible." He strode to the parlor and found Joanna looming over the firewood. An uncomfortable expression clouded her fine features.

"Ah, Miss Fagan, here you are," Peter said. He reached the fireside table, picked up the silver box, and adopted a puzzled expression.

"Hey, are you okay?" she asked.

He eyed Joey with a frown. "I'm fine, thank you. Just recalling a recent discussion with Mrs. Milford." He replaced the box on the table. "Well, we'd best be off."

His guest looked awkwardly from the firewood to Peter and back.

"Please, Joanna." He gestured to the door. "We're running late."

Chapter Six
A Difficult Assessment

In the front hall Peter searched the small closet for Victoria's overcoat and hat.

"Shall we be off?" he said, offering her the coat.

"Yes, thanks."

She slipped into it and crossed her arms, warming herself. He passed her the hat and she accepted it, but didn't put it on. Peter donned his overcoat and hat and together they headed for the carriage house. They found William astride one of the horses, Car standing close, holding the animal steady.

Peter cleared his throat. "Gentlemen, our surprise guest is departing. Have you anything to say before she goes?"

With Car's help, William dismounted. He approached Joanna and extended his small hand to her. "Thank you, Miss Fagan. I hope to see you again soon."

Peter's heart swelled. Good manners were paramount, and William behaved splendidly. Joanna's intimate reaction surprised him.

"Oh! Buddy, buddy, buddy ...." She knelt down and wrapped her arms around William, her voice soft and husky. She let go, looked into his eyes, and traced a finger from his temple to his chin. "Stay dry for me, okay?" William nodded and Joanna kissed his forehead.

Standing once more, she turned to Car. "And thank you, "she said, smiling, "for all your help last night. You're quite the fisherman, Car." She leaned forward and gave him a peck on the cheek. Peter suppressed a smile as Car blushed, uncharacteristically speechless.

She stepped into the carriage while Peter checked the harness. He climbed in beside her, pulled a lap robe from the rear and covered her. She smiled and thanked him, still clutching Victoria's hat. He continued to stare at her.

"Is something wrong?" she asked.

Peter thought he detected discomfort in her eyes.

"Your hat," he said.

Joanna eyed the hat with a puzzled look, examining it from all angles. It was one of Victoria's more ornate pieces, covered with flowers and finished with ribbons. A busy hat, but suitable for church, and Peter had always thought it a nice one.

"I … um … I don't usually wear hats, but thanks anyway." She extended her hand, as if to pass it back to him.

Peter frowned. Perhaps there was some truth to Mrs. Milford's assessment. All women, at least women of good breeding, wore hats—especially to church. If she was unfamiliar with hats, perhaps she lacked the means to buy them, and really was of humble birth. Maybe she did collect the match safe, but had a change of heart. She certainly looked troubled when he found her in the parlor. Regardless, they were running late.

"Miss Fagan, we are on our way to church. Heads are covered in the house of the Lord. Now, please put on that hat."

She made no move, but seemed to be considering a counter argument. She glanced at Car and William, who viewed their exchange in silence. Whatever she struggled with, when she spoke, her good sense prevailed.

"Oh. Right. Church. If you could just show me how …." She turned the hat over in her hands. "I mean, which part goes in the front?"

Peter placed the hat on her head, gathered the ribbons and tied them under her chin. He looked down to see her cringing, and found a sweetness in her discomfort.

"There now," he said. "You look lovely. Shall we be off?" Nodding to the boys he shook the reins and they left the house.

On the trip to church Joanna seemed dumbfounded by everything. Her gaze lingered on certain streets, and as they progressed her features gave way to fright. She asked once or twice about buildings they passed, but was silent through most of the ride. Peter thought she was trying to get her bearings. He wondered if she hit her head, in addition to her ribs, when she fell into the lake.

Mass had already begun by the time they arrived, and they slipped into a pew at the back of the church. Joanna seemed to follow the rituals, but she didn't sing the hymns. Understandable, he thought, considering he was never comfortable singing aloud, even in times of thanks and praise. Victoria was the singer in their family....

Lost in his memories of his late wife, Peter didn't realize the sermon had concluded. The rustle of rising congregants brought him back to the present and he turned to assist Joanna, who also remained seated. She was staring straight ahead, hands in the prayer position, index fingers pressed against her lips. Peter thought she was praying, but then a large tear rolled down her cheek. She blinked, producing another tear. He pulled out his handkerchief and passed it to her. Joanna accepted it, but made no attempt to wipe the tears away. He leaned close and whispered, "Is everything all right?"

She gave him a sidelong glance, shook her head and looked away again. Peter thought she looked pale.

"Are you in pain?" He reached for her ribs. Joanna shook her head again.

"Would you like some fresh air?"

She nodded.

He took her gently by the arm and ushered her outside. She was slight, he thought observing her for the first time today.

And much too thin. Had she eaten any breakfast? Peter hadn't noticed. They sat on the front steps.

"What is it, Miss Fagan?" He touched her arm. "Joanna, what's the matter?"

She gave him a frightened look but said nothing, trembling beside him. Peter hesitated and, though it seemed inappropriate, he put his arm around her and gave her a reassuring squeeze. She crumbled at his gesture, collapsing into his chest as her hat fell to the ground. She sobbed hard into his overcoat.

"There, now. What's all this?" Peter rocked her gently, all awkwardness forgotten, soothing her as if she were William. He held her until the tears subsided.

"Better now?"

She nodded and sniffed.

He took the handkerchief from her, wiped the tears from her cheeks and handed it back. "Would you care to discuss it?"

Joanna stiffened like a cornered animal, desperation mounting in her eyes.

"I don't even know where to begin, but if what I think happened really happened ...." She seemed to shake inwardly. "Peter, you don't know me from Adam, and I'm scared to death if I tell you everything, you'll think I'm crazy."

He chuckled at the notion. "I disagree with your conclusion. It's true, I don't know you, but you strike me as a rational individual."

Joanna swallowed hard and ran a hand through her hair. Peter followed her movement and thought her short hair oddly becoming.

"Okay, you're a doctor. Is it possible to experience some sort of aftershock after a situation like yesterday? Because it's the only logical explanation I can think of for my circumstances."

"Honestly, Joanna, since I don't know the entirety of your circumstances, I can't give you an informed opinion until I have been fully informed."

"Wow." Her tone showed signs of mirth. "You are a logical man, aren't you?"

"Logic is one of my strong suits. Please," he begged her with a trusting smile, "test my belief in your rationality."

Her delicate features remained clouded with doubt. "Would you mind if we spoke in the carriage? It's a little cold out here."

She collected the hat and they walked back to the carriage. He offered her his hand and as she raised her skirt to climb in, he caught sight of her bare feet.

"Dear God in Heaven! Where are your shoes?" He forced her onto the bench, simultaneously covering her with the lap robe. "No wonder you're cold. You'll catch your death!"

Still admonishing her, Peter climbed onto the bench.

"This is highly irresponsible! I've just fished you from a freezing lake! You invite pneumonia with this sort of behavior! Why on earth didn't you say something?" Pounding a fist to his lip, he took in a hard breath, searching his mind for logical answers. He seldom lost his composure, but this woman was such a puzzle.

"Were they lost in the water?" he offered aloud, staring at the church.

Joanna hung her head and answered in a timid voice. "If my take on this is right, then they are my only proof—I mean, my only hope—of gaining your trust."

Though Peter heard her speak, wrapped in his frustration, he was no longer listening. He stared hard at her, willing an answer to come to mind. The woman beside him was an enigma. Yesterday's confidence had been replaced with mystified uncertainty; her easy manner contrasted sharply with moments of fear. Her short hair and low voice conjured a young man, but belonged to this befuddling young woman who could bring the dead back to life, yet had no knowledge of something as basic as a hat. She attempted to meet his gaze, but like a child caught in a lie, she lowered her head, as if sensing his grasp of the inconsistencies.

He continued to stare at her, willing himself to calm down. Confounding though she might be, she had revived William yesterday, and regardless of how she accomplished it, Peter was indebted to her. The least he could do was help her in what seemed to be her hour of need.

"Joanna," he said softly, "you saved my son's life. I want very much to understand your dilemma, and help you as best I can. I owe you that much." His hand covered hers in a tacit offer of security. "Please, tell me everything."

She blinked back fresh tears, eyed him for a very long time, and took a deep breath.

"I lost my husband not quite a year ago."

Chapter Seven
A Cat and a Clue

Joanna spoke. Peter listened, eyes drawn to her hands as she talked about Martin. Her voice was calm, but her hands moved with passion. Palms raised, she described their beginning. Hands clasped, she articulated their life together. Fingers pressed over her heart as he learned of Michael's birth, and fisted anger over the errant bullet that killed her husband.

As she spoke Peter marveled at her ability to impart the story. His own tale of loss shared similar elements. His feelings for Victoria seemed an uncanny parallel to her love for Martin, but to voice it? He would never consider doing so. Still, he found a surprising measure of comfort in hearing grief expressed in blunt, though earnest, dialogue.

"Roughly a week after his death, I began running every day." Joanna paused, passing her fingers through her hair. "When I run, I remember the good stuff and I can cope. But when I stop, all I remember is the void, and it's a pretty dark place." She faced him. "I'm not really sure where I'm going with any of this."

He raised a shoulder. "Nor am I, but it seems your loss feeds both your confidence and your fear."

Brows arched, Joanna eyed him in silence.

"Last night," he continued, "your actions were decisive. This morning I caught a glimpse of uncertainty. You seemed uncomfortable, out of place." Peter stroked his chin. "Perhaps losing Martin has rendered you quite lost in this world."

"I think you nailed it," Joanna said. "Literally."

Her last word caught his attention. "Can you elaborate?"

"Oh, God." Her voice wavered. "I don't know if I can put this into words yet. I wasn't sure until we drove to church. Everything's so different. I thought I'd eventually see something familiar, but nothing is as it should be. The truth is I really need to talk to somebody about this, but I'm terrified of what you might think of me once I tell you." She took a breath and drew in her shoulders.

She reminded Peter of a child about to take her first leap from a great height, unconvinced she would survive. He patted her hand in an attempt to reassure her. "Joanna, I'd like very much to help you, as you have helped me." Her tears welled again and he felt the fear in her trembling hand. "Please," he said, coaxing her, "William's life. I owe you a great deal. Please continue."

Joanna nodded and shifted in her seat. "Okay, but some of this may be pretty hard to swallow. For starters, I'm lost."

Peter's hand remained over hers. "I sensed as much, please go on."

"No. I'm worse than lost. I didn't want to admit if but … Peter, I have no clue how—or how long—it will take to find my way home. And my son, he's … he's—"

"I thought he was safe with your mother."

She nodded. "He is, but getting home, back to the fu—. Oh God, what a nightmare!"

The church doors opened, and parishioners streamed out. He gave her hand a reassuring squeeze. "There's no need to invoke the name of the Lord. I can *help* you."

"Even if it means staying with you?"

She lowered her head as if anticipating a blow. Peter realized he wanted very much to see her regain the strength and spirit she possessed at their first meeting. He had helped others all his life, though only once offering shelter in his home, and Car had grown to be an indispensable member of the family. How could he deny anything less to the person who revived his son?

"Look at me," he said, lifting her chin. "Joanna, you are welcome to stay as long as you like." The weight of her relief reached his fingertips as she sighed, eyes closed.

"Why Peter Hastings!" A bright, intrusive voice exploded in his ears. "Who *is* this charming girl?"

Peter and Joanna turned to find a stunning young blonde, impeccably dressed in burgundy, with a head full of lustrous curls that were barely contained by a matching broad-brimmed hat. She smiled expectantly, her face a vision of playful flirtation.

"Good day, Elizabeth." Peter raised his hat, adopting a passive tone. "This is Miss Joanna Fagan. Joanna, allow me to introduce Miss Elizabeth McNair."

He saw Elizabeth give Joanna a calculated stare, and his stomach clenched. Joanna, to his complete shock, responded with unexpected theatrics of her own.

"Pleased to meet you, Elizabeth." She leaned across Peter and extended her hand. "I'm a distant cousin of Peter's."

Peter shot Joanna a look of perplexity and fought to keep his mouth closed as she elaborated on her fabrication.

"I'm just in from San Francisco for a visit."

"Ah." Elizabeth relaxed her stance, accepted her hand and added a degree of warmth to her smile. "Well, I am a dear friend of Peter's. I'm sure he's told you all about me." She leaned into the carriage. One hand reached Peter's arm and she let it rest there.

Peter flinched, glanced at Joanna for a fraction of a second, and saw her eyes travel to his captive arm. Then he watched, dumbstruck, as Joanna called upon some inner voice or instinct—he didn't know which—and change her demeanor. She leaned closer to Elizabeth, letting her hand rest on Peter's knee as she did so.

"Actually … no." Joanna's voice took on a purring quality that rivaled Elizabeth's. "But I've only just arrived, so we're still catching up." She paused, and, to Peter's relief, she changed the subject.

"My goodness, it's so much colder here!" She leaned even closer to Peter. "How do you manage?"

Elizabeth, shedding any pretense of warmth, tightened her grip on Peter's arm and leveled her gaze at Joanna. "My dear Miss Fagan, the natives of Chicago are born to withstand her rigors. We're quite capable, as Peter can attest." She smiled at Peter who said nothing, splitting his glances between them.

"I can well imagine." Joanna flashed a restrained smile. "Peter, shall we?" She patted his knee and leaned back. "My poor California bones need a fire."

The subtle fury of their exchange had him in a quandary. He felt as if he were at the center of a brewing storm.

"Of course, how thoughtless of me." He raised his hat and picked up the reins. "Good Day, Elizabeth. Please give my regards to your father."

"Oh no, you don't!" Elizabeth recovered with a playful grin. "Not until you agree to come to dinner. Father hasn't seen you in months and he would love to meet your little cousin."

With obvious discomfort, Peter cleared his throat. How could he politely refuse her?

"This Saturday," she insisted.

To his utter surprise, Joanna settled the matter for them.

"Saturday would be perfect," she said. "What time shall we come?"

"Five o'clock," said Elizabeth, still smiling at Peter. "Until then!" She released her grip and waved goodbye.

Peter set the horses in motion, passing an occasional stunned glance at Joanna. Once they were out of congregational earshot, he glared hard at her.

"Who *are* you?" he demanded.

"Who am I?" Joanna gasped her reply. "Who the hell is she?"

"Don't swear," he said. "It's unbecoming."

"Sorry," she replied, "but where I come from 'hell' is not much of a swear word, and quite frankly I had other words in mind. She's a real piece of work ... little cousin. Where does she get off?"

Peter was lost. This woman possessed a foul mouth and a ready lie. She moved him from empathy to exasperation in a single breath, and he failed to keep the latter out of his voice.

"What on earth are you talking about?"

She laughed, maddening him further. "Peter, I think your friend has a thing for you."

Peter's gaze remained uncomprehending.

"A crush. She likes you, Peter."

He dismissed the notion with a shake of his head. "I still don't understand. Why lie to her?"

"Two reasons. When I first met her she looked a little jealous, and I thought she might be your girlfriend. I told her I was your cousin so you could avoid a fight with her later."

"And?" Peter gestured for more.

"And cousins rarely marry in my neck of the woods. It was my way of saying I wasn't her competition." Joanna rubbed her forearms. "But then she laid a hand on your arm, and you reacted like it was a snake. You looked like a deer in the headlights. All of a sudden I thought maybe I should give her a reason to think otherwise."

"Deer in the headlights?"

"Oh yeah, you probably don't have those yet." She waved her hand as if dismissing the thought. "Anyway, it seemed to me that her attention wasn't welcome."

Peter shook his head, pressing her on. "And the other reason?"

"Listen, if I am really welcome to stay with you, you're going to need a logical explanation for my presence and the truth, as I'm beginning to understand it, is not at all logical." She rubbed her temple as if fighting a headache. "A visiting cousin may not have been the best choice, but it was all I could think of with Princess there staring holes into me."

Peter suppressed a smile. "And the real reason for your presence?" he asked. "Why are you so lost?" He watched as her confidence wilted again.

"Can I tell you when we get back to the house? There's something I have to show you."

He nodded, but before long he began debating aloud, searching for her logic. "I thought you were an honorable person, and then you lie like a card sharp to a total stranger."

Joanna offered an emphatic response. "First, it's card shark, and second, I have never lied to you, Peter, and I won't start now."

"No, it is card sharp, someone who skillfully deceives others at poker. A shark is a predatory animal with no knowledge of card games. And lying to Elizabeth McNair is a secondary issue for me. It was the cunning …." He paused, unsure how to describe the nuances of a gender so foreign to him. "You behaved quite like her, and I didn't consider you capable, given what little I know of your nature."

"Well, I'm not really like that." Her voice dropped and her eyes held steady. "But I am a woman, and Elizabeth McNair is like, super femme. She's … she's all cat."

Peter gave her a puzzled look as she raised a hand and lowered it, as if debating how to continue.

"You just looked so uncomfortable, so I decided to fight fire with fire. For your sake, I tried to let her know, in her own language, that she couldn't just sink her claws in unchallenged. If I crossed a line, I'm sorry."

Brows raised, Peter smiled. "So you came to my rescue?" He bowed slightly and tipped his hat to her. "Again I am in your debt, but why, then, did you accept her dinner invitation?"

Joanna frowned. "Well, since I acted purely on instinct, and I didn't know the nature of your relationship with her, I thought we could use Saturday to either repair the damage or permanently declaw her. Not that I have a clue how to go about either one."

"You would do that for me?" Peter was still mystified, but touched nevertheless.

"After you hear the rest of my story, whether you believe me or not, you're going to understand that I owe you a great deal more than you owe me." She braved a look in his direction and he smiled, pleased to see another glimpse of her spirit.

"I do wish you could elaborate on this mystery for me. Must it wait until we get back?"

Joanna held firm. "Honestly, I'm not trying to beat a dead horse here, but my *mystery*," she emphasized the word, making quotation marks in the air, "is pretty far-fetched, and I need every shred of evidence available to me before I say another word."

"Really, Joanna!" Peter laughed. "You seem to think I'll have you locked away once I hear your story."

"That's exactly what I'm afraid of. Can we please talk about something else?"

"Anything you wish."

"So, what's the deal with Elizabeth?"

"The deal?"

"What's the story between you two?"

"There is no story." Peter sighed, staring straight ahead. "She was a friend of my wife's. She always seems to—" He paused for a moment, unsure how to continue. "Her forward nature is quite troublesome, and I find myself uncomfortable in her presence."

Joanna grinned. "Ah ha! So, that *was* dread I saw when she put her hand on your arm."

She leaned forward to catch his attention, sincere regret in her eyes. "I'm sorry, Peter. If I had seen it sooner I would have claimed to be your fiancé instead of your cousin."

He let out a hearty laugh. "Ah. If only we could turn back time."

Joanna stiffened.

"Be careful what you wish for," she muttered quietly.

Chapter Eight
Secrets at the Carriage House

As they made their way home, Peter explained that Elizabeth McNair was a neighbor of the Sullivan family and a life-long friend of Victoria's.

"Victoria had no sisters, so she enjoyed having a friend to discuss subjects she would never broach with her brothers. She was so completely immersed in a world of men that she felt abeyant in the feminine arts. She yearned for female companionship and was thrilled to find a girl who navigated life by means of her feminine intuition. Victoria once told me Elizabeth uses her gender as her father does his surgeon's tools."

Joanna held up a hand. "You said Victoria felt 'abeyant.' You mean, like, absent or missing?"

Peter nodded. "Her character lacked nothing. Her mother died when she was a baby and she was the only girl in the house. Her father raised her as he had her brothers. And yet, she was like the bloom on a lush magnolia, distinct from the greenery, but born of the same branches."

He continued, eyes fixed on the road. "I think her feminine qualities were naturally rooted within her, and flourished without her notice. I always thought they were finely suffused with the paternal upbringing she experienced. She was, to me, the essence of feminine." His rich tone trailed to a whisper.

"Wow."

Her soft response pulled him from his reverie. Peter cleared his throat and changed course.

"Victoria was a valued member of her household, not some jeweled object, artfully placed and feeding on attention. My experience with women is limited, but I count Elizabeth McNair among the jeweled objects. Since I lost Victoria she seems more intent on inserting herself in my path. It's disconcerting." He looked to Joanna and found her wearing a curious expression. He frowned. "Is something wrong?"

"No. Not at all. That was just a really touching description of your wife. You're an eloquent guy, Peter. Even your dig at Elizabeth was smooth. I'm not at all surprised she's attracted to you."

"I would prefer she weren't."

Joanna smiled. "Peter, if it wasn't Elizabeth it would be some other woman. In fact, I'd be willing to guess there are several women who would love to spend more time with you."

As they rounded the corner to Chapman Lane, Peter felt the heat in his cheeks and Joanna noticed.

"What? Are you embarrassed? Wow again, Peter! Clearly you have no sense of yourself." His puzzled expression spurred her on.

"Look at you!" she said, raising a finger for each point she made. "You're kind, generous, that voice of yours could stop a train ... and all that thick hair!" Her hand darted close to his head, and retreated. "You're like some knight in shining armor. Sooner or later you'll be somebody's champion."

Peter froze—caught by the echo of Victoria's claim of chivalry, given voice now by this puzzle of a woman. He eyed Joanna, but found her attention focused elsewhere. Following her gaze, he beheld one very dour Mrs. Milford standing on the front porch, holding a dirty sweater in one hand and an odd looking pair of shoes in the other. They dangled from some kind of string, and called to mind a pair of dead rats, swinging by their tails. Still jolted by the knightly comparison, he turned to Joanna. Her smile had wilted.

"I am so busted," she whispered, eyes closed.

"I beg your pardon?"

"She found my shoes. That's what I wanted to show you."

"No. You spoke of knights and champions."

"Oh, that," she said, staring at the porch. "Well, I could use one right about now. It seems I'm about to face a dragon."

Peter thought of Victoria, years ago, declaring him her champion. Joanna was so different in appearance and manner, yet she possessed sparks of Victoria's direct nature and all of her sincerity. Her dilemma seemed to warrant some measure of heroism. If he was a knight, was she his fair maiden? His just cause? A sense of warmth stirred within him. It was nothing like his first meeting with Victoria, yet he felt a growing need to shepherd this woman through her mystifying situation.

Watching her tremble, Peter released a broad smile. He felt a measure of joy in this newfound sense of purpose. He had no idea where it would lead him, but he basked in the warmth of it just the same.

"Joanna, from this point on you are a guest in my home. Stay with Car in the carriage house. I will speak to Mrs. Milford and then come for you. It's time I heard the rest of your—" He smiled, imitating her finger gesture. "Mystery."

The horses entered the driveway and Car bounded from the carriage house with a grin. "Found yer shoes! Figured ya'd be back to get 'em." One look at Joey and he abandoned the smile. "Guess I might've put ya in a bit of a spot there, Joey. Sorry 'bout that." He steadied the horses as Peter descended, and then climbed up beside her. Peter glanced at them.

"Car, Joanna will be our guest for a few days. Please entertain her while I speak to Mrs. Milford." Before walking away, he turned to Joanna. "Don't worry. Stay with Car and everything will be fine."

Once inside the carriage house Car unhitched the horses and led them to their stalls as Joey stood by, watching him.

"Can I be of any help?"

"Nah, I'm good wi' this. Mind the dung."

He pointed out some fresh manure and she raised her skirt, revealing her bare feet. "I can help you, though. Come with me, Mate." He linked arms with her and led her up a set of stairs. Car opened a door and beckoned her inside.

"Behold m'garret. Make yerself at home. I won't be a tic." He disappeared through another door and returned carrying a pair of thick socks. Joey smiled as he tossed them her way.

"Have a seat, put 'em on." He gestured toward a sofa by a fireplace.

Joey put on the socks and glanced around. The room had a small sitting area and a separate room, probably a bedroom, off to one side. There was a dining area of sorts and a sink, but no real kitchen.

Car sat on the floor opposite her, his back against the stone wall, regarding her with half a smile. "So, yer stayin' with us for a while, eh?"

"I guess so. I hope that's okay."

"Fine by me. This tree could use a bit of a shake." He produced a cigarette and a match. "Care for one?"

She shook her head.

Car lit the cigarette. "Well, don't mention this to the doc. He'll have my head."

With a finger to her lips, she asked, "How did you manage to find my shoes?"

"Found 'em when I was stackin' fresh wood in the parlor." He exhaled into the fireplace and pointed across the room. "Why'd ya hide 'em in the logs?"

"I didn't hide them. I just kind of stuffed them out of the way, and forgot to grab them before I left this morning."

"So, ya came back ta get 'em?"

"I did, but I have a very bad feeling that my home isn't there anymore." She hugged herself. "Actually, I'm afraid I might be here for a while."

"That's terrific, Joey. Stay as long as ya like. But, if ya don't mind my askin', how the devil does a home go missin'?"

She sighed heavily. "Car, it's a long story, and I promised Peter I'd tell him first. Can I fill you in later?"

"Sure. I'll be here." A steady stream of smoke filled the air. "I love a good story."

Joey eyed him carefully. "How do you know it's going to be so good?"

"Well, let's see," Car said, stroking his chin. "Summer's long over and yet yer out splashin' about in a cold, dirty lake. Ya rise from the depths of it with Will in yer arms, swimmin' like a mallard, then pump the life back inta him as if ya were born to it." He pulled on the cigarette and paused to exhale. "Yer a lass, but ya slink around the docks lookin' like a boy, and ya know how ta swear like one, too. Oh yeah," he finished dryly, "yer a real snore."

"I see your point." Joey settled onto the sofa and curled her feet under the skirt, watching him. "So, what's your story, Car? How did you come to be here?"

"Ah. That's a pretty good story, too."

"As it happens, I've got some time on my hands."

"Well, the long and short of it is, me mam died, and Doc was there when she passed. I think it was pretty obvious I had nowhere ta go, so he offered me a spot here. That was several years ago, back when Conall and Maeve were still around."

"Conall and Maeve?"

"Yeah." He smiled, as if recalling a good memory. "The Dennaheys. They looked after the place back then. Today it falls ta Mrs. Milford and me."

At the mention of her name, Joey twisted in her seat. "You know, I don't think that woman likes me very much."

Grinning, Car shook a finger in her direction.

"Now, don't go around thinkin' yer special! She's a bitter berry, that one. Sour ta everyone who gets a taste of her." He stopped for a moment, seeming to consider his thoughts. There was a touch of compassion in his voice when he proceeded.

"Her heart's in the right place, Joey, it just got caught on a nail some time back. And since it gives her the occasional trouble, she shares it with the rest of us, is all." He took a final drag and tossed the cigarette into the fireplace, turning to exhale up the flue.

Clutching her sore ribs, Joey laughed. "You're a crack up, Car."

They both heard the door to the carriage house slide open. Car was on his feet in an instant. He touched Joey's forearm. "Hey," he said softly.

He raised two fingers imitating a cigarette, and shaking his head he followed it with a single finger to his lips, indicating the need for silence. Joey responded, repeating his cigarette gesture. Then she poked her index finger down her throat, indicating wretched disgust, followed by a shake of the head and a finger to her own lips. His secret was safe.

"Yer a bit of a hoot there, yerself, Joey." Laughing, they walked downstairs and found William Hastings waiting below.

"Hey, little mister!" Joey called out.

William bobbed his head. "Oh, Miss Fagan, you *are* here!"

"Please, call me Joey, or Joanna. I mean, we're going to be friends, right?" William surprised her. He stopped short and straightened himself.

"A gentleman must call a lady by her last name."

Joey melted.

The earnest display of decorum raised a sudden swell in her heart for her own son. She could easily picture Michael saying something similar in a year or two, and the thought brought on a wave of anxiety. How would she ever get back to him? She dropped to her knees, hungry for a child's touch.

"Oh, William! From the moment I met you I thought you were a consummate gentleman." She opened her arms, and he tumbled into them, unknowingly quelling her fear.

"You call me whatever you like." She tousled his hair and kissed his forehead, wishing he was Michael, but grateful for his innocent presence. She hugged him longer than she intended, and then released him. "Call me Miss Fagan in front of others, and Joey or Joanna when we're alone. It will be our secret. Okay?"

William's eyes were clouded with doubt. "Are you sure it's allowed?"

"It's allowed by me, and that's all that matters."

A mischievous grin appeared. William leaned close and whispered, "Joey is a boy name."

She grinned back. "Well, kind of. But my hair is short like a boy."

"I'll call you Joey," he said, looking around the room, "when no one else is near."

She laughed at his discretion and glanced at Car, who knelt down and extended his hand in a conspiratorial shake. "You betcha, boyo! She's a Joey by me any day." Car tilted his sandy head toward the house. "So what's the scuttlebutt, Will? Hear anything interesting?"

The boy swallowed before answering. "Well, Mrs. Milford is very angry."

Car gave Joey a wink over William's head. "We all know the words ta that tune. Anything else?"

"She doesn't want Miss Fa—" William stumbled over her name. "Jo … Joey. She doesn't want Joey to stay with us." He dropped his head, and then raised it with a look of conviction. "But I do!" He blurted out.

Joey felt the color drain from her face, and Car must have seen it too. He put a hand on each of them. "Listen up, you two. I've been down this road before, and I know, as sure as I'm breathin', that once the doc has made a decision, no one will change his mind." He crossed his arms with an air of finality. "I'd stake m'life on it!"

"Say, Will," Car's toned softened, "shall we give Boots and Coco a treat? I don't think Joey's spent much time with horses. I bet she'd get a kick, ya know?"

William scampered to one end of the building and returned with two apples.

"Would you like to feed the horses, Joey?" He whispered her name.

She took his hand, smiling. "I've never fed a horse. Will you show me how?"

"Sure," he turned to the stalls, musing. "Never fed a horse. Car, did you hear that?"

Car laughed. "Will, I learned early, our Joey is full a surprises. I'm just waitin' for the next one."

Joey faced the horses. Coco was a dark brown mare with a streak of white running down the center of her face. Boots had a chestnut red coat, and cuffs of white hair above each hoof. Joey wasn't afraid, nor was she completely at ease. Save for a few riding sessions at summer camp, she had no experience in her favor.

"Okay, William," she said, keeping a polite distance, "which horse is your favorite?"

"Oh. I love them both," he said solemnly, "they match, like Car and Molly."

Joey gave Car a questioning look.

Car changed the subject, stroking the dark brown horse. "Now, Will, I thought yer favorite was old Coco here."

"Oh, Coco is very gentle," he explained, "and she's the tallest. I can see everything from her back. But Boots is just as kind." Both horses sniffed the air and leaned toward William, who still held the apples. "Are you ready to feed them, Joey?"

"I'll just watch this time."

William held out both hands, palms flat, and offered each horse an apple. After the snack, they lowered their heads, allowing him to stroke their long noses. Car stayed close at hand throughout. The door slid open and Peter stepped inside.

"Joanna?"

Everyone faced Peter, who responded with a genial smile. "Mrs. Milford is preparing lunch. Son, can you help Car while I speak to Miss Fagan?"

Car pulled William into a friendly hug. "We were just about to spiff up the stalls. Right, Will?"

As they were leaving, Joey heard Car quietly admonish him.

"What am I goin' ta do with ya, Will? Molly's m'best kept secret, man."

Chapter Nine
Confession

O kay, back in the '80's there was this movie." Joey curled her hands into fists. "No, there was this *story* called *The Terminator*, about this guy who goes back in ... oh shiii ... eesh!"

Palms out, she took a step back from her host hoping to stop his expected protest. Her frustration gave way to a pleading look. "Please pardon my language, but there is no way in hell this will ever sound plausible."

Peter sat behind his desk, elbows on the arms of his chair, index fingers steepled and braced against his lips. At the moment he looked a lot like a principal and Joey felt too much like a student trying to explain her way out of trouble. They had been here only a few minutes, but to Joey it seemed like forever. Her running shoes were on the desk between them, in her mind a reasonable representation of a Chicago that didn't yet exist, if only she could convince him. She sighed and tried again.

"Okay, let's just focus on the shoes. Have you ever seen anything like them?"

He shook his head.

"Good. Now what's different about them?"

Peter separated his hands. "Everything."

"Can you elaborate?" Joey leaned forward from the other side of the desk.

He picked up a shoe. "Well, I don't see a heel."

"Right. You don't run in heels. That's asking for trouble. Anything else?"

"This check mark has an interesting shine."

"Yep, the swoosh. It's phosphorescent, it glows in the dark or something. What else?"

Peter's eyebrows arched. "Phosphorescent?"

Joey bit her lip. "Mmm … fluorescent … phosphorescent … one of the two. My science is weak, but it's basically a material that reflects light. It's meant to help others see a runner in the dark. I never really thought about it. I usually run during the day."

His fingers played near front of the shoe. "This material reminds me of a honeycomb."

"It's nylon. The fabric and the pattern work together so your feet can breathe as you run. They don't get too sweaty."

"The sole is not made of leather. What is it?" Peter kept the shoe in his hand.

Joey slid her finger along the bottom of its mate. "Rubber. Maybe a couple of steps beyond the rubber used for tires."

He nodded, indicating some measure of comprehension. "Such as those on a safety bicycle?"

She snapped her fingers. "Exactly! Like on a bike. But you've never seen it used on a shoe before, have you?

Peter shook his head.

"So, we agree these shoes are unlike any you've ever seen before. Right?"

Another nod.

"Well, here goes." She met his gaze with effort. "That's because most of these materials haven't been invented yet." Joey slowed her speech, adding weight to her words. "You won't be able to buy a shoe like this for at least 50 years." She held her breath, waiting for his reaction.

Peter was a stone wall. He set the shoe on the table and stared at her, eyes blank, face void of expression. A seed of dread sprouted in the pit of her stomach.

"Peter, I bought these shoes in the year 1993. The last time I put them on was October 21st, 1993. Yesterday I went for a run in a Chicago that doesn't yet exist." Her eyes remained locked on his. "I have no idea how I did it, but somehow I traveled one hundred years back in time."

Joey continued to stare at the statue that was Peter Hastings. Finally, sensing defeat, she looked down at her shoes. They sat on the desk, dirty and small and decidedly unimpressive. If this were a courtroom drama the case would be lost. The man before her was not a lawyer but a physician.

Christ!

She gripped the sides of the table, fighting panic. What was she thinking? Of all the people she could confess this to, she chose a man who could probably get front row seats to a lobotomy. Comprehending the magnitude of her mistake, Joey picked up the failed shoes and placed them out of sight. She sank into the sofa across from Peter and rubbed her temples.

"I should have bought the Air Jordans," she mumbled.

Well, there was no taking it back now. Her feet were firmly planted in his soil. She clung to a weak notion that the concept might grow on him.

"Peter, for God's sake, please say something. I just told you I came from the future. Surely that raises a few questions in your mind."

He had returned to his principled stance. Leaning back in his chair, he eyed her quietly, judicial index fingers tight against his lips. When he finally spoke his rich voice held a note of sympathy.

"Is it possible you hit your head prior to landing in the water?"

Joey gave him a feeble smile and shook her head. "As explanations go, it would certainly help, but I'm afraid not."

Peter shrugged. "Joanna, I'll admit your shoes are very different from any I've seen before, but that simply makes them foreign to me, not from another time." He leaned forward, stroking his sideburns. "You asked me earlier if the shock of an event such as yesterday's could bring this about."

"Could it?"

"Joanna, please understand, I have virtually no experience in neurology or psychiatry, but for lack of a better explanation, I think that's our best choice. Perhaps I'll speak to—"

"NO!"

In a flash, she was on her feet and leaning across the desk. Peter froze in mid-sentence, and the implication of her sudden move registered within her. She stepped back.

"Please," she said, "put yourself in my position. If you found yourself alone in the world, would you want the only person who befriended you telling your bizarre story to others?"

"And I ask you: try to understand mine. Imagine a prolonged encounter with a stranger, under extraordinary circumstances, and then imagine that stranger asking you to believe the impossible."

"Okay, point taken." She paced the floor in front of the desk and then made her way to the windows. "There's got to be some common ground here." Leaning against the window frame, she asked, "If this is shock, how come I remember everything about 1993, and nothing about 1893?"

Peter gave her a curious look. "Such as?"

"I don't know … daily life."

"All right then, exactly how does daily life in 1993 differ from today?"

She gave her host an enthusiastic smile. "Where do I start? Peter, it's amazing! Everyone travels by car, even by air. Airplanes are a huge industry. Personal computers are fast replacing typewriters. They're working on something now called the Information Super Highway. I don't really know much about it, but it's supposed to be really cool."

Peter remained still, and Joey took it as a positive sign.

"Let's see, daily life." She checked the room for inspiration. "Wind-up clocks are long gone. Fireplaces are still around, but mostly for decorative or sentimental reasons. Homes are heated by natural gas or electricity. There's a telephone in every house—cordless is big. Oh! And there's a new kind of phone, a cell phone. Well, it's not that new, but I don't have one. Um ... doctors use pagers." She paused. "Oh! And movies, like *The Terminator*! Man, I wish you could see that one." She caught sight of her reflection in the window.

"And women! They vote. They work outside the home. And many of them have short hair." She turned to find Peter with a distinct crease in his brow. Her smile faded and she reached for her tea.

Peter shook his head. "Computers? Pagers? Movies? Joanna, you're not making any sense."

It took both hands to steady her tea cup. "I suppose now you *really* want to call your friend."

Peter remained seated and stoic. Between them lay a gulf of uncomfortable silence, and Joey waited, dreading the words that would end it. Finally, he exhaled heavily and addressed her.

"Maybe we should concentrate on what you know about the present."

There was no faking an answer to that question. Joey slumped against the window frame. "Well, you've got me there, Peter. I haven't a clue."

"Then concentrate, Joanna. Try to recall anything about the year 1893, anything at all. Focus on what you do know."

She flinched at the variation of Martin's pet phrase. Hearing it come from Peter was odd, but comforting. Nevertheless, he was right. She needed to give him something concrete about this century. She didn't want him to think of her as a lost cause. Lost causes are cast aside and put away. She couldn't risk that. Then she would never get home. Joey scanned her thoughts and threw out a name she had always associated with the turn of the century.

"William McKinley? Isn't he the president?"

"No, although he would be an excellent choice."

Joey lowered her voice. "He'll get there at some point."

"I beg your pardon?"

She looked up. "Never mind."

Peter still wore an expectant look. She tried again. "Taft?"

Shaking his head, Peter supplied the answer. "President Cleveland. Grover Cleveland. Try again. Can you think of anyone else who's made the papers recently?"

She threw out a more sensational name, culled from childhood rhymes. "Lizzie Borden?"

Peter smiled. "Excellent. What do you remember about her?"

"Well, if memory serves, she was tried for the murder of her parents, but she was acquitted."

"That's right. She was found innocent a few months ago. It made the national news." He leaned forward with an encouraging look. "Can you remember anything else, anything specifically about Chicago?"

Joey shrugged and shook her head. "I don't know. Do you still have today's paper around?"

Peter frowned. "I'd rather you try to remember on your own."

"Listen, I understand your logic," she countered, "but if this is some sort of shock-related thing, maybe looking at a newspaper will dredge up a greater number of memories."

"You raise a good point." He pulled the paper from the desk and extended it to her. Joey spread it out in front of her.

"Oh my God!" she cried.

Peter sat forward. "What is it? You remember something?"

"The World's Fair! The Columbian Exposition! That's going on now? It never occurred to me … wow!" She smiled. "I would love to see that!"

He frowned again. "You mean to tell me that you, a resident of Chicago, have not yet visited the Columbian Exposition. Joanna, it's been open for nearly six months!"

"Look," she said, trying to keep her frustration in check. "I really don't know how to convey this without offending you. I've been in Chicago, just not in your time zone."

Peter's stoic expression revealed a decided lack of amusement.

"Okay, okay," she held up a hand. "No luck with that one. There must be something else here." She scanned the remainder of the front page, which was littered with stories related to the fair. One smaller headline caught her eye. She let out a cry and looked up at Peter.

"Okay, I found something, but this really supports my theory, not yours." She swallowed hard. "I can tell you about something that's going to happen this week ... something awful."

Peter's voice approached a growl. "Joanna, I am running low on patience."

"Please, look at this." She pointed to a small headline. It read. HARRISON HOSTING AMERICAN CITIES DAY AT EXPO.

"Yes? Go on."

"This Saturday is the 28th of October. Mayor Carter Harrison will be at the fair with a group of civic dignitaries. I think he's giving some sort of closing speech."

He scanned the text with a smoldering impatience. "That's not a prediction, Joanna. That's all stated in the article."

She held up a hand. "Please, bear with me. Growing up, I learned about the history of Chicago. We learned about the stockyards, the Great Fire—"

"And?"

"And we learned that on October 28th, 1893, Mayor Carter Harrison, one of the most beloved citizens in Chicago, was shot and killed by a mad man named Prendergast."

As before, Peter's face registered nothing.

"Peter, the mayor will be dead by Sunday." Joey collapsed onto the sofa, clutching her sides. "Oh my God," she said softly. "Oh my God."

*　　*　　*

Peter remained silent for a long time, regarding her. He was convinced she had suffered some form of memory loss. But time travel? Mayor Harrison murdered? Her revelations shed an unflattering light on her sanity. Still, her ability to maintain cogent discourse contradicted this odd imbalance.

With some hesitation he decided to treat her claim with a modicum of respect. After all, her basic thought processes seemed intact. If he found no answers through written research he might be forced to discuss her case, on a hypothetical basis, with his brother-in-law, Richard, a neurologist. He walked to the sofa and sat down beside her.

"Joanna, it took a great deal of courage to reveal this to me. I appreciate your candor, even if I don't quite know what to make of it. I think, at present, this is best kept between us."

Fear stole over her fine features. "So, you don't believe—"

He held up a hand. "Let's not worry about my belief, let's worry about reuniting you with your family. Now, I promised you a place to stay and I am a man of my word. Should we meet anyone else during your stay, I will introduce you as my distant cousin visiting from San Francisco."

Joanna let out an anxious breath. "Thanks. But what are we going to do about the mayor? Shouldn't we at least try to warn him or something?"

Peter rose from the sofa and began pacing. Her prediction was odd. Harrison was an extremely popular man. Still, politicians can't please everyone, and in twenty-five years Harrison had surely cultivated a few foes. Had Joanna been purposefully evasive about her origins? Did she, as Mrs. Milford suggested, live among unsavory characters? Men who would consider assassination to achieve their means? He eyed her critically. She remained on the sofa, her brow creased with worry. If she was involved in something dire, then he was sure she wanted no part of it. Her desire to warn Harrison was proof of that. He reached for his quill pen and wrote the name Prendergast, but then ran a line through it.

Assassination? It was a notion as far-fetched as her futuristic roots. Whoever she was, she didn't seem like a street urchin, but she wasn't completely herself. The last thing he intended to do was allow her to confront the head of the city with some sort of personal doomsday message. Her sanity, or loss thereof, remained his first priority.

"We have at least a few days to address your concerns about the mayor. Let's start with your family." He raised his pen, "I'll need your current address and the names of any living relatives. I'll make inquiry with the police, see if anyone is looking for you."

Joanna rolled her eyes, but complied. "You won't have any luck, but okay."

"Nonsense. With a little effort I'm sure we can—oh, Mrs. Milford. I didn't hear you come in. Kindly remember to knock when the door is closed." He stood and offered Joanna a hand. "Is lunch ready?"

The housekeeper nodded, eyeing Joanna, a downward curl dominating her thin lips. Peter thought her worries were unnecessary. Joanna would be with them a few days at most, and it was unlikely this charming waif would upset the natural order of the household in such a short time. As they left the parlor he gave Mrs. Milford a reassuring smile. What could possibly go wrong?

Chapter Ten
The Story of Car

Aknock on the front door interrupted lunch, and Peter excused himself to attend to two injured boys. One walked in cradling his arm. His brother favored a swelling black eye. Their stern father stood between, denying them the pleasure of further destruction.

As Peter dressed their wounds, he thought of William. It pained him greatly that he had no siblings, despite the potential for bloodletting among young boys. He worked in silence, grateful that at least William had Car. Despite their age difference, the young Irishman was a wonderful companion, kind, patient and willing to indulge William in all manner of horseplay. Given the circumstances, Peter counted himself lucky to have found Car so long ago, and luckier still, that the boy had remained with him....

In 1883 Peter completed his studies at Rush Medical College and followed in his father's footsteps, serving with various charitable organizations around the city to help those in need.

Late that summer he spent the better part of one hot day at a busy charity clinic. After a rushed lunch he stepped outside for a breath of fresh air, though given the dog days of August and the stagnant, clotted air, there was little difference between the clinic and the sunbaked street.

As he stretched his arms to unbind his muscles, he watched a small boy approach. The child was young and scrawny, seven or eight, Peter guessed, and he pulled a heavy load with a rope. It was looped over one shoulder and under the other, fashioned like a harness and attached to some sort of litter. Though he couldn't make out the contents, Peter guessed it was an ailing relative.

"Good afternoon, sir. I'm Car Madigan. Would ya be a doctor, then?" The boy paused to catch his breath. "If so, I wonder, could ya see to me mam, please? She's a bit under today, sir."

Charmed by the child's pleasant disposition, especially in light of his burden, Peter smiled, approaching the litter. "Of course. I'd be happy to help your—"

He was close enough to see he could do nothing for the woman. It appeared she had died a few hours earlier. Car took no notice of Peter's observation. He launched into a brief history of her illness.

"Her color's off, sir. And she hasn't eaten well in days, though she'll take water when I can find it. She cold now, but I had to use her blanket for the litter. She's bound to warm up once I find another."

Peter stared at the blue figure, and then the boy. He squatted down beside the child and pressed a fist to his lips, watching him. Car Madigan was bleary-eyed, with ribs visible through a threadbare shirt, pants tattered and too short, revealing blackened bare feet. The boy was gaunt, exhausted, and in dire need of a bath. But he stood erect, tired eyes rimmed with hope. Car returned Peter's scrutinous gaze and responded to it with a surprising level of diplomacy.

"Forgive me, sir," Car said, gesturing to himself. "Since she took sick, I gave her my portion of the water for drinkin' so bathin' wasn't—" He swallowed hard. "I'll stand well back while ya help her."

Impressed, Peter addressed the young man in soothing tones. "No need to worry, Car. Getting clean is easy, getting healthy takes a little work. But that's why you're here, isn't it?"

"Yes, sir. Well, not for me. I'm fit as a fiddle, but Mam's a bit lower than usual."

Peter marveled at the boy's courage. Car was anything but fit, and if Peter guessed correctly, the boy was quite alone as of today.

"Where's your father, son?"

"He died, sir, a few weeks back."

"Do you have any family in Chicago?"

"No, sir. Just me mam."

"Car, when did you last eat?"

The boy averted his gaze and kicked at the dirt. "Oh, I've had a bite here and there."

Peter laid a hand on his shoulder. "Tell you what. Let's let your mother sleep here for a moment. We'll go inside and find something to eat. While you get some nourishment, I'll get her a blanket and a space to sleep inside. You can sit with her after your meal."

Car swayed at the offer, confirming Peter's suspicions. He untied the makeshift harness and led Car inside. After settling the boy in the kitchen with one of the Sisters of Mercy, he retrieved the body and laid it near the other corpses they had accumulated. He found a piece of cloth and covered the woman as if to warm her.

Normally he wouldn't go to such lengths, but the mix of desperation and hope in young Car's eyes took hold of him. The child displayed a sense of responsibility beyond his years. The only thing Peter could offer him was the comfort of knowing he'd done everything possible for her before she died. Peter didn't like lying, but he could justify this ruse if it was helpful to the boy.

Once he had arranged her as peacefully as possible he found Car, upbeat and animated, chatting with the Sisters over a bowl of soup. He smiled as Peter approached.

"Here's the doc who's helpin' her. Is she feelin' better, sir? Yer all aces, Doc."

Peter smiled, giving nothing away. "Would you like to sit with your mother now?"

Car stood and thanked the nuns. He turned to follow, but stopped. "Might I take her some water, sir?"

"Oh, she won't need any just yet, she's still asleep. Come with me."

As they walked Peter prepared his speech, inadvertently borrowing from a conversation he'd had with Conall when he was no older than this boy. Just before they reached her, he stopped and knelt close to Car. He began to speak, his rich voice low and soothing.

"Car, your mother is deep asleep and when she wakes up," he paused, cupping the boy's chin in his hand. "Son, you need to know something. When she wakes up, your mother will be with the angels. Do you know what that means?"

Car nodded and tears welled but he didn't blink, only stared at Peter, wide-eyed and silent.

"You were very strong to bring her all this way. She'll reach heaven knowing you did everything you could to get her here safely. Now, I want you to sit with her, and tell her anything in your heart. Tell her good bye. She can't respond but she will hear you. She'll want to hear from you one last time. Do you understand?"

Car swallowed hard and nodded. "She's been feelin' down for a long time now."

"I promise you, she's not feeling down any longer." Peter squeezed his shoulder. They reached his mother and Peter squatted beside Car once more. "I need to attend to a few things, but when I return we'll talk more over supper. All right, son?" Car nodded, and Peter walked away forming a loose plan.

The normal procedure in such cases was to pass the orphan into the hands of the Sisters of Mercy. Peter knew he had no intention of doing so, though he didn't dwell long on his motives. Perhaps it was because he was new to his profession and his heart hadn't yet hardened to situations such as this. Perhaps he did it for Conall and Maeve. He knew they would welcome this boy since they had no children of their own. Or perhaps it was because Peter had lost his own mother as a young boy. He understood the agony of such a loss, and he didn't want Car to endure it alone. He decided this little fellow deserved some comfort along his dark path.

After cleaning his instruments, he informed the Sisters that Car's mother had died, but told them the boy had local relatives and Peter would see him delivered safe into their hands. Within the hour he returned to Car, only to find him fast asleep. He picked up the boy and made his way home.

Conall and Maeve met them in the driveway. Maeve took the child and Peter instructed her to clean him well and dress him in an old nightshirt until they found some proper clothes for him.

"Will he take his meals with us, then?" Conall asked, unhitching the horses.

"Of course," Peter responded. "As long as he is here, he will be treated as family. He can sleep in my old bedroom."

Car didn't join them for dinner that night, instead giving in to a high fever. Peter, Conall, and Maeve took turns watching over him, and each one caught small pieces of his past as he babbled in his delirium. He was one of several children, most of whom had died in Ireland. The last four members of the family set sail for America, and he lost a baby sister in the crossing. His father died in Baltimore and then his mother's health, already compromised, failed her shortly after they reached Chicago.

Peter noted that, even when incoherent, the boy maintained his polite tone. This cemented his belief that Car was essentially a good child who merely stumbled on the wrong side of circumstance. Bringing him home was the right thing to do.

Children enliven a house and, as Peter surmised, Conall and Maeve Dennahey were happy to help this one find his voice. Young Car thrived under their care, eager to please and always gracious. Car devoted himself to the Irish couple, doing everything asked of him. Before long he anticipated their needs and tackled chores without prodding. He was in awe of the horses, and Conall spent many hours with him, teaching him how to care for them, manage and ride them.

In many ways, the timing of his arrival was perfect. The Dennaheys were getting on in years and didn't move as deftly as they once had. Car eagerly took on the tasks that required too much of them physically. Conversely, the energy he radiated kindled their spirits and kept them "in the hunt" as Conall would say, "for a wee bit longer."

In Car's eyes, Peter was 'the doc' and he remained forever grateful to his benefactor, pledging like a knight to serve him always. Peter asked only that he learn his letters, maintain his disposition, and do as Conall and Maeve instructed. Without any formal discussion, Car Madigan became a permanent member of the Hastings house....

"So I said m'good-byes, fell asleep beside her, and woke up a week later in Maeve's arms. I thought I'd joined me mam. Here was this angel, singin' ta me like a harp itself. Not a bad nap, a'tall," Car finished, smiling.

Joey and William sat together on the garret sofa, mesmerized by their storyteller. Car lay on his side, propped up on one elbow, his feet close to the fire, finishing a cigarette. They had adjourned to the carriage house after lunch.

"So, from my perch, even if somethin' bad befalls ya, there's generally good luck right around the corner. Ya just have ta scour the bushes a while ta find it." He nodded in her direction.

"So what's your story? Y'promised ta tell, ya know."

Joey blushed. "Boy, where do I start?"

"The beginnin'. Where else?"

Laughing, she looked at William and then at Car, grinning cat-like across from her.

"Well," she began slowly, "I told all this to Peter, and he said I should keep it a secret."

Both boys leaned in, curiosity piqued, but it was young William who hastened to reassure her.

"Oh Joey," he said solemnly, "this is the best place for secrets. Car tells me all his and I tell him all mine. Yours are safe, I promise."

Car nodded. "Yep. We've a pact." He reached out to William, who took his hand. Both boys extended their free hands to Joey, inviting her to join their circle.

"If ya join us now," Car said, giving Joey a playful wink, "why it'll be forged anew! We'll be stronger than ever."

William nodded in agreement, staring wide-eyed at Car, his awed expression revealing absolute hero worship.

Joey laughed and took their hands.

"Okay, but you're probably not going to believe this." She looked at William, and leaned in closer to both of them, whispering, "But I swear everything I'm about to tell you is tr—"

Everyone froze at the sound of the carriage house door sliding open, but a distinct knock on the door of the garret coaxed huge grins from Car and William. William bounded from the sofa and opened the door. Joey couldn't see the newcomer, though she remembered the name as soon as William uttered it.

"Oh Molly! We have a new member and she's about to tell us her secret. It's a big one! Come and meet her."

"Aye aye, Cap'n," said a sweet voice from beyond the door. "M'sparraw told me we might have a new member, so I hurried right over."

Into the garret stepped a lovely young girl. Molly Hannafee was a slight little thing, barely five feet tall, her hair a sun-dappled shade of red. Her eyes were blue like Car's and her brogue held the same Irish magic. Joey glanced at Car. His eyes were on Molly and his expression mirrored William's look of awe. Only in Car's case this wasn't hero worship. Car was in love. Joey smiled and stood up.

"I'm Joey Fagan." She extended her hand. "It's a pleasure to meet you."

The four of them spent the afternoon together. Joey told them her improbable tale, imploring them to keep it a secret. She told them about all the fantastic things she could think of, like airplanes and astronauts, and rockets to the moon. She told them about Michael's favorite things, ice cream that comes in thirty-one flavors, lifelike toy dinosaurs, and bright-colored blocks that clicked together to form a building.

In turn, they peppered her with questions. Did all the girls have short hair? Could Pullman cars fly in the future? Did the moon have a fancy hotel, and a good place to feed your rocket once you arrived?

When Joey ran out of steam, she asked Molly about herself. In the spirit of the game, Molly launched into a story tailor-made for William's imagination. She told them she was actually the daughter of a mighty leprechaun, but she'd been stolen away by an evil man who intended to hold her in exchange for her father's pot of gold. She snuck away in the night, boarding a ship to hide from him. Unfortunately she fell asleep and by the time she awoke, they'd sailed half way to America. Not long after she arrived she bumped into Mr. Calder, Peter's next door neighbor. He looked remarkably like her father, only much taller, and she told him so straight away.

"An' he says t'me, 'Well, I've no daughter of me own t'look after me, would ya be willin'? An' I says, 'Deal!' An' I've been here ever since, carin' for Mr. Calder as if he was my Da."

Though he'd heard it before, William was still taken by Molly's story. "A leprechaun! But, tell Joey how you can still see him. She won't believe it!"

"Ah, it's easy. I see him when it rains. He slips inta town on every rainbow." She smiled at Joey and squeezed William who was sitting on her lap, wrapped contentedly in her arms.

"An' speakin' a Da's, I'd best get back ta Mr. Calder. He'll be needin' m'help with dinner."

Everyone stood, but Molly seemed inclined to linger. Joey, without missing a beat, took William by the hand and led him to the door.

"Come on, William. Let's go on ahead and find your father."

Chapter Eleven
Marshall Field and Company

Over breakfast Monday morning Peter announced his plans for the day.

"Joanna, I'm taking you into town for a new pair of shoes. Victoria's are too small and you'll invite scrutiny wearing what you own."

"Thanks, but Victoria's skirts are long enough. My shoes stay pretty well hidden."

"Nonsense," he replied. "You need new shoes. You will buy new shoes. I'll take you to Marshall Field's. You can browse the store while I run over to the Rush Medical library. I need to gather some research material."

"Don't get me wrong," she said, setting down her fork. "I'd love to go into town, and to check out Marshall's, but there's no need for new shoes. I don't plan on being here that long."

"Joanna, this is not a discussion. You will come with me to town and do as I tell you.

Joey crossed her arms. Peter's authoritative tone would take some getting used to.

"How about this? I'll go to Marshall Field's as long as we can stop by City Hall while we're in town. If you recall our discussion yesterday, I have a very good reason for going there."

Peter pinched the bridge of his nose with his thumb and forefinger. "Joanna, I think it best if we start with something simpler. I thought a trip into town might help improve your memory."

"My *memory*," she said, putting quotation marks in the air, "may be just as easily improved at City Hall as at Marshall Field's. Why not visit both places?"

She watched as Peter's hand slid from his nose to his cheeks, stroking his broad sideburns, still deep in thought. She was about to raise another point when he responded.

"Our schedule will be busy. I'll consider a visit to City Hall only if time permits."

"Then I'll buy a pair of shoes so fast it will make your head spin." Joey's response coaxed giggles from William and Car. "Now, if you'll excuse me, I'll go get ready."

Excited by the prospect of seeing her city in all its 19th century splendor, Joey raced upstairs to use the commode. This had fast become a dreaded task, in part because of the primitive nature of performing the act, but also because it was Mrs. Milford who cleaned the commode. Despite Car's insistence that she wasn't a bad sort, the woman seemed antagonistic and Joey cringed at the thought of giving the housekeeper any additional reason to find fault with her. On her way downstairs, the muffled sound of a flush reached her ears, and Car stepped from a room Joey had never entered. Hope flickered inside her.

"Car, what's in there?" She pointed to the door he'd just closed.

"What d'ya think? It's a powder room."

"With a toilet … that flushes?"

The sandy-haired Irishman rolled his eyes in mock exasperation. "What else would flush in a powder room?" He opened the door and showed her an antique-looking toilet and a tiny sink with a faucet.

"Yes!" She raised a fist in the air and pumped it back to her chest. "Oh, man, do you know how great this is?"

"Well, it's no cause ta celebrate. It's just a powder room."

"No!" she gushed. "It's dignity, it's privacy, it's technology. Oh, man, it's …."

Car let out a hearty laugh. "It's what I'll get ya for Christmas if it means that much to ya!"

After donning a coat and the dreaded hat, they left for town. Along the way Joey asked Peter and Car all about home technology. Peter explained that after the Great Fire in 1871, plumbing was added into the design of many new homes, but his residence predated the Civil War. It had escaped the fire and remained largely in its original state. Over the years he made some improvements, adding living quarters off the kitchen for an aging Conall and Maeve, a powder room before his wedding, and the bathtub after William was born.

Peter admitted his home lacked many modern conveniences, but said he could live happily without them and Joey smiled. Given his tenuous treatment of her claim, she sensed he was a man uncomfortable with change. She felt much the same way, though it never occurred to her that living in a simpler time would be as difficult as embracing emerging technology.

As they traveled closer to the center of town, Joey noticed a distinctly foul smell in the air. At first she thought they had passed a dead animal, but instead of dissipating, the stench grew more intense. The others didn't seem to notice. She tried her best to do the same, but soon it seemed the atmosphere no longer contained any oxygen, only the egregious reeking tang now invading her sinuses. Finally, she could stand it no longer.

"My God, what is that awful smell?" She abandoned all pretense and waved her hand frantically in front of her nose. "It's like somebody filled Soldier Field with dead elephants or something. How can you stand it?"

Peter passed her his handkerchief. "That's the stockyards and slaughter houses. You've never smelled it before?"

She shook her head, hoping to keep breakfast down.

"The air will clear again soon." He gave her an odd look, but said nothing more.

They arrived at Marshall Field's and Peter escorted her inside, but within ten feet of the entrance Joey stopped in her tracks and tugged hard on his arm.

"Peter, there is no way I can shop here." Her protest came in a fierce whisper. "This is way over the top! I'll break your bank."

They stood in the midst of over sixty thousand square feet of opulence. The magnitude of the store wasn't overwhelming, but the price tags on the entry displays were another matter. To their right stood a mannequin on a platform, attired in a milk-white, gold-accented, silk evening gown, complete with a mink-lined cape and hat. A placard at the base read 'Complete Ensemble Available for $5000.00.' To their left, another platform held a majestic Persian rug for a mere twenty thousand. Other signs of luxury—shawls from India, Belgian lace and Irish linen—were strategically placed, and everything boasted a 20th century price.

Joey whistled. "Five thousand dollars for an evening gown?"

In 1893? If the dress was really an indicator of current pricing, then she'd be lucky to find shoes for less than one hundred dollars. Joey refused to drop someone else's hard-earned money on something she didn't need. Leaning close to Peter, she pointed at the evening gown.

"Peter, I didn't even spend a grand on my own wedding dress, and I bought it one hundred years from now! How can everything cost so much? Doesn't everyone earn, like," she paused, glaring at the Persian rug, "five bucks a week or something? How can they possibly afford this stuff?"

"Calm down," he admonished her, "you're only here to buy shoes."

One look told her he was equally at a loss to explain the grandeur. "Victoria always shopped here," he admitted, "but she didn't spend lavishly. Let me think for a moment."

"Let's just go. I can live without the shoes. Please?"

She knew he was in over his head, and decided with a little more pleading he might concede. She was about to make her case when a sunny voice interrupted her from behind.

"Shopping for my dinner party? May I join you?" Elizabeth McNair appeared beside Peter.

"Actually we were just leaving," Joey muttered, though no one heard her. Peter spoke over her, startling Joey because he sounded as if he were actually happy to see this woman.

"Elizabeth!" he exclaimed. "What perfect timing!"

Joey's mouth fell open.

"Yes!" he said. "Joanna would love some company today." He took a tentative step backward. "She's here for shoes. Her … ah … her trunk hasn't yet arrived."

"And a new dress for my party?" Elizabeth asked, cooing. "She'll need something nice."

"Of course, of course." Peter swallowed hard, eyeing the expensive gown. "Buy a dress for Elizabeth's party while you're here."

Joey stood silent, shell-shocked at his proposal. Did he honestly expect her to shop with the wily Miss McNair?

The cat from the church?

Evidently he did.

"In fact, why not enjoy lunch after you've finished? Elizabeth, have them put it on my account." His hand flew erratically around the room. "Joanna … whatever you want." He backed away. "I'll be busy until one o'clock. I'll … I'll pick you up out front." He attempted a casual wave as he reached the front door. "Enjoy yourselves."

And then he was gone.

Joey was still staring after him when Elizabeth spoke.

"Well that was a first," she said. "Usually he's in a hurry to get away from me, but today I think it was your turn."

Her frank assessment roused a laugh from Joey. She looked at her unwanted companion. Elizabeth returned her gaze, assessing her.

"So ... you're here for shoes and a dress."

Joey shook her head. "Honestly, just the shoes. My ... trunk should be here by Saturday. Peter loaned me a few of Victoria's old things, but her shoes are too small."

Elizabeth gave her a wry smile. "Joanna, you seem uncomfortable. Is it because of the store, or because of me?"

"A little bit of both. I don't really know you," she paused and gestured to the evening gown, "and I don't shop at this level of extravagance."

"Oh, that," Elizabeth said, waving a dismissive hand. "They're just putting on a show for the visitors to the fair. One can certainly spend extravagantly at Marshall's, but they cater to all tastes and incomes. Have you ever been here before?"

"No." Joey averted her eyes.

Not in this century.

"Well, don't let this gown deter you. Marshall Field is a genius. His store is an amazing place. You know, Victoria and I loved coming here. Come on. I'll show you around."

Elizabeth was right. The store was a veritable cathedral of material goods designed for the 19th century citizen, yet it held relatively little for Joey. Like Peter's house, it was a living museum, a snapshot of antique commerce. There was a heavy emphasis on fabric and sewing-related notions, a stark reminder of a skill Joey lacked, but one as common as cooking to women of this era. Hats, which she considered a seasonal need, dominated one floor, a testament to their prominence in current daily dress.

For the men, Joey discovered a novelty called the paper collar and cuffs. The idea that a man might 'freshen' his outward appearance in such a way intrigued her, and she made a mental note to keep an eye on the cuffs and collars of all the men she encountered.

Elizabeth expressed delight at Joey's interest in such simple things, and seemed to relish her role as hostess for the excursion. They fell into an easy rhythm. As they wandered from floor to floor Joey found that, despite her loyalty to Peter, she actually enjoyed Elizabeth's company.

Once she understood the pricing structure, Joey relaxed considerably. There was a unique repetition to everything. Wealthy shoppers could buy the five thousand dollar evening gown. For the budget conscious Marshall's offered a humbler copy, produced by one of the house seamstresses, for about twenty five.

Elizabeth took the lead in every department. The sales clerks knew her by name and treated 'our Miss McNair' with the utmost courtesy. She, in turn, would inquire about an item and either be shown samples or be assured of notification as soon as it became available.

By the time they reached the shoe department, Joey was ready to take a break. The staff offered Elizabeth a warm greeting and expressed pleasure at meeting Joey. After seating them comfortably they procured box after box of—to Joey's mind—horrendous shoes. In truth, they were all boots, stiff-looking high-heeled affairs in an odd range of bright colors. Most reached mid-calf, and all hosted a dizzying array of hooks and laces. Joey was assured that with winter approaching, this was the most logical choice.

"Well, I'm just here for a short time," she said, hoping it was true, "and my home is in California where winter is milder. Do you, by chance, have any summer styles left?"

"Why, of course, Miss Fagan. I am sure we can find something to suit you." The salesman, a Mr. Markham, turned to his colleague.

"Mr. Burnside, would you kindly check the remaining stock of summer shoes? Miss Fagan prefers something lighter."

In very short order, they repeated the entire process. Boxes were opened; heels were too high. Over Elizabeth's objection, she finally settled on an unobtrusive pair of dark shoes. They sported the lowest heel she could find and featured the shortest leather upper, offering her greater freedom of movement. She held onto the new shoes and asked Mr. Markham to wrap her running shoes instead. She caught his judgmental glance at her footwear as he took them to the counter.

Elizabeth explained that Joey was the cousin of Dr. Peter Hastings, and she had been instructed to sign for him. Would the gentlemen consider it an acceptable arrangement?

After a successful check with the billing department, they completed the transaction. Last, the clerks collected their packages—Elizabeth had made purchases in other departments—and assured the fine ladies that all boxes would be held safe by the doorman until their departure.

"That's great," Joey told the clerk, "really great."

"Thank you, Mr. Markham, Mr. Burnside." Elizabeth extended her hand to the lead salesman. "Dr. Hastings will be so pleased by your accommodation."

Markham accepted her hand and held it as if it were porcelain. "Any time, Miss McNair. We are always happy to serve you and your guests." He bowed.

Joey, not wanting to seem ill-mannered, extended her hand as well. Mr. Burnside, the young associate accepted it, and she startled him with a standard grip, giving his hand a firm shake in return. She repeated the gesture with Mr. Markham, aware she lacked Elizabeth's finesse but incapable of offering a limp wrist.

"Thanks a lot," she said. "I really appreciate it. You guys are great."

Joey thought they looked at her oddly, but each man returned her handshake and wished her a good day. She turned to leave but sensing an opportunity to rid herself of her hat, she removed it and turned back to the salesmen.

"Could you please put this with my old shoes? I ... I may want to see about a new one."

Markham's eyes flickered, but he accepted the hat. "Why of course, Miss Fagan."

"Thank you!" She walked away, but her sense of relief was tempered by a remark from Mr. Markham.

"I think our Miss McNair is performing a private charity today."

She glanced over her shoulder as Mr. Burnside nodded in agreement. Joey considered returning to defend herself, but decided against it. If the mark of social status was an over-adorned flower pot, she would rather be perceived as poor and hatless than proper and presentable. Besides, she had no desire to establish herself here; her only wish was to find a way home to Michael. Squaring her shoulders she returned to her shopping companion.

As they left the shoe department, Elizabeth took Joey by the hand. "And now, my new friend," she said, pulling her toward a wall of gleaming elevators, "since I was able to help you, perhaps you can help me."

Chapter Twelve
A Saucer of Milk

They dined on chicken stew served on white china in the Marshall Field's Tea Room, an elegant space offering respite to weary shoppers. At Joey's prodding, Elizabeth spoke about her life and family.

"Well, I'm one of three children and, by virtue of my gender, I am my father's biggest disappointment." Her tone showed no trace of the feminine lilt she used in public conversation.

Joey was puzzled. "Why by virtue of your gender?"

"Because I, the lone female in the family, was the only one to reach maturity; both my brothers died young."

"I'm so sorry."

"So was my father." Her reply was frank. "My younger brother died of pneumonia and my father was devastated. But when my older brother died in a hunting accident, he lost the heir to his fortune, his business, and the continuation of his name. It broke his heart and very nearly broke his spirit."

"But he still had you."

"Yes, but a daughter is nothing compared to a son. My loss would have been mourned, but much easier to bear."

"But … but that's medieval!" Joey stammered. "Did he actually tell you that?"

"No, not directly," Elizabeth replied. "Joanna, my father is from the South. He would never state his feelings in such bold terms."

Joey regarded her companion in silence. Elizabeth seemed different. She had abandoned her bright tone, and her speech held no trace of a sugary inflection. This was like meeting an actress after a performance. This Elizabeth was nothing like the character she played on Sunday, or the decorous hostess who bantered with store clerks. Joey didn't quite know what to make of her. Elizabeth returned her look and continued.

"He always planned on passing everything to my brothers, but once they were gone he sold everything and retired. He was very successful in grain and livestock. These days he enjoys his hobbies and waits for me to find a suitable husband."

"Is that your only option? I mean … were you ever interested in the business? Were you disappointed when he sold it?"

Elizabeth smiled, sipping her tea.

"Honestly, no. I wasn't raised to understand it and I never visited the office. Unlike Victoria, who always wanted to emulate her father, I had no desire to work at a stockyard."

"So, now you're on the hunt for a suitable husband."

Joey had suspected Elizabeth's interest in Peter was matrimonial, but when she considered the era in which she now found herself, the idea made sense. What logical goal, other than marriage, could there be? To her surprise, Elizabeth laughed at her observation.

"Officially, yes. I am considered an eligible young lady in this town, a desirable match. In that regard, I am quite social, highly visible in society."

The tone of her response caught Joey off guard. Guessing there was more, she pressed her.

"And unofficially?"

Elizabeth cast a quick glance around the room, leaned in closer and spoke in a hushed tone.

"Unofficially, a suitable husband is the *last* thing I want."

Joey blinked. "I'm confused. I thought I detected a pretty keen interest in Peter when we met you on Sunday."

"Oh, I'm interested in Peter. In fact, he is the only man in Chicago who interests me, but not because I hope to marry him."

"Huh." Joey frowned. "You're full of mysteries, aren't you? If you don't want to marry him, what do you plan to do with him?"

Elizabeth grinned. "I need his help in keeping my father's fortune."

Joey shook her head. "I don't get it. Once he dies, wouldn't it go to you?"

Elizabeth exhaled in frustration. "It should, but, as a woman, I am considered incapable of handling money. Of course, not all women are subject to this, but my father is adamant about my well-being. If I marry, my father would rest easy, and ensure my comfort by bequeathing his fortune to my husband. Legally, it would become his money, not mine."

"Whoa! That really stinks! My parents don't have much, but I'm sure when they go everything will pass to me."

"Well," Elizabeth sighed, "perhaps in California men hold women in higher regard than they do in Illinois."

A server reached their table carrying a dessert tray. "Oh my, they look delicious," Elizabeth said, purring over the selection. "But, I must pass. Joanna, would you care for dessert?"

Joey declined and thanked the server, amazed at Elizabeth's ability to change her demeanor so smoothly. She eyed her companion and considered another point. "Couldn't you talk to your father? Ask him to reconsider?"

Elizabeth shrugged. "Unfortunately, the conversation was never open for discussion and I wasn't aware that it should be. My upbringing was focused on preparation to become someone's wife. My skills aren't without merit. I can entertain, persuade and dissuade. I can manage most men. But certain things in life require more skill than I possess, particularly where my father is concerned." She paused. "You know, I wasn't really aware there were other ways to live until I met Victoria."

Joey nodded. "She was pretty cool, from what I can gather."

"Oh no. Victoria was warm-hearted to everyone she met."

"Sorry. Where I come from the word 'cool' means interesting in every way."

"Hmm ...." Elizabeth pondered the word, fingertips caressing her teacup. "Used in that way, yes. I think it's an apt description. Like me, she moved quite easily among men, but not because she was raised to complement them, because she was groomed to stand among them." She closed her eyes for a moment, reflecting, Joey thought, on her old friend.

"You know, I think her father did her a disservice, though she gained from it in the end. Victoria was groomed to be an anomaly and I, to be a wife. She met Peter and became a wife. I hold all suitors at bay, hoping to become an anomaly." She stared into her cup and then raised her eyes with a rueful smile. "Victoria may have been bound by convention, but I learned a great deal from her."

"Bound by convention? How so?"

"Why just as you are, just as I am. Victoria wanted to be a physician like her father, and though he encouraged her to study hard and think logically, he wasn't willing to put her in a position to break any barriers or, as he told her, to be broken by them. He forbid her request to apply for college." She shook her head at the memory. "His decision devastated her."

Joey, still rooted in the 20th century, failed to understand. "What's the big deal? Women go to college. I went to college."

Elizabeth gasped. "You went to college? That's quite an accomplishment, Joanna, so few of us are given the chance. Miss Addams said only five percent of American women today are able to gain admission to the halls of higher learning."

"Wait. You mean Jane Addams? *The* Jane Addams?"

Elizabeth nodded and raised her cup in salute. "You're a college graduate. So you teach? Are you a teacher?"

Joey felt uncomfortable with the lie, but it was easier than trying to explain marketing. "Yes, I'm a teacher. I guess it's given me a greater measure of independence. I tend to forget that. But life is a little different ... out west."

Elizabeth nodded. "I think that's why I like Marshall Field's so much. I am independent here."

Again, Joey was thrown off. "What's so independent about shopping at a department store?"

"This is the only store where I can sign for things myself. Of course, my father pays the bill, but he doesn't need to be here with me as he would at other stores. Only Marshall's accommodates women in such a way."

"Wow. I didn't realize ...."

"Did you know you're sitting at the first decent restaurant in town where a woman can dine unaccompanied by a man? Every other reputable eating establishment denies entrance to a lone woman. She must be escorted."

Joey's hand flew to her mouth, muffling a gasp. "You're kidding! That's discrimination."

"No doubt you know of Elizabeth Cady Stanton. Her work for women's suffrage has gained recognition, but little success. Like most of the challenges women face, gaining the right to vote is an arduous battle. Dining unescorted is just one instance of our frustration."

Joey lowered her eyes with a growing twinge of shame. She knew women couldn't vote until 1918, but never gave serious thought to anything else they might be denied. Of all the choices available to her, all the rights she took for granted, she never would have counted dining alone as one of them. And yet they were hers to enjoy thanks to the hard work of so many women who came before her. There were big names like Stanton and Anthony, even Jane Addams, Chicago's own feminist icon. But thousands of nameless others helped pave the path to the equality she trod upon so casually in her own time.

"I'm so sorry, Elizabeth. Life in California is much easier for a woman. I feel spoiled by comparison."

"Don't be sorry." Elizabeth waved her hand as if batting a fly. "I never gave it much thought until I spent time with Victoria. We used to go everywhere together. She took me to my first lecture. Jane Addams spoke about the hardships young girls face in moving here. The depravity of their living conditions, the dangers they encounter, the scam artists who separate them from their money or their families—shocking. I had never known hardship in my own life, so it never occurred to me how distinctly it existed for others."

"And now that you know ...?"

"I'd like to be of some help to them. Victoria and I used to do things together for unfortunate women." She stopped for a moment, sipped her tea and sighed. "To be perfectly honest, I am not at home in humble conditions. Victoria was a master at ignoring the squalor." She wrinkled her nose. "I was never comfortable, though I did try."

"Don't feel bad, Elizabeth." Joey thought of the outreach programs she and Martin worked on at the hospital. "There are many ways to help people."

"Precisely. That's why I need Peter."

Joey eyed her carefully. "So, I'm still drawing a blank. How can Peter help you?"

"I want him to agree to become my legal guardian."

"Elizabeth, you're an adult. You don't need a legal guardian."

"Yes, but my father insists on management of his heir and estate by someone trustworthy." She let out a small breath and adopted a pleading look. "Joanna, my father is getting on in years. Please don't misunderstand me, I have no desire to usher him to an early grave, but I do want to settle the matter of a financial successor without having to walk down the aisle to do so."

"Is he frustrated by your current ... marital status?"

"No, in some ways he's as easy to play as the men who pursue me."

Joey was taken by surprise, not just by her remark but by the path their conversation had taken.

"Please, don't think ill of me," Elizabeth continued. "I have been active in society long enough to recognize the motivations of many who pursue me. In their eyes I'm a first class ticket to a Pullman-Car lifestyle. I am not willing to allow that, out of respect for my father's lifelong effort, and because it should be my money to dispense with as I see fit. I plan to support women's suffrage and other worthy causes."

"Touché!" Joey raised her cup. "So, how does Peter figure into all of this?"

"Well, I've been planning for several months now." She leaned close and slipped into a smile. "I feed my father subtle hints about the men who call on me, allowing him to develop a less-than-favorable impression of them over time. He's convinced I know how to discourage the wrong kind of man, but he does hope I'll find someone suitable." She raised her brows with a mischievous grin.

"In the interim, I asked him to consider appointing a guardian, purely as a precaution, while I mingle in society. Someone like him, a gentleman of good standing in the community, someone with a solid work ethic, and no interest other than protecting his fortune and my well-being … a man he trusts and respects, someone young enough to manage my affairs but old enough to have no misguided motivations where I'm concerned. Someone like—"

"Peter!" Joey finished for her. "Wow, Elizabeth. You're good. You're like a feminist secret agent or something."

"Feminist secret agent?" Elizabeth looked puzzled.

"I just meant you've thought this out well."

"Perhaps a little too well," she said. "My social persona is flirtatious. Since Peter lost Victoria, our paths seldom cross and when they do his discomfort is evident. Approaching him is difficult enough, discussing this with him seems nearly impossible. I thought you might be able to help me."

Joey laughed. "He did tell me on Sunday that he found your forward nature troublesome, and you are kind of uber femme. But, hey! He is coming to dinner on Saturday."

Elizabeth nodded, extending her cup in Joey's direction. "Yes, but if you recall you accepted the invitation for him. I doubt he would have done so on his own, and a dinner party is hardly the place to discuss a proposition such as mine."

"Good point." Joey scanned the room, thinking. "Well, he's a doctor, and his office is at the house. Have you ever visited him for medical reasons? He would never refuse to *treat* you." She mimed her quotation marks. "Once you're inside his office, just give him your pitch."

"My pitch?" Elizabeth arched her delicate brows.

"I mean tell him your idea."

"Yes, but I'm afraid a single discussion won't be enough."

Joey reached across the table and patted her forearm. "Elizabeth, I can handle advance PR on this project." She thought of her work at Michael Reese. "I know how to sell a new program."

Elizabeth gave her a blank stare. "You sound so certain, but I'm afraid I don't understand what you mean."

"Oh." Fighting semantic frustration, Joey clenched her fists, searching for a better explanation. "I just meant I can convince him to listen to you."

"But what will you say?"

"Well, first we have to eliminate fear. I think Peter's afraid you want to marry him. Once we eliminate that obstacle, he'll be more receptive to your idea." She frowned. "But, he's not the kind of guy who would jump on board with anything underhanded. He won't want to deceive your father."

"But there would be no deception involved on Peter's part." Elizabeth was adamant, emphasizing her points with her fingers. "He *would* be a good administrator. My father *does* respect him, and his involvement would be minimal, requiring a monthly meeting at most."

Her hand remained in the air. "In truth, I come closer to deceiving Peter, though only slightly. My idea, where he's concerned, is to highlight my father's mortality, and impress upon Peter that assuming guardianship will ease my father's mind. Both statements are true. The only falsehood is my search for a husband." She glanced down at the tablecloth. "Peter feels strongly about serving the community. I intend to appeal to his charitable nature. The official logic is to involve him only *until* I find a husband. For my part, I will continue to circulate in society as if I am searching for one. From what you've told me, as long he knows I'm not after him, I doubt he'll give it much thought." She raised her eyes to her companion.

Joey saluted her with her tea cup. "I believe you've thought of everything. Well, for my part, I can eliminate the fear of marriage, and ask him to listen to you without rushing to judgment, *and* I can make him promise not to give you an answer until we meet again on Saturday. That will give me a few extra days to work on him. How does that sound?"

Elizabeth relaxed into a warm smile. "It sounds more possible than ever before. Joanna, if he agrees to this, I will be forever in your debt."

Joey raised a fist in the air. "Hey, Sister. Solidarity! Right?"

Elizabeth gave her a funny look. "Solidarity?"

Joey laughed. "Let's just say I'm with you in the fight against feminist repression. It must be getting close to one. Let's go."

Chapter Thirteen
Into the Fray

A s they descended the steps to the main floor, Joey scanned the crowd coming through the entrance. The women were more humbly dressed now, and they moved faster, as if they lacked the luxury of time. They came in singles and pairs, chatting as they walked. Joey thought they were shop girls on lunch breaks or household help running errands for their employers. A heavy stream of shoppers flowed toward the back of the store. Joey asked Elizabeth where they were headed.

"Oh, they shop downstairs in a bargain room filled with returns and last year's styles. It's a good place for those who can't afford something current, but still want a quality piece. Would you like to see it?"

Once she heard the word bargain, Joey was interested. If she really needed a dress this week, she would feel much better spending Peter's money on cheaper clothing. "Do you have time?"

"Of course. Come with me."

They joined the throng and made their way downstairs. It was as Joey expected—a bargain basement of sorts where women stood at tables and racks, scrutinizing the merchandise. She stopped to examine a formal dress on the end of one rack, priced at a dollar fifty. Joey smiled. This was her kind of shopping. This particular dress might be out of date, but from her perspective they were all out of date.

They wandered around for a few more minutes and Joey, certain by now she would return, decided she had seen enough. As she turned to Elizabeth, she caught sight of a familiar face at the checkout counter. It was Molly Hannafee, Car's red-headed young girlfriend. Joey tapped Elizabeth on the arm and pointed.

"Oh! I know her. She works for Peter's neighbor. I want to speak with her, maybe offer her a ride home. Will you come with me?"

Elizabeth smiled, pressing Joey's forearm. "Certainly. We will have to hurry though. She's leaving through the side entrance."

Joey glanced back at the checkout counter but Molly was no longer there.

"This way," Elizabeth said, guiding her to the wall on the left. "A girl pressed for time can leave through the side and avoid the incoming crowd. It leads to an alley, though, and it's not a pleasant passage."

Molly neared the door and Joey called out to her, but the room was too noisy. Joey moved quickly, pulling Elizabeth along. Their shopping trip had been a wonderful surprise. She had gained a new perspective on the rules governing a woman in 1893. Now she hoped for a working girl's take on life in this era.

They reached the door and Joey tried to pull Elizabeth through, but her friend gripped the door frame, stifling a cry. One hand flew to her nose, fighting the stench of the alley, and Joey followed suit. The passageway was littered with debris, and more than one unfortunate soul made camp against the weathered brick of the opposite wall. Far worse, about ten yards away a filthy-looking man held Molly from behind, one arm wound tight around her waist. He flashed a lewd, brown, and nearly toothless grin. Molly cried out, struggling to break free. He raised a grimy arm into the air, the neck of a bottle clenched in his fist. With one broad swing he brought it down on her beautiful red head. Molly slumped in his arms as blood spurted from the gash. The man dropped the bottle and proceeded to drag her down the alley.

Joey gave Elizabeth one quick order.

"Go find Peter. Now!"

Then she turned, sprinted down the stairs and ran full speed after the attacker, anger churning inside her. Ignoring the roar of protest from her ribs, she closed the distance quickly, emitting a guttural cry as she ran. She leapt the final foot and landed on his back. The three of them tumbled headlong into the filth with Molly at the bottom of the heap. The man slid to the right, face down, muttering in surprise. Joey, still clutching his back, took advantage of his disorientation. She grabbed a handful of his matted hair, curled her fingers tight around it and slammed his head repeatedly into the dirt beneath her.

"LEAVE! HER! ALONE!" Her ribs throbbed with every word.

The man whimpered and slackened under her. She knew she'd hurt him, but didn't believe for a minute he was defenseless. She was right. As she loosened her grip on his head, he turned quickly, forcing her to one side. Joey lost balance, but only for an instant. She landed in a crouch at his feet.

The man, still turning in her direction, was laughing—*at her*—a sneer on his weathered, whiskered face.

Anger surged hot through her veins, overtaking the pain in her side.

Still laughing, he faced her, supporting his weight on his elbows. His legs were apart, giving Joey the only opening she really needed. She hammered the toe of her new shoe into his filthy crotch.

"Bastard!" she hissed.

"How! Dare! You!" She raised her voice, landing each kick in time with her words.

"YOU! FILTHY! SCUM!"

By the time she stopped, the man lay curled in the dirt, hands defending his anatomy, no longer inclined to laugh or fight. Joey took advantage of his incapacity and tried to pull Molly away, but her injured ribs protested. A small crowd had gathered at a safe distance and Joey called to them.

"Someone help me…."

Most heads dropped, a few feet shuffled. Two girls in identical brown dresses eyed each other as if considering her request, but no one moved. Joey watched them squirm and fought a rising sense of exasperation.

"PLEASE!"

The pair in brown broke away from the crowd and made a cautious approach. Together they gripped Molly from under her shoulders and began to drag her back toward the door. Suddenly one of them screamed, dropped her hold, and backed away. Joey felt a hand on her ankle. One glance back told her the attacker was sitting again, still dazed, but not finished yet. Blind fury obliterated all remaining reason; Joey wasn't finished yet either.

She pivoted on the heel of the ankle he held, raised her other foot high in the air. Tapping into every ounce of her anger, she kicked him full in the face. The man cried out. His head snapped back and blood flew from his nose and mouth, spraying her clothing. The force of the kick robbed her of her balance and she fell on top of him. Overtaken by the storm within her, she slammed her knee into his crotch again and again, pounding his bloody face with both her fists, berating everything about him with every blow she landed.

"She … likes … GENTLEMEN!

She … likes … men … who … BATHE!

She … likes … men … with … TEETH!"

In her fury, Joey became a tightly wound coil of wrath, every muscle wracked with indignation, hating this man. And he became, through the veil of her rage, the man who shot Martin. He became every man who ever hit, hurt, or raped a woman. She responded as his judge and jury, meting out vengeance for anyone who had ever suffered a loss at the hands of someone like him. A growing chorus of voices sounded dimly behind her. She put her fists together, hoping desperately for greater force and pounded at his chest, growling like a wild animal.

"Don't you *ever*," she struck him again, "hit another girl! Don't come near this alley *ever again*." She separated her hands, gathered his collar with one hand and raised the other high in the air, preparing to smash his face again. "And don't you *ever*—"

Someone grabbed her blood-caked fist from behind. Joey screamed and turned fast, her free hand searching for the new attacker. She landed a good blow to his shoulder before she heard his deep voice.

"Joanna. Stop. That's enough."

It was a command spoken softly, but with absolute authority.

It took her several seconds to understand that it was Peter, his face set in stone, his grip painfully tight, willing her to abandon this. Panting heavily, and incapable of quelling the need for vengeance, she began to shake. The logical part of her brain understood the fight was over, but the emotional side wasn't willing to submit. As she looked at Peter, the anger seething within recoiled into the center of her being, building force as it spun tighter, seeking an outlet. It started low in her throat and rose like a volcano. Rearing her head back she released an ear-splitting scream and filled the air with all her remaining anger.

When she finished, Peter dropped her hand and she leaned over—exhausted—hands on her knees, gasping for air. At length she looked up and saw Peter scowling, eyes burning with a fury that threatened to match her own.

"He- could have- raped her," she panted. "Even- killed her."

Peter's brows rose a fraction of an inch, but the fire in his eyes remained bright and barely contained. She knew he was angry with her, but couldn't think clearly enough to grasp why.

With one hand covering her ribs she straightened, met his gaze, and began to defend her actions.

"I had to- do something…."

Peter failed to respond; he was a proverbial statue. She glanced at the crowd behind them. A few had begun to move along, but many remained frozen in place. The women who stayed met her eyes. The few men who had gathered looked away, seeming to share Peter's disapproval. Turning back, she softened her voice and nodded toward Molly.

"Please. Help her. She works for your neighbor. Can't we take her home? Please?"

The plea seemed to have a reasonable effect. Peter huffed with force, air rushing fast through his teeth. He looked to the sky, silently dismissing her. Behind him Joey spied Elizabeth, eyes wide, her hands covering much of her face. This situation was beyond her 19th century skill set. Joey knew she was on her own.

Peter looked at Molly and vague recognition seemed to register within him. She lay on the ground, moaning softly under the care of the girls in brown. Car sat beside her, looking gravely agitated. A manager from the store appeared, offering assistance. Peter asked if he had summoned the police, and then directed him to take Molly inside the building. He requested a few medical supplies and once they arrived he proceeded to dress her wound. While this transpired someone handed Joey a towel and she absently wiped the blood and dirt from her face and hands.

Once he finished, Peter instructed Car to bring the carriage to the entrance of the alley. He thanked the store manager for his assistance and approached Elizabeth, conversing with her in an inaudible tone. Joey, still raw from the whole experience, watched from the side. The store manager lingered nearby. She noticed him and a thought occurred to her.

"Excuse me, sir?"

"Yes, ma'am?"

"I don't mean to tell you how to run your business, but you might want to hire a security guard for that side door exit. I can't imagine she was the first girl ever attacked out there. If I may—"

"No you may not!" Peter interjected with a firm hand on her elbow, steering her away from the manager. "Thank you kindly, Mr. Selfridge. We'll be on our way now." He prodded Joey ahead of him, toward the exit.

"Elizabeth, would you escort Joanna, please? I believe she's still upset."

Without another look in her direction, Peter gathered Molly into his arms and strode out the side door. Fuming, Joey hung back and fell reluctantly in step with Elizabeth. They proceeded through the alley toward the main thoroughfare.

"That was very foolish … and very, very brave!" Elizabeth whispered, a hint of reverence in her voice. "I think you saved her life. If you hadn't intervened, God only knows what would have happened to her."

Joey responded without emotion. "Raped for sure, maybe worse."

Elizabeth stopped and clutched her arm. "This illustrates Miss Addams lecture perfectly. She spoke of young girls who are tricked or forced into sexual servitude. I think he was going to rape her and then sell her to a brothel."

Joey shook her head. "Did you see that guy? I seriously doubt he was that enterprising." The hate crept back into her husky voice. "Then again …." She shuddered. Many young girls disappeared in big cities at the turn of the century and Chicago was no exception. They were raped, murdered, or swallowed by dirty alleys like this one, and never seen again.

As they neared the carriage, Elizabeth turned, clutching her arm. "How did you *do* that?"

Joey took a good look at Peter, lips pressed tight as he passed Molly to Car in the rear of the carriage. "Oh man. How much did he see?"

"We saw you kick him in the face, and hit him ... there." She gestured awkwardly at her pelvic area. "What *else* did you do to him? Where did you learn to fight like that?"

"Well, I ... I just—" She held her tongue, feeling stumped. This was no time to discuss self-defense classes. "I don't know. It's a California thing. I just got so mad at the guy."

Suddenly overwhelmed, Joey dropped her hands to her knees and took in deep cleansing breaths. She tilted her head in Peter's direction and offered Elizabeth a small grin. "I think I'm in a bit of trouble with him. Is he terribly angry?"

Elizabeth nodded, still amused.

"Just so you know," Joey said with a conspiratorial smile, "he finds *my* forward nature troublesome, too."

Elizabeth giggled and pulled her farther away from Peter. "Promise me we'll do this again," she whispered, blonde curls bouncing.

Joey shrugged. "Well, I can't guarantee you a fight next time, but—"

"What a day! You are quite something, Joanna Fagan." Elizabeth's carriage pulled up. She handed Joey her packages, squeezed her hand, and nodded toward Peter.

"Don't worry about Peter. Let him vent. If he's too over-bearing ... well, I've seen firsthand what you'll do to a man who crosses you. If it comes to blows I am not at all worried about you."

Elizabeth waved to Peter and hailed her driver, signaling her intention to leave.

"I'll see you on Saturday."

Joey watched her carriage pull away, took a deep breath and turned to face one decidedly angry Peter Hastings.

Chapter Fourteen
Persistence Through the Aftermath

Without so much as a look in her direction, Peter extended his hand to help Joey into the front of the carriage. She seated herself, acutely aware of the chill in his manner. Peter climbed in beside her and took the reins, guiding the horses through the crowded streets. Joey gave him an occasional sidelong glance, hoping to engage him, but his attention remained fixed on the road ahead. At one point she tried to speak, but with a raised hand he stopped her before she could utter a sound.

Behind them, Car held Molly close, whispering soft words of comfort. Molly sat beside him, her head resting on his shoulder, her face ghostly white. Car was nearly as pale. Joey's heart went out to him. The thought that he nearly lost Molly chilled her, reminded her too much of losing Martin. She crossed her arms over her chest and hugged herself, yearning to be anywhere but here. Quite unexpectedly, Peter interrupted her thoughts, finally deigning to speak to her, though it was in clipped, matter-of-fact phrases.

"Your hands are bruised, your clothes are blood-soaked and you smell foul."

Before she could respond, he cut her off again, citing a long list of demands and never once looking in her direction.

"Once we are home you will give Mrs. Milford your dirty clothes so she can attempt to rid them of the stench. You will go directly upstairs, clean yourself thoroughly and then wait for me in the parlor. Do not speak of this to anyone. Not a word! Do you understand?"

Joey stared at him, struck by the anger in his voice. "Lighten up, Peter."

"DO YOU UNDERSTAND?"

The force of his words rekindled her fury.

"EXPLICITLY!" she spat back.

They remained silent for the rest of the ride. Peter stopped at the front gate and nodded toward the house, indicating she should get out of the carriage. She made her way to the front door as Peter drove on to the Calder residence. Mrs. Milford met her there, blocking her entry.

Joey attempted to explain. "Peter said—"

"Don't you dare cross this threshold. And it's Dr. Hastings to you. Good God! You smell like the bottom of a privy. Go to the back door and wait for me. And take off those filthy clothes! Of all the—" Mrs. Milford slammed the door in her face, grumbling as she did so.

Joey made her way around back and waited, fighting a sense of defeat. Only when Mrs. Milford appeared at the back door did she begin to undress. The housekeeper shoved an old blanket in her direction.

"The bath is ready. Go straight upstairs, and don't touch a thing. I've just polished." she said, wagging a stubby finger. As Joey walked away, Mrs. Milford bent to retrieve the dirty clothes. "Filthy guttersnipe," she muttered.

Joey froze.

"What did you call me?" she asked, turning around.

"You heard me," the old woman snapped at her. "You're nothing but a filthy guttersnipe!"

Before Joey could respond, Mrs. Milford unleashed a verbal tirade.

"Why he allows you to stay here is beyond me. If it was up to me I'd toss you out on the street right now," she bellowed. "This is not your home. Leave! Go jump in the lake. Swim back where you belong, you conniving little sea snake! I know exactly what you're doing here, and I don't like it. Not one bit!"

"Mrs. Milford, you don't know the first thing about me." She shook her head, the echo of Mrs. Milford's anger still sharp in her ears. "I ... Jesus! What is *with* you?" She clutched the blanket tight, fearful of losing what remained of her composure.

"Cursing, swearing." The old woman chided her. "Taking the Lord's name in vain. What else will you take? Answer me that! You're the worst kind of sinner and I hope you rot in Hell. Now get out of my sight!"

Stunned into silence, Joey entered the house and walked up the stairs. "Wow," she mumbled. "Don't sugar-coat it, lady. Get in touch with your inner feelings."

Still smoldering, she entered the bathroom and sighed. The housekeeper had some serious issues. Joey dropped the blanket and removed the binding from her ribs.

Once she slipped into the hot bath, her mood shifted. The heat softened her anger, and as she scrubbed away the dirt and blood, her ire dissipated along with the grime. Peter was right. Both hands were bruised at the knuckles, and the bones at the base of her palms were tender. Her ribs were raw as well, still throbbing from the exertion of the fight. Her foot ached. She landed wrong after the last kick.

Despite everything, she felt good. For the second time this week she'd done something incredibly right. It was odd. She'd never done anything heroic in her life, and now twice in three days. It was unbelievable. The entire situation was unbelievable.

Joey surveyed the small bathroom. No matter how comforting the water felt, she couldn't completely relax. Not here. Mrs. Milford was right about one thing. This wasn't her home. Not by a long shot.

Home.

Joey ached to go there. Not just the physical place, but the sense of being somewhere familiar, where stuffed animals lay amid picture books; where her favorite flavored coffee—fluffy coffee, Martin always called it—beckoned her with its hazelnut scent. Home, where Michael was probably playing with Gran's dog right now.

Joey fought fresh tears. God, had it only been two days? Would she ever see him again?

Thoughts of home brought Martin's sweater to mind. She longed to get lost in it and curl up by a warm fire, but Mrs. Milford hadn't yet returned it to her. Joey entered her bedroom resigned to wearing another stiff-necked blouse and long skirt. She dressed slowly, donned Car's thick socks and left the room. Her thoughts returned to Peter as she headed downstairs.

Though he seemed to share her perspective on some things, for some reason he was furious over what happened today. The thought of losing her only real ally weighed heavily on her, and she walked to the parlor dreading their next encounter. Unlike Mrs. Milford, Peter really had some control over her life at the moment. If he considered her actions unforgivable, then she would be out on the street and forced to rethink basic survival in addition to finding a way home. Joey wasn't ready to face that. Not today.

Regardless of the nature of his anger, in this instance, perhaps Elizabeth had a good point. She should just hold her tongue and let him vent. It might not be easy, but it was far easier than sleeping on a park bench. She placed a hand over her unbound ribs as she reached the doorway.

"Okay, Peter," she whispered. "Bring it on."

Peter faced the fire, one hand on his hip, the other pressed against the wall. He didn't acknowledge her entrance. The tick of the grandfather clock paced her movement and she glanced at it, surprised to learn it was already past five. Joey made her way to the fireplace, sat on the small stool and cradled her knees in her arms. They watched the flames in silence.

"How's Molly?" Joey asked.

Peter continued staring at the fire. "She is confused and in pain. I gave her a strong sedative so she'll sleep through the night. Luckily, her hair is quite thick. I think it actually absorbed some of the blow. Still, head injuries can be unpredictable." He paused, and a look of profound sadness seemed to wash over him. "But in this case, I am confident she will recover."

Joey let out a sigh of relief. She still didn't understand why Peter was angry, or sad, but she didn't really care. Molly was safe and that was all that really mattered.

As late afternoon gave way to early evening, the silence lengthened. The quiet was broken only by the steadfast tick of the clock, marking their isolation. Joey didn't want another argument, but it seemed that disparity over the incident hung between them like a heavy curtain. She felt compelled to discuss it and move on. She spoke first.

"Peter, I'm completely in the dark here. Please tell me why you are so angry with me."

After an uncomfortably long minute, he finally let out a great breath and met her eyes.

"Joanna, as a guest in my house you are considered, first and foremost, a lady. As such, I expect you to act like one and follow the rules dictated by society. I found your flagrant disregard of social decorum today appalling!"

"But, she—" Joey stood, challenging him.

He held up a hand, silencing her.

"Second, I expect you to conduct yourself in a manner that reflects well on my place in the community and on the reputation my profession demands."

"But, I—"

With a withering look, he silenced her once more.

"I suspected your origins were somewhat lowly, but after today, after watching you behave like some anarchist run amok at Haymarket Square ...." Peter let out an exasperated breath. "I won't have it. Do you understand? I will not stand for such coarse behavior. Not while you are under my patronage."

Before she could respond, he exploded, punctuating his frustration with a hand in the air.

"A woman possessing even an *ounce* of gentility would never stoop to the level you embraced today! I will not tolerate such a shoddy display from you ever again. Fistfights may be acceptable in your household, but not in mine. Should trouble arise in the future, you will call upon me to handle the situation. Only those lacking refinement go grousing around in the dirt, fighting like a street urchin. If you wish to remain here, you must never stoop so low again. Do I make myself clear?"

His last remark, though phrased as a question was, without doubt, a demand.

"Very." Joey responded, her voice husky with an undercurrent of defiance. She crossed both arms over her chest, tacitly negating her response.

They stared at each other, locked in a silent impasse.

Joey was on the brink of unleashing her anger when she thought of Elizabeth. Acutely aware of exactly where—and when—she was, she knew her only recourse was to concede. Rankled, but determined to maintain peace, she did so to the best of her raw-nerved ability.

"Peter, I am truly sorry for offending your sense of social propriety, for compromising your social standing, and for any damage I may have inflicted on your professional reputation." She looked at him without wavering. "It won't happen again."

That was all she could manage. Still fuming, she turned to leave before she said anything she might regret. A few steps from the doorway she paused, waging an internal debate. When she finally turned to face him, her husky tone never wavered.

"Just for the record, I'm not a bit sorry for stopping him." She closed her eyes, debating the consequence of voicing one final thought. Defiance overruled reason and she held her head high as she volleyed her last remark.

"You know, I can't help but wonder. Would you be this angry if it was William I pulled away from that swine?" She saw him flinch, though just barely. "Now if you'll excuse me." Without waiting for a retort, she left the room.

Joey headed straight for the front door, half worried that Peter would follow. She needed fresh air and she wanted to find Car. As she lifted the latch, an exasperated howl came from the parlor.

The chill evening air shocked her as she descended the porch steps—a perfect antidote for the heat boiling inside her.

She inhaled deeply, though not without pain, allowing cold air into her lungs, cooling her anger a little more with every breath. Once inside the carriage house, she climbed the stairs to the loft and knocked on Car's door. He opened it right away.

"Got a minute?" She offered an uncertain smile.

Car grinned wide, pulled her in and gave her an enormous bear hug.

"For you—I've got hours!"

His loft was colder than the main house, but a strong fire burned in the fireplace and Car ushered her to the sofa. He tossed her a blanket and settled onto the hearthstones opposite her. Joey felt relief for the first time since the fight. This garret was a safe haven, stress free and always open to her.

"How's Molly? Did Mr. Calder let you see her?"

Car fished around in his pocket, producing his tobacco and paper.

"Oh yeah! Well, not Calder himself. After I put up the rig and horses I snuck back through the brush and waited outside 'til the Doc left. Then Mrs. Johnson, his cook, let me sneak in for a tic." He rolled the cigarette into a perfect cylinder and twisted the ends together. "Poor Molly's a wicked headache, but Doc gave her somethin' strong. Ya know, my girl's got some spunk, but you—" He lit the cigarette, drew deeply and released a thick stream of smoke. "You've a real fire in yer belly, Joey. What you did took guts."

"Thanks, Car," she grinned. "Too bad you didn't see the whole fight. I think you would have appreciated it."

"I didn't see all of it, but Nora O'Shea—one of the girls helpin' Molly—she filled in the blanks." Car made a show of squeezing his knees together. "Remind me never ta cross ya with yer new shoes on."

Joey laughed and settled deeper into the couch. She pulled the blanket over her shoulder and laid her head on her arm. "Listen, I never said a word to Peter about you and Molly. I just told him I recognized her from next door, so I think your secret is safe." She chuckled at the thought of Peter, probably angrier with her now than he had been in the alley. "Besides, he's a little preoccupied with my lack of decorum at the moment. I believe he thinks I'm some sort of thug."

"Yeah." Another stream of smoke flew from Car's lips as he nodded. "He doesn't know what ta make of ya. Well, good. Keep him guessin', I say. Yer all aces there."

Joey grinned at his enthusiasm and pulled the blanket closer, stifling a yawn.

Car pointed at her. "Ya know, Joey, yer the best thing he's come across since … well, since *she* died. Doc's been in a bit of a trance since he lost his missus. So what if he's mad. At least he's finally feelin' somethin'."

Joey closed her eyes, half-listening, half-smiling. Car was like a loyal little brother. She could let her guard down with him, tell him anything. He might not believe her story, but he didn't seem troubled by it. His casual acceptance of her was the only buoy she had today, and she clung to it now, grateful for the comfort of his friendship. Sitting in his garret, enjoying his easy banter, was like basking in sunlight, and the warm fire softened her frayed nerves.

"Glad to oblige," she said.

"Hey, don't ya go noddin' off on me now. Mrs. M will have dinner on the table soon." Car took one last pull on his cigarette and tossed it into the flames.

Joey yawned again, fatigue fast replacing spent aggression. Food was the farthest thing from her mind, and she had absolutely no desire to face Mrs. Milford again. Or Peter, for that matter.

"Please, Car? I'm not hungry and I'm in no mood for strained conversation. Be a bud. Let me catch a nap. Please?"

Car stood and added another log to the fire. "Well, if Peter's as mad as ya say, then maybe it's best." He patted her shoulder. "Y've earned yer forty winks, Mate. I'll cover for ya."

Joey mumbled her thanks.

Chapter Fifteen
A Somnolent Illusion

She was aware of two things: the rhythm of her feet, and the steady sound of her breath. The air played in and out of her lungs as she moved, again and again. She enjoyed the symbiotic relationship she shared with this place, accepting the air and releasing what she no longer needed, back into the trees all around her.

Joey was running. The route was unfamiliar but utterly breathtaking. It was a well-traveled path in a dense wood. The trees were majestic, taller than anything she'd ever seen. The forest offered a canopy of shade in variegated color. Sunlight cut through the branches, scattering fractured rays onto the forest floor. The fall air was crisp and the leaves were at the height of their color, adding bursts of orange, red and yellow to the dense landscape.

A symphony of wildlife played here, and every few yards she encountered something new. Squirrels chattered as they leapt from branch to branch. Songbirds hidden in the foliage sang in sweet, melodic phrases. A frog bellowed low in a nearby creek, and the soft breeze offered perfect relief as she ran. Keeping a good pace was easy. Her ribs were completely healed. Joey smiled as she took everything in. It felt great to be here, wherever here was, and to run again.

The trail cut hard to the right, and curved in a graceful arc up another tree-laden hill. She saw another runner at the top of the curve, a man. Like everything else on this trail, he looked stunning ... and familiar. Despite the fall weather, he wore only a light tee shirt and shorts and he must have had quite a run. His cheeks were flushed, and his body glistened with exertion. He stood smiling amid the ferns and waved her over. Joey looked around to make sure the gesture was intended for her. His grin expanded, as if he was amused by her uncertainty. Everything about him seemed so familiar. Still, Joey hesitated. It couldn't be, could it? She wasn't quite sure. Then his laughter reached her and she knew.

It was Martin.

He flashed a playful grin and turned away, indicating she should follow.

"Mac, wait up!"

Joey bolted after him, desperate to know it was really him. He disappeared into the greenery but she could hear him through the trees.

"Come on, Pix," he teased. "Get the lead out."

Fueled by the sound of his voice, she ran full force along the trail, taking the curve with ease and heading fast up the incline. Ecstatic at the prospect of a reunion, a belly laugh escaped her. The trail veered sharp to the left and she stayed with it, agile and light, anticipation mounting inside her, guiding her along. Twenty yards past the last curve she heard him again, this time from behind. She pulled up short and turned around, panting. He was only a few yards back. He had stepped off the trail into the brush, and he was leaning against a giant maple tree.

"My God, it really is you!" she gasped, working to find normal breath.

"In the flesh!" He said, chuckling.

He was beautiful.

Joey thought of every picture he graced back at the townhouse. None of them did him justice. There was a brilliance about him now that surpassed any other likeness, but it was definitely Martin. His blue eyes still held a flash of mischief, and his sandy hair softened his jaw defining that look ... that mixture of resolve and compassion she knew so well. He glanced at his chest.

"Okay, not exactly flesh, but ...." He cupped his fingers, inviting her to join him.

She took a tentative step in his direction. "Can I ... touch you?"

"I don't know." He lifted a shoulder and spread his arms. "This is your dream. Let's give it a try."

In three strides Joey was home, her head burrowed into his chest, lost in the scent of him as quiet tears spilled down her cheeks. He gathered her close, his arms tight around her.

"Well, do I seem ghosty?" he whispered.

Laughing, she wiped her eyes. "No, you're great. Different, but great." She brought her hands to his face. "Man, I've missed you!" Her lips reached his, and as she kissed him desire suffused with her joy, adding greater force to her embrace. Her hands slid from his neck to his chest, and she leaned into him, finding firmer footing. He responded as he always had, answering her unspoken need with equal intensity, one hand almost feather-like at the back of her neck, the other rediscovering the small of her back. She shivered. This was so unbelievably different from their last encounter....

Random visions of the night he died rushed through her mind: infectious smile before he turned, terrified expression when he faced her again. The way he fell forward, and his grip on her arm as he clung to her, to the remnants of his life. Finally, the smile of acceptance and the way he relaxed as he let go.

Suddenly Joey felt very selfish, caught up in her own fulfillment, mindless of what he'd been through. She softened her kiss, and pressed her hands against his chest. Backing away, she studied his face. "Martin, I'm so sorry...." His final moments replayed in her head, and left her struggling for words. Nothing seemed appropriate. "Did it hurt?" she asked. "At the end? Were you in a lot of pain?"

He pulled her close. "I think you got the worst of it," he whispered.

She melted into him. There were so many questions, so much she wanted to say. "You know, Michael's been great," she spoke into his chest. "He's such a trooper." A thought struck her and she fought the catch in her throat as she looked at him.

"Can you ... see him from here?"

With a hint of a smile, Martin answered her.

Tears fell and she gave in to them, sobbing into his chest. He rocked her ever so slightly, brushing his lips across her temple, into her hair.

"He's so... beautiful... and so—" Joey forced her words through the hitch of emotion, "So much... like you." A new rush of tears choked her. "But he's... alone! And I'm ... I'm—"

"Easy, Joey. He's not alone."

He held her as she cried, held the fragile pieces of her. Gradually her uneven breath steadied and she managed to collect herself.

"Mac, losing you took me someplace I never expected to go. It's cold and closed, and I'm still lost. I just want to go home to Michael."

"I know," Martin whispered, holding her. "You'll find your way, Joey. You always do." His hands slid down her shoulders and clasped hers. "Come with me. I want to show you something."

Martin led her further into the brush, away from the trail. They walked hand in hand, their movement effortless despite the dense terrain. Other questions came to mind.

"So, what's it like after death?"

He suppressed a grin and adopted an officious tone. "Sorry, Ma'am, I'm afraid that's classified information."

"Oh, come on! Throw me a bone, Mac. At least tell me you're happy."

"Can't you tell?" He flashed a genuine smile.

Looking around, she gestured to the trees. "Well, it's really beautiful here." She squeezed his hand. "As long as you're all right, that's all I really care about."

Martin stopped and lifted her into his arms. "I'm fine," he said softly.

She wrapped her legs around his waist and her arms encircled his neck, the ache of longing once again aroused by his embrace. She kissed him gently, so grateful to hold him. She wanted only to love him now, and revive for him the part of her that died along with him. But if this was only a dream, venturing further down this path would only bring a new sense of loss upon awakening. Joey couldn't risk it again, not at that level of intensity. With a heavy heart, she released her grip and slid back to her feet. He cupped her chin in his hand, and raised her eyes to his.

"It's all right, Joey. You're close."

She gave him a puzzled look. "Close to what?"

He answered with a small grin and a lift of the brows. Clutching her hand, they continued through the brush in silence.

A few minutes later they reached a clearing the size of a basketball court, rimmed by trees on three sides. As they made their way toward the opening, Martin grew playful again. "Okay, get ready for something amazing." He pulled her along. "You can see everything from here."

In the distance, the Chicago skyline came into view. Bright sunlight sparkled on the lake and made mirrors of every skyscraper window. She looked at Martin and back at the clearing.

"Wow. Where are we?"

"I call it the Intuitive Vista. It offers a different perspective to whatever's on your mind. The view gives you something new to consider."

"That would come in handy in the land of the living," Joey muttered.

"It's there, Joey. People get a few good glimpses throughout life, if they bother to look."

She smiled. "I guess metaphysics factors heavily in your new surroundings."

"Oh, it factors heavily everywhere," he replied.

"Well, teach me, Mac. How does it work?"

Martin grinned. "This is really cool. Okay, close your eyes, take a deep breath and clear your mind."

Joey complied, easing her grip on him as she inhaled.

"Now, look again," he said, tilting his head toward the vista.

Joey opened her eyes. The skyline was gone, replaced by a sunset view of the waterfront. It looked as if they were right on the dock. A few dying rays clung to the edge of the western sky. A lone figure stood at the pier, looking out over the darkening lake. Water dripped from his clothing. Joey recognized him at once.

"That's Peter," she murmured.

"Mmm, looks like he lost something." Martin draped an arm over her shoulder. "Or maybe found something. Either way, seems like he could use a friend."

"I am—" she faltered. "I mean, he is a friend. Although, I'm not sure he thinks of me as one."

Martin said nothing.

Joey took a step back. "Why are we looking at this? What are we doing here?"

"Getting a new perspective."

"On Peter?" She frowned. "He's a good guy, very kind, but rigid, set in his ways."

"Does he look like that now?"

Joey studied the figure, stark and alone against the blunt backdrop of the waterfront.

"He looks unsettled," she conceded.

"Don't give up on him, Joey. He lost his mooring, just like you. Help him out."

"Help him?" She frowned. "How? What am *I* supposed to do?"

Martin grinned. "Remember what my granddad always said. "In helping others ..."

"... we help ourselves," she finished, chanting in a monotonous tone.

"And there it is." He stood behind her, strong arms around her waist, his chin resting on the top of her head.

"There's what?" Joey closed her eyes, leaning back, enjoying his touch, reveling in the memory of the solid sense of self Martin always called forth within her. When she was with him, she was truly complete.

"The key," he whispered.

Martin felt so real. So strong. So different from Peter. "Did you say something?" She barely heard him.

When she opened her eyes the vision before her remained, now shrouded in fog. Martin stood alongside her, holding her hand. Joey sighed, looking at the image of Peter Hastings. What on earth could she do for the man other than give him a premature heart attack? In her brief association with him she had managed only to take him to emotional extremes. How was that helpful? As she stared across the clearing, a fog swallowed the image of Peter in a veil of heavy white mist.

"I don't know, Mac."

Martin laughed softly, his voice fading. "Come on, Pix. Focus." His hand slipped from hers and she reached for him, but the fog was everywhere now and Martin was lost. She could still hear him, though his voice was distant.

"Concentrate, Joey. You can do this."

"Mac, please! Do what?" she called after him. He didn't answer.

She stumbled blindly forward, arms out, searching, not yet ready to lose him. Just as fear began to overtake her, she felt his hand on her shoulder and she clung to it, determined to keep him from slipping away.

"Thank God," she murmured, rubbing her cheek against the back of his hand. "I don't want to lose you ever again."

"What?" Martin's voice was deeper.

His change in tone surprised her. "Please, I need you."

"Joanna, wake up."

Peter shook her gently.

"It's after eight. You really should eat something."

Chapter Sixteen
Prelude to Affinity

"Whoa … that was weird." Joey let her hand slip from Peter's. She was back in the garret, the dying embers glowing crimson in the fireplace, a kerosene lamp burned from a hook near the door. "Where's Car?" She yawned, her voice thick with sleep. "He said he would wake me."

"He's taken Mrs. Milford to visit her sister."

Joey gave him a guarded look. "I'm kind of surprised you're speaking to me." She opened her arms intending to stretch, but contracted them quickly, clutching her left side. "Ow! Man, that hurts!"

Peter arched a brow. "Your ribs?"

She nodded.

"Shall I rebind them for you?"

"Maybe." Joey eyed him cautiously. "Maybe not."

"Afraid I'll render you unable to breathe? Or bind your arms to your sides?"

"Something like that."

"Well, your feet would still be free to oppose me, a far greater danger, I suspect."

As he folded the blanket Joey thought she detected a smile. With half a laugh she lifted her skirt, exposing her feet. "You're safe, big guy. I'm not packing any heat."

"Packing any heat?"

"I'm not wearing shoes. Given your size, I'm at a considerable disadvantage."

"If it came to blows, given your expertise at fisticuffs, I suspect we're on even ground." He collected the lantern and gestured toward the stairs. "Please, come down and have some dinner."

They left the garret in silence and entered the main house through the back door. Peter led the way from the kitchen to the dining room where a covered plate sat on the table.

"Will you join me?" she asked.

"Are you sure you want my company?"

Joey took a seat. "Truce, okay? I fought a little dirty earlier. Sorry."

"Apology accepted. I suppose I was a bit harsh myself." He turned toward the hutch.

Joey lifted the cover from the plate and picked up her fork.

"Peter, this is your home. You are perfectly within your rights to ask me to live by your rules while under your roof." Her voice softened. "Though a cheat sheet would be nice." She rebounded with energy, taking a bite. "Mmm, good chicken."

From the hutch Peter retrieved a decanter and two glasses. He sat across the table from her.

"Would you care for some brandy?"

Joey raised her eyebrows. "You mean the stuff I drank on Saturday? Maybe just a sip. I'm more of a wine girl." She took another bite.

"A wine girl?"

"I prefer wine, but to be honest with you, a drink of some kind sounds good tonight."

"Because …?"

"You have to ask?" She set down her fork.

"Because of your street fight?"

Examining her sore hands, Joey nodded. "You're not going to get mad again, are you?"

"No." He shook his head, poured the brandy, and passed a glass of the caramel-colored liquor across the table. "In fact, I've been thinking about what you said—"

"That was anger talking," she interjected, returning to her meal. "My apologies."

Peter inclined his head in a gesture of acceptance. "Actually I was referring to your parting words: Would I have been as upset if William had been the one in danger?"

"Oh ... and ...?" Joey lowered her fork.

"And I think I still would have been appalled. You should have seen yourself." He pinched the bridge of his nose and shook his head. "Most unsettling. But I must admit, had it been William I would have been far more grateful than angry." He raised his glass. "It was good food for thought, though at the time I didn't particularly care to digest it."

She raised hers as well, taking her small victory with grace. "You have a lovely way with words, Peter. Thank you."

"I am curious, though," he said, "it seemed the attacker never had a chance. Where did you learn to fight?"

"Are you sure you want to know?"

"Please."

She remained silent for a moment, and set down her fork, appraising him. She could try to come up with an explanation suitable for this era to appease him, but she rejected the idea. Joey needed to keep as much of her own experience alive in her heart, even if it moved beyond the bounds of believability for Peter. He was kind enough to take her in and brave enough to let her stay. She needed to believe he was strong enough to accept her as she was.

"Well," she began slowly, "there's a place in town called Impact Chicago. They offer self-defense classes for women. Our neighborhood is moving toward gentrification, but it's not there yet. Soon after we bought the townhouse a young woman was beaten and raped not far from our place." She paused and glanced at Peter, looking for a confirmation of sorts. He lifted a hand, indicating she should continue.

"Martin still pulled the occasional night shift, and he was uncomfortable leaving me alone so I took the class to ease both our minds." She drank from her glass. "I never used any of it before today. Despite what you must think of me, I don't go around beating people up on a regular basis."

Peter struggled visibly with her explanation. Self-defense classes couldn't possibly exist in 1893.

"Do men still protect their women in … in your neighborhood?"

"Sure, but in my *neighborhood,*" she mimed her quotation marks, "women are empowered. We're much more independent. Most of us don't consider ourselves in need of protection."

After she finished her meal, Joey set her plate aside and let her fingers slide over to the brandy. She moved the glass in a circular motion, swirling the contents.

"Listen, I know you can't quite grasp where—*when*—I come from, but today was a real eye-opener for me. Elizabeth taught me a lot about how women live in this era. The restrictions are surprising. I take a lot of freedom for granted in my own time." She sipped the brandy. It was much stronger than port, nearly attacking her throat on the way down, but it did have a warm, pleasant finish. She stared at the glass and continued.

"I think some of what she told me kindled some flame of anger deep inside me. The attacker simply poured gas on it when he hit poor Molly." She looked up at Peter. "And I still say Marshall Field's should put a security guard at that door."

"An excellent suggestion. I'll speak to the manager about it later this week." Peter's brown eyes brightened. "We never did discuss your shopping trip. Did you enjoy yourself?"

"Speaking of protecting your women," she adopted a mock-stern tone, "you all but abandoned me to the clutches of the vicious Miss McNair."

The pattern on the tablecloth suddenly commanded Peter's attention, and Joey grinned, watching his cheeks flush bright red.

"I am sorry," he said.

She reached across the table and squeezed his hand. "Don't be. I actually had fun with her. Elizabeth is quite something, Peter. I can see why Victoria liked her so much."

"Oh no!" His face acquired a tortured look. "Not you, too."

"Yes, me too," she said. "On the surface, she's a classic example of an age-old feminine stereotype. I'm just beginning to grasp the limitations women have in 1893. Your present day society caters so completely to men; it takes some getting used to." She took another sip from her glass.

"As for Elizabeth, if I put on my psych hat, I'd say she uses the only skills she was given in order to maneuver more deftly in the limited space society has given her. She's got a keen eye for an opening, and she makes the most of every opportunity. Victoria was right. She operates with the precision of a surgeon."

She glanced at Peter. He had leaned back in his chair and was eyeing her critically, arms crossed over his chest.

"Interesting observation," he said. "You sound as if you are familiar with psychology? You've studied the subject?"

She cringed under the intensity of his gaze, but held firm on her decision not to shy away from the truth. She could fake her way through encounters with others, but she needed to be completely herself with someone, and though it might be difficult for him, Peter was her only choice. Like it or not, he was her patron. She needed his acceptance and his support. Speaking frankly about her situation was her only means of convincing him it was true. Still, there was a fine line between telling the truth and discussing a future he could never verify, one he would never live to see. Even honesty required a good deal of caution.

"I'm by no means an expert, but I did take Intro to Psychology as a freshman at UC."

"UC? The University of Chicago?" His voice lost its depth. "That's impossible. They don't admit women."

She fought the urge to laugh, her amusement tempered by the thought that most everything she told him would be unbelievable.

"They don't in 1893, but they will eventually. I double majored; Business and English Lit, 1986," she said. "I did an internship in the PR department at Michael Reese and joined them full time after graduation."

"Michael Reese Hospital? Here in town? You work for them?" His tone climbed higher with every question.

"Not now, in the future. Internship in the spring of 1985, full time since the fall of 1986," she smiled over the rim of her glass. "I handle marketing for internal and external programs."

"Marketing? What sort of job is marketing? I'm aware of no such term in medicine."

"Well, medical care is a product, and products can be marketed. Remember all the expensive displays at Marshall Field's?"

He nodded.

"All marketing. They were selling the dream of a priceless Persian rug and an enchanted evening gown, offering the customer a vision of how grand life could be." She sipped her brandy. "The displays are designed to make the shopper feel like everything she buys is as special as an expensive evening gown."

"Well, there's no need for your *marketing* in a hospital." He borrowed her quotation mark gesture, slashing his fingertips through the air. "The goal of medicine is not to sell dreams."

"Not dreams." Joey ran a hand through her hair. "Well, maybe, sweet dreams. My job is to market security. At Michael

Reese, you will be treated by competent physicians who care about your well-being, who have a sincere desire to restore your health. You can rest well, knowing you're in safe hands."

"That's absurd," Peter scoffed. "You're stating the obvious." He leaned back in his chair, pursing his lips. "Still, I suppose we should stop in tomorrow, see if anyone can identify you."

She shook her head. "Waste of time, Peter. I won't have a job there for another ninety-some-odd years. Not a single soul will recognize me."

Peter didn't seem to be listening. "It must be where you learned your chest compressions. I wasn't aware they had adopted the technique."

"No, I took CPR in high school, and again in college, but Reese does offer it in their community health programs. A friend of mine manages the—"

Overhead came a heavy thud, followed by a cry and they exchanged a mutual look of surprise. Joey was already out of her chair.

"Oh man, that was Michael!" She sprinted from the dining room, one hand clutching her side, the other raising her skirt. "I bet he fell out of bed."

Peter stood, but froze at her words. "You mean William," he called after her.

He'd almost forgotten she had a child of her own, and, of course, upon hearing a cry in the night she would naturally think of him. Just as well to let her tend to William, he thought. Besides, the boy adored her. He had missed her at dinner and would, no doubt, be delighted to wake up and find her beside him.

Peter stood and pushed his chair close to the table. Joanna Fagan was a complete mystery. A college graduate? Highly unlikely. An employee of Michael Reese Hospital? She contradicted that statement as soon as she uttered it. Still, her assessment of Elizabeth showed signs of critical thought. She received an education somewhere. She was indeed a mystery, and, street fights aside, a pleasant one.

Peter collected her plate and took it to the kitchen. Back in the dining room, he wound the clock and extinguished the lamp, then collected the glasses and decanter and carried them to the parlor. As he made his way up the stairs he heard Joanna speaking in low, animated whispers. It sounded like she was reciting a poem. He moved quietly, hoping to listen without disrupting.

"... no, ten new friends!" She finished the poem, tickling William.

"I like Tumble Bumble, Joey. Do you know any more?"

"Sure, I know tons of them. But maybe our next one should be something to help you get back to sleep. This is called Goodnight Moon. You're a little old for the poem, but I think you'll like it."

Peter reached the doorway and stood just out of sight, watching them. Joanna lay on the bed with her back to the door, her body curled protectively around his son. He didn't approve of that sort of coddling, but she seemed to have her own way of doing things. Rather than ruin her moment with him, Peter decided he would advise her later.

"In the great green room," she began, "there was a telephone and a red balloon."

"Excuse me," William said. "What is a telephone?"

"Well, it's a ... a ...."

Curious to hear her response, Peter leaned against the doorframe.

"It's a device you use to speak to someone very far away."

"Like my mother?"

"Kind of like her, but the person you speak to has to be on Earth."

"Oh."

The longing in his quiet voice added so much weight to the word. Peter ached for the boy and considered entering the room, but Joanna countered quickly and he held back, listening.

"Your mom is in heaven, isn't she?"

"Yes, ma'am," he whispered.

"You can still speak to her, you know. It's tricky, and it's only possible when you sleep. Even then, it happens very, very rarely."

Again, Peter fought the urge to enter the room. It did William no good to fill his head with nonsense. But, as before, her words held him at bay.

"Earlier tonight I had a dream about someone I lost, but also about someone I found."

"You lost someone?"

"I lost my husband. He died, just like your mom."

"You can't get them back." William's voice was very small. "It's hard without them."

"Very hard, Sweetie. I miss him every day."

"I miss her, too."

Joanna kissed his cheek and held him close. "Oh Buddy, I think she knows. Maybe someday she'll visit you in a dream and tell you herself."

"If I sleep now, will she come?"

"There's only one way to find out. Shall I tell you the story now?"

"Yes, please."

Joanna began again, her voice low and soothing.

"In the great green room there was a telephone and a red balloon, and a picture of the cow jumping over the moon. And there were three little bears sitting on chairs, and two little kittens and a pair of mittens …."

As she spoke, Peter admired her cadence. She was a good storyteller and the low rasp in her voice, combined with the rhythm of the poem, had an altogether pacifying effect. The words were simple but comforting to the ear. Whether he agreed with her methods or not, he had to admit she had a way with children.

"… and good night to the old lady, whispering 'hush.' Good night stars … good night air …" Her words lingered, barely audible. "Good night noises everywhere." She finished in a whisper, climbing carefully from the bed.

William was nearly asleep. Joanna leaned over his little body and gave him one last kiss.

"She's out there, buddy, and she's watching over you." Turning, she found Peter smiling.

"Thank you," he whispered.

She shook her head and returned the smile. "No. Thank you. I needed a kid fix."

"A kid fix?" he chuckled. "Joanna, your diction is baffling at times."

Chapter Seventeen
Suggestion and Surprise

Eugene Prendergast lifted the last stack of newspapers onto the cart and cast a sidelong glance at his employer. The horses bristled, eager to move as Mr. Meacham barked delivery orders to the driver. Meacham was gruff, but approachable, and he appreciated a good work ethic. Prendergast, confident in his abundance of ethics, felt sure this would work in his favor. He only needed four dollars.

'It's for a good cause,' he would say. 'To further the Lord's work,' he would say. 'Repaid within two months,' he would say. Meacham would understand. He was strong in his faith; he would understand that a vengeful God needed an instrument. He needn't know Eugene was His instrument, or that God's instrument needed a gun.

No.

Mr. Meacham only need know that Eugene was doing the Lord's work. The rest would be revealed in due time. The corner of his lip tightened. He bit back a smile and nodded to his boss.

"A word, Sir?"

Peter and Joey spent the remainder of Monday night talking in the parlor, which Joey thoroughly enjoyed. Without meaning to, Peter often made her laugh. At times his thoughts were as old-fashioned as the era, and at others, remarkably progressive.

He firmly supported allowing women access to higher learning, but was baffled by their desire to vote. He said a man's voice should speak for an entire household, and his house had always been united in political discourse. Why waste good paper on such repetition?

Joey loved the blank stare she received as she argued for the sake of widows and women who'd been abandoned. By his logic, those women went without a voice. Without a vote, who would speak for them?

Peter did manage a comeback, touting local charity as the voice who spoke on their behalf.

She countered, asking if Jane Addams, the woman who established Hull HouseH, was given special dispensation to vote for those she assisted. Peter acknowledged her point in silence. He attempted a reply, but offered her nothing save an exaggerated intake of breath. His baffled look was worth ten Persian rugs and she told him so. He laughed aloud. They reviewed her shopping trip and the pressure from Elizabeth to buy a dress. Peter offered to pay for one, but Joey refused.

"If it doesn't make you too uncomfortable," she told him, "I'd rather borrow from Victoria's closet and save you the money. If I can figure out a way home before Saturday, I'll be out of your hair, and no longer burden to your household, or your bank book."

"Joanna, you are not a burden. Bewildering perhaps." He tipped her a smile. "Regardless, if you're still with us, dinner at the McNair's will be formal. You'll need something else."

She deferred again, saying, "Let's just cross that bridge when we come to it."

On the subject of Elizabeth, Joey kept her promise, assuring Peter the young lady had no designs on him, but was eager to request his help on another matter. "Out of respect for her friendship with Victoria, I hope you'll hear her out; and for the generosity she showed me today, I hope you'll consider it. She plans to stop by sometime this week."

Peter consented and pressed her for more detail, but Joey only laughed and said he was in for a pleasant surprise. "Who knows?" she teased, "you may find a new friend in her as well."

Soon after, they retired for the night.

Tuesday morning Joey woke feeling comfortable for the first time since her arrival. She dressed and went downstairs, half-dreading another encounter with Mrs. Milford. To her relief, she found Car and William eating breakfast alone.

"Morning, guys. Where's Peter?" she asked, pouring a cup of coffee.

"On Tuesdays he runs a clinic at Hull House," Car passed her the bread basket. "If it's busy, he'll be there most of the day."

"You're kidding. *The* Hull House? As in Jane Addams' Hull House?"

Both boys nodded.

"I didn't realize he knew her." She smiled to herself. He had said nothing the night before.

Joey had studied Jane Addams in school. Her establishment, Hull House, offered child care, medical care, legal aid, and English language instruction for immigrants at a time when virtually no one else did. She supported assimilation and championed civic reform—not just in principle, but in practice. She even served as the garbage inspector for her ward to help improve sanitation standards.

"Cool," she said, buttering a slice of toast. "So, what's up with you guys today?"

Car and William stared at her, sporting a matching pair of puzzled looks.

Joey sighed. "What are your plans for the day?"

"Well," Car grinned. "Will here has his lessons with Mrs. M, and I've a few things to do in town, and that is *what's up* with us today." At the mention of his name, William stood, excused himself, and went in search of his dour instructor.

"Hey, can I go with you?" Joey asked, warming her hands on her coffee cup. "I need to check on something at City Hall."

She hadn't yet warned the mayor, and, given Peter's reaction to her defense of Molly, Joey thought it wise to go without him. His interest in her prediction was minimal at best. If she went to City Hall alone, she wouldn't compromise him in any way.

"Trackin' down yer ancestors?" Car whispered.

She nodded. It was as good a reason as any, and despite his acceptance of her, even Car probably had his limits. "I thought I'd check the local records."

"Fine by me, but let's keep this on the Q.T. We don't want to upset the doc." He stood. "I'll get the carriage. Y'd best gather yer hat and coat."

A few minutes later, she met him outside.

"Hey, where's yer hat?" Car eyed her bare head.

"Don't go there, Car." Joey made a show of her feelings, sticking her finger down her throat. "That thing is an eyesore."

Climbing in beside her, Car fought off a frown. "Joey, every woman wears a hat. Ya know?"

If this were Peter talking, Joey would already have the hat on her head, but Car would not win this fight. "Listen," she said, "if you want to go parading around in a flower pot, be my guest." She made a sweeping motion with one hand. "I'm taking a pass today."

Car adjusted his cap and gathered the reins. "A pass, 'eh? All right, then. Off we go."

They made quiet, steady work of the trip, and the scenery changed gradually. Houses and trees gave way to pedestrians and storefronts, growing in density as they neared the center of town. Eventually, Car found his voice.

"Lookin' up relatives, eh? And here I thought y'd be takin' a swim."

"A swim?" Joey frowned.

"I heard Mrs. Milford bashin' away at ya yesterday, while I was waitin' ta slip next door."

"Oh yeah. Go jump in the lake and swim back where you belong." Her voice trailed away.

"Ya connivin' little sea snake!" Car laughed, fisting her shoulder, but she didn't react. "Come on, Joey, I'm just havin' a laugh. Don't be mad."

"I'm not mad, I'm thinking." She replayed the bitter words in her mind, and suddenly found some sense in them. "Oh man, Car! What if she's right? What if the water is my way home?" She gripped his arm, excitement mounting in her voice. "What if it's that simple? I mean, I fell into the lake in 1993 and surfaced now, maybe that's the way back."

Car stared hard at her.

"Listen, after City Hall, can we go back to the dock?"

"Sure, but—"

"No buts, Car. I really think I need to try this, and I need your help to do it."

"Boy, yer askin' a lot. What if ya drown?"

"Don't be silly. I know how to swim. If Mrs. Milford is right, then I'll resurface in 1993. If she's wrong, I climb up the ladder and we head home, no harm done."

"Well if she's right, and ya do go back—I mean forward—the doc'll be a bit upset with ya. And since *you* won't be here ta yell at, he'll be upset with *me*."

Joey grinned. "I think we both know his bark is worse than his bite." Seeing a cloud of doubt on his face, she added, "Come on, be a bud! I'm asking a lot but, after yesterday, isn't there any way you could return the favor?"

Car pulled to a stop and shook his head, but returned her grin in kind. "Say n'more. I'm at yer service." He offered her a seated bow, his open palm extended toward her. "After what ya did for Molly, I'll throw ya inta the lake m'self, if that's what ya really want."

"Car, you are the best!" She squeezed his hand and stepped down from the carriage.

"My chores'll take about an hour. Once I'm back we're off ta the docks."

Car slapped the reins down and the carriage rolled away. Joey mounted the steps, wondering how she should approach the mayor. Every idea she had seemed either overly dramatic or entirely unrealistic.

Mayor Harrison, your life is in danger.

Mr. Mayor, I've had a vision you need to know about.

Mr. Harrison, don't go home on Saturday night. Your life depends on it.

Nothing seemed right. She began to understand Peter's reluctance. How does one warn of impending doom without sounding like a complete nut job? Still debating the right approach, she entered the building but stopped midstride.

This City Hall was smaller, but much prettier, than its 20th century successor. The main entry opened into a great round hall. A lavishly carved staircase spiraled to the upper floors of the building. Joey marveled at the craftsmanship in the woodwork and the complexity of the tiled floor. Four colorful murals adorned the walls, each depicting a stage in the growth of Chicago. She stepped into the center of the hall and looked up. The staircase leveled off just below a stained-glass dome. Sunlight filtered through the glass, giving the rotunda a churchlike hue. Joey swelled with native pride, thrilled to see her city in its youth.

A gentleman brushed her as he swept past and she surveyed the scene before her, watching people head for offices and appointments. Across from the staircase, a concave reception desk conformed to the shape of the great rotunda. As Joey approached, a man standing at one end raised his voice in anger.

"They're a danger to us all and something must be done! Another life was lost yesterday."

"My dear Mr. Prendergast," the desk clerk huffed, "the mayor is well aware of the city's grade crossings. The increase in accidents is unfortunate, but unavoidable, given the crowds attending the fair."

There was no mistaking the name.

Prendergast.

Eugene Prendergast? The man who assassinated Carter Harrison? She moved closer, hoping for a better view.

"Nevertheless, I must speak to him. In addition to the railroad crossings we have other critical matters to discuss."

She ventured a peek. Prendergast was said to be barely older than Car, but his hardened features aged him. His hair was jet black, as were his eyes. His cheeks were thick and full, framing a mouth that was mostly lower lip, pouting and angry. For a slightly-built man, he seemed menacing. She took a place in line behind him. Should she speak to him?

To Prendergast?

"I'm terribly sorry," the clerk said, "but Mayor Harrison is out today, hosting a group of civil engineers."

"Well, they must take a tour of the grade crossings," Prendergast commanded, leaning across the counter. "They need improving. It's a matter of life and death to those who cross the railroad tracks."

"Excellent suggestion." Condescension rippled through the clerk's response. "Perhaps they will inspect them later today."

"See that they do," Prendergast said, handing the clerk a postcard. "And give this to the mayor right away. It's his last chance to right a grievous wrong. He'll know what it's about."

Last chance?

Joey shuddered. She needed to say something, but what?

Suddenly, Prendergast turned on his heel and collided with her. She tumbled back, but remained upright thanks to his strong hand, which caught her by the wrist. Mouth agape, she looked from the hand to the assassin.

"My apologies, Miss. Are you hurt?"

Joey stood speechless, shocked to be in the grasp of a notorious murderer. "I ... I ..."

"Perhaps you should sit down."

The pressure on her wrist helped Joey find her voice. On impulse she leaned close to Prendergast. "Don't do it," she whispered.

His thick black brows lifted and Prendergast eyed her critically. His hold tightened and his face turned red. "I have no idea what—"

"The mayor." Joey paused, anxious to keep her thoughts in order. She'd come here to warn Harrison, not to counsel his assassin, but here he stood. It would be foolish to waste the opportunity. Prendergast was only slightly taller than Joey. She leaned close to his ear. "I know what you're planning," she whispered. "Please. Please, don't do it."

His clench intensified. Her hand grew red from the loss of circulation, and she tried to pull away. An elderly, bespectacled man in the line beside them coughed. Joey looked over, half-worried he overheard, half-hoping he would intervene. Prendergast reinforced his iron grip and she faced him again. He kept her close and answered her, his breath hot on her cheeks, reeking of stale beer and tobacco. She turned her head in a vain attempt to escape the odor.

"Devil!" he hissed. "I am His instrument. You will not stop me." He raised her arm, squeezing tighter as if to emphasize his point. Joey recoiled. The man beside them appeared ready to speak, but Prendergast glowered at him, daring him to defend her. The fellow closed his mouth and averted his gaze. Prendergast returned his attention to Joey. "I will right this wrong," he whispered. "Now, be gone, Devil. Be gone!"

He flung her wrist down and bumped hard against her shoulder as he strode past. Joey stood mute, wiggling her fingers as she watched him go. A voice broke her stupor.

"May I help you?"

She turned to the desk clerk. How much of their conversation did he hear? Did it matter? Her plea was in vain. She eyed the clerk, hoping for better luck with her original plan.

"Man," she nodded in Prendergast's direction, "he was in a foul mood."

"Oh, he's a constant complainer. Today it's the guard crossings; tomorrow he'll fuss about the General Counsel. I ignore most of what he says." He gave the postcard a cursory glance. "I'll just file this with the others." He flicked the card into a nearby wastebasket. "Now, what can I do for you today, Miss …?"

Joey watched the postcard disappear. "Fagan. Joanna Fagan. I'm afraid I'm on the same mission as your last guy. Is the mayor really out, or were you just saying that?"

The clerk shook his head. "Mr. Harrison is out all day. Can I help you?"

Joey debated his offer. She could borrow some paper and write a note, but his mail was probably screened. Whoever read her warning would treat it with the same deference given to that postcard. She sighed. "Will he be back tomorrow?"

The clerk nodded. "He begins every morning right here," he pointed to the massive desk, "between seven and eight thirty. He likes to be out among the people before things get busy."

Joey thanked him and turned away. In an effort to shake the memory of Prendergast, she approached the murals. The first showed Fort Dearborn, Chicago's first settlement where Indians, fur traders and the militia conducted business along an idyllic, forested lakefront.

The next mural featured Chicago's path of growth, highlighting railroads, water trade and industry. In one section cattle awaited slaughter at the stockyards. Another featured Cyrus McCormick's reaping machine, which reinvented farming and helped establish Chicago as a leading grain port. The last section showed trains and boats, loaded with meat and grain, outward bound to feed an emerging nation.

Joey rediscovered an unexpected point in history in the third mural, the raising of Chicago. The image illustrated a remarkable feat. To accommodate a new sewer system, much of the town was elevated roughly nine feet into the air. In the mural a monstrous building was surrounded by hundreds of workmen, manning thousands of the jackscrews used to raise each structure. Joey was surprised to read that George Pullman, inventor of the railroad car, was involved in the effort.

The last mural captured the Great Fire of 1871. On one side, violent flames leapt into the night sky, burning three quarters of the city in less than three days. The far end showed Chicago rebuilding at dawn. Efforts began quickly, according to the plaque, and Chicago took full advantage of the craftsmanship of its immigrants, enabling an architecturally stunning recovery.

Captivating as the fire mural was, Joey was drawn back to the raising of the city. The impressive visual realization of a massive structure, raised manually, fairly begged for her attention. Joey pored over the mural until a pudgy, gloved finger tapped on the image of young George Pullman barking orders to his crew.

"It's a shame he didn't apply his industrious nature to more noble pursuits."

"I beg your pardon?" Joey turned to find a stout young woman standing beside her.

"It is a pity he didn't pursue his later projects with an eye toward civil advancement."

Joey eyed her curiously. "But he invented the Pullman car which created jobs. Doesn't that aid civil advancement?"

Though shorter by at least three inches, the newcomer had an admirable air of self-possession. She gave Joey a calculated stare. "I consider the creation of jobs a tremendous benefit," she said, "but when the creator demands more of his employees than is democratically appropriate, the advance is hardly beneficial."

Joey shook her head. "I'm sorry, I'm not following you."

The young woman smiled. "There is no need to follow me, dear. I am not moving. Unfortunately, neither are Mr. Pullman's employees." She extended her hand. "You're new to Chicago? Welcome. I'm Jane Addams."

"*The* Jane Addams?" Joey said. "It's an honor to meet you. I'm Joanna Fagan ... from San Francisco." She glanced at the mural. "So, Pullman is a bad guy?"

Addams nodded. "He requires his employees to live in a town of his own making. He pays them only pennies more than he charges in rent, and doesn't," she leaned closer, "give a tinker's damn if they've anything left to feed themselves." She straightened and stepped back. "If the only mark of a good man is his sense of fairness, then Pullman is not a good man. He is indeed, as you say, a bad guy."

Joey was at a loss for words. She wasn't sure when the Pullman railroad strike occurred, but given Miss Addams' frustrated description of the man, it couldn't have occurred yet.

"Well, justice has a way of finding guys like him. I'm sure he'll answer for his behavior eventually." She smiled at the reformer. "What brings you to City Hall?"

"Garbage." Addams glanced at the clock as it struck the hour. "Always garbage. It was a pleasure, Miss Fagan." The solid figure advanced down the hall much like a boxer, Joey thought, headed for a fight in a familiar ring.

Car was nowhere in sight when Joey emerged from the building, so she perched on a ledge at the main landing, visible but out of foot traffic. People moved past her, the speed of their gait recalling her recent failure. She scanned the crowd, pondering the ethics of her goal. Did she land here expressly to help the mayor? Was she right to try and prevent his assassination?

Her first answer was yes. Regardless of how odd her message might seem, she felt compelled to deliver it. She'd already had a hand in unwittingly saving two people this week. Maybe saving lives was her purpose here. Didn't things happen in threes? Maybe the third time was the most critical because she had foreknowledge of the event?

Or maybe not.

The first two incidents involved no foresight; she'd simply reacted as they occurred. In the mayor's case, she knew exactly what would happen, and roughly when and where it would occur. Harrison had been gunned down in his home shortly after a late dinner on Saturday the 28th of October.

Joey rubbed her wrist, remembering the black-eyed assassin. Confronting him had been useless. It probably only renewed his determination. She forced herself to focus on Harrison. Though she recalled few of his accomplishments, she knew he was popular and had served several terms.

Harrison's influence on Chicago was vast. How would history change if she saved his life? She wished she'd read more of Martin's science fiction novels. She remembered a few random stories about time travel, but thought of it only as a unique plot device.

Some science fiction theorists would argue that, even if she succeeded, Harrison was bound to die by some other means because his death was already ordained by time. Others would take the leap, and consider how such a save might affect the future. The outcome seemed to be an even toss. In some cases intervention made the world a better place, in others the main character returned home to face the worst kind of nuclear annihilation.

Vague interpretations, but they were the best she could recall, and she thought the odds of doing something helpful were slim. Still, warning Harrison seemed like the decent thing to do, even if it came to nothing. A shout interrupted her thoughts, and she saw Car waving enthusiastically. Certain she could do nothing more today, she joined him at the carriage.

Chapter Eighteen
A Test and a Tale

Are ya sure about this, Joey?" Car crossed his arms over his chest. A cold breeze passed between them as they stared at Lake Michigan.

"No, but I have to give it a shot. I don't know what else to do."

Car spoke quietly, eyes on the water. "Ya know, when ya told us yer story on Sunday, I thought it was for Will's benefit." The lines in his brow deepened. "I gotta be honest with ya, I don't think this'll work a'tall."

Joey laughed. "Peter doesn't believe me. Why should you?"

Car gave her a curious glance. "Some of what ya say does set y'apart, and I don't think yer loony, but I still can't make out what happened on Saturday." He pointed to a nearby building. "Will was over there. I was busy, loadin' the carriage when I heard a splash." He fisted one hand into the other, emphasizing his last word.

"We didn't know what it was, but it sounded big, and we looked out over the water. Peter turned t'ask Will if he'd heard it, and realized he was missin'. He was just about ready ta dive in when up ya came with Will in your arms. It just struck me funny, ya know?"

"I know. I wish I had an explanation for you. Now, turn your head, I need to lose the skirt."

"What?" Car exploded with surprising force. "What in the name of all saints are ya thinkin'? Have ya gone daft, Joey? Ya can't go walkin' about in yer bloomers. That ain't fittin'. Ever!"

"Relax, Car. I wouldn't be caught dead in those frilly things." She lifted her skirt to her knees. "I've been wearing my running tights ever since I got here." Bending over, she removed her new shoes, unfastened the skirt and wiggled out of it.

Eyes cast down, Car launched a new argument. "Now, don't tell me yer gonna run home in yer bare feet."

She smiled. "Ever heard of Zola Budd?"

"Can't say's I have." The wind playing in from the lake seemed to pass through his voice, making it colder.

"She does it all the time."

Car grabbed her arm and pulled her back down to the bench. "Joey, ya know how all this looks, don't ya? And ya do know there's a general curiosity as to the whereabouts a yer sanity?" His fingers dug into her flesh. "Don't ya?"

Joey placed her hand over his and shook her head. "Car, I'm sorry. You're so easy-going. I tend to think you're down with this."

"Down wi' this?"

"I tend to think you believe me."

"I want ta believe ya." His grip eased. "But, it was a whole lot easier when we were sittin' by the fire tellin' stories than it is now, with you half-naked and no hat, about ta jump inta that Irish Sea of a lake."

"Please." She squeezed his hand. "I have to try this, Car, and you promised to help. Come on. Don't freak out on me now. Please?"

Car whistled long and hard through his teeth. "Ya make a man long for his local, Joey, but a promise is a promise." He reached for her hand and they walked to the edge of the dock.

"See the ladder?" Car pointed to the right. "That's where I pulled ya in."

"Okay." Joey stepped to the edge like a runner to the mark. After a deep breath she faced Car. "Once I jump in, count to a thousand. It should take you about ten minutes. If this doesn't work, I'll be up long before you reach three hundred." She eyed the lake. "But just in case …."

Car grinned. "Ya don't want ta have ta chase after me, or walk home soakin' wet."

She gave him a hug. "You're a nut, Car. Thanks."

He squeezed her tight and then took a step back, regarding her. "Look at ya. Out here tryin' ta dive into another century, and ya think I'm a nutter? Tsh!" He mussed her hair.

Laughing, she put her hands on either side of his face and kissed his forehead. "That's for you, and this," she pecked his left cheek, "is for William. This last one," her lips met his right cheek, "is for Peter." She dropped her hands. "Take care of each other, okay? Hug Will and Molly for me. And quit smoking before it kills you. Oh! And thank Peter for me. I don't know what I would have done without him."

Car laughed again. "Any more and I'll be needin' a quill pen. Is that all?"

Joey grinned. "You can give Mrs. Milford a hug."

Car let out a hearty laugh. "Well, now yer just stallin'."

"Remember, this *was* her idea." She gave Car an unsteady thumbs up and squared her shoulders. "Here goes nothing." With a final wave, she stepped off the pier.

The water seemed like liquid nitrogen. Joey held her arms tight to her chest. *Think of Martin, think of Martin,* she chanted, trying to ignore the cold biting into her skin, seizing her muscles. Her goal was to match her first experience. She held her breath, hoping that when she returned to the surface she would be home.

Clutching her sides, she realized Peter never did rebind her ribs. She would have to walk home. She hoped it was warm enough. Her lungs pressed harder against her chest, demanding an exchange of air. She did her best to ignore them, picturing Michael playing at her mother's house, his blanket, Fuzz, beside him. She closed her eyes, holding the vision and let the seconds pass.

Only when she began to worry about getting back to the surface, did she allow herself to move. She'd sunk deeper than she realized, and, as before, the cold settled in, slowing her movement. Panic threatened to take over just as she burst through, and she gulped in air, again and again, grateful to draw breath in any century. She braved a look up at the pier.

It was empty.

Joey let out a shivering sigh, dropped her head and made her way to the ladder.

Odd ... that was all it took, evidently. She'd done it. She was home. Equally as odd though, was the twist in her stomach, the uneasy sense that she'd left something significant behind. A familiar voice interrupted her thoughts.

"Jesus, Mary and Joseph! Yer lips are blue! Gi' me yer hand!"

From the bottom of the ladder, Car reached for her. Joey considered diving back down, but her body refused to comply.

"Sh-Sh-Shit! Shit! Shit!" she slammed a fist onto the water. "Damn it all to hell!" She managed a defeated grin as she swam to the ladder. "S-s-s-so much for that theory."

Car caught her and pulled her to the first rung.

"Look at it this way," he said, "ya get ta kiss everyone yerself." He laid a hand on her shoulder. "C'mon, yer freezin! I should a brought an extra lap robe."

"I'll ... b-b-be ... o-k-k-kay." She gripped the ladder, but didn't budge.

With one arm around her waist, Car pulled her up and swung around behind her. "Move it. If I bring ya home dead I'm in worse trouble than if I'd come home without ya."

Near the top Joey faltered. "Oh no ya don't!" Car pushed her rear end. "Forgive m'manners, but we're not home yet!"

With one forceful heave he had her on the dock. Joey landed on her knees and crawled away from the edge.

Car pulled her to her feet. "Ya got ta move, Joey!" He put an arm around her waist and steered her toward the carriage. "Ya got ta keep movin'."

She managed a thin laugh. "I know it up here," she pointed to her temple, "but my legs are too cold to cooperate."

As they walked she managed to shake some life back into her limbs. Once they reached the carriage, Joey put on the skirt.

"T-t-turn around, Car, I need a sec." Hoisting the skirt, she shed her tights and wrung the water from them. She debated removing the blouse, but decided it would keep until she got home. "Okay, all c-c-clear." She grinned, tights in hand, teeth chattering.

Car jumped onto the platform, pulled her up beside him and wrapped her in the lap robe. Joey pulled it tight and sat down, hugging her knees close to her chest. Car placed his cap on her head and put an arm over her shoulder, rubbing vigorously. She offered him a grateful smile.

"Man, I'm glad you stayed! How high did you count?"

"I made it over one fifty, but I was countin' pretty fast after seventy five." His usually merry eyes held little light, and worry lined his brow. "Ya gave me a fright, Joey."

"I still think I was on to something." She nudged him. "I won't put you through it again, Car. Promise."

"Thanks." He rubbed her arm again, affectionately this time, and then picked up the reins. "Glad to know yer still with us. Guess yer here 'til ya remember yer address."

Joey let out a frustrated huff. "Car, I know my address. I gave it to Peter on Sunday. He hasn't found my home because it doesn't exist yet." She dropped her head in defeat.

Nothing had changed. She still had no idea why she was here. Her attempt to warn the mayor had failed, and she'd just proved she couldn't simply swim through time on a whim. She was no closer to getting home, and there was no point in trying to find a non-existent neighborhood. If she tried, she would probably discover some god-forsaken sewing sweatshop overworking its child labor. It was altogether too depressing to think about.

They traveled in silence, Joey occasionally breathing into the opening of the lap robe to warm herself. As they made their way inland the lake wind died away and the air grew warmer. She loosened her grip on the robe and put on her socks and shoes. The need to stave off cold air gradually shifted to the standard discomfort of damp clothing. She glanced at Car.

"I hope Mrs. Milford is off today. She's bound to give me a piece of her mind if she sees me like this."

Car laughed. "Our Mrs. M, and a piece a her mind." He pointed to his temple. "Lord only knows I've enough of 'em rattlin' around in here. Joey, she may seem hard, but she's givin' ya the only thing she has ta offer."

"You hinted on Sunday she'd been at odds with you in the past. What happened, Car?"

"It wasn't any one thing really. She showed up ready ta run things her way, but certain traditions set by Conall and Maeve were still in place." He turned the carriage onto Michigan Avenue. "I guess ya could say we all struggled, seein' things change."

"I don't understand. What changed?"

"Well, for starters, Maeve passed on. We needed a new cook."

"But how did you guys manage to land somebody so disagreeable? I would think Peter and Victoria might prefer someone a little more upbeat."

"Upbeat?"

"Happier. Friendlier. Not such a ...."

"A grumbler?"

Joey grinned. "Exactly!"

Car settled back and put a foot on the rail, "Well, Victoria was heavy with Will and not feelin' a'tall well. She took to her bed and the doc was busy lookin' after her. Conall and I did what we could, but none of us men were worth much when it came ta cookin'. So, Peter put the word out and along came Mrs. Milford. All business she was, walked right inta the kitchen and took over. Her cookin' got her the job. She plays that stove like a grand piano."

"But she was grouchy even back then?"

"Not grouchy so much as bossy. The changes started small, so's ya'd barely notice. One day she said she'd get more work done if she lived here. In the beginnin' she lived with her sister and walked in every day, so Peter offered her my old room. I was already downstairs. Conall needed the company. We slept just off the kitchen, and kept the place goin'. Conall and I doin' what we'd always done, and Mrs. Milford handled the housework as Maeve used ta do."

Car stopped speaking and they traveled a while in silence. The wind shifted and Joey wrinkled her nose, sure she would never be able to ignore the smell of the stockyards.

"Will was barely a year old when … em … Conall gave out." The back of Car's hand passed over his lips. "He was gettin' on, ya see. By his own account he'd lived a good life, so he left without regrets, and I understood, though I was sad ta see him go." He cast Joey a sidelong glance. "He and Maeve were saints ta me."

She gave his forearm a sympathetic squeeze. "But, once they were gone?"

Car sighed. "Once they were gone, Mrs. Milford announced she needed the rooms by the kitchen. By then she was a part a the place. Victoria had come ta count on her, and that old lady loves Will somethin' fierce." His voice trailed again.

"So, she wanted the rooms by the kitchen, and Will needed a room of his own. I was feelin' big for my britches, what with takin' over for Conall, so I moved inta the garret."

"Did that cause a problem?"

"Nah, but Mrs. M. had a nephew she wanted Peter ta hire, and she pushed hard ta make the impression he could do a better job than me." He broke into a good imitation of her.

'You know, my Tom has a lot of experience with horses. Tom can keep the tools sharp, and shiny to boot,' she'd say. At times she poked a bit harder, sayin' things like, "I'm not sure Car can handle that, Peter. He didn't do so well last time. I'll bring Tom 'round, show him how it's done." He gave Joey half a grin. "It was all a bit devilish on her part."

"Something had to give. What finally happened?"

"Ah, Peter put a stop to it. One day I was weedin' the beds out front, just out a view, when inta the parlor she came, complainin' about somethin' related ta me. Well I froze, listenin' to her bash on. Mind ya, I was beginnin' ta feel alone, what with Conall and Maeve gone, and Mrs. M always on about m'skills. I thought maybe I'd be out on the street soon. But Peter, he went deep with his voice—stopped her, then and there." He sat up straighter and delivered an impressive, though higher-pitched, imitation of Peter.

'Mrs. Milford,' he says ta her. 'You have made it quite clear that you find Car's contributions to this house lacking. Let me be frank. You are wrong. Car has always served us admirably. I suspect your comments are driven by a desire to secure a position for your nephew. Am I correct?'

"And Mrs. M. admits she's only tryin' ta help young Tom out, so Peter says ta her, he says, 'Car is a member of this family, and even if his work fell short, he would still have a place at my table. Should the need arise I would be happy to interview your nephew, but at present we are well and fully staffed. Do you understand?'"

Brows raised, Joey gestured, indicating he should continue.

"And Mrs. M. nods, but Peter isn't finished." Car called upon his baritone again. "Finally, I will not tolerate any more negative remarks about Car. He handles his responsibilities well, and never has an unkind word for anyone. If you wish to remain here, you would do well to follow his example. Do I make myself clear?" Car took a deep breath. "And evidently he did, because she never said another word about it."

Car pulled his foot from the rail and leaned forward, an elbow on his knee.

"I felt a bit bad, overhearin' like I did, so a few days later I offered her a lift to her sister's, so she'd have more time ta visit. Kind of a peace offerin'. Well, she took me up on it and we moved on. Now I take her anywhere she needs ta go. It's pretty much past between us, but she still gives me a hard word every so often. Sure, she's a bit sour, but she don't mean ya no harm, Joey. Not really."

Joey sat quietly, considering his tale. The hostility she'd encountered was no worse than Car's, and he had endured her insults for years without complaint. She eyed him, feeling lucky to have his friendship. As much as she needed Peter's kind patronage, she needed the warmth of Car's good nature. If he could withstand Mrs. Milford, then so could she.

"Thanks, Car. I'll keep it in mind if she goes off again."

As they trod along she asked, "So, what was it like growing up in Peter's house?"

"Ah, it was grand," Car smiled. "For a time it was just the four of us, Peter, Conall, Maeve and me. We had some good craic."

"Crack?"

"That's Gaelic for fun."

"Oh." She shrugged. "What happened to Peter's parents?"

"Well, he lost his mam young like me, ta typhoid. It was just the three of 'em, until Peter's da returned from the war."

"Did you know his father?"

"Nah, he passed on before I came." He leaned back against the bench. "Maeve always said half of him died in the war, and the other was just waitin' ta join his wife. When he finally passed, she said it would ease his soul ta lay down beside her again. He was a stern ol' guff, by all accounts."

"Huh. He sounds a little like Peter."

"Ah no, Joey. Doc wasn't always like he is now. Quiet, sure, but always friendly and kind. And when he met his missus, well he lit up brighter'n the White City." Car smiled. "Boy, she was somethin'. Pretty on both sides, she was. A shiny coin, that lass."

"Pretty on both sides? Like front and back?"

"Nah, silly. Inside and out. Ya know, yer somethin' like her, but rougher."

Joey laughed. "Thanks, I think."

"I mean rough 'cause yer not afraid ta fight when ya think somethin's wrong. Yer not afraid ta get dirty defendin' yer point. Mrs. Hastin's wasn't afraid either, but she had a gift for makin' a point without stirrin' up trouble. She could get people ta see her side so well that before long they'd be believin' it was their side all along. You," he said, nudging her. "Yer a scrappy lass, and ya don't think twice about kickin' up a little dirt."

"Believe it or not, Car, I never kicked up any dirt in my own time." She surveyed the landscape as they clopped along. The structures grew smaller, and the trees taller, as they drew closer to home. "In my own time I take care of my son, I work, pay my taxes, and I run. I live a pretty boring life, but here," she sighed. "Life is so different here. I get frustrated."

"Yeah. Yer a real piece of flint, aren't ya? Cross ya too hard and the sparks fly, but I like that about ya, Joey. Ya kept Molly from a terrible fate yesterday, and ya sure lit a fire under the doc. He's been cold ever since his missus died, and he's too fine a man ta live out his years that way. He needed a spark."

"Car, I'm not sure making him angry constitutes a spark."

"Believe me, any reaction from him is good. He needs ta move on, for Will's sake if nothing else."

"Well, given today's failure, I guess I'll still be around to set him off. I just hope I can clean up before he gets wind of my little swim. I'm sure he'd have something to say about it."

Car gave her a sweet smile. "Maybe, but like ya said, his bark is worse than his bite."

Chapter Nineteen
The Tenacity of Reptiles

Just after they turned onto Chapman Lane they spied Peter and William studying something in the flower bed next to the front porch. William waved and ran to the carriage, eyes alight with excitement.

"Car! Joey!" He covered his mouth after saying her name and cast a worried glance back at his father, but Peter remained focused on the patch of ground. William reached them, shouting. "We found a tortoise! He's digging for something."

The wayward pair grinned at each other and Car reined in the horses, stopping the carriage in the drive. "Ya don't say, Will. We'd best have a look at him, 'eh, Joey?"

Passing Car his hat, Joey stepped down, pulled one hand from the folds of the lap robe, and reached for William. "Where is he, buddy?"

"Over here," he said, pulling her along. "Come on!"

Car joined her and they followed William, who related the adventure from the beginning.

"I was playing outside and I found a tortoise moving in the grass. He walked from the trees all the way to the house. Now he's digging for something."

As they reached the source of the excitement William dropped Joey's hand and knelt on the ground. Peter sat on the porch steps, his back against a column, watching the reptile. He noted Joey's odd appearance with a lift of the brows. She held up a hand to ward off questions.

"I'll explain later," she said, kneeling beside William.

"Well, what d'ya make a that?" Car leaned over the busy animal. "What d'ya suppose he's diggin' for, Will?"

"I don't know. Maybe he's looking for food."

"Actually, son, he's digging a bed for himself. He's preparing to hibernate."

William frowned, staring at his father. "What is to hibernate?"

"Good question, son. This little fellow will sleep all winter long, and he's making his bed underground."

The child's eyes registered alarm. "But it will be too cold outside! Can't we make a bed for him in the house? He can sleep in my room. Please? I'll take care of him."

Peter opened his arms and cupped his hands toward William. "Come here."

The boy joined his father, taking care to give the tortoise a wide berth. Peter turned him around so they could watch the spectacle together, wrapping his arms around the boy's waist. William leaned back against his father's chest, his little body rigid with worry.

"There is no need for concern, William. A tortoise is a reptile. He doesn't feel cold the way you and I do. Once the days grow colder, he knows it's time to dig a hole and go to sleep."

William persisted. "But it's freezing cold outside in the winter."

"Yes, but your tortoise will be underground. For him that's like being inside a house. The ground around him is warmer than the air above. He'll be just fine. In fact, next spring, if we're vigilant, we may see him dig his way out again."

"But there's no air in the ground."

"Actually, son, there is a good deal of air in the dirt, and your tortoise is very small. He won't need much air when he's hibernating.

William wavered at this prospect. "You're sure he'll be warm enough?"

"Absolutely." Peter hugged him. "Speaking of helping animals, could you give Car a hand with the horses? I'm sure they're ready for a few carrots. Joanna and I will keep an eye on your tortoise."

"Yes, sir." He bounded out of his father's arms and went straight to Car who was still leaning over the reptile.

Car grinned at William. "Ya wanna ride on m'back?"

"Could I?"

"You betcha, boyo!"

William scrambled up and they were off. Peter turned his attention to Joey. "Are you cold?" He pointed to the lap robe.

She took a quick breath, hoping for the best. "A little," she admitted, opening her arms to reveal her damp blouse. "I took a dip in Lake Michigan today."

Peter's features hardened. His eyes darkened and the crease in his forehead returned along with his frown.

"You did WHAT?"

In a flash, Joey was on her feet and at the porch. "Keep your voice down! I was just testing a theory."

"What do you mean you were testing a theory?" Peter's voice was calm, but Joey heard restrained anger in every word.

"I … don't look at me like that! Yesterday after we returned from Marshall Field's I was advised to go jump in the lake."

"What? And you—? Who—? Who would say such a ridiculous thing? And why on earth would you act on such misguided advice?"

"Listen," Joey said, pressing her palms together, "I know you struggle with the story of my origins, but from my perspective the suggestion made sense. I fell into the lake in 1993, but surfaced in 1893. On some level, getting back that way seemed like a reasonable theory, and I wanted to test it."

Peter glared at her. She held her ground, matching his gaze. Finally he raised a hand to his face and pinched the bridge of his nose with his thumb and forefinger. He was either deep in thought or battling a nasty headache. Joey eyed him, silently chiding herself for instigating it. After a long silence he let out a frustrated exhale.

"Joanna, an incident like this, coupled with your aggressive behavior yesterday, does not strengthen my belief in your sanity. I may not believe your story, but I did think you possessed the ability to function in society." He paused, glancing at the tortoise. "Your action today calls everything into question."

Joey took a deep breath and scanned the yard, searching for a counter point. She found nothing. She understood his perspective all too well. If their situations were reversed, she would argue, though not as eloquently, with the same sort of logic. But she had no choice. Just as she had to jump in the lake, now she had to try to convince him it wasn't an irrational act. She shrugged in defeat. There was no way she could win a faceoff with this man. From his perspective, she had no logical line of defense.

"May I sit down?" she asked.

Peter gestured to the steps beside him. "By all means."

Joey sat quietly near the opposite column, keeping her distance from his chilled reply. She racked her brain for a logical way to explain herself. Elbows on her knees, she rested her chin in the cup of her hands, watching the tortoise burrow slowly into the ground. He was a steady worker, but he had a long way to go to reach his goal. Joey could relate to the enormity of his task. The thought struck a chord. With renewed determination, she raised her head.

"Okay, Peter. Let me start by saying I understand your point of view. I know this seems like another bone-headed move on my part, but try to look at this from another angle."

She braced herself and mounted her defense. "Take this tortoise. Poor William is convinced he's digging his own grave because he lacks the experience you have. He doesn't understand the life cycle of a tortoise, but you do. You've seen this before and you know how it turns out."

She had Peter's attention, but his expression bore a measurable level of skepticism. Joey willed herself to proceed cautiously. This might make sense if she worded it properly.

"In a way, I'm something like the tortoise; only going for a swim is the act you can't understand. It seems crazy to you, but only because you lack my experience. Just as it's hard for William to understand that an animal can sleep safely underground for several months, it's hard for you to believe my passage home may be through a body of water."

Peter said nothing for an agonizingly long time. Rather than press him, she crossed her arms, awaiting his reaction.

"My dear Joanna," he said, with no trace of humor. "Although I applaud the creative nature of your analogy, you left gaping holes in your hypothesis, the most obvious being that, unlike your friend here," he gestured toward the reptile, "instead of accomplishing your task, you sit here beside me soaking wet and stinking of the lake. How do you explain that?"

Joey shrugged, still determined to make her point, and desperate to keep the discussion from escalating.

"Well, you've got me there, Peter. It didn't work for me today, but suppose it didn't work for the tortoise the first time out either. William said he started over by the trees. Suppose the little guy has been digging all morning, hole after hole, only to run into tree roots. He had to change course and dig elsewhere."

Peter gave her a withering look. "Am I to assume you plan on diving into other bodies of water until you find one that leads you home?"

Joey laughed gently. "Somehow I don't think that's how it works in my case. Unlike this guy, I can't go just anywhere. I think my fate is tied to Lake Michigan."

"How comforting," Peter said dryly. "At least we'll know where to find you, should you try this nonsense again."

"Oh, come on." She chided him. "Crazy as it sounds to you, it was 1993 when I fell into the lake, and I have a son back there—*then*—whatever." She pulled a hand through her hair with greater force than usual. "And the lake ... well, the lake is the only link I see so far. I just had to give it a try. If it's any consolation, I don't think I'm likely to try again anytime soon. That water is freezing cold."

The corner of Peter's lip softened. "And dirty. Swimming off the Chicago pier is ill advised, regardless of your intention." He glanced at her wrist. "How did you get that bruise?"

Joey drew a blank. Admitting the full extent of her mission would only start another heated discussion, eradicating any semblance of the truce she thought they had reached. She kept her tone light, and her eyes locked on the tortoise.

"Oh. I was jostled in a crowd downtown and lost my balance, and a gentleman—" She swallowed, hard-pressed to think of Prendergast as a gentleman. "A strong-fisted gentleman kept me from falling." She traced her finger along the bruise. "I guess he had a pretty tight grip."

"Was this at the dock?"

"No, it was while I was waiting for Car to finish his errands."

To her relief this seemed to be a satisfactory answer. Peter's interrogation ceased, but he concluded with a note of caution. "Stay closer to Car if you venture out with him again. I do not want you involved in another street fight." His tone wavered between frustration and acquiescence. "Not that you couldn't acquit yourself, should the situation arise. I would just rather it didn't."

Sensing their fragile truce remained intact, Joey stood, offering a warm smile. "Done. I'm pretty grody. I'll go clean up."

"Grody?"

She grinned. "A cross between gross and dirty, compliments of the lake."

Peter stood, but held her departure with a heavy hand on her shoulder. The weight of authority resonated in his deep voice.

"Joanna, I fear you may misunderstand me. I am not at all happy with your actions today. Your behavior in no way reflects rational thought."

His judgmental tone held her in place.

"Let me be clear. Up to now, I've been researching your condition on the assumption you suffer from some sort of amnesia. Your aberrant behavior leaves me no choice but to consider other neurological disorders. Listen carefully." His grip tightened, emphasizing his message. "Do not, under any circumstances, attempt something this foolish ever again. Irrational acts lead to dire consequences. Don't force me to consider them."

His dark eyes pierced hers. "Do you understand?"

"Yes." Joey held his gaze. "I understand completely." Her eyes shifted to the hand on her shoulder. "May I go now?"

Peter released his grip and she walked into the house.

I understand that you seriously doubt my sanity. She went up the stairs and entered the bathroom.

I understand I am inches away from being carted off to a nuthouse. She pulled down the tub and turned the spigot. Her fears rose along with the bath water. She shed her dirty clothes and slipped into the hot bath.

I understand that, despite your good will, I am completely alone here. She dunked her head under the water and stayed there. *I understand I may never get home.* Slowly, she resurfaced.

"And I understand now that I may never see Michael again." Then silent tears, unleashed by her last revelation, began to flow.

Chapter Twenty
Administrative Atonement

On Wednesday morning Joey awoke determined to get through the day without upsetting Peter. Although she regretted nothing she'd done since her arrival, she was keenly aware that his patience had been sorely tested and she wanted to restore his confidence in her. After taking breakfast with Car and William she went straight to Peter's office, knocked twice, and poked her head through the door.

"Got a minute?"

Peter, head buried in a reference book, met her with a look of pleasant surprise. "Joanna. Please, come in. What can I do for you?"

"Actually, that's what I wanted to ask you," she said, leaning against the doorframe. "You've put up with a lot from me and I'd like to make it up to you." She gave the office a cursory glance. "Is there anything I can do for you today?"

Peter rubbed his sideburns, considering her offer. "I can't think of anything at the moment. Perhaps you can be of help to Mrs. Milford."

"I've offered. She doesn't want my help." She gave him a pleading look. "Come on, there must be something I can do. Typing? Filing? I'd like to earn my keep."

Peter raised a finger. "There is one thing, but I'm afraid it's a bit of a job."

"Please," Joey said, "I've got nothing but time."

"Hmm, my filing system has fallen away since ...." Peter closed the book and walked over to a small closet. "Well, it's been untouched for several months. Perhaps you could do some filing."

Joey grinned. "Gladly! Just show me what you want done—" She stopped and whistled. "Holy smokes! How many months are we talking here?"

Peter averted his eyes. "Each pile represents one month."

Together they surveyed five shelves laden with paper and separated into stacks. Joey whispered the count, her voice gaining volume as she finished, "… thirteen, fourteen. Whoa. No filing in fourteen months. What did you do, lose your secretary?" She drummed her fingers on the nearest pile, grateful for the chance to help, already imagining a busy day.

"Yes, I did," Peter said quietly.

Joey took no notice, eyes locked on the project. She fanned a stack with her thumb. "Okay," she said, nodding. "This is doable. I can handle this. So, how do you normally file? By month? By vendor? Do you have an old file I can use as a guide?"

Peter nodded. "I'll show you what was done previously. Follow me."

He led her to a small room at the back of the house where several hat boxes were stacked against the wall. One lay open, and contained what appeared to be sewing scraps, squares of fabric and loose ribbon. Peter selected the closest box. "Each box contains a year of receipts and patient information, all wrapped by month. Everything is ordered alphabetically within a given month. Here," he pulled a packet from the box. "This is February, 1892. Use this as your guide."

"Oh, I get it." Joanna fingered the ribbon on the packet. "The receipts are folded into the cloth and tied. How cute is that?" She smiled. "Let me comb through this one and then I'll get going on the others. Mind if I work in the parlor? I don't want to disturb you."

"The parlor would be fine."

Armed with a sample, some fabric and ribbon, Joey followed him back to the office. She collected the first three stacks and headed for the parlor. She spent the better part of the first hour at the desk, poring over the sample and discovered almost nothing was typed. Nearly every receipt was handwritten. The penmanship was beautiful, and every scrap of paper showed a flourish in calligraphy, but some were frankly hard to read, and there wasn't much variation in the style of paper. Joey was fascinated. Thanks to Martin, she had plenty of exposure to medicine, but she'd never seen receipts for morphine and cocaine.

"You wouldn't find cocaine in a GP's home office in 1993." She shrugged. "Then again, you wouldn't find a GP with a home office."

"Just what do you think you're doing?" Mrs. Milford loomed in the doorway, thick hands pressed into ample hips.

"I'm giving Peter a hand with the filing." Joey gritted her teeth and went back to her work.

Mrs. Milford stomped across the room, barking as she moved. "How dare you do Mrs. Hastings job! You have no right to take her place."

Joey drew a sharp breath and set the receipts on the desk. No filing done in fourteen months. That must have been when Victoria died. He'd even admitted losing his secretary. Left untouched all this time, Peter must have exposed a fairly raw nerve in allowing her to do this, and she hadn't even noticed. Still, it was none of his housekeeper's business.

"Mrs. Milford," she said slowly, "I am not taking anybody's place. I am trying—"

"Oh, I know exactly what you are *trying* to do," the old woman interjected. She had reached the desk, and towered over her. "Take advantage of a good man and settle into a nice life, all fine clothes and fancy new footwear." She mimed her jibes with mincing steps and pointed feet, as if dancing. If it were anyone else, Joey would be laughing at the impersonation, but the razor slash in Mrs. Milford's voice carried no trace of humor.

"Listen here, *young miss*, you can take a girl from the gutter to the great room, but she still smells like the sewage on the street, and I know a street rat when I see one."

Temper rising, Joey stood, palms out, as if to hold the woman at bay. "Mrs. Milford, I can't change your opinion of me, and I don't intend to be around long enough to try. As for this—" She pointed to the papers on the desk. "I'm doing what Peter asked me to do. That's all I know. If you have a problem with it, take it up with Peter. Now, if you will excuse me, I have work to do." Glaring hard at the woman, Joey picked up a handful of paper, silently daring her to respond. Mrs. Milford turned on her heel, muttering as she left the room.

Once she was alone, Joey let out a breath and reached for the back of her neck, fingers massaging tight muscles. Peter's housekeeper was always so hostile. She dropped the papers and turned to the window, hoping for a peaceful distraction. The clouded sky matched her mood. She twisted her neck back and forth, seeking release from the encounter. Mrs. Milford was really the only nightmarish element to this whole bizarre adventure. She could have landed someplace far worse, and though the woman was frustrating, she was bearable. Joey debated talking to Peter about her, but decided against it. He had enough on his mind. With a sigh, she returned to her work.

By the time she finished the first three months, the sun threatened to break through the clouds. Joey walked across the hall to the office for the next round of material, still rubbing her neck. Peter was alone, in between patients. She entered the room quietly and headed for the closet. He gave her a studied glance, frowned, and returned to his medical journal.

"Everything okay?" she asked.

He set the textbook on the desk. "Your case is proving difficult to diagnose. I've found several cases on memory loss, but not a single one resembles yours."

"That's because I haven't lost my memory."

"Joanna, you have virtually no memory of current events, either local or national. You can barely name a president after Lincoln, and when you do recall a name, like Grant, you can't remember a single detail about his term."

Joey sighed. "I know it seems like amnesia to you, but I guarantee you it's not."

"Well, barring any definitive proof, it's the only explanation I can accept thus far."

"Hey!" Joey snapped her fingers. "What about teeth? Fillings? Do dentists fill cavities yet? Would that prove I'm from the future?" She opened her mouth and pointed to a filled molar.

Peter shook his head. "Joanna, dentists have been filling decayed teeth since the 1840s."

Joey scraped a hand through her hair and let it rest at the base of her neck. "There's got to be a way to convince you."

"And I'm sure we'll find a way to unlock your memory." He retrieved his book. "Eventually."

Peter buried his head in his text and Joey set about collecting another round of material to file. As she closed the closet door, the sun moved from behind a cloud and flashed through the window beside her.

"Damn it!"

"Joanna, must you always resort to swearing?"

"Sorry." She stood, head down, the palm of her hand pressed hard against her right eye.

"Something in your eye?"

"No," she replied. "I just looked right into the sun. Now I see tracers. I'm getting a migraine." She rubbed her palm back and forth. "Man, I hate these."

"I'm familiar with migraines." He spun his chair to the wall and reached for the medicine cabinet. "I can help. Let's get you some laudanum."

Joey raised her free hand. "Thanks anyway, but I can never keep anything down with one of these. Believe me, I've tried every drug in the book. I just have to ride it out."

"Do you experience them often?"

"I used to get them all the time when I was younger, but they tapered off after college. Since Martin died they kind of came back again, and in the last few days ..." She shrugged. "It's probably stress-related."

"You're sure? Laudanum is very effective for headache."

"Relax, Peter. I'll be fine. Don't get me wrong, migraines suc—" she stopped and let out a sigh. "Okay, this is just a monster headache with some serious vomiting thrown in for the big finish. Nothing more. I'll get through it. I always do." With one hand covering her eye, she left the room.

They passed the remainder of the morning in relative silence. Peter counseled a steady stream of patients and left at one point to visit Molly Hannafee. Joey's pace slowed considerably, but she made a pale appearance from time to time to gather more material.

Around two o'clock, Peter entered the parlor and pressed her to join him for a late lunch, but Joey declined, knowing what lay ahead. The initial flashing symptom had passed, and now the right side of her head throbbed incessantly. She could do nothing except wait for the nausea.

Just after four, as Joey was walking back to the parlor with her last load of filing, a knock interrupted her. Shading her eyes from the afternoon light, she opened the door and found Elizabeth McNair standing on the front porch.

"Hey!" she said, drawing her into the front hall, "it's great to see you." Joey led her into the parlor. "So, I guess this is the big day, huh?"

Elizabeth nodded, looking at the packets strewn around the room. "What's all this?"

"Oh, I'm just trying to help out," she replied, rubbing her temple.

"Maybe you should take a break. You don't look well."

"Headache." Joey brushed her comment aside. "I'll get over it." Anxious to focus on something else, she studied Elizabeth.

"You look kind of nervous. Do you know what you're going to say?"

Elizabeth smiled. "I do, but I am nervous. I want this to succeed. Any thoughts?"

"Well, I've been greasing the wheels for you. He knows you're not after his name, and that you have a business proposition, so I think he'll be relatively open to your proposal."

"Thank you, Joanna. You've been a great help."

"No problem." She raised a finger. "I do have one more thought."

"Please. I am open to suggestion."

"Set aside your public persona today. Talk to Peter like you spoke to me over lunch. I think the flirting makes him nervous. Just be frank with him. He'll be pleasantly surprised to see it coming from you." She rubbed a hand over her stomach. "I think he'll respond to an honest plea."

Elizabeth pressed Joey's hand in hers. "Thank you."

Smiling, Joey nodded toward Peter's office. "You go, girl."

Elizabeth walked across the hall, knocked on the office door and entered. Joey raced to the powder room to begin the third phase of her migraine.

Chapter Twenty-one
Candor and a Cure

Peter stood as Elizabeth entered. He accepted her proffered hand and led her to a chair. "Thank you for seeing me today. Joanna told you I was coming, but I asked her to refrain from revealing my purpose." He nodded, watching her carefully. The overt charm Peter always associated with her was absent and it surprised him as much as her frank statement.

"Peter, I am here on behalf of my father and if he knew I was here he would be angry."

"Is this about your father's health? Is he uncomfortable asking for assistance?"

"His health is a motivating factor, but my well-being lies at the heart of this matter."

Sufficiently intrigued, Peter listened as she described her father's heartbreak for his sons, and his desire to see her marry so he could settle his financial affairs. Then she confessed she was not ready to take such a step. Relief flooded his mind and he leaned forward.

"How can I be of help?"

"Peter, because I fear my father might force me into unwanted matrimony, I asked him to consider selecting a guardian, as a precaution in the event that his health fails him before I marry.

Guardianship? Of Elizabeth McNair?

Peter nodded in silence, indicating she should continue.

"After due consideration, Papa concluded he could entrust the task to you. Please understand, he does not actively seek this arrangement, but it would ease his mind in his advancing years." Elizabeth leaned forward. "He plans to approach you on Saturday. I'm here today because his request is unusual and I didn't want you taken by surprise."

"I confess, Elizabeth, I am utterly surprised, and deeply honored that your father thinks so highly of me." He stroked his sideburns. "I will further admit your strength of character is such that I never considered you in need of guardianship. Still, I understand your father's desire to secure your future." Peter sat motionless, one hand resting on his desk.

Elizabeth waited patiently, no batting of lashes, no sighing, no effort to win him over. He found himself comfortable with her for the first time in memory.

"This will require some cogitation on my part." He reached for his pen and toyed with the quill feather. "On Saturday I can arrive early and speak to your father, but I'd like to understand his expectations before I consent to assuming the role."

Elizabeth gave him a warm smile. "Your need for contemplation is exactly why he selected you. You're a careful man, Peter. Your scrutiny alone will bring peace to his heart. Now, about dinner this Saturday ...."

Nearly an hour later, they emerged from his office. Peter escorted Elizabeth to her carriage and told her he looked forward to Saturday. As he watched her pull away, he realized he meant what he said. Victoria, and Joanna for that matter, had been right. Elizabeth McNair was a woman full of surprises.

After she left, he returned to the house and went in search of Joanna. The parlor was empty save for a few hat boxes and fourteen thick, neatly-tied packets aligned against the wall, dated in simple, printed penmanship.

Peter went upstairs and knocked on her door. Receiving no answer, he guessed she might be resting and peeked in to verify his assumption. The room was empty, but her skirt and blouse were laid out across the bottom of the bed. One quick check of the armoire confirmed that her running clothes were missing. Peter stormed into the hallway, anger rising. Did nothing he said yesterday make sense to the woman? He checked the window at the front end of the upstairs hall, scanning the street for her. Would she actually go back to the lake? A small movement caught his eye. Joanna's green sweater contrasted against the gray stone bench in the corner of the front yard.

She sat, knees close to her chest, rocking back and forth with William by her side. Quite suddenly she turned and retched violently into the bushes behind her. With a shake of his head, Peter descended the stairs. By the time he reached them, Joanna was seated on the ground, her head resting on the bench, eyes closed, William stroking her hair.

"How long have you two been out here?" he asked.

She didn't move, but she did answer. "Not too long." Her voice held none of its customary energy. "I needed fresh air and William was kind enough to join me."

"Miss Fagan isn't well, Papa. I'm helping her."

She gave William a weary smile. "You've been a big help, buddy. Thanks a lot."

Peter frowned. "Well, it's dinner time. You should probably have some broth."

Joanna covered her stomach with her free hand. "No way. I want to stay outside. The air out here is helpful."

I'll stay with you," William offered.

Joanna gave him a pat on the arm. "No, sweetie, you should eat with your dad. I'll be fine."

Peter sat on the other end of the bench, watching her. "How is the headache?"

"Not bad at the moment," she replied. "The intensity drops after I throw up, but then the pounding comes back. It builds until I blow again and then it starts all over. Today it's been a pretty vicious cycle, longer than usual."

Peter noted her pale cheeks, and moved to check her forehead.

"Go." She waved him away with a faint smile. "I'll be okay. Please, guys, eat your dinner. I don't even want to think about food."

"Well, then. I'll be out again to check on you shortly. Come along, William."

She lowered her head and closed her eyes. "I'll be right here."

Some time later Peter returned.

"Joanna? Are you awake?"

Yawning, she opened her eyes. "What time is it?"

"Coming on seven. Please, come inside." He helped her to her feet. "If nothing else, you should have something to drink."

"I think I could manage water now. Water sounds good, actually. Thanks."

Joey entered the parlor and sat on the stool by the hearth. Peter returned and handed her a glass.

"Drink this."

She took a small sip.

"All the way down."

"Easy, too fast and I'll spew. Besides, it tastes funny."

They argued half-heartedly for several minutes and Joey did her best to appease him, drinking nearly half the glass. Finally, she convinced him to take it back.

"Please. Enough. My stomach is already churning, and I am really tired of puking."

Peter set the glass down and eased into the chair across from her. Stretching her legs out, Joey leaned against the wall and pointed at the table. "Hey, Peter. What is that little silver thing?"

He lifted the small, pillow-shaped box. "You mean this? Why do you ask?"

A slight mist shrouded her thoughts. "Well, it's cute, but I can't think what it's used for. Is it a pill box or something?"

"No, this is a match safe. It was given to my father for services rendered in the Civil War."

"Is it like dog tags, or do you use it to store gun powder?"

"Dog tags?"

Joey laughed longer than she intended, but couldn't seem to stop. "Sorry. Where—*when*—I come from, soldiers wear identification tags around their necks, and at some point somebody renamed them dog tags. The name stuck. Your box has initials on both sides, so I thought maybe it was some kind of identification." She laughed again. "So your dad must be WH, and USG is for United States Government." She shook her head, trying to clear the mist. "It seems like an odd way to identify someone, but it's pretty." She took note of Peter's narrowed eyes and wondered what thought lay behind them.

"This is not for identification," he said. "It was a gift given to my father by Ulysses S. Grant. At some point during the war, he saved the life of one of Grant's closest advisors. Why do you wish to know?"

Joey put a hand on either side of her head and closed her eyes. The headache was fading, but so was coherent thought.

"Mmm, I remember seeing it on the table my first night here. And, the weirdest thing ... the next morning I found it in the pocket of Victoria's skirt as I was dressing." Her arms felt heavy and she dropped them to her lap. "I put it back on the table right after breakfast." With effort, she forced her eyes open and looked at Peter. "What's the matter?"

He wore a stern, closed look. In a foggy corner of her mind, an alarm sounded. Joey sat forward. "Oh God, did I do something wrong again?"

For a long time he said nothing, and then his features relaxed. "You've done nothing wrong. I just remembered something I need to ask Mrs. Milford."

Her stomach churned harder. She rubbed a hand over her belly and changed the subject hoping to ease the unexplained tension.

"So, how was your day?"

"Productive. I haven't finished researching your condition, but all my books seem to reinforce your theory."

"Of time travel?" She raised her head.

"No," he countered, "of amnesia. According to my references, none of your symptoms fit."

"I already knew that, but I understand your need to check."

"I also saw a fair number of patients today, all of whom will survive their ailments."

Joey grinned as the churning sensation subsided. "Well done, Dr. Hastings. And how was your visit with Miss McNair? Will she survive as well?"

"She is, it seems, well versed in the art of survival."

"Wow! I guess she cut right to the chase."

Peter chuckled. "There was no chase involved, Joanna. You do express yourself oddly. Let's just say I never expected to be asked to administer her fortune. That was quite a surprise." He sighed, staring at the ceiling. "I'm not quite sure what to do."

Hands back on her stomach, Joey replied. "The right thing. Isn't that what you always do?" She rolled her head from side to side. "Hey, I feel kind of funky. What did you put in that water?"

"Laudanum," Peter said. "I tried to get you to take it this morning, but you refused. It really is helpful for headache."

Joey graced him with a lazy smile. "Comes on fast." Her head felt heavy and she had to work to keep it erect. Finally she gave up and let it rest against the stones. "Weird. My head is still pounding, but the pain seems to be over here." She gestured to the wall beside her. "And my stomach is queasy, but at the moment I don't think I care."

However, in that hazy instant, she realized she did care. Bile rose fast in her throat and she sat up, searching for a suitable receptacle. On the far side of the hearth she grabbed a brass bowl filled with kindling. Joey dumped the contents and vomited. Peter joined her on the floor, though he could do nothing but watch her suffer.

"Told you," she chided him, one hand over her mouth.

"Yes, you did, and I should have been better prepared. You're a quick thinker. Considering what you already expelled today, I thought you might avoid it, but vomiting is a possible side effect of laudanum. How are you feeling now?"

"Exhausted, but … whoa … really kind of lit now, flying lit, bottle of wine lit." She giggled leaning against him, her limbs thick and slow. "What is laudanum anyway?"

"It's a potent pain reliever. Now, I suggest we go upstairs so you can get some rest."

"Sounds good." She made a futile attempt to stand. "A little help?"

Peter pulled her to her feet, and kept one arm around her waist as they made their way upstairs. "Why did you change into your old clothes?" he asked.

She let out a lazy guffaw. "Ha! Bet you thought I was headed for the lake again."

He shrugged and smiled. "It did cross my mind."

Joey leaned against him, groggy but content. "You know, Peter, you have a really nice smile." Through the fog, she felt him stiffen beside her. Laughing, she looked up once more. "And you're cute when you're uncomfortable, too."

His features relaxed. "And you are—how did you put it— lit? Thank you for the compliment, but you didn't answer my question. Why change clothes? Another trip to the lake?"

Through the haze of laudanum she fought a familiar wave of frustration. "Walk four miles in bright sunlight, while spewing up the last of a migraine? Whoops! Sorry." She missed a step and stumbled against her host. "Peter, you give me credit for stamina I don't have." They reached the top of the stairs and he relaxed his grip on her waist, but she held tight to his arm. "I just wanted to be more comfortable ... oh, God."

Joey stiffened. One hand flew to her mouth and she broke away, reaching the commode with seconds to spare. After another round of violent upheaval she collapsed, leaning against the side of the commode.

"Please, God. Let that be the last of it," she said. My stomach must be empty by now."

Peter leaned against the doorway watching her. "I wish I could be of more help to you."

Joey shook her head. "Martin used to say vomiting is one of life's truly solo endeavors. Besides, you did help. The pounding is gone." She tried to move. "But my feet are MIA, too. Be a bud? Give a girl a hand?"

One strong arm reached for her and she was on her feet.

"Can I have a wet towel and a glass of water?" She eyed him cautiously. "Just water, though, okay? I am sufficiently stoned and pretty close to pain free."

Peter smiled. "I can tell—just water and a cold cloth. Can you stand on your own?"

She nodded. "I think so."

He released her and went downstairs to fulfill her request.

Chapter Twenty-two
Impress and Impart

I t's open." Joey called after the knock on her bedroom door.
"You're awake." Peter wore a look of genuine surprise.
"Here is the cloth you requested."

"Great!" She plucked it from his hand, leaning forward from her seat by the fireplace.

He set the water on the bedside table while she scrubbed her face and neck.

"Ah. Much better." Rolling the towel lengthwise, she placed it behind her neck and pressed it into her muscles. "What is laudanum, anyway? I was really buzzed at first, and I'm still flying, but now it feels more like I had an Irish coffee."

"It's an opium tincture, a combination of morphine and codeine." Eyeing her curiously he gestured to the bed. "Wouldn't you rather lie down?"

"Not until I'm sure I won't—" She mimed a gagging reflex. "Your little cocktail came with an unpleasant surprise, but it knocked out the headache. Now my neck is killing me."

"Your neck is stiff? Perhaps I can be of some help."

"Would you? Thanks."

Peter sat beside her on the floor. She turned at an angle and he pinched the muscles on either side of her neck.

"Ow! Go easy. Those are live wires!"

"Live wires?"

She looked back at him. "Never mind. They're just touchy."

Peter frowned. "Joanna, your muscles are as stiff as railroad ties. How can they be so taut?"

"Just another piece of the migraine pie." She arched her back and pulled away from him.

"This isn't going to work," she said, shifting her position, "unless I sit here." She moved in front of Peter, resting her back against his knees. Then she wiggled against him, forcing his legs apart.

"I … um …." Peter faltered, but complied.

He touched her with tentative fingers and then retreated.

Joey reached for his hands. "Don't shy out on me now. Dig in."

He shifted on the floor behind her and began again.

"That," she sighed, settling against his chest, "is much better."

Ginger-light strokes moved over the knots under her skin. "Too hard?"

"No. Just right."

For a time they didn't speak. Joey lay still, enjoying the sensation of strong hands on her skin. She hadn't had a massage in nearly a year. Peter kneaded one muscle with the heel of his hand, just the way Martin used to. She tilted her head to one side, vaguely unsettled by the comparison.

"You must be exhausted," he said, thumbs working another large knot. "I counted fourteen bundles in the parlor. Given the severity of your headache I'm impressed you managed to do any filing, let alone finish the job. Thank you very much."

"I'm just glad I could finally do something other than make you angry."

"You don't make me angry, Joanna." Peter chuckled. "Well, at times you do. More often than not you confound me.

The logic of our discussions this week seems obvious to me, but when I hear your perspective I am forced to reconsider my own."

"So my turtle analogy had some merit?" A quiet laugh slipped from her.

"It was a tortoise. And no, I drew the line at that one."

Joey arched her back and pulled away. "Well I think you might be reliving some of your frustration. You're pushing pretty hard. Can you back off a little?"

His hands left her neck. "My apologies. That was unintentional."

"You know," she said, twisting her head, "in some spots you could touch me with a marshmallow and I'd squirm. "Look, it can't be easy having some stranger in your house. God knows you're entitled to react. Can you work on my temples?"

"Interesting," he mused, fingers tracing light circles on either side of her forehead. "It is just as rigid up here."

"I know. I have a hard line running from here," Joey tapped the base of her neck, "all the way to the top of my eye. And when the flashing stops and the headache starts, I just want to grab a knife and cut this side of my brain out."

Peter resumed with feather strokes. "Of all the pain one must endure in life, I'm pleased migraines aren't among my burdens. Unfortunately, they seem to be one of yours."

"Oh, I've endured far worse."

"Mmm … the loss of your husband?"

"Man!" She shivered at the memory of Martin's death. "Talk about losing your breath! It was as if someone reached down my throat and ripped out my lungs. I couldn't breathe right for weeks."

Peter's hands slid from her temples to her neck. "That's an apt description."

"What was it like for you?" Joey asked, tilting her head to accommodate his touch. "I know it's a stupid question. I'm sure it was very hard."

"It's still very hard," he said softly.

"What was she like? I mean, you've heard an awful lot about Martin, but I know next to nothing about Victoria."

Peter frowned. "What would you like to know?"

"I don't know … anything. What was her favorite color? What do you remember most about her? What do you miss?" She glanced up at him. "How did you guys meet anyway?"

"Well," Peter began, "it was on the day we met that I had trouble breathing. Victoria stood out like a cluster of goldenrod in a field of heather. She, quite literally, took my breath away."

"What was she like?" Joey angled to one side to better see his face.

Peter averted his eyes. "She was much more at home in the world than I. We used to go to Hooley's—well, now it's the Powers Theater—quite often. She loved the bustle of town as much as the serenity of Lincoln Park." He let out a slow breath. "I can't recall a favorite color because, from my perspective, she loved all color. I remember her excitement over the arrival of crocus in early spring, and the charcoal clouds that swept in before a heavy summer storm."

"We worked together at Hull House in its early days." He smiled to himself. "Victoria so admired Jane Addams. One day we met a young girl, only seven or eight years old. The poor child had a withered arm, rendered useless by some unspeakable act of violence. But she had the loveliest green eyes—bright green with just a touch of white, much like a semi-precious stone."

He stopped for a moment.

"I didn't notice her initially. She was such a shy little thing, but Victoria saw her right away. She knelt down and asked her, 'How can a girl get eyes as pretty as yours?' Well, the child opened her mouth in such surprise." He paused, errant fingers played with his sideburns and Joey fought an urge to still his hand.

"Before that moment, I think her infirmity defined that child, and she was thrilled to be noticed for another feature. She became devoted to Victoria, followed her like a puppy whenever we visited. And Victoria always called her Jade. Princess Jade. Eventually everyone did." He looked at Joey. "Victoria made that child feel special. She gained a great deal of confidence, overcame her shyness. I credit Victoria with that. She had a talent for making everyone feel special."

"She sounds very nice. I wish I could have met her."

Peter gave her a kind smile. "I think she would have enjoyed your company, too."

"You know," Joey said, closing her eyes, "you and William sound a lot alike when you speak of her. Someday he's going to grow right into that voice of yours."

"Victoria used to call him *my little physician*," Peter said. "She even gave him a black handbag that looked similar to my medical valise. She filled it with old kitchen utensils for surgery, even fashioned a homemade stethoscope for him, using old cabinet door handles and ribbon." He laughed.

"She wound cotton around the ends of the handles, so he could put them in his ears. And William would walk around for hours wearing them, the third handle tight in his little hand. He approached everyone saying, 'Lissen to yo hawt.' Car probably still has a mark on his chest."

The thought of Car and William together, two unlikely but well-suited playmates, was comforting. Joey wished Michael had a buddy like Car, someone to look up to in the absence of his father. She glanced at Peter. "So, what happened? How did you lose her?"

He looked away without answering. The silence gained length. Joey sat forward, suddenly uncomfortable with direct contact.

"Peter, I'm sorry. I didn't mean to pry."

After a moment he let out a great breath. "I'm not offended by the question. It's simply that I've never spoken of it to anyone."

"Maybe you should hold off—"

His hands pressed into her shoulders, no longer massaging; it was as if he sought her support.

"It was late August, and we had gone to town ..." His tone wavered, giving cautious voice to this terrain. "... for no specific reason I can recall. Car dropped us off on Michigan Avenue. Victoria wanted to take a stroll by the lake before heading home."

His voice steadied as the story changed course.

"It had been a busy year for me. I served on the board at Hull House and co-chaired another charity with Charles, Victoria's brother. William was thriving, Victoria was consumed with him, and I was swept up in my practice and my professional obligations."

Anxiety formed in the pit of her stomach and Joey crossed her arms.

"Victoria was very excited. She kept hinting at a secret, but refused to tell me more, only saying she wasn't ready yet. I suspected she'd bought tickets to something special, like Sarah Bernhardt. She and Elizabeth used to plan many things together."

Joey felt him shift behind her. "Michigan Avenue is a busy thoroughfare, but it is considered safe. However, on that day ...." He paused, and one hand left her shoulder, curling slowly into a fist. "There was a vendor selling flowers and Victoria asked me to buy her a bouquet. As I was paying him, she walked closer to the road, looking for Car. I remember hearing a clatter of hooves. A man on horseback moved through the crowd more swiftly than he should have—"

Joey took a shuddering breath and Peter flinched.

"Something spooked the horse. The animal reared up directly in front of Victoria. He struck her as he was coming back down. I saw his foreleg extend out, searching for the ground. His hoof connected with her abdomen. She was thrown back *so hard*. Her head connected audibly with the macadam, and she lost consciousness."

His left hand slid back and forth across her shoulder seeking, Joey thought, some sort of sanctuary. She reached for him, stilling his hand.

"The sequence is clear in my head, but at the time everything seemed to happen at once. I raced over, the horseman was already with her, then suddenly Car was there and we lifted her into the carriage and started home. She woke up along the way."

There was a desperate note in his half-hearted laugh.

"The first thing she said to me when she came around was, 'Please tell me you have the flowers,' and I thought to myself, well, she's going to be all right. She'll be sore, but it will pass. I examined her once we reached home and the odd thing was—*she was fine*. She was lucid and laughing and her usual self. She complained of pain in her abdomen, and of headache, which I expected. So, I gave her some laudanum and put her to bed. In the next few hours I took care of things downstairs. William was only three, and needed much more attention than he does now."

He stopped speaking and Joey ventured a look in his direction. Peter seemed detached from his narrative, fist close to his lips, eyes locked on the window.

"I was reading to him in the parlor when she screamed. Of course, we both ran straight upstairs, with Mrs. Milford behind us." Peter pressed the heel of his hand against his forehead.

"Victoria lay in bed, thrashing and screaming, 'the baby, the baby!' And I told her, 'William is fine, he's right here.' I thought ... well, I've misjudged, she's out of her head. She has a more serious concussion and she'll need heavier sedation to allow the brain to heal. I asked Mrs. Milford to take William to Car and return with my valise. I didn't want to leave her alone. After they left I pulled the coverlet back so I could check her abdomen and—" Peter's fist returned to his lips. His voice rose considerably and lost all its resonance. "That's when I saw the blood."

Joey gasped, squeezing his hand.

"I should have known! I'm a doctor, but I behaved like a husband. I should have had someone else examine her, someone more objective. *I should have known!* I was so preoccupied, I missed all the signs. There ... there was another baby." Tears spilled down his cheeks, and he brushed them away.

"The kick from the horse dislodged the placenta, causing a miscarriage. The baby was ... it was another boy. So small. She was barely four months along. She'd suffered early miscarriage in the past, so she kept this one from me. She wanted to be sure ...."

Peter cleared his throat, eyes focused on the nighttime sky. "By the time the hemorrhage was under control Victoria was delirious with pain, arms locked tight around her head. I gave her a generous dose of morphine. It took a great deal of time, but eventually the drug reached her."

Peter sighed and leaned his head against the wall, tears still rimmed his eyes. Joey waited quietly. When he finally spoke again his voice was barely audible.

"Once she let go, that was it. She never woke up again." He seemed to grow tense behind her. "Three days later ..." he whispered, "... she was gone."

Fourteen long months of silence broke free and Peter fell forward, sobbing into her shoulder. Joey drew her knees tight to her chest and braced her feet on the floor to support him. She said nothing, but held tight to his forearm, hoping it was enough; hoping that in telling her he found some small measure of release from this self-decreed conviction.

In truth, she thought it unlikely because she knew first-hand that a loss like his created a void—vast, immense and filled with regret. The hole would gape, ragged and open, in the heart of the one cursed with the burden of survival. She pressed her hands over Peter's, grieving for his loss as well as her own. They remained so for a long time, bound by mutual tragedy Joey didn't move until his tears subsided.

Once he was quiet she simply took over. She pulled him to his feet, led him to his room and helped him into bed. Peter never spoke. After removing his shoes, she covered him with a blanket and sat beside him, stroking his hair until he fell asleep.

Morbidly charged by his tale she returned to the guest room, pacing about like a caged animal. She tried to lie down, but in minutes she was up again treading the floor.

Again, she questioned the logic of her presence here. Desperate for answers, she thought of her dream. Is this what Martin meant when he told her not to give up on Peter? Perhaps, if she had never come here, Peter would have carried this guilt to his grave, the burden adding more misery to the lines on his face.

But, was there really any relief in giving voice to such a tragedy? Didn't she know, firsthand, that it still cut sharper and deeper than any knife? Sure, it helped to get it off your chest, but the loss remained. What then was the value? Had she helped Peter? Had she, in any way, heeded Martin's dream-induced call?

Though she cursed herself for it, Joey couldn't help wondering if her gesture tonight had any bearing on the future. Ever since she considered the consequences of saving the mayor, she began thinking about the personal ramifications of her interaction here. Why had Martin come to her in a dream, and so pointedly suggested that she help Peter? Was it because Peter was an earlier incarnation of Martin? Was reincarnation even possible?

If it was, would her actions somehow set in motion a positive outcome for another life? Joey had felt an odd connection between the two men more than once. *But reincarnation? Of Martin?* If that were true, could changing a life in one century affect that life in another? A life with her? Joey shook her head. What a self-centered notion, she thought, remembering the utter despair in Peter's voice. *Shame on you.*

This was simply one human being reaching out to another, finding common ground in tragedy. To hope for personal gain from it was the lowest form of greed she'd ever experienced. In that instant she felt no different from the man in the alley, indiscriminate in her desire to get what she wanted.

Shame on you.

She wanted to kick herself as hard as she had kicked Molly's attacker.

Man, she thought, looking around, *where is the laudanum when you really need it?* Knowing deep down that it held nothing for her, she climbed onto the bed and cried herself to sleep.

Chapter Twenty-three
Another Night Visitor

Peter felt a hand caress his face, and turned his cheek to meet the palm. A cool cloth passed across his brow and covered his closed eyes. Gentle hands pressed the fabric into his lids, an unexpected, soothing sensation.

"That's very kind of you," he murmured, "but not really necessary."

"Shh," she whispered. "You've had quite a day, try to relax."

Peter froze. Not Joanna's low tone, he thought, but a voice soft as silk and all too familiar. He pulled the cloth from his eyes and sitting beside him, smiling like an angel, was Victoria. He opened his mouth to speak, but so like the day he met her, Peter found no words and no breath.

She arched her brows in greeting, her eyes hinting at mischief, beyond beautiful. Peter thought all his memories of her were faulted, cryptic compared to the vision before him. Golden blonde hair framed her face and her smile touched his heart, warming him from within. Peter reached for her cheek. It was warm and flush, firming in his hand as her smile spread.

"Even now you take my breath away."

Victoria brushed brown locks from his forehead and stroked his cheek, her feather light fingers tracing the outline of his jaw. He sighed, at home in her touch, enjoying a serenity he never thought he would experience again.

"How can this be?" he asked.

"Well, tonight you stumbled upon a door and since you summoned the strength to open it, I was able to pass through."

"Can you stay?"

She pursed her lips. "I'm afraid that's not possible."

He looked at her, a combination of love, longing, and loss welling within him. Peter was overjoyed by her appearance, but terrified of its fleeting nature. "Victoria, your end was the hardest burden I've ever had to bear, and though I thank the Lord for allowing me to see you again, my gratitude will turn bitter at your departure. I don't know how you came back, but I'm certain I haven't the strength to lose you a second time."

She shook her head. "You're stronger than you know." Delicate fingers smoothed the lines on his brow. "I'm sorry my death was such as it was. You were so attentive and sad. I was with you, but had no way to reach you."

Peter frowned. "I don't understand. You were quite unconscious."

Victoria glanced around the bedroom. "It's difficult to explain. All I know is that for a while—before I passed on—I was here with you. Not in body, but in spirit. It was odd and new, but very natural. After a time, I knew I had to leave." She favored Peter with a gentle smile. "But I am here now."

He watched her carefully as she spoke. This was his dearest, his Victoria, sitting on the bed they had always shared, and for reasons he might never understand, God had allowed her to visit him tonight. Despite the temporary duration, he vowed to make the most of his time with her. Sitting up, he adjusted the pillows behind him and opened his arms.

"Come here."

She joined him, wrapping herself in his embrace, resting her head on his chest, stroking his arm with her free hand. For Peter it was the same, and though he smothered her in his arms, she was to him like a blanket to a child, warm and reassuring. In this moment he was whole again. He sighed and kissed her hair.

"You've had an exciting week and a very intriguing houseguest," she said.

"Mmm, Joanna Fagan. She's an interesting case, but I'm afraid her situation is beyond my professional grasp. I'd rather confer with your brother, but I promised to keep her affliction confidential." He let out a long breath. "It's proving difficult, though. I suspect Richard would fare better with her, and devise a more logical course of action."

"Don't doubt your ability, Peter. You have within you the means to help her, but if your frustration impedes your progress Richard is an excellent neurologist. It's a shame Father never credits him for his dedication to his field."

"Victoria, unfortunately for Richard, your father's abiding faith in traditional medicine is too well entrenched, and at his age he is not inclined to change his mind." He looked down at her and smiled. "I don't want to talk about Richard or your father. I want to talk about you."

He gave tender kisses to her forehead, the tip of her nose, her lips. She responded, pulling him closer. Memories of moments like this filled Peter's heart and he reacted, passion weaving through his adoration. His kiss was slow and intense, revealing his desire for her, and for all he had lost when she left him. She was the half that made him whole, and like a man who has lived long without nourishment, Peter took everything she offered. "Perhaps I don't want to talk at all," he whispered, his lips still close to hers.

The sound of her laughter was a peal of soft bells rung randomly, every new pass creating a joyous song of its own. She had always been an angel in his eyes, perhaps now she really was one. He cupped her chin. "There is no other light quite like you, Victoria. It's been dark since you left."

She raised his palm to her lips, kissed it, and nestled her cheek in its warmth. "Then I think it's time you found a new source of light."

"No," he said firmly, shaking his head.

She sat up and cupped his face in her hands. "My darling Peter, there is all manner of light in the world. Not every light is a wife. There are friends, companions, colleagues. You've hidden yourself away since I left. It's not good for you."

He shrugged. "I live a quiet life, but I do manage."

"A managed life is a meager existence. There are many who suffer as you do. You're a kind man, Peter. If you won't seek light for yourself, use what lies within you to light a path for others ... perhaps for your guest."

"Light a path for Miss Fagan?" He gave her a weak smile. "I'm hardly a beacon these days. Every attempt to assist her ends in failure. The issue of her sanity is constantly in question. Whenever I address her bouts of irrationality, I sound like a crusty benefactor upbraiding an unruly ward."

"I thought she behaved very well today."

"Oh she did! I quite agree." He studied the blanket. "But who knows what she'll do tomorrow? For a reasonably steady individual, her behavior is as hard to predict as the weather."

Another sweet peal of bells tolled as Victoria laughed. "Sometimes, my love, we stumble on exactly the problem we are meant to solve, whether we want to—" She lifted his chin with her fingertips, forcing his gaze. "—whether we have the means to, or not. Consult with Richard if she leaves you no other choice."

"I gave her my word I would keep her confidence."

Victoria crossed her arms scowling. "You promised to help her. If involving Richard leads to success, how can you oppose that?"

"Darling, a man's word must be worth something. I already lost you, and I very nearly lost William this week. I have little left but my integrity, and that I intend to keep."

Victoria sighed. "When you find no other recourse, just remember you can always talk to Richard." She surveyed the room, hugging herself.

"You know, it's fitting somehow that I return to the place where I last saw you." Mischief lined her blue eyes as she flashed a smile. "I can't stay much longer, but perhaps there's enough time to change your last memory of me." She leaned in to kiss him. Peter held up a hand.

"Once you've gone, how will I find you again?"

She laughed again. "I'm not sure that will be necessary. So, for now ...." Hands on his shoulders, she leaned close and silenced him.

Her breath was apple sweet, her desire apparent. She moved and Peter responded, pulling her close, willing her to become a part of him again. As their passion intensified he felt a wondrous surge of heat burning from within. He grasped her hair, intending to take her and never let her go. Victoria was stronger, her hold more powerful, and Peter found himself blissfully lost in her energy. He yielded to her, accepting her strength. Her lips slid to his neck, his chest. She moved upon him in a magnetic, compelling rhythm and he reacted, growing hard beneath her. He struggled anew, desperate to shed his clothes. Desire became need, boiling within him. She seemed to sense it and her lips rediscovered his, but this time her kiss hungered for more.

It was as if she sought his very soul. Her tongue overtook his, her lips enveloped his, her body pressed insistent upon him. She exerted amazing power. Peter wanted desperately to couple, but she held him easily at bay. Eyes closed, he hungered for his release. Just when he felt he was reaching a pinnacle, she reared her head, let out a tremendous cry and in a manner he had never before experienced—*she entered him*. Her spirit invaded his mortal coil, reuniting with his in an explosion of heat. The force of her pervasion shocked him. It wasn't a physical entry, but much, much more—as if her soul had gained access to his entire being. Peter held his breath as he felt her embody him, trembling as her spirit ignited him. The purity of the moment was unearthly, unnerving and all-encompassing. With a shuddering gasp, he opened his eyes.

He was alone.

Chapter Twenty-four
Analysis Paralysis

Peter bolted from the bed as if it were on fire.

What, in the name of Almighty God, just happened?

If that was a dream, then it was the most vivid nocturnal specter he had ever experienced. Peter flinched. He was completely alone and yet certain she had been here. Even now, he could feel her, a remnant of that unbelievable rush remained. The whole experience gripped him and he shivered, though he wasn't at all cold.

Brandy. He thought abruptly. *I need a brandy.*

In seconds he was downstairs, retrieving decanter and glass, which he carried straight into the parlor. The fire was nearly out, and he stoked the flames with the kindling Joanna had scattered earlier. The flames grew stronger and Peter added a log. He settled into a chair and glanced at Joanna's unfinished glass of laudanum. He debated drinking it, but he knew laudanum would dull the senses and separate the user from the experience. Peter wanted very much to reexamine his recent encounter. It was far too vivid to consider it merely a dream. He poured generously from the decanter and took a liberal drink from his glass.

The day had been long, with unexpected revelations occurring throughout. From Elizabeth's request for guardianship, to Joanna's office contributions to … actually, Joanna had contributed far more to his day than mere filing. Shifting in his chair, Peter stretched his legs toward the fire.

Ever since their first meeting, Peter had enjoyed discourse with Joanna, but he never thought her capable of culling such a guarded story from him. What he spoke of tonight—such a dark place and time. As a matter of survival he never allowed himself to think about it. Yet she pulled it from him as casually as one might pluck a flower from a field. In fact, she shed tears alongside him. Given the similarity of their circumstances he supposed it was natural. Regardless, her ability was uncanny.

Was his confession the door to which Victoria referred?

Reliving the worst experience of his life? It must be. It was horrid, voicing aloud his abominable failure. Yet, in a ragged way he felt purged of guilt after laying bare the mistake that cost him the love of his life, and a second son. Peter pinched the bridge of his nose and ran a hand through his untidy hair.

And what of her suggestion to consult Richard?

Among the many things he missed about Victoria were their occasional discussions over his more compelling cases. Though she was not formally educated in medicine, coming from a family of physicians she understood the process of reaching a diagnosis.

It was always a pleasure to share the details of a case with her and watch her mind at work, at times shedding light on an element he had overlooked. She was the perfect confidante and counselor. Peter often thought that, given the opportunity, Victoria would have made a fine physician. However, in Joanna's case, she was wrong. Joanna had begged him to keep her condition confidential, and he felt duty bound to honor her request, despite his inability to treat what he now believed was a neurological affliction. Peter sighed and drank again from his glass. The brandy warmed him, though it was a feeble echo of the fierce heat he experienced when Victoria entered him.

Exactly what had happened in that moment?

There were certainly carnal elements in the experience, but it moved far beyond the physical. The instant it should have become the peak of physical fulfillment it became radically spiritual. It was amazing in its way … *and not peacefully so.*

The best analogy he could call forth were a few random encounters between Old Testament figures and the Lord. Abraham's sacrifice of Isaac. Moses and his burning bush. Those Godly exchanges left both men trembling in the presence of the Almighty. Though, for Peter, the sensation bore some measure of the Biblical, he never feared his wife. Quite the opposite, in fact. And the moments leading up to her entrance were intensely physical. He flushed at the strength the memory still held for him. But when she entered him, when her soul embodied his being, *by God he did tremble.* Peter reached for the decanter.

He drank again, this time concentrating on the sensation of the brandy coursing down his throat, warming him from within. He closed his eyes and traveled with the drink deep into his core, hoping to find some insight lurking there.

Nothing came to mind.

He drained the glass, shamed by the notion of using alcohol to understand his experience. The last of the liquor entered his system, this time quelling, as laudanum might, any further thought toward logic or insight. Peter sighed.

The Lord moves in mysterious ways.

A bitter laugh escaped him. Weak as it seemed, it was the best conclusion he could draw this evening. His fingers played across the table and came to rest on the silver match safe—another oddity. Mrs. Milford insisted it had been stolen, and Joanna admitted tonight that it was in her pocket. The two incidents were connected somehow, but Peter had neither the energy nor the inclination for further rumination. He secured the fire, gathered the glassware and put it away.

Once upstairs, he checked in on William. Regarding the sleeping boy, Peter saw elements of Victoria in the shape of his nose, the arch of his eyebrows. Things easily missed in broad daylight were apparent as he lay sleeping. Another warm rush welled from within. He loved William dearly. Pressing two fingers to his lips, Peter kissed them and laid them on the child's forehead. Turning quietly, he left the room.

Down the hall he paused between the doors to his room and Joanna's, and debated looking in on her. What passed between them tonight was still a matter of great sensitivity. Should he find her awake, it might lead to another discussion, and Peter had no words left. He longed for sleep. Still, she had suffered a massive migraine, and she was in his care. Besides, she drank enough to ensure eventual sedation. Peter bet on the laudanum and opened the door.

Joanna lay curled in the center of the bed lost in her boyish clothing, eyelids swollen from tears shed earlier, blankets pushed aside. In stark contrast to William, she didn't look at all peaceful. Even in her sleep she looked as if she struggled mightily with something, and it—whatever it was—had bested her. Her gaunt frame suggested unnatural frailty and the realization pained Peter. Evidently the drug offered no respite from the stress of her situation.

Was he doing enough for her? Could he really help her? Or find her family? Peter rubbed his sideburns, frustrated by his lack of progress, but at least he understood the source of her suffering. Perhaps providence determined their meeting, guiding Joanna to one who trod the same black path. In that sense, Peter felt a kinship with her that he shared with no one else. In that dark place they were as one. He pulled the covers over her. She shifted and drew them close.

"Shamejoey, shameonyou."

Her words were slurred, but Peter heard them. He sat on the bed, puzzled. What on earth could she possibly have done to warrant any shame? He passed a hand through her hair, attempting to soothe her. Joanna recoiled from his touch and curled tighter—if that were possible—into whatever lonely place she now occupied. A soft, high-pitched sound escaped her. It took Peter a moment to understand that she was crying in her sleep.

He could try to waken her, and coax from her the source of her angst, perhaps help her find some path to absolution. But he was tired, and, as he had confessed to Victoria, hardly a beacon. He could barely help himself, let alone another. Still, Victoria's words stayed with him. *If you won't seek a light for yourself, then use what lies within you to light a path for others.*

He placed a hand on Joanna's shoulder, but made no other move. She didn't pull away this time. At least that was something. He sighed, watching the deep red glow of the fireplace.

It was something of a shock when Joanna's hand clutched his. He looked at her. She was still asleep, still crying, but the troubled look on her face had eased somewhat.

"Missyoumac." Her voice was thick and slow. "Justmissyou."

He gave her shoulder a gentle squeeze and slipped his hand over hers and whispered, "I know exactly how you feel."

Chapter Twenty-five
Breakfast of Consequences

Eugene Prendergast walked down Morgan Street, head held high, his mood as swollen as his wallet. He stepped into a cobbler's shop just past the alley. The counter wasn't manned, but he heard activity behind a dark curtain.

"Mr. Petty?"

A short man with a bristly gray mustache drew back the curtain. "Ah ... Prendergast? We spoke Monday? For the black boots?"

"No sir, the pistol, the used pistol you advertised. I trust it's still for sale?"

"Ah. That's the man. Now I remember. Yes, but the price is firm." A pair of grey eyebrows knitted together, nearly matching the mustache. "Four dollars for a pistol in excellent condition."

The blade sight was missing, but Prendergast hadn't noticed and Petty didn't point it out.

Prendergast worked hard to keep from smiling. His vengeful God did provide. "Yes, yes. I understand. May I see the weapon?"

Petty set the gun on the counter, nudging it forward for inspection. "A .38 caliber five shooter."

Prendergast nodded, touching the letters on the cylinder. "U.S. Revolver Company?"

"Good gun. Hole puncher. Stop anything in its path."

Prendergast made for his wallet, but hesitated. "Bullets are included?"

Petty frowned, made a show of his internal debate. Even loaded, the piece was only worth three and two bits. He nodded at his customer and produced a leather pouch. "They are today."

Prendergast laid his money on the counter. "Praise be. You're a fair man, Mr. Petty. The Lord smiles on the righteous." He collected his purchase and left the shop.

"Indeed, he does," Petty said, pocketing the cash. "Praise be."

Thursday morning dawned, and with it came Joey's conflicted feelings. Her desire for some transcendental gain remained laced with guilt. She ventured downstairs, uneasy about facing her host. Peter was at the dining room table reading the newspaper, his empty plate pushed to one side.

"Good morning," he stood as she approached. "Think you can hold down breakfast?"

"Well, my stomach is still a little delicate, but I am starving, so ...." She took a seat.

"Excellent."

Joey served herself a tiny portion of eggs and toast, but couldn't shake the guilt she carried. Even now, greedy as it seemed, the desire remained with her. She still wished for a positive change in her contemporary life as a result of her actions in the past. Peter's voice pulled her from her reverie.

"I think you'll find that fork useful." She raised her head and watched his smile fade. "What's the matter, Joanna?"

With a weary exhale, she pushed the plate away, set her elbows on the table, and hid her face in her hands. "I feel so guilty," she said.

"Whatever for?"

"Boy." She drummed agitated fingers on the table. "The explanation is pretty convoluted. I'm not sure it's even worth discussing."

"If this involves anything I spoke of last night," Peter said, "I never intended—"

"Whoa!" She raised a hand. "It's nothing you said at all, so don't go there, girlfriend."

"Girlfriend?" Peter grimaced, but pressed on. "What is it, then?"

Joey waved a hand, mumbling. "Sorry about the girlfriend thing. It's just an expression." She took a deep breath. "Okay, let's start at the beginning. I told you I came from the future and you don't believe me."

"Joanna, my personal belief has no bearing on—"

"No need to defend," she volleyed. "I wouldn't believe me either. For now, let's just agree we have a difference of opinion regarding my *background*. May I continue?"

He shrugged and nodded.

"Well, from my side of this argument—that time travel is possible—there are theories about how an intrusion from one time period might affect another."

"Meaning?"

"Meaning, because I'm here, it's possible that what I do in 1893 *could* change the outcome of events yet to come." She noted Peter's doubtful expression and attempted to reframe her argument.

"Okay, skip the time travel part for now. Think about what happened on Monday. If you hadn't taken me to Marshall Fields, then I wouldn't have interrupted the attack on Mr. Calder's employee."

"And?"

"And the course of Molly Hannafee's life might have taken a vastly different turn."

Peter nodded.

"Now, if you agree, then there's room for the idea that my presence here may alter the course of your life in ways you'll never know, because now they're destined to change, based on my presence."

"I'm not sure I can accept your theory."

"Well, consider this. It already happened for you."

Peter sat stone still. Joey laughed.

"Come on, think about how we met. The dock? William?"

"Oh." Lines deepened on his forehead. "If you hadn't been in the water, then William—"

"Exactly," Joey said, "but it's not the reason for this discussion, though it is related."

"How so?" Peter crossed his arms, regarding her.

"Well, the conclusion you probably drew, regarding William, was related to a thought I had last night." She cast her eyes down. "A wish really."

"Please, go on."

"I don't know the formal name for it, but there's a school of thought that believes if a time traveler affects life in the era visited, it's possible any change wrought will affect future events, maybe future lives." She looked across the table, hoping her words made sense.

Brows raised, Peter showed no sign of comprehension.

Joey sighed. "Okay, circling back to the beginning, you asked me why I felt guilty. It's because I went to bed wishing that, in traveling back here and helping you, I might set in motion a new course, one that prevents Peter's death in 1993."

His eyes narrowed. "I think you meant Martin."

Joey stiffened. "I ... I said Martin."

"Actually, you said my name."

"Did I really?" Groaning, she dropped her head. "Oh man! See how confusing all this becomes? What a mess! I feel terrible, hoping to benefit from your circumstances. What a self-ish, selfish thing! And still, I want it! God, I hate myself today."

Deep-throated laughter erupted from Peter's side of the table. Joey looked up. Peter was still shaking and he burst out again at the sight of her shocked expression.

"What's so funny?"

"You are!" He stopped to catch his breath. "Joanna, you harbor guilt for something that, based on your own belief, will never affect me. If future events play well as a result of your being here, then congratulations! You already saved William's life. I've gained by you. Why shouldn't you gain by me?" He shook his head, still smiling.

"If I follow your theory to its natural conclusion, when you return to the future whatever you find will have no bearing on me. I'll be long gone in 1993, so I'll never be affected." He pushed her breakfast back to her. "You place a great deal of unnecessary guilt on your plate. Stick with the eggs. Much healthier for you."

Joey cocked her head and picked up her fork. "I guess I never thought of it that way. Seems like you have a better grip on all this than I give you credit for."

Still smiling, he shook his head. "I confess, I've exhausted the medical library and found nothing relating to your claim of time travel. I do understand it is real for you, and given your demeanor—certain incidents notwithstanding—I can accept that you believe it, even if I don't."

Her brows arched in reluctant acceptance. "I guess that's something...."

"Barring any definitive proof, it's the best I can do. Now, please eat."

Joey took a tentative bite and gave Peter a satisfied nod. He offered her coffee and she extended her cup.

"Now, what would you like to do today?"

Eyes visible over the rim of her drink, she studied her host. "Hmm ... I haven't given it much thought. I do want you to check my work on those files."

"Of course, but that won't take long." He grinned broadly. "If you could do anything today, what would it be?"

"That's easy," she smiled, setting down her cup. "I'd pay a visit to the mayor."

Peter's grin disappeared and Joey mounted her defense.

"Oh, come on! You asked."

"Yes, I did." He sighed heavily. "But it wasn't what I had in mind."

Joey crossed her arms. "What is so wrong with trying to warn a man of mortal danger? How can you oppose that?"

Peter paled as she spoke. Pinching the bridge of his nose, he drew a careful breath.

"Hey, are you okay? You look a little funny."

"I'm fine, thank you. Your last question brought a recent dream to mind." He cleared his throat and adopted an officious tone. "Regardless, this returns us to our earlier conversation, and from my perspective it is a question of belief. Because I don't believe your theory, I have no interest in doing anything to promote it. I think it detrimental to your recovery."

"How so?"

"To rush down to City Hall and deliver dire warnings and grim predictions." Peter's voice took on an edge. "It separates you further from rational thought. People will question your sanity, and mine, for allowing you to do such a thing."

"Look," Joey countered, "from my perspective I am not sick, I am lost, so I have nothing to recover from. And since I don't think of myself as separated from rationality, I promise you, I won't behave like some stark raving lunatic. I just want a moment of the mayor's time, to tell him—"

"Tell him what?"

"Good question. I struggled with that one on Tuesday."

A sharp intake of breath came from the other side of the table, and Joey felt a sick twist in her stomach.

"On Tuesday?" Peter's voice gained half an octave.

It was an unfortunate slip. Her cheeks flushed crimson as Peter leaned forward in his chair.

"What do you mean *on Tuesday?*"

Color crept slowly up from the top of his collar. Joey remained silent.

"Do you mean to tell me that, in addition to your little swim, you attempted to speak to the mayor of Chicago?" Displeasure framed his question.

"Did you?"

Then it gave way to mounting indignation.

"Well ... *did you?*"

Her shoulders slumped and she nodded.

Peter slammed his fist onto the table and Joey flinched along with the dishes. He rose from his chair in a fury. Locks of hair scarred his brow, darkening his features as he paced back and forth across the room, one fist pounding away at his lips. He stopped, stared at her and attempted to speak, but mustered only a cry of exasperation.

"How could you?" he hissed finally, turning away.

"How dare you!" He spun back around, finding words for his anger. "I thought after our recent discussion you understood what was acceptable under my roof."

"For what it's worth," she said quietly, "he was out of the office."

"It's worth nothing! Whether you saw him or not is beside the point. That you disobeyed me, ignored my wishes, and have absolutely no regard for my rules—that is the point!"

Joey held her breath. It was, in part, true. She had only agreed never to engage in a fight, but following the argument after Monday's incident, she fully understood that her need to warn the mayor was beyond the bounds of Peter's acceptance. In that respect, she did disregard his rules, but with Harrison's life at stake, she didn't regret her breach of ethics.

"Well?" he demanded, one hand on his hip, gesturing toward her with the other. "Have you anything to say for yourself?"

"Nothing that will appease you."

"Ah ha! You can't even summon the decency to apologize!"

She shook her head. "No, I can't, because I'm not sorry."

"What?!"

Joey stood, knowing full well this was a fight she would lose. Determined to hold her ground, she summoned every fragment of courage she could find.

"Peter, I would rather risk angering you and save a man's life, than live by your rules and see him die. I didn't tell you I went to City Hall on Tuesday because I knew it would upset you."

"Oh, I am far beyond upset." He began pacing again. "I am indignant. I am furious!"

"And I'm just trying to keep the mayor alive. Maybe when he dies, you'll finally believe me."

Peter gave her a smoldering stare and Joey found it hard to maintain eye contact.

"How is it you know of this, Joanna?" The slick undertone in his voice was something she hadn't heard before. It was even more unsettling than his anger.

"I told you. History class. If I have to be stuck back here, the least I can do is try to prevent a murder."

"Could it be you *know* the man who plans to kill him? Is that what lies at the bottom of this?"

"What are you talking about? I don't know him, I only know *of* him. I've never even met—" She covered her mouth, stopping just short of a lie.

She had met Prendergast on Tuesday.

"Ah ha!" Peter raised an accusing finger. "So, you do know him. At least you finally remember something. Perhaps he's the man you ran from, prior to falling into Lake Michigan. Is that why you can't remember, Joanna? Because you wish to forget? Because someone you know plans to commit a horrible crime, and you can't live with the knowledge? Or perhaps you planned it with him, and the guilt of carrying it out sent you to the lake and erased your memory?"

"My God, Peter. Is that what you think of me?" Joey leaned on the tabletop for support. "You honestly think I'm capable of murder?"

He raked a hand through his dark hair, scowling at her. "I don't know what I think, but if you know Mr. Prendergast, tell me now, because one way or another I will find out."

"I don't *know* Prendergast. I bumped into him at City Hall on Tuesday. He's the man who bruised my wrist." She shuddered. "Since I couldn't warn Harrison, I ... I told Prendergast I knew what he was planning. I begged him not to do it. That's why he grabbed me so hard. I think I freaked him out."

"You freaked ... *what?*"

"I think I scared him. It's a common expression where—when—I come from."

"Joanna, I am tired of your common expressions. This simply must stop. I warned you before. Be careful or this will end badly for you."

She dropped her head, ready to concede, aching to start the day over. "I know. Car said—"

"Car? Was he involved? By God, I will have his head—"

"Don't you *dare* bring Car into this!" she snapped. "The whole mayor thing was my idea and I acted alone. Car thought I was looking up relatives. He gave me a ride into town, nothing more. I didn't tell him a thing." She pointed to herself. "You're mad at *me*, Peter. Let's keep it that way."

In an instant he was across the room, towering over her, hands fisted, voice as black as his eyes. "I am not mad, Joanna, I am angry! You, on the other hand are *Stark! Raving! Mad!*"

He strode past her before she could rejoin. Seconds later, the front door slammed.

Dear God, what have I done? Joey sank to her seat, feeling sick to her stomach.

"Well, well, well," Mrs. Milford sauntered into the dining room, "seems our little street rat chewed right through the welcome mat."

The housekeeper's smug expression was too much. Joey leaned forward and vomited onto her plate. With great delicacy, she wiped her mouth with her napkin and placed it on the table. She faced her adversary, determined to keep from shaking.

"Breakfast was delicious, Mrs. Milford, but I seem to have lost my appetite. Now, if you'll excuse me." She nodded her head and left the room.

As Joey reached the front hall, she heard hoof beats and caught a glimpse of Peter on horseback, on his way, she feared, to orchestrate her undoing.

Chapter Twenty-six
The Prank, the Prophet, and the Prognosis

Coco moved at an aggressive clip and Peter fumed in the saddle, still reeling from the shock of Joanna's defiance. In his house, strict deference to the rules was expected of everyone. He had been adamant about this on Monday, and yet she disregarded him the very next day! Anger and confusion battled within him as he rode into town. Ever since Joanna's arrival, his well-ordered world had shifted into uncertainty. In five short days he found himself, much to his dismay, deep in unfamiliar territory.

Joanna was a lovely woman—he could admit that—maternal to William, friendly to Car, and an engaging companion. She had settled easily into their lives, and his general feeling regarding her grew warmer with each passing day. She was, in her way, an endearing mystery.

But a charming personality did not excuse willful disobedience. Her defiance left him duty bound to step back and review her situation from a more professional stance. It was her congeniality, he thought angrily, that led him to such a lapse in judgment. He needed to approach her case based on her behavior, not her personal nature.

First, though she knew herself quite well, she'd lost complete touch with the present which revealed an irrational state of mind. Second, her contention that she came from the future was a direct cut to her sanity. Last, her certainty that the mayor would die on Saturday was an unsettling thought. The fact that she named the assassin shed a different light on matters.

This Prendergast ... she knew him by name and admitted meeting him on Tuesday. Could he be the cause of her illness? Perhaps, in despair after Martin's death, she fell in with Prendergast, learned of his plans, and had run from him, rather than participate. Peter stroked his sideburns, considering the theory. It didn't make sense. Joanna was not a woman inclined to run from things. Far from it. Ever since he met her, when adversity arose, she chose to stand and fight. Fleeing trouble was unlike her. Creating it, he thought rolling his eyes, was entirely another matter.

Two logical steps were open to him. One: locate Prendergast and force a confrontation. That ought to shake her memory. The other: break his promise of confidentiality and consult Richard. Her admission this morning left him no alternative. It was clear that under his care neither Joanna's behavior nor her memory had improved. He debated his lapse in personal ethics, but remembered her stance when she told him she wasn't sorry.

Well, confidentiality be damned! He wasn't sorry either. He turned onto Calumet Avenue ready to seek the opinion of his brother-in-law.

Peter had always considered Richard a fascinating man. The only Sullivan who pursued neurology, after medical school he spent six years perfecting his expertise at Friend's Hospital in Philadelphia, a facility for the insane. He returned to Chicago in 1890, to help Northwestern University expand their School of Neurology and Psychiatry. Peter tethered Coco to a fencepost in front of a Federal-style building and knocked on the front door.

"The esteemed Dr. Hastings!" Richard beamed, embracing Peter. "My God, man, it's been months. What a pleasant surprise! Please come in."

Piercing blue eyes marked every member of the Sullivan family, and Peter always thought Richard's were a natural complement to his magnetic personality. They demanded attention, but it was his quick wit and affable charm that captivated everyone. Peter gave his brother-in-law a sound clap on the back.

"It's good to see you, Richard. You seem engaged as ever," he said, taking in the disheveled office.

The room was a living tribute to a mind constantly on a quest. Books lined the shelves, but, like an intellectual flood, they spilled from their natural boundary. They were splayed across tables and armchairs, providing clues to the subject of a given day. A nearby desk was littered with paper, the haphazard arrangement of which was, no doubt, logical to his host.

"Tell me," Peter said, pointing at the desk, "What holds your attention these days?"

"Ah! Most interesting." Richard settled into one armchair after clearing another, and entreated Peter to join him. "I have a new batch of students and we have the good fortune this fall to be treating a fellow who believes he's the resurrected Christ. He thinks he's here to save us all. My goodness, he's a nice break from the usual disorders."

Peter leaned forward. "Any indication what brought on such a belief?"

"Cerebral scars give evidence of a blow to the head, so we must consider a physical trigger. His accent places him somewhere in the south, which could indicate a rigid upbringing. Rural southerners often embrace faith with open zeal. These may well be contributing factors in this particular case." He stroked his silver mustache with a thumb and forefinger.

"He was discovered wandering the streets, admonishing sinners," Richard said. "Normally a case like his would go straight to Dunning, but his physical injuries let the police to remand him to Mercy Hospital, and he was placed in my care.

Papers found on his person identified him as Steven Wilson, but that is not yet verified. We call him the prophet."

"He sounds fascinating."

"Oh he is. Best puzzle I have had in a good long while. Personally, I am of the opinion he harbored his delusions long before he suffered any physical injury, but I'd like to see what my first-year students will deduce. I'm taking them on practical rounds shortly and we will assess him today. Would you care to join us?"

"If it's not an imposition." Peter studied his friend. "If I may, what is the goal of practical rounds in neurology?"

"It mirrors the rounds done in traditional medicine, though it's a new technique for my field. We expose the class to the mental imbalances they will one day treat. Students examine patients, and engage them to reach a diagnosis, then propose possible treatments. We repeat the process continually to develop good diagnostic skills. Our graduates enter the field with some solid experience." He glanced at his pocket watch and rose from his chair. "Let's be off. With you here we'll make a game of it somehow."

Peter hesitated. Every Sullivan was considered gregarious, but Richard's sense of humor often bordered on the jocose. He loved taking a good-natured poke at others when presented with the opportunity. Over the years, Peter enjoyed the retelling of Richard's more outlandish exploits, and on occasion he'd even been the victim of his wild humor.

As a medical student Richard confounded the sternest of his professors, a Dr. Jensen, playing a prank that took a full semester to complete. Once a week, young Richard snuck into class and shaved one quarter inch from the legs of the professor's desk. In the ensuing weeks, Jensen's puzzled countenance enlivened an otherwise dreary hour. By the end of the term, the desk was nearly without legs, and poor Jensen had perfected a befuddled expression. Richard made three-inch reparations before the final exam, and restored mystified order to the professor's world. Peter eyed his brother-in-law, wary of taking part in his favorite pastime.

As they crossed the campus Peter relayed general news, but said nothing of his real purpose in coming. He decided to wait and see if the rounds provided him with some new option for Joanna. In turn, Richard spoke of his students who were, judging by his tone, dear to him. He was the only Sullivan who never married.

"These new boys are bright, but overconfident. We've just begun the term, yet they're convinced they know everything. Ooh!" Richard slapped his forehead. "I have an idea. Peter, the perfect game for today. You won't have to do a thing, just be your usual, stoic self."

Peter glared at his brother-in-law, his brow creased in disapproval. Richard laughed.

"That's the look I'm after! You'll see what I'm onto in no time."

Peter shook his head, chuckling. "You're mad, you know. One day they'll arrange a room for you here, if you're not careful."

Minutes later, they entered a quaint, red-brick building and approached five young men gathered in a gray alcove. All shared the look of casual confidence worn by men certain to conquer new fields. Richard winked at Peter and greeted his class with a merry smile.

"Gentleman, allow me to introduce my colleague, Dr. Peter Hastings. He is here to assess your diagnostic skills. Separate the men from the boys, so to speak. I advise that you keep your wits about you. He's one of the sharpest minds I know."

Arms crossed over his chest Peter obliged Richard well, dispensing a generous dose of unease in his greeting. Raising one hand in a gesture that bordered on the dismissive, he droned, "... Gentlemen."

More than one Adam's apple rose and fell in response.

Grinning too broadly, Richard clapped his hands and rallied the class. "Let's begin with Mrs. Greer, shall we?"

They entered a small, drab room and encountered a matronly, gray-haired woman. She paced before a barred window and paid no attention to her visitors. One hand flew about as she moved. She covered her mouth, swept her forehead, tapped her chin, and rubbed the back of her neck, all the while mumbling in breathy tones.

"It's gone, I tell you, gone. He stole it! Stole it right out from under my nose. Mr. Greer will be most upset. Oh, dear." She raised her eyes to the group and her skittish hand, like an uncertain bird, fluttered around in search of another place to land.

"Dr. McBride, would you be so kind?" Richard gestured to a burly, competent-looking fellow standing close to the wall. The young man nodded.

McBride questioned the woman as a detective might. He asked about the painting, the intruder, and the night of the theft. Her answers varied widely, lacking any trace of logic. She even changed her description of the painting. When asked for details of the culprit, Mrs. Greer looked at McBride as if he were dim.

"Well, isn't it obvious?" she huffed. "He wore a small shoe! A bigger foot would have been discovered. Oh!" Her hand flew to her temple. "Oh dear! Mr. Greer will be most upset!"

"How long has she been here?" Peter whispered to Richard.

"Three months," he returned quietly. "She snapped after the death of her husband."

Peter blanched. Joanna had suffered the loss of a husband.

The students, he noted, seemed painfully aware of their quiet exchange. Given their discomfiture, Peter suspected they thought it was a discussion of performance. Richard confirmed his suspicions.

"Whisper to me at least once during each evaluation," he said quietly, fighting a grin.

As the rounds progressed Peter noted that every room was small, spare, and devoid of character. Starch white cots matched bare white walls, not even a chamber pot in sight.

Richard explained that austerity helped clear the mind, and moveable objects only became weapons in irrational hands.

After Mrs. Greer, they observed an older man who shared his head with three other personalities. The attending student engaged two of them, and their stark differences highlighted a seriously divided mind. Next, they examined a ten year-old boy with no communication skills. He huddled in a corner, rubbing his head against the wall, oblivious to the student assigned to him. The fourth room held a fiercely agitated young woman. She was small and dark-eyed like Joanna, sitting on the floor, chained to the wall by wrist and ankle. She repeated the phrase *'the poison'* and screamed incessantly at the poor fellow who attempted to reach her.

"Evers, let's put her back in the tranquilizing chair. Immobility may calm her. Boys, give Evers a hand and meet us in the hall."

"The tranquilizing chair?" Peter asked, watching as they struggled to transfer the frenetic young woman.

Richard nodded. "Ben Rush's technique, it's old but useful. The patient is seated and restrained at the joints. A box covers the head, blocking vision and reducing cranial movement. The overall effect pacifies the nerves. It can take time, but patients do calm down eventually."

Peter shook his head. "But you address only the symptoms, not the illness."

"Quite correct, but in her case the condition appears to be permanent. I'm currently researching the work of a man named Burkhardt. He experimented with calming patients by removing a portion of the temporal lobe. It's drastic, but she's a good candidate if we adopt the procedure."

Peter frowned. "How so?"

"Well, she's in a constant state of agitation, and the procedure eliminates that condition. She's an indigent, no known family, so we're free to work with her aggressively. I'm not entirely settled on lobectomy as a course of treatment, but if it eases chronic suffering, it merits investigation.

Peter shuddered. "Cutting away at the temporal lobe…."

Richard lifted a shoulder. "In cases like hers we have limited choices. The tranquilizing chair is one, being chained to a wall is another. A lobectomy eliminates the need for those options. Peter, the woman is in a near-constant state of distress. As her physician, I must consider any technique that might benefit her. Ah! Here come the boys. Let's move on."

During each assessment Peter had, without realizing it, played his part to perfection. His brow remained creased, his arms crossed, one hand occasionally stroking his sideburns. In essence he appeared to be what Richard claimed he was, and as the hour progressed faces fell as each man began to question his professional prowess.

As they neared the last room, Richard whispered, "Peter, this was a stroke of genius. See how they're squirming. What fun!"

Although he masked it well, Peter was aghast at what he had witnessed. Joanna had trouble minding authority, and a fantastical belief in her origins, but she shared nothing in common with these poor creatures. A strong will and a tendency for disobedience were no match for the illnesses found in this place. Confounding though she might be, Peter concluded that her behavior in no way warranted commitment to an asylum. Still, he would discuss her case with Richard in theoretical terms, to determine some helpful course of treatment for her.

At last they reached the room of the prophet.

"Dr. Benson." Richard addressed the only man yet to perform an evaluation, "he's all yours."

If one tried to envision a prophet, Steven Wilson would not be the conjured image. Built like a featherweight, and possibly in his thirties, he had no defining features. His hair was either dark blond or light brown depending on the light, and his eyes were blue gray. Peter thought he looked like an altogether forgettable figure. Wilson stood by the window, offering them a beatific smile.

"Welcome, dear lambs. Blessed are those who seek for they shall find—"

The sermon stopped abruptly as Wilson caught sight of Peter. He cocked his head, staring hard as if trying to place him in memory. After a moment he adopted a scowl. "What is this? My betrayer is among you today?"

Jaw clenched, the hand under Peter's chin curled slowly into a fist, though no one noticed. The prophet approached with hands graceful and open, no animosity in his movement. He stopped inches from Peter. His tone was light, but his proximity intimated a challenge.

"So, you return again. You walk among the flock as I do, my dear Judas?"

Despite being singled out, Peter held himself in check and said nothing, his expression set.

The prophet turned to the students, one hand raised in warning. "Tread carefully, my lambs. It was once my destiny to fall by his hand. Today that fate awaits another, possibly one of you. But, as before—" He favored Peter with an acidic smile. "He acts with the best of intentions."

Peter scanned the students as Wilson returned to his window. He cast a glance at Richard, who appeared delighted by this turn. Given the false pretense given for Peter's presence, the prophet's psychotic claim seemed to solidify the discomfort in which the students were already mired. The proof lay in cleared throats, lowered heads and shifting feet.

"What are *your* intentions here, Mr. Wilson?" Dr. Benson spoke with authority.

"I am the Lord, thy God, here to save you all, to gather my flock and return to my father."

Benson nodded toward Peter. "Perhaps Judas stands before you today, not to betray, but to beg your forgiveness, to be saved as well."

Wilson pursed his lips, but countered quickly. "My young disciple, we are all destined to repeat our roles on this earth. I can assure you he is here to betray."

"Your response assumes reincarnation, and a basic tenet of God's law is the belief in one life and one eternal resting place.

"Ah, but I am not a reincarnation," Wilson rebounded. "I am the resurrection and the life. He who believes in me will live, even though he dies; and whoever lives and believes in me will never die."

Benson rejoined quickly, pointing at Peter, his calm voice holding the challenge.

"What, then, is Judas? By your own admission he cannot be a reincarnation. Is he not a resurrection as well?"

Wilson looked momentarily stumped. Benson pressed on.

"What if it is he, not you, who is the true God among us? What if your Judas is actually Jesus, the true resurrection and the light? What if you are the imposter, the betrayer?"

Wilson huffed and swept a commanding hand around the room.

"Know this," he announced, advancing on Peter as his voice gained force. "*I am the Lord thy God!* Thou shalt not have false gods before me. There is no other. *I* am the one true God!" The prophet stopped within inches of Peter. He was a good deal shorter, but the vehemence of his oratory minimized the difference.

"You come to betray," the prophet whispered, circling him. "Tell me," he taunted, leaning close to Peter's ear. "Will there be a kiss?"

As he had all morning, Peter stood, statuesque and opaque. The effect was as agitating to the prophet as it had been to the students. Wilson adopted a different tone, his cadence revealing his suspected southern roots.

"Why do you hound me?" he sneered, tapping hard on Peter's chest.

Richard inched closer and motioned McBride to stand behind the prophet.

"Demon!" Wilson spat. "I cast you out in Gatlinburg. I put you down in Frankfort. How can you be here? *Will you never die?* Must I cast you out again?"

The prophet lunged at Peter, but McBride moved faster, pinning Wilson in a great bear hug. Another student left the room, calling for restraints, and within seconds the incident was over. While the enraged prophet was being subdued the rest of the group stepped into the hallway.

"Well done, Benson." Richard shook his hand. "Your first breakthrough." He turned to the others. "Simmons, Riesman; contact the authorities in Gatlinburg and Frankfort. Inquire about any unsolved assaults or murders, particularly among the clergy. Our prophet may have a criminal past after all. Evers, I want you and McBride to spin our prophet on the gyration bed, see if that will calm him down. "

Dr. McBride emerged from Wilson's room.

"Excellent job, McBride! Your timing was precise." Richard surveyed his class. "I expect diagnoses and treatment plans on my desk by tomorrow morning. Now then. Dr. Hastings and I have a good deal to discuss. Good day, gentleman."

Richard clapped Peter on the back as they retreated down the hallway. "Well played!" he said quietly. "You showed remarkable resolve throughout. I'm famished. Let's have lunch."

Peter gave him a sidelong glance. "So long as we start with a brandy."

Chapter Twenty-seven
Guarded Betrayal

Here's to the prophet." Richard raised his glass. "He always entertains."

They sat in a quiet establishment near the campus, each man sipping a brandy. Peter returned the gesture, drinking as his host regaled him.

"You know," Richard said, "I love my job. I have no need to attend the theater. It comes to me and I'm paid to watch it."

"Well, you can keep your drama and theatrics. Give me a good book and a warm fire." He glanced at his brother-in-law and thought of Victoria. "I derive far more pleasure in knowing someone else enjoys the action."

"Well, today you were a consummate actor. What a performance!" Richard chuckled, and drank from his glass. "My boys were fidgeting long before you met the prophet, but after he identified you as Judas—" He took another sip of his brandy. "My goodness, that was epic! Each man felt sure he was your victim."

"Only for you, Richard." Peter suppressed a grin.

"You played it like Shakespeare, still as stone, even when he advanced on you. If he ruffled you at all, I failed to notice."

"He did shake me in calling me Judas. It was an uncanny choice."

Eyes alight, Richard set down his glass and leaned across the table. "How so?"

"I came here today seeking advice on a patient of mine, and I'm breaking a confidence in doing so." Glass raised, Peter nodded at his brother-in-law. "Your prophet may be false on many fronts, but he showed remarkable insight in that instance."

"Well, you have my full attention. Tell me about this patient you're betraying, Judas."

Peter scowled. "You are not helping the situation."

"Evidently you aren't either," Richard said, laughing. "Otherwise you wouldn't be here." He settled back and adopted a gentler tone. "Please, tell me everything."

Pinching the bridge of his nose, Peter lowered his head, waging an internal debate. He had come intending to discuss every detail of Joanna's case, but after facing five examples of true mental incapacity, he found he was loath to do so. Compared to the cast of characters he'd just encountered, Joanna was of sound mind. Still, her belief in time travel and her subsequent actions placed her within their range. Her theory couldn't be rationalized or excused, and it was why he came here in the first place. He drew in a long breath and began carefully.

"I'm treating a patient who claims to come from the future."

"Say!" Richard interjected. "That rivals my prophet. Man or woman?"

Peter frowned. "For the sake of confidentiality, let's leave gender aside."

"Oh, then it's a woman!" Richard clapped his hands like a child beholding a new toy. Peter gave him a disapproving look, but Richard ignored it and leaned forward, eager for more of the story.

"Last Saturday I witnessed the revival of a drowning victim. My time traveler performed this feat using methods unfamiliar to me."

"Ah," Richard settled back into his chair, "then it's a man."

Peter crossed his arms, his lips reduced to a thin straight line.

"Oh, all right! I'll stop guessing. Please, continue. What were his methods?"

Utilizing Richard's chosen gender, Peter continued. "He used a variation of Maas's chest compressions and another technique that I'm still researching. It was quite fascinating. He saved the victim's life. And he is generally well-behaved, but we've had a few incidents which call everything into question."

"Such as?"

"There was a fight in an alley. Granted, a woman had been attacked, but my patient threw some rather vicious blows. Like your prophet, I considered it a possible clue to his upbringing."

"Has it led you anywhere concrete?"

"No."

"Does your patient know his full name? His address? Have you looked into those? Did you make inquiry with the police?"

"Yes, yes. I've done everything." Peter reached for his brandy. "He professes to be a native of Chicago, but the address he provided is nonexistent. His surname is common enough, but no one by that name is missing in any precinct I've checked."

"Hmm … intriguing. How did you meet him?"

"We pulled him from Lake Michigan. He called for help with the drowning victim and Car pulled them from the water, which brings me to another incident." He sipped from his glass. "My time traveler is of the opinion he arrived here courtesy of the lake. Two days ago he attempted to return home."

Richard leaned closer. "Do you mean to tell me your man jumped into Lake Michigan? Oh, Peter, this is rich! Please bring him in! I would love an hour with him."

"No. Your cases today convinced me my patient is not without his faculties. In fact he is quite capable of functioning in society. I just need advice on helping him remember his origins."

"Hmm …. Any sign of physical trauma?"

"Nothing. He took a good blow to the ribs, but no head injury. The water was quite cold. I've considered the possibility that the temperature of the lake induced trauma to the brain, but found nothing to support it."

"How often do you see him?"

"Daily. He's been staying with us since Saturday."

Richard's brow furrowed. "That's ill-advised. An unbalanced stranger in your home …."

Peter raised a hand. "He poses no threat to anyone in the house. We all get on quite well with him, save for Mrs. Milford."

"If memory serves, she doesn't get along with anyone."

With half a grin, Peter acknowledged his observation.

Lunch arrived and each man concentrated on his meal. Peter regretted admitting Joanna was a houseguest, but it couldn't be helped. He debated voicing the most compelling piece of his argument, her dire prediction about the mayor, but decided against it. The more he spoke, the more he truly felt like Judas. He had only come in search of advice. Revealing anything more would compel Richard to demand an audience with her, and his instincts told him it would be a step too far. The sudden rush of protective feeling for Joanna struck him as odd. Shifting uncomfortably in his seat, Peter cut into his brisket.

"Well—" Richard wiped his lips with his napkin. "Maybe your goal is misdirected. If you have fully indulged his delusion of time travel, and I suspect you have, let's take a lesson from Benson's case. Perhaps the truth of his present situation lies in what your patient considers his past. You've already explored what he believes is his current address and found nothing. Check on his local ancestry."

Peter lowered his fork. "He does claim to be a native of Chicago. You think it could lead somewhere?"

Richard shrugged with an amiable smile. "I never know. That's the beauty of my profession, but investigating his past could lead you closer to his true story and perhaps to the origin of his trouble."

"You know," Peter said, "that's not a bad thought. Perhaps when faced with someone he identifies as a great-grandparent he finds a parent."

Richard beamed and slapped the table. "That's the spirit!" He fingered his brandy glass, firing off instructions. "Look into his lineage. Have him take an active part in the project. If he hedges, it could be a sign he has something to hide."

Richard continued, caution in his voice. "Make careful note of his reaction. Don't attempt this without Car nearby. Pursuing this might set him off, like Wilson today. Say, how is my little Irishman?"

"Car? Sunny as ever, and not so little anymore."

Grateful for a break in topic, Peter spoke at length of Car's relationship with William; how he coached him in the care of the horses, how generous he was with his time and attention. This reaffirmed, for Peter, his good fortune in taking Car into the fold. He had grown into a capable, admirable young man.

It also occurred to him that his reason for taking on Car mirrored his need to shield Joanna. Aside from the trials she put him through he still believed she was a good person who had somehow lost her way. Though as an adult—one with a child no less—it was unlikely she would remain in his household. That thought gave Peter some cause for lament. Despite her unpredictability, she was a lively addition. He would miss her conversation, and her company.

Peter shook his head, clearing his thoughts.

If nothing else, his visit here had brought him full circle, and reaffirmed his original inclination to give Joanna a private chance to resolve her problems. With the issue firmly settled in his mind, he decided to say nothing more to Richard, but use the advice offered and see where it led him. If the path became darker … well, perhaps he would be back. But if it proved fortuitous, then Joanna would recover, with all credit due to Richard. Only when her health was fully restored would he tell his brother-in-law the complete story. Secure in his decision, Peter gave Richard a broad smile.

"What of you, my friend? Anyone on your horizon aside from your students? Has the woman destined to catch you finally crossed your path?"

Richard put forth a solid laugh and pushed his plate to the center of the table. "Peter, my work is my wife, and my students are my sons. I love them all with equal aplomb and I drive them to equal corners of my world, just as I was driven years ago."

Peter listened with a twinge of regret. Richard had the makings of a good father and a devoted husband. It pained him to see the man cling to those who didn't really belong to him—not in the long run. He thought of his own father. Men do tend to force their young along the path to maturity, convinced they will dominate by virtue of their lineage. How a child survives the force of such a thrust is up to the individual.

Perhaps Richard, as the oldest, never married simply to protect anyone who warmed his heart. Perhaps he didn't want to put a woman through the rigors he perceived his father had designed for him. Perhaps, given his interest in the workings of the mind, he recognized this early in life and set a course he could live with at the end of the day.

But this was pure speculation. Of all the Sullivan children, Peter knew the least about Richard. Of course, he gave of himself generously, entertained everyone with his many colorful stories and outrageous pranks, but Peter knew little of the man who actually sat by the fire at the end of the evening. He was a man who always put others at ease, made others happy. But was Richard a truly happy fellow? Peter departed soon after lunch, hoping very much that he was.

Chapter Twenty-eight
Commitment

Joey and William were crouched beneath a tree at the edge of Chapman Lane when Peter arrived. Heads bent together, they remained engaged in their examination until he was nearly upon them.

"What have you there, a bit of buried treasure?" he asked, reining in Coco.

William grinned. "Jo… Miss Fagan found cicada eggs." He stood and handed his father a leaf. "See the little balls on the back? Those are the eggs. She says when the leaves fall to the ground they crawl into the dirt and sleep, just like my tortoise."

"Interesting."

Joey cast him a wary-eyed glance as she stood. "William has the makings of a biologist," she said, one hand shielding her eyes from the afternoon sun. "He has a knack for finding all kinds of creatures."

"Sounds like you two have had a good day," he said. "Say, William, would you like to guide Coco into the stable?"

William reached for his father, grinning broadly.

"Here you go, bud." Joey clasped her hands together in a makeshift stirrup. "Step on up." She lifted him from her cupped hands, and with Peter's guidance William settled into the front of the saddle.

"Can't Miss Fagan ride with us?"

"Oh, I'll walk back." Joey locked eyes with Peter. "If that's okay with you."

Peter nodded and nudged the horse, giving William soft words of encouragement as he led the animal down the lane. Joey remained by the tree and watched them go, dreading the discussion to come.

The explosion at breakfast left her dangerously close to a precipice. Her nerves, already frayed, had her trembling like a cornered animal. She'd considered leaving while Peter was out, but running seemed like an admission of guilt, and he already thought her guilty of insubordination. She decided to face him like an adult. If she left today it would be by choice. She would not act like a fugitive.

Still, she dreaded his return all morning. The thought of their next meeting churned away in the pit of her stomach. At lunch, Mrs. Milford added to her anxiety, setting out plates for the boys, but nothing for Joey. When William inquired about her meal, Mrs. Milford told him, "William, we don't waste food in this house. Joanna didn't finish her breakfast. If she wants to eat, she may have what she left on her plate." In a voice thick with false charm, she added, "I've kept it warm for you. Shall I bring it out?"

Refusing to be bested by someone so petty, Joey politely declined.

As Coco turned into the driveway, she took heart in their small exchange. Peter raised his son with an iron rod. She hadn't seen him parent with much warmth, and it relieved her to see him display kindness to William. But he wouldn't necessarily extend her the same courtesy. Not today.

In Peter's house a rigid line ran through the core of every relationship, including hers, and if she had truly crossed that line, then he would have her committed. The threat had stayed with her all day, gnawing away at her courage. The decision to stay and face him could land her in an insane asylum, but she clung to the belief that Peter was too logical to take such a drastic step.

Now, however, she wasn't at all sure, and the gravity of their next encounter held her in place. Any apprehension she felt before today paled in comparison to the case of nerves she had now. She straightened her back, took a deep breath and forced herself to walk back to the house.

In Peter's absence, Joey had formed a loose plan. She would look for a room at Hull House. She might be more at home with a group of women who, by the very nature of their work, seemed out of character with the times. It seemed like a safe choice, and, in truth, she couldn't think of another.

Heart pounding in her ears, Joey crossed her arms as she reached the driveway. Peter was already walking back to meet her, his expression impossible to read—always a bad sign. She stopped under the shade of the elm tree, gripping the corner fencepost for support.

"How did he do?" She worked hard to adopt a casual tone.

"Rather well," Peter said, glancing back at the carriage house, "though I need to take him on longer rides now. He's ready for more time in the saddle. Once he's comfortable, he can concentrate on management of the horse."

"Hmm …." She tried to sound engaged. "That makes sense."

They faced each other in a gradually extending silence. Joey broke first.

"Listen," she spoke quietly, "I know I've worn out my welcome. Maybe it's best for me to go. I think I've come up with a suitable alternative."

Peter frowned at her announcement. From her perspective his eyes hardened, and the resolve she perceived in them frightened her. She swallowed hard, and gave voice to her suspicion. "Unless your sudden departure this morning was to make other plans for me."

Peter averted his eyes as if ashamed. Joanna gasped, convinced his reaction was a confirmation of her worst fears. She dropped her head, shocked at her accuracy.

That was it, then. He intended to commit her. The one location to be avoided at all costs was about to become her home. She tried to swallow, to breathe, but her throat constricted and she could do neither. In silence, she cursed her stubborn streak. Her lack of compliance had come at the price of her personal freedom. This was the consequence Peter threatened, and though she was sure it would be discussed, she never thought he would act so decisively. Not yet ....

Suddenly even the sun seemed to lash out at her, its brilliance shedding too harsh a light on her circumstances, exposing every detail of the corner into which she had painted herself. She managed a small breath and mustered everything left within her just to face him.

"Oh ..."

As soon as she spoke her strength began slipping away, as air might escape through an undetected hole in a balloon. Grappling for the fencepost, she desperately hoped she sounded nonchalant, but it was hard to hear her own voice. "So do you take me there, or do they come here with a straitjacket?"

His mouth dropped open, registering shock, she thought, at her understanding. He said nothing, confirming all her suspicions. There was a ringing in her ears and her legs turned to rubber.

"Peter, please. I prefer the street to an asy—." She tried to draw breath, but the world was void of air. She sagged against the fencepost, her words a whispered panic. "Please, let me go now ...."

The sun faded out everything around her. Her legs gave way and she slid down the fencepost as the last of the air escaped the balloon. Peter called out from far away.

"Joanna! You're white as a sheet! Here," he instructed, guiding her head into his lap. "Lie still and try to breathe."

"Please." Her voice was thin, and close to breaking. "Don't do this."

"Shh … take a breath … that's it … now another. Why do you say this? No one is coming for you." He stroked her brow. "If you want to leave, you're free to go. I haven't made any dire arrangements for you."

She blinked and let out a small cry. Tears of relief mingled with confusion, but normal breath still proved elusive. It was difficult, but she forced herself to look at him. "I thought … when you turned away … I thought for sure …."

In an earnest display of contrition Peter shook his head, negating all her darkest fears. As they fell away, her lungs found air. Freed from her dreaded fate, Joey broke down and sobbed her relief into the crease of his trousers.

"Hush now," he whispered, passing her his handkerchief. "You misunderstand me. Shh … it's true. I did go to an asylum today, but only to seek advice from a colleague, not to send you away. This is still your home, if you wish to remain here. Hush now," he said, stroking her shoulder.

In time her tears subsided, but she lacked the courage to face him. Eyes locked on his trousers, she asked. "Then, why did you look so guilty?"

"Because," he sighed, "I betrayed your confidence in doing so."

"Oh." She took a long, slow breath. "Well, I disregarded your orders, so, in a way, I guess we're even."

Neither spoke for a time. They sat quietly, the silence broken only by the oddly staggered breath drawn in the aftermath of tears. Peter kept a hand on her shoulder.

"Your colleague," Joey said. "Did he want to commit me?"

"No, not at all, but he was most anxious to meet you."

"Was the discussion helpful?"

"Not tremendously." Peter said. "I came away with one reasonable idea, but after what I witnessed, I'm not at all confident it will help."

"Witnessed? You mean our fight?" Her shoulder tensed, but he pressed against it with his hand.

"Calm down. I was referring to the residents of the asylum. Joanna, you may have an unrealistic belief in your origins, but I can say with conviction you don't belong in such a place."

She relaxed considerably and shifted to face him. "Where does that leave us, then?"

He let out a half-hearted laugh. "Damned if I know."

"Listen to you," Joey said, wiping away the last of her tears. "I really should go. I'm totally wrecking your vocabulary."

"No." He shook his head. "No, you shouldn't. I made a promise. Ah, your color is returning." She moved to sit up but he pressed her shoulder. "Not just yet. Give yourself another minute." She complied without argument.

"My memory is faulty at the moment. What promise are you referring to?"

"I made two, actually. I offered you my home, and I said I would help you find your family." He brushed the remnant of a tear from her cheek. "After today, I intend to keep both of them regardless of how angry I may be with you."

Joey moved to sit up again and Peter didn't stop her. Leaning back against the fence post, she drew her knees to her chest.

"Peter, you had no idea what you were getting into with me. It's unfair to hold you to such a tall order. I know my being here gets to you."

He released a fraction of a smile.

"My way home is my problem, and any attempt I make to solve it will only drive you crazy. You had a nice quiet life going before I came along. I don't want to make any more noise than I already have." Joey paused, offering him a chance to react. He said nothing, so she continued.

"Hull House might be a better fit for me. Here I'm an oddity. There I might seem normal, and if they aren't aware of my background, they won't make a fuss if they wake up one day and find me gone."

Peter shook his head. "There's no need to leave."

"Be reasonable. Think back to this morning. I'm a thorn in your side. Given everything you've done for me, I think leaving, giving you back your normal routine, is the best way to show my gratitude." She took a breath. "Peter, I can't change what I know about myself, but I think I can live quietly elsewhere, and not arouse any suspicion while I try to resolve things."

Peter studied her carefully. The last twenty-four hours had been exacting for both of them. Actually, the last several days had been challenging. The emotional cost was evident in her tired eyes. He couldn't fault her logic. Hull House would be a good place for her. But after this morning Peter resolved to find the key to her particular, and comparably minor, affliction. He wanted to solve this mystery with her, and see her regain her health. But there was something more. Peter realized that it wasn't just the kinship they shared in tragedy. He genuinely enjoyed her company and he would miss her if she left. The thought startled him and he shook his head, unsure what to do with it.

"Honestly, Joanna, I think—whether I believe it or not—I can live with your problem, and I still want to help you. The only thing I can't embrace is this threat against the mayor. The man is adored by almost all of Chicago. To think someone would raise a hand against him is madness. Your insistence leads me to conclude that somehow you are connected to this Prendergast fellow. I don't think you could commit murder, and I know you don't run from things. Why did you run from him?

I didn't run from him, Peter. I don't know him. I only know that on Saturday night, shortly before eight o'clock—"

"You know the time of death? How can you be so sure? There must be a link, Joanna. No other explanation fits."

"The one I gave you fits, but you won't realize it until it's too late."

Peter huffed, but held his tongue, anxious to avoid another escalation. "All right, instead of racing to City Hall, let's locate Prendergast. Surely he'll recognize you, and shed some light on all this nonsense. Will you agree to abandon your quest for Harrison in favor of a meeting with Prendergast? It could be beneficial to your recovery."

"Screw my recovery. I'll meet Prendergast because it could be beneficial to the mayor's life, but I still want to warn Harrison."

"No." Peter crossed his arms. "We must meet Prendergast and ascertain his motives. Until then I cannot accept this mortal danger nonsense. Carter Harrison is a man of the people. He's very popular."

"Lincoln was popular," she countered. "Look what happened to him."

He had come to expect an opposing view from her, so he wasn't surprised when she tried to hold her ground. He fought back a smile and responded softly, but with authority, feeling much like a teacher lecturing a student.

"Joanna, Lincoln was a very popular man who committed a very unpopular act. He led the country to war against itself. Any man who plays such a divisive role garners a host of enemies. His assassination, though hard to accept, wasn't hard to understand. Harrison is different. Yes, the press takes him to task, and the Women's Christian Temperance Union frowns upon him, but he is a friend to all men, gentry and immigrant alike. I can assure you he will come to no harm."

They sat quietly, Joanna staring at the ground, Peter at the far side of the yard. She opened her mouth more than once, but didn't speak. He knew she sought an answer that would appease him, yet keep intact her own view of the situation, and he admired her for it. It was one of the things he'd come to enjoy about her. He waited patiently, curious to hear her answer.

"Everyone has enemies, Peter, but … okay. I can't pretend I don't know what's coming, but in sincere appreciation for everything you've done I will give up on my mission to get to City Hall. I owe you that much."

He noted that she made no mention of the mayor, only City Hall. It was a clever acquiescence. Part of him wanted to point out the omission, but he decided to let it go. He planned to keep her busy for the next two days. He would give her no opportunity to warn the mayor until Sunday. By then her prediction would be proven wrong, which would set her on a path that might lead to a revelation of what created this odd mental dilemma in the first place.

"That's the spirit."

Echoing Richard's encouragement, he pressed a reassuring hand over hers. Peter felt as if he might be able to help her on his own after all. He might achieve what Richard called a breakthrough. He smiled as he watched her, admiring her resolve and his own cleverness in handling the situation.

Chapter Twenty-nine
A Fair Proposal

Friday dawned with a touch of Indian summer and a brightening of spirits. Peter awoke with a plan to lighten the mood and show Joanna the best of Chicago. And if their excursion helped her come closer to present day reality, then so much the better.

At breakfast, he said nothing of his intentions, but his poorly concealed mirth didn't go unnoticed. After finishing his meal he read the paper, but scanned the table frequently, brown eyes betraying his delight. Joanna called his behavior into question.

"What's up with you this morning? You look like the cat who ate the canary."

"Oh, nothing."

Car grinned from across the table. "I don't know, Doc. Sounds ta me like there's a whole lot a somethin' hidin' behind that nothin'."

"I'm with you, Car." Joanna said. "Come on Peter, throw us a bone."

Even William joined in, asking, "What is it, Papa?"

"Well," he said, setting the newspaper aside, "I thought today might be the perfect day to show Joanna the

Columbian Exposition. Why don't we all go? It will be gone come November."

Mrs. Milford stood abruptly, scowling. "No thank you. I have better things to do than go prancing around in public, enjoying myself at other people's expense." Collecting the serving platter, she stomped from the room.

"Mind the nails, Mrs. M.," Car called out. "Sounds like y've one in yer shoe."

Peter stared after her. His housekeeper had a grave temperament at best, but since Joanna's arrival she'd been positively dour.

"Wow. You would do that for me? Thank you!"

He turned his attention to Joanna, pleased by her reaction.

Car stood, stretching his lanky frame. "Sounds great, Doc. But if ya don't mind, I'll stay home and give Mrs. M. a hand today. Winter's not far off and there's a bit yet ta do about it. I've seen the fair six ways ta Sunday, but gettin' Joey there, well that's grand."

"May we ride the Ferris Wheel? Please, Papa?"

"I think," Peter answered slowly, enjoying William's anticipation, "that's the *first* thing we should do."

With one enthusiastic whoop, the boy was out of his chair.

"Now, now," Peter said, "let's finish breakfast." He turned to Car. "You'll need to take us down to Jackson Park and pick us up again this evening. We'll use the Midway entrance and avoid the Court of Honor crowd. What do you say?"

Car nodded as he left the room. "Whatever ya need, Doc. I'm yer man."

William attacked his breakfast and Peter sat quietly, observing Joanna. The Columbian Exposition was a showplace for technical innovation. A time traveler should have much to say about it, and he was eager to see her response. At the moment she appeared lost in thought, but her fine features were alight with excitement. She glanced up from the table and caught his eye.

"What?" she said, brows arched.

"It's nice to see you smiling."

"Peter, this is a phenomenal opportunity. I'm pretty jazzed."

He gave her a blank stare.

"Jazzed?" William's face was a miniature reflection of his father's. "What is jazzed?"

"Jazzed is excited." She turned to William. "I'm excited, just like you, buddy."

After breakfast, Peter collected his Expo brochures while Joey and William donned their coats in the front hall. William had just put on his cap when Peter rejoined them. He reached for his own coat and retrieved Victoria's hat. Joanna groaned.

"What is it?"

"Oh please," she said. "Please don't make me wear that froufy thing again."

"For goodness sakes, Joanna. Women wear hats. Everyone wears hats. You are not properly attired without one. While you're a woman of this house, you will wear a hat." He gave her a stern look and thrust the hat in her direction. "This is not open for discussion. Put it on."

"Mmhh …." Her lips disappeared behind a clenched fist.

Peter watched her, well aware she would mount a defense, and curious to hear it, though he fully intended to dismiss her argument.

"Do you—?" she stammered. "Did Victoria—?" she sighed. "Peter, I'm not used to wearing something so busy. Do you have anything simpler? Not so fancy? Anything?"

The desperation in her voice left him chuckling. He turned back to the closet. "Is that all? I should have known. You ladies like variety. Yes, Victoria has—*had*—several hats. Try this."

He produced a navy blue hat. It was a half-height top hat that had neither flowers nor ribbons. Joanna accepted it with an audible sigh of relief.

"Thank you. This is much more my speed." She donned the hat and smiled. "Scores?"

Peter and William exchanged puzzled looks.

"I meant, how does it look?" She tilted her head to one side, offering another view.

"Beautiful," they replied in unison. Peter pressed William's shoulders as they laughed. He offered Joanna his arm and they left the house.

On the drive to Jackson Park, William joined Car on the bench while Peter and Joanna poured over the brochures in the back.

"A 22,000 pound cheese? How bizarre!" Joanna laughed.

William turned around. "It's the biggest cheese in the world. It's from Canada."

"Canada? I would have guessed Wisconsin. Hey, it's in the Manufactures and Liberal Arts Building, and this Electrical Building looks interesting, too."

"I thought you would prefer the Court of Honor, or the Women's Building," Peter said.

"Well, since we're limited on time I want to see things everyone will enjoy, and, no offense, but a massive shoe exhibit doesn't excite me at all. I've seen enough shoes this week."

Peter suppressed a smile. "What about the Court of Honor?"

"If we have the time, I would love to but—" She lowered her voice and nodded toward William. "I don't know how long little legs will hold out. Doesn't this thing span, like, seven hundred acres or something? She pointed at the Manufactures Building brochure. "Besides, it says the roof of this building has a great view of the Court of Honor."

"Yes, it does. If we time it properly we can watch the incandescent lights go on from the roof. It's quite something. I'd like to show you a few of the international buildings, too."

"Ooh!" Joanna shuffled through the material. "I'd love to visit the Japanese one, the Ho-o-Den, and this German village looks really sweet."

Peter nodded, handing her another leaflet. "We'll see the German Village on the Midway Plaisance. And the Wooded Island is a good place to break for lunch. You must see the

French building. It's a reproduction of one wing of the palace at Marseilles."

"Sounds great!" Joanna grinned, holding up another paper from the pile. "Check this out. Ireland built a replica of Blarney Castle. How cool is that! Have you been there, Car?"

"Great beer at the castle, Joey. Bend an elbow for me if ya get there today."

"Norway sent a Viking ship." William announced. "A *real* Viking ship. May we see it, Papa?"

"Of course we can." He leaned close to Joanna, pointing at an illustration of the ship. "Rumor has it Norway sent it to remind us they arrived here long before Columbus."

"Well, I'm in for all of it. Thanks, Peter. It's very sweet of you to take the trouble."

"No trouble at all. I brought William once, and I've come alone on a few other occasions. I want one last look before it closes." He leaned close, his voice low. "And I think we're due for some respite, you and I."

By way of an answer she clutched his arm, grinning as she did so. "Have you seen Little Egypt? The belly dancer? Do you think she's still there?"

"Oh, she's a big attraction on the Midway. I can't imagine she would leave before the fair is over. I expect we'll find her, along with the Dahomey tribe from Africa."

"Oh!" William whipped around in his seat. "They eat people! Mrs. Milford said they've eaten ten members of their tribe since they arrived!"

Peter winked at Joanna. "Then I suggest you keep your distance, son. You don't want to tempt them." He scanned the brochure. "They create the most interesting music using only a few handmade drums. With any luck we'll hear them perform."

"Speaking of music," Joanna fanned the papers in her lap, "is Souza still playing here?"

Peter gave her a curious look. "You're familiar with John Philip Souza?"

"Sure," she rejoined. "March music, big on the Fourth of July, very patriotic stuff. My dad loves his work. He's a defining composer of American music. Do you think he'll be there?"

"His orchestra often plays at the Court of Honor, and I suspect he will play the close of the fair, so it's possible he'll perform today. I'm glad you remember him."

So, she knew Souza.

Peter leaned back, thinking he should have taken Joanna here much sooner. This excursion could open a veritable treasure chest of insight into her mysteriously disjointed sense of time. Suddenly the fair seemed ripe with potential for remembrance. He smiled to himself. This could be a very good day indeed.

Chapter Thirty
The Midway Plaisance

At the corner of Cottage Grove and 60th, Car pulled up to the sound of a lively street band. Peter laid a hand on his shoulder.

"We'll meet you right here around seven-thirty this evening. Is everyone ready?" The trio stepped from the carriage and crossed the street, hands linked, William between Peter and Joanna.

"Oh, man!" Joanna bobbed her head to the music. "That sounds familiar."

"Ah," Peter said as they turned the corner. "A Negro quartet."

"You're kidding, right?" She stared at him as they approached the band.

"About what?"

"The African Americans," she whispered.

"You mean the Negroes?"

She responded with an elbow to his side, and a look of profound mortification. The vehemence of her reaction surprised him, but Peter held his tongue.

The band was deep in the throes of a lively tune. Everyone smiled as they passed, but few lingered. Joanna hung back, tapping her foot in time with the music, her brow lined in concentration. Peter sensed she was trying to remember something and he stood silently by, watching her.

As the song ended she raised her head and blurted, "That's Ragtime! That song has Scott Joplin written all over it."

Peter suppressed a smile. If she was familiar with Ragtime music, as a current, popular form of entertainment, it helped place her in this century. Better yet, she could name a composer. He'd never heard of Joplin and gave little thought to the Negro music, though he did enjoy it. Before Peter could respond, a raspy voice sounded behind them.

"Hey. Scott. That lady knows your horn!"

Joanna faced the band. They were a clean-shaven, smartly dressed group. A young man holding a coronet stepped forward and bowed.

"How do you do, ma'am. I am Scott Joplin."

"No way!" She seemed pleasantly shocked, extending her hand as she strode toward him. "Sir, it is an honor and a pleasure to meet you. That song was wonderful."

Joplin eyed her hand, and then scanned the crowd, nervous eyes settling on Peter. Peter nodded almost imperceptibly and Joplin accepted the tip of her hand, bowed quickly and released it.

"So you know my work?"

Joanna nodded and pointed at his coronet. "I thought you played the piano."

Joplin gave Joanna a penetrating stare, and cocked his head to one side. "I play both, Ma'am. This is my first visit to Chicago, but I frequently play in St. Louis and Texarkana. Perhaps you've seen me perform there."

"I … I can't remember exactly where I've heard you, but I really like your stuff."

Joplin offered her a pearl-white smile. "Would you like to hear more of *my stuff*?"

"Can you play The Entertainer?"

"The Entertainer?"

"You know." Joanna nodded her head. "Daa da duh da. Duh da. Duh da." She stopped and shrugged. "Oh. I guess you haven't ... never mind. Please, play your favorite song."

Joplin said something inaudible to his band. Joanna returned to Peter and William as the group launched into another tune. She swung William's hand back and forth in time with the song, soliciting easy laughter from the boy. A few minutes later the music ended with a flourish. Peter thanked them, dropped a few coins into a hat on the ground and they entered the Midway Plaisance.

As they walked, Peter watched Joanna, but remained silent. If nothing else, the encounter with Joplin had given him two cities to research. It occurred to him that today could be filled with incidents such as this and he needed to determine how to discuss her experiences without arousing her frustration. He thought it best to let her talk and see what he could glean from her. It was William who opened the conversation.

"So you knew him, Jo—Miss Fagan?" William corrected himself with a guilty look on his face.

"William, please call me Joey." She turned to Peter. "Do you mind? I've been with you guys for nearly a week and using my surname is just too formal. William is a good boy with impeccable manners. Calling me Joey won't diminish that in the least, and Miss Fagan is such a mouthful." Her brown eyes widened. "Come on, what do you say?"

Peter squatted beside William. "Since it's what the lady prefers, you may call Miss Fagan by her first name, but—" He raised a finger in caution. "Other than Car she is the only adult you may address in such a way. Do you understand?" William nodded. "Very well, then."

"Whew! Thanks." She tucked her hair behind her ear. "So to answer your question, no, I never met him, but I have heard his music. I think he's from St. Louis." She cocked her ear in the direction of the midway. "Speaking of music, I think I hear your African drummers."

A question about St. Louis died on Peter's lips. "That will be the Dahomeys. Let's go!"

They rushed down the midway, slowing as they came upon a hot air balloon ride. Directly opposite lay the Dahomey Village. An infectious rhythm pulsed from inside the compound. They ventured in, rounded a corner, and entered an open square. A crowd had gathered at one end, the African drummers at the other. The center remained empty. The Dahomeys had bright, boldly painted faces, and wore costumes which left much of the anatomy exposed to the elements and to the audience. They sat in a row on the ground, drums nested in their crossed legs. One strong drum led a commanding beat, inviting visitors to the spectacle. Softer drums echoed. Some beats faster, others slower.

Peter, William and Joanna stood at the front. The drumming pattern intensified and Peter looked around for William. The child had gripped Joanna's waist, his head half-buried in her skirt. She crouched low and wrapped him in her arms. Peter smiled at her gesture. The rhythm continued to gain speed, and just as it reached a pinnacle everything stopped. Then a single, even pounding broke the silence. A base drum joined in, creating a new and different pattern. Moving in time with the drums, the Dahomey women entered the square. William hid his face and Peter knelt beside Joanna, explaining what he'd learned from previous visits.

"This is very rare, virtually unheard of in warfare. These women are the warriors for the tribe. They lead every battle and are said to be fearsome fighters. The man who brought them here told me they decapitate their foes right on the battlefield."

Ten women, as sparsely clad and oddly painted as the men, overtook the square moving in time with the incessant pounding. Each one carried a spear and, on cue, they thrust them fast in one direction or another, sometimes hoisting them high in the air, other times performing mock battles. There were dramatic leaps, fierce shouts, and absolute precision. The drummers punctuated each thrust with an exacting drumbeat.

Suddenly the drums were overpowered by a ferocious battle cry, shouted in unison by all ten women. The women lurched toward the audience, then stopped, heads erect, spears pointed out, frozen before the startled crowd.

No one moved.

A lighter rhythm began, effectively releasing the women from their service. The Dahomey warriors rose to their full height and fled into a thatched hut. With a collective sigh, the crowd gave the tribe a thunderous round of applause. Peter stared after the women as a lone drummer played soft easy beats, providing ambience for the unique little village.

"Amazing," Peter said. "I've seen them perform three times and still they mesmerize. I could never imagine a culture where the women wage war and yet it exists. The world is full of unexpected surprises."

His comment drew a laugh from Joanna. "I'll take that as a hopeful sign," she said.

Before he could reply William interjected. "Papa, may we please go ride the Ferris Wheel now? Please?"

"Of course, William. Lead the way."

"Holy crow" Joanna exclaimed as they neared the great attraction. "That's not a Ferris Wheel. It's a monster."

"It's 265 feet tall," William said, chest puffed with pride.

"Oh my God, are those boxcars? Where are the little chairs?"

"Inside the boxcars, of course. There's no need to invoke name of the Lord, Joanna. " Peter laughed as they moved forward. "Each car holds 40 passengers."

"I thought this ride would be boring," Joanna said. "But I've changed my mind."

The line moved quickly as the operator could fill six boxcars at once. Joanna remarked on the efficiency of the system as they rose slowly above the Midway. William scrambled from one section of the car to another, pointing out favorite buildings and fountains. Peter and Joanna remained in one place, enjoying the expansive view. William gave a shout when he spotted the Viking ship.

"Ah." Peter pointed to the right, feeling a sense of pride. "The Manufactures Building, the largest building in the world; it covers more than forty acres."

He pointed out the Wooded Island, home of the Japanese Ho-o-Den.

"Wow, it's like an emerald ring on a big concrete hand." Joanna said.

"It isn't all column and plaster." Peter led her to another corner of the boxcar. "There's plenty of greenery throughout the park, and Lake Michigan provides a nice blue border, don't you think?" He looked down to find Joanna wide-eyed and smiling.

"I think it's breathtaking," she said softly.

After stepping off the Ferris wheel, William tugged at his father's hand, urging them on to the Streets of Cairo.

"Now, this is where we'll find Little Egypt, the belly dancer. She's quite a spectacle."

"And the camels." William said, skipping ahead. "Papa, may I ride one?"

Peter nodded. In very short order William was astride one of the enormous mammals, holding fast to a colorful pommel. Grinning from ear to ear, he waved fanatically as an Egyptian boy coaxed the camel to stand and led him down the street. Although the ride consisted of a single loop around the famous thoroughfare, it was enough to satisfy a young boy's fancy. William slid from the animal looking most pleased.

"Well, what was it like?" Joanna asked.

"Smelly," Peter said, passing a hand over his nose as another camel ambled by.

"And his hair was scratchy, but it was fun."

They wandered up the narrow street, but found the venue for Little Egypt closed. "Not to worry," Peter said. "I'm sure she'll be dancing this evening."

Rounding the bend, they came upon a snake charmer playing an eerie little tune on a simple flute. The music held sway over a large snake rising from a nearby basket. With one look at the reptile, Joanna and William clung to Peter, watching from the safety of his coat. Peter remained unruffled until a ruddy-cheeked teen either fell forward or was pushed by one of his friends. The snake flared its hood, jerking toward the boy, its open mouth revealing an intimidating pair of fangs. The crowd emitted a collective gasp and took a united step back, and the frightened boy scrambled back to join them. The snake charmer continued to play until the snake retracted its hood and retreated back into the basket. The charmer, without missing a note, slipped a lid over the top of the basket with his bare foot. His final act prompted a massive sigh of relief and a firm round of applause.

Peter, still holding tight to William, eyed Joanna. She had relaxed her stance and stepped away, but held her arms tight across her chest. He laughed. "You'll jump a man twice your size in a dirty alley, but you cower before a performing snake."

"Absolutely. I've never seen a cobra without a thick sheet of glass between us. That one was too close for comfort."

"We're nearing the German Village. Perhaps you'd like a brandy to steady your nerves."

"I'll pass on the brandy, but I'd love to see the German Village."

They entered a quaint tavern and found a table. Peter ordered a drink and allowed William the luxury of a few sweets, including a paper cone filled with caramel coated popcorn and peanuts. William offered them to Joanna and his father before taking any for himself.

"Hey! Cracker Jacks! I love this stuff. Thanks, buddy!" She tousled his hair.

Peter regarded her thoughtfully. "This is your first visit to the fair? You're quite sure?"

"Yes. Why?"

He sipped his brandy. "That candied popcorn is only available here. A man named Rueckheim sells popcorn and sweets in town. He combined them into a treat just for the fair."

Joanna reached for Peter's brandy and took a sip. "Oh, it will live on after the fair. Mark my words, it will become a staple in the American diet."

Peter retrieved his glass. "Joanna, that's silly. Sweets will never become a staple of the American diet."

"But Joey said in the future people eat sweets whenever they like." As soon as he spoke, William clamped a hand over his mouth in a guilty rush.

Peter glared at Joanna. "Does he know your entire story?"

She nodded, putting an arm around William. "He does. And before you let it ruin our day, let me say it was told in the spirit of fun."

Peter drained his brandy and shook his head. He leaned close to William. "So Joanna told you she comes from the future?"

"I won't tell anyone, Papa, I promise. Please don't be angry." He eyed Joanna. "I'm sorry."

She pecked his cheek. "It's okay, buddy. He would have figured it out sooner or later."

Peter spoke just above a whisper. "Listen carefully, son. Joanna can't remember where she's from, but it isn't the future. Now, you mustn't tell anyone her stories, because people will think she's sick and take her away to a special hospital. Do you understand?"

"I don't want anyone to take her away."

"Nor do I, so we must keep our lips sealed." He pressed his index finger to his lips. "Not a word. Understand?"

"Not a word." William said.

"Thank you," Joanna sighed.

"Whatever for?"

"For handling that well, and for not wanting to see me taken away. That was sweet."

Peter waved a dismissive hand through the air. "There was nothing sweet about it. You came to me with a problem and I intend to see it resolved." He rose from his chair. "Now, ah ... I believe the Glass Works are near here."

William scrambled from his chair and soon they were absorbed in the world of Libby Glass, where men stood around a huge fire, manipulating large glass tubes into enormous vases and bowls. In another corner, craftsmen sat at tables close to a smaller fire, blowing and bending tiny tubes of hot glass into delicate objects.

"That was cool," Joanna said as they walked away. "It must take years to master the skill."

"Which piece did you like the best?" William asked.

"I don't know. They were all so pretty. How about you, William? If they were to blow something special just for you, what would you like?"

The boy spoke without hesitation. "A camel. And you, Papa?"

"I honestly don't know. I'll have to give it some more thought."

"A Dahomey drum?" William offered.

"Or a warrior woman," Joanna said, brows lifted.

"We already have one warrior woman in the house, and I value my head far too much to risk another. I think a drum would suffice."

"And you, Joey?" William asked. "What would you choose?"

Her features clouded as she glanced from Peter to William.

"Joanna, what is it?"

She looked up, eyes glazed with unshed tears. "Last fall Martin and I took Michael to a crafts festival on the waterfront. They had blown glass there. He loved it and I just miss him." Her voice cracked and she covered her face with her hands. At length she released them and ventured a smile. "I lost Michael when I landed here, but thank God I found you guys."

She turned to William. "You know the little metal baby buggy on the shelf in the parlor?"

He nodded.

"I'd like a glass version of that. It's so quaint it reminds me of you guys, but—" Her voice grew hoarse. "It's for a baby, so it reminds me of Michael, too."

Peter placed a hand on her shoulder. "We'll find him, Joanna."

Chapter Thirty-one
Women: Commended and Considered

W ell, Joanna, this is the Women's Building. Are you sure you don't want to go in?"

They stood at the entrance of a grand Italian villa and Joey recalled her flippant remark about a shoe exhibit. Though she was largely ignorant of what lay inside, she knew the Columbian Exhibition was the first time America publicly acknowledged the contributions of its women. There had to be more to this place than shoes.

She thought of Elizabeth McNair and the nameless others who struggled to advance without upsetting the natural order of a patriarchal society. How many succeeded, and to what degree? Susan B. Anthony and Elizabeth Cady Stanton had the money and social standing to fan the flames of the Suffragette movement. Local heroes, like Jane Addams, had the tenacity to generate change from the bottom up, but who else lent a hand?

Joey assumed only a few prominent achievers were featured inside, inspiring others to fight convention. She took a breath. This building was the closest she would ever come to the birth of the women's movement. Feeling sufficiently humbled, she turned to her host.

"Peter, if we have the time, I would love to."

They traversed the first floor at a casual pace, taking in displays of a modernized hospital and kindergarten. Joey was surprised at the early instance of professional daycare. Children of the fair workers played in the drab classroom.

If the kindergarten seemed lackluster, the hospital was even more so. Medical tools considered modern in 1893 looked sinister to Joey. However, women played a far greater role in medicine than she realized. They introduced new sterilization techniques, and improved the design of hospital beds, chairs, stretchers and splints. She shuddered at one advance, a speculum for gynecological exams. Metallic and large, it looked painfully intrusive. Joey tapped the glass case that held it.

"They've got a long way to go with this puppy."

"I beg your pardon?" Peter stood a few feet away, engrossed in a display of surgical tools.

"This *improvement*," she said, miming her quotation marks, "has yet to meet plastic."

"Plastic?" he said, offering her his arm as they moved away.

"A material that doesn't get cold like metal, *much* easier on the anatomy."

They passed a multitude of paintings and statues, all done by women, and the library boasted over 7000 works by female authors. Contributions from foreign countries lay scattered throughout the building. William enjoyed the swords and jewels of Isabella of Spain, who financed Columbus's voyage to America. To Joey's relief, there wasn't a single shoe in sight.

They reached the second floor and found a working kitchen where Joey learned that over 140 innovations had been developed by women. Among them: the first tiled kitchen floor, a commercial oven and an early refrigerator. They saw a Josephine Cochran dishwasher and a clothes washer invented by Margaret Colvin.

"I understand why women would be motivated to improve home appliances," Joey said as William tugged at her hand, "but I had no clue they did so many."

"You won't believe the science room," he said, pulling her along.

The first thing visible in the next room was a display celebrating the astronomer, Maria Mitchell. Joey studied the book and photograph, the first time a face accompanied a name. Mitchell looked like she had little time to sit for a picture, but her eyes held steady, committed to the task. A quote attributed to her was printed on a placard below:

"First, no woman should say, 'I am but a woman.' But a woman! What more can you ask to be? Born a woman, born with the average brain of humanity, born with more than the average heart, if you are mortal what higher destiny could you have? No matter where you are, nor what you are, you are a power. Your influence is incalculable."

"You are a power. Your influence is incalculable. Wow," she said softly. "I had forgotten all about Maria Mitchell."

"Is something troubling you?" Peter stood by the glass case, observing her.

Joey gestured around the room. "Peter, less than a handful of these women are remembered in 1993. Take Ms. Mitchell here. When I think of astronomers, it's Copernicus or Galileo. Mitchell doesn't even cross my mind, and she's well documented. I had no idea women played such a large role in shaping the world. Almost every name is new to me, and none are honored—or even remembered—for their effort. I feel a bit ashamed."

Peter leaned across the case, forearms braced against the glass. "You bear shame for the strangest things, Joanna."

Eyes downcast, she ran her fingers along the edge of the case. "Peter, being here reminds me that the lifestyle I normally enjoy is due to these women. They fought for it, but didn't live to see their success. In 1993, I take my rights for granted, so yes, I feel shame for my ignorance." She let out a breath. "If I ever have a daughter I'm going to teach her all about these women."

Peter smiled. "Your appreciation is admirable. I think that's a fine idea."

William raced up to them, his small face flush with excitement. "Papa! Joey! Come this way."

They found William around the corner, dwarfed by a massive mural of a stormy seascape. At one end was a battered ship, stranded on an outcrop of jagged rocks, a bright red light shining on its deck. At the opposite end another boat cut across the water, the green light on its bow announcing its arrival.

"The red ship is in trouble, but the green ship is coming to help," William said.

According to the placard, the lights, Coston Signal Flares, were envisioned by a chemist who died of exposure to the chemicals of his trade. His wife spent ten long years bringing his vision to life, eventually outfitting Union Army vessels with the invention. Martha Jane Coston then traveled Europe and gained international adoption for her flares. The placard stated that the Civil War era resulted in eighty-six patents awarded to women for industrial inventions.

"Wow!" Joey tapped the card. "This proves my point. Mrs. Coston's flares probably helped the Union win the Civil War, and she's virtually unknown. The patent is in her husband's name." She hugged William close. "I really like this painting, buddy."

"You do seem to enjoy art, Miss Fagan."

"Jane? What a pleasant surprise!" Peter offered Jane Addams his hand and cast a dubious glance at Joey. "You're acquainted?"

"Miss Fagan and I admired the murals together at City Hall on Tuesday. She said she was a visitor, but didn't mention the name of her host." She inclined her head. "It's good to see you, Peter."

"And you." He cleared his throat. "So, you know each other?"

"Our encounter was brief, but," Addams smiled, "for a woman seemingly not of our time, she shows a keen interest in history."

"Not of our time?" Peter gave Joey a look of alarm.

"Pardon my blunt interpretation, Miss Fagan," Miss Addams said, turning to Joey, "but at our last meeting I was struck by your lack of historical knowledge."

"I'm not offended," Joey replied, glaring at Peter. "My historical knowledge was pathetic. I've learned a lot since I arrived here."

Peter seemed to regain his composure. "What brings you here, Jane?"

"I'm giving a lecture." A clock near the stairway announced the hour. She smiled as she moved away. "It was a pleasure to see you again."

"Hey," Joey whispered, watching her go. "I would never share my story with anyone outside your home."

He nodded. "I thought not, but her choice of words rattled me. It's already noon. I suppose we should go as well. We still have a lot of ground to cover."

They made their way out through the back of the building, which offered a stunning view of the lagoon and the Wooded Island.

"Whoa!" Joey stopped midstride. "And I thought the view from the Ferris Wheel was cool."

"I'm glad you like it." Peter bent down to William. "Son, shall we ride a gondola today?"

"Yes, sir!" William replied, running toward the loading area.

Within minutes they were skimming across the tranquil lagoon. The oblong boat wound its way around the Wooded Island and docked on the far side, in full view of the Manufactures and Liberal Arts Building.

Armed with chicken kebabs and orangeade, they strolled along tree-lined footpaths strung with festive Japanese lanterns. Inside the garden they settled under a large sycamore tree. Peter spread his coat out on the grass for them. William ate his chicken with abandon and finished first. Eyelids drooping, he took a sip of his drink.

"Want to put your head in my lap?" Joey reached for him. William joined her and laid his head on her thigh. He drifted off, soothed by the stroke of her hand.

Peter lay on his side, propped on one elbow. He pulled meat from the stick in small pieces, chewing slowly as he watched Joanna care for William. A soft breeze played through his hair.

He had difficulty reconciling the two facets of her. Inside the Women's Building Peter thought she seemed fractured, when discussing the women celebrated there. Now, caressing William as he fought the weight of fatigue, she seemed whole—almost happy. She had a son somewhere in the world. He believed that to be true. Peter wasn't inclined to indulge her delusion, but he wanted her to speak freely. With luck, she might give voice to something that tied her more definitively to the present.

Initially Peter was uncomfortable with the connection she and William shared, but he wouldn't rob the boy of a maternal influence, however tenuous. He decided their budding relationship might be mutually beneficial. The sight of them together, ensconced in that place between waking and sleeping, reserved—in Peter's mind—for mother and child, brought him unexpected peace.

"There," Joanna whispered, "I thought his tank was about empty."

"His tank?"

"He looked like he could use a nap," she clarified, reaching for her chicken. "Does he still nap every day?"

"It's rare, but with so much excitement it's natural for him to tire quickly. I thought letting him nap would gain us more time in the evening. There's a good deal left on our list."

"Don't feel like you have to cram everything in on my account. I'm sufficiently blown away already. Anything else would be cherry."

"Blown away? Cherry?"

"Mmm," she nodded, sipping Orangeade. "Have you ever had an ice cream sundae?"

"Yes."

"With all the great stuff? Chocolate sauce? Whipped cream? Cherry on top?"

He nodded.

"Well, I just meant the day has been an explosion of surprises—blown away." Her hands burst into the air as she spoke. "As for cherry, I just meant anything else I see will be a bonus, like the cherry on a sundae."

"You do have an odd way with words. You remind me of Car. He's full of unique phrases, but they come from his homeland. Fagan is an Irish name, but where do your roots lie? What is your maiden name?"

"Lawrence," she said. "My maiden name is Lawrence and Mom's was Brown, so I guess that makes me British on both sides. Hastings is British too, right?"

"Yes, it is. My family immigrated at the turn of the last century."

"Hmm … I have no idea when my ancestors crossed over, but I'm glad they did." She smiled. "This will sound silly, but I really like Chicago in either century. I never gave much thought to how it grew. Have you seen the murals at City Hall?"

Peter nodded.

"I hadn't. They don't exist in 1993. The whole building is gone. They really brought the last few decades to life." Joanna lapsed into silence, taking in the garden around them.

"And that's where you met Jane Addams?"

She nodded. "I'd never really envisioned the raising of the city. Jane filled in a few blanks for me."

William shifted on her lap and she lowered his head onto her coat. Freed from his sleeping form, she stretched out face-down, propping herself up on her forearms. Her fingers played through the grass.

"Peter, can I ask you something that's really none of my business?"

"Yes, but I may not answer." He played idly with an empty skewer. "What would you like to know?"

Joanna spoke to the ground in front of her. "It's about Mrs. Milford. It seems like she's not a very happy person."

"And?" He prodded.

"Oh, I don't really know where I was headed." She raised her head. "She strikes me as an odd part of your household. No offense. I mean, I know it takes a village to raise a child." Her voice faded and she tugged on a blade of grass. "Even though she seems like an odd fit to me, I don't think she does to you. I just wondered why."

"Hmm." Peter rolled onto his back, hands behind his head, and stared through the branches above. "Good question," he said at length. "You're right, I do think she fits, but I never stopped to consider why. I suppose she reminds me of my father."

"Whoa. Didn't see that coming," Joanna said. "Care to explain?"

Peter spoke softly, eyes fixed on the sky. "The day she arrived she entered the house in much the same way my father did when he returned home from the war: very stern, very serious. I remember trembling at the sight of him." He laughed. "If I'm being honest, I do believe I trembled before Mrs. Milford as well."

The unexpected peal of laughter from Joanna sounded remarkably like Victoria. Peter smiled and continued.

"The house was in complete disarray. Maeve had passed on, Victoria was bedridden and we were in dire need of help. I contacted the agency and they sent Mrs. Milford. She marched in scowling, asked to see the kitchen, and told me she would tidy up and make lunch. When she finished we discussed the terms of her employment and that was that. She came every day after, always frowning, confronting her chores as if they were enemies."

"And the connection to your dad?"

Peter offered half a smile. "He was very much like her. He rose each day harboring some sort of frustration I never quite understood, attacking his work as a soldier takes to battle. It seemed nothing brought him any joy. As I grew older I came to understand he was embittered by many things, though I can only guess at a few of them. He—" Peter halted and pinched the bridge of his nose.

"We were not close, but I always felt some empathy for him. There was little I could do but try to be a good son. Mrs. Milford harbors a similar frustration. I do believe she finds some measure of joy in my home, and she adores William." He looked at Joanna.

"I suppose it is odd I would hire someone so like my father. Maybe, she's with us because I want to help her as I never could help him, like repaying an old debt, or righting an old wrong."

Joanna lowered her forearms to the ground. "You're very kind, looking out for people as you do. You carry a lot on your shoulders, though."

"You think it's wrong?"

"No. I think it's gallant, but it seems like you actually bear guilt for their frustration. It's interesting you would take it to that level." She rested a hand on his arm. "You're a brave man, Peter: dealing with the loss of your wife, the ghost of your father, the wrath of your housekeeper, and my little mess all at the same time." She grinned. "You thrive on challenge, buddy. I'll give you that."

"It may have escaped your notice, but I've made very little progress on any front."

Joanna broke into another echoing peal of laughter. "Maybe so, but you still get points for trying."

Chapter Thirty-two
Electric Encounters

The center of the Electricity Building was dominated by the Edison Tower, a massive beacon of light that captivated William as soon as they entered. Forty thousand multi-colored bulbs flashed and faded in perfect rhythm to a song that played when William pressed a button.

"What would you like to see?" Joanna asked as they watched the lights twinkle.

"Whatever you like." Peter shrugged. "I prefer medical advances. Technical innovation holds little for me."

"Seriously?" She nodded at the display. "In a few years those lights will be in every house."

Adopting a pained expression, Peter replied, "Please tell me they are not accompanied by carnival music."

"God, no!" She laughed. "If they were, people would head for insane asylums just to escape the noise.

"Please, Joanna. Must you always invoke the name of the Lord over trifles?"

"News flash, Peter. Electricity is hardly a *trifle*." Joanna enlisted her quotation marks. "It's a game-changer. Why are you so indifferent to this kind of innovation?"

"I suppose I am old-fashioned. Perhaps if the Great Fire had burned my house, then advances in home improvement might have piqued my interest, but it didn't and I remain happily ensconced in my older, simpler home."

"Well, at least you embraced the flush toilet." Joanna smiled and linked arms with him. "Come on. Let's check out the Tesla stuff."

The first thing they encountered was a phosphorescent lamp. The lamp itself meant little to Peter, but the word 'phosphorescent' struck him. Joanna had used it on Sunday. He didn't know how she knew the word, or applied it to a pair of shoes, but he felt certain this represented a solid blow to her fantastic claim. He cast her a sidelong glance.

"Joanna, what do you make of this?"

"Oh! A florescent lamp," she said reading the placard. "Okay, phosphorescent. This is what I was telling you about on Sunday."

Since she made the connection, Peter pushed her. "You told me this wouldn't exist for at least another fifty years, yet here it is."

"Well," she countered, "it had to start sometime."

"Hardly evidence of the future, wouldn't you agree." To his surprise she laughed easily.

"Peter, this is where it begins." She waved a hand around the room. "Do you see any phosphorescent shoes around here? Tesla invented the technology, but the application to footwear hasn't happened yet. Eventually all kinds of things will glow: shoes, bowling balls, nail polish." She tugged at his arm. "I know you think I'm nuts, but it's true. Come on."

They found William, open-mouthed, before a display of illuminated glass tubes bent in a myriad of spirals, squares and stars. One lamp actually spelled the word *light*.

"Neon! I didn't realize Tesla did neon. Now, imagine any word you can think of lit up like this." She leaned close to William and whispered, "I've seen it."

William giggled.

Peter expelled a weary sigh. "Come along, you two."

Within the hour they were ready to leave, but William wanted to watch at the Edison Tower one last time. They approached just as the synchronized song ended. The crowd disbursed and William headed for the front, anxious to press the button and watch the lights dance.

Joey begged off for a quick trip to the restroom, but didn't return to the display. Her shoes were uncomfortable. She settled onto a small bench, rotating her ankles, and watched the lights from a distance.

"May I join you? My feet ache unmercifully." A tall, striking brunette with large brown eyes approached the bench.

"Sure, have a seat." Joey moved to one side and gave her new companion an amiable smile. "Are you enjoying the fair?"

"Well, yes I am, but not as a visitor. I work here. I'm with the Westinghouse Electric Corporation." She extended her hand. "My name is Bertha Lamme."

"Really?" Joey gave her hand a firm shake. "I'm Joanna Fagan. Are you an electrician or an administrator for the exhibit?"

Miss Lamme smiled. "Everyone assumes I am a docent. You're the first person to guess in broader terms." As she leaned closer a wisp of hair slipped from her bun. "Actually, I'm an electrical engineer."

"No way!" Joey said. "There can't be many women engineers in the US right now. That's really cool!"

"Well, my reception here was certainly cool enough. The bulb boys don't quite know what to do with me." Bertha laughed, pulling her hair back into place. "I am the first woman in this country to hold a degree in Electrical Engineering. Some of the men still don't believe me."

Mouth slightly open, Joey extended her hand again. "The first female Double E. It's an honor to meet you! That's a hell of an accomplishment!"

Bertha laughed, renewing the handshake. "Thank you for your candor. I happen to think so."

Joey's brow furrowed as she beheld the young woman. "No offense, but you seem awfully young." She nodded at the exhibits. "Have you been at this long?"

Miss Lamme shook her head. "No, I graduated from Ohio State in the spring and joined the company at the end of the summer. This is my first big assignment. I'm here to assist in dismantling our exhibits." She began rubbing her ankle. "The fair gives me the chance to see most of our projects working in one place. My feet don't like it, but they have no voice in the matter." She surveyed the room. "Are you here alone? I seldom see women in this building."

"My friends are over by the Tower, but I did ask them to come here. I wanted to see—" Joey paused, choosing her words carefully, "how everything works."

"Well, I'm glad. It's nice to speak to a woman." She cocked her head in the direction of the tower. "Your friends don't honestly like that gaudy music box, do they?"

"Well, one of them is not yet five, and children tend to enjoy light and motion, and it does catch the eye." She looked at her companion. "What? You don't think it's pretty?"

Miss Lamme offered half a nod. "It has charm, but what useful purpose does it serve?"

Joey gave the tower a circumspect glance. "Well, you've got me there. I think only Vegas—" she caught herself. "I mean, I can't imagine a practical application for it … except maybe a bunch of slot machines." She finished in a whisper.

"Exactly." Ms. Lamme spoke over her. "The tower was built only to attract attention, I'm proud to represent a company that strives to achieve more."

"I take it you don't think much of Mr. Edison." Joey fought back a smile.

"Edison. Ha! The man is an unethical swine." Ms. Lamme fairly spat her words.

"A swine?" Joey was surprised by her vehemence. "How so?"

"In my industry, everyone knows Mr. Westinghouse won the contract for this Exposition fairly. His bid was lower than Mr. Edison's."

"I had no idea they competed for the job. So, Edison lost the bid. Was that such a big deal?"

"It was to Mr. Edison. After he learned of his loss, his company, General Electric, prohibited the sale of their light bulbs to Mr. Westinghouse."

"That sounds kind of petty," Joey replied. "There must be tons of bulbs at this fair. Seems to me like the guy walked away from some easy revenue. If I were Edison I would have jacked up my price on bulbs rather than prevent their purchase."

Bertha laughed. "Then you have a good head for business. There are over 90,000 incandescent light bulbs in use at the fair. Supplying them was a great opportunity for someone smart."

"So who supplied the light bulbs?"

"My boss." Bertha said, laughing at Joey's puzzled expression. "Mr. Westinghouse had his team create a new kind of light bulb, a double stopper. The design is distant enough from Edison's to survive patent scrutiny. So, you're right. Edison lost the bid and the chance to make any money on light bulbs."

Joey eyed the tower. "Did he think to take tower orders, for town squares or something?"

"I can't say, but I think it highly unlikely. Even if he had, since the banks failed in the spring, few cities can afford so costly a trinket, especially one that serves no useful purpose."

"And you're all about useful purpose." Joey grinned. "You're quite something, Bertha."

The song ended and Joey stood with some reluctance. "It's been a real pleasure, Ms. Lamme. I suspect you will prove very useful to Mr. Westinghouse and his Electric Corporation."

"I shall certainly try." She stood and clasped Joey's hand in both of hers. "The pleasure was mine. I'd best check the transformers now. Good day." Turning, she slipped into the crowd.

"Made a friend, have you?" Peter asked as Joey reached him.

"More like a role model."

"I beg your pardon?"

"Well, she's not from Chicago, so I'll never see her again— even if I am stuck here." She looked over her shoulder. "I can tell you this, though. I'll never forget her."

Peter nodded. "William and I need to attend to ourselves before we continue. We'll meet you out front, all right?"

As he entered the restroom, Peter considered her last remark. What if Joanna really were, as she put it, *stuck here*? What if they never found her family? The question played in his mind. He knew William and Car would be delighted, and he …. Peter cleared his throat. Of course, she would be welcome, but would she want to stay?

She got on well with everyone, save for Mrs. Milford. The thought of his housekeeper brought a new frown. He remembered her accusation of theft on Sunday morning. Days later Joanna mentioned discovering the match safe in her pocket and returning it to the table. Peter was certain Joanna wasn't a thief. So why had Mrs. Milford insisted she was? Exactly why did she find Joanna so distasteful? He abandoned the thought as soon as he stepped outside.

Ten yards away, Joanna stood in the grip of an angry-looking stranger. She appeared to be resisting him, yet she argued as if she knew him. William bolted to her side.

Peter hurried after him. "Excuse me, sir. Do you know this woman?"

"This one?" the stranger responded, raising Joanna's arm. "I know her for a crazy devil."

The man was short, thickset, and had a dark air about him. His bulky hand held fast to Joanna's wrist. Peter reached her side, unsure if he should separate them.

"Your name, sir?"

"I'm Eugene Prendergast." The man said. "And I don't appreciate her wild accusations."

Peter took a breath at the name. "So you know her? She is a friend? Perhaps a relative?"

Prendergast pulled her closer, and Peter moved to intervene, but Joanna ignored him. She pulled free from his grasp and huffed at Peter. "I don't know him from Adam, I'm just trying to prevent—"

"Odd you should mention Adam." Prendergast said. "He and his wife suffered a fitting fate, didn't they?"

Peter stared hard at the man. "Sir, do you mean to say this woman is your wife?"

This brought a cutting laugh from Prendergast. "Not on your life, sir. I'd never marry a devil who spouts wild stories as she does."

"She's not a devil!" William shouted. "Take it back."

"Silence, William," Peter said, then returned his attention to Prendergast. "But you do know her?"

"I don't know her, but I know she doesn't understand the work of the Lord." He leaned close to Peter, voice low, breath stale. "She thinks she *knows* things. I think she's touched," he said, tapping his temple

Peter stood stock still. She did purport to *know* things. Did Prendergast know about her claim of time travel? What on earth was her connection to this man? He eyed Prendergast carefully.

The stranger before him smelled like he frequented a local pub, but his shoes were solid, and he wore a clean coat and hat. He wasn't a street rat, but his countenance was unsettling. Could Joanna, in her grief, have fallen in with this man? Did she come to her senses and flee, only to land in Lake Michigan?

Had the association been so disagreeable as to affect her memory?

Peter glanced at Joanna. She showed no sign of fear, but did seem rattled by his presence. He glanced back at Prendergast. The man still hadn't provided a definite answer on the length or nature of his relationship with Joanna. Peter tried again.

"Please answer my question, sir. How long have you known her?"

"I've known the likes of her ever since I learned the ways of the devil's temptation," he sneered, "but I never set eyes on this one before Tuesday." He pointed a thick finger at her. "And may God keep you from my sight in the days ahead."

"I told you I didn't know him." Joanna looked at Peter, every bit as angry as Prendergast.

"That's right," Prendergast said. "You don't know me, and you don't know a thing about me. I'm a God-fearing man. Now, stop with your wild talk."

He glared at Peter. "Sir, she has taken leave of her senses. The woman is in need of a physician. See that you get her some help." With a mighty 'humph' Prendergast turned on his heel and left.

"The woman is in need of a big, fat drink," Joanna muttered, rubbing her wrist as he walked away.

Chapter Thirty-three
Storming the Beach

Within minutes of entering the Manufactures and Liberal Arts Building, Joey wanted to leave. The immense structure made her feel like an ant in a shopping mall, and the monstrous exhibits reinforced the notion. They walked the length of the East/West corridor taking in gargantuan displays from all over the world.

Though she tried to get interested, Joey couldn't shake the memory of their encounter with Prendergast. Peter actually thought she might have been his wife. Pfh! And *he* questioned *her* sanity? Of all the stubborn, old-fashioned values .... Did a woman always have to *belong* to somebody in this age? The nerve ....

They skipped the French exhibit. Joey gave no more than a nod to its elaborate entrance. She cared little for the English porcelain and said nothing about the German armor. Peter must have known she was upset; he made no attempt to slow the pace she set. When they reached the U.S. exhibit William raced over to the 128 carat, canary-yellow Tiffany diamond.

As she watched it sparkle from its velvet rotating perch, Joey conceded the place left a lasting visual impression. Movement in any direction led to the best and brightest the world offered, all of it shining beneath the natural light of the glass ceiling. The trouble was it was too much to take in, especially after bumping into Prendergast.

William gave the diamond its proper due, whistling in awe. By contrast, Joey barely shrugged her approval. As they moved on, Peter placed a hand on her back, steering her toward the exit.

"Why don't we walk along the lake? William's Viking ship is north along the shore," he said. "The French Pavilion is up this way, a perfect place for an early dinner."

Delighted by the news, William ran down the steps and raced to the water's edge, dodging the small waves, laughing as he came within inches of soaking his feet.

Joey remained on the steps, eyes locked on Peter. Though his expression gave nothing away, she sensed he was trying to make amends. She nodded and accepted his arm.

William's boat floated alone in the shallows, framed entirely by the lake. Black and gold shields spanned its length, reflecting the afternoon sun. The head of a fierce dragon adorned the bow, a mighty tail lashed out from the stern, and a colossal striped sail billowed from the central mast. Joey thought the ship more impressive than the diamond they left behind.

"You know," Peter said, nodding toward the vessel, "they sailed their exhibit here from Norway just to prove the voyage could be done."

"Is that so?" She looked directly at Peter and pulled her hat from her head, daring him to challenge her. The cool air brushed her skin like a salve, soothing the burn of her frustration. She faced the wind, enjoying the rush of air, and decided to try to talk through her anger. Maybe meeting Prendergast brought Peter a step closer to believing her prediction, if not her entire story. She softened her tone. "Listen, thanks for the break. That last building was too much."

"Any particular reason?"

"Prendergast kind of ruined the mood."

"You seemed out of sorts." Peter spoke with his eyes on William. Armed with a stick and down on his knees, the boy was already fifty yards ahead of them, digging in the rocky sand.

"Oh, I pretty much ran the gamut of human emotion in the last hour." She took a deep breath and held it. "So," she said, expelling the word with restrained annoyance. "What did you think of him?"

Peter stopped walking and cast her an unreadable glance. "I thought he was a disagreeable fellow."

"Yeah, I got the same vibe on Tuesday."

"Vibe?"

"Feeling. I had the same feeling when I met him on Tuesday." She rubbed her wrist. "He's got an iron grip, I'll give him that." She edged closer to Peter, fighting her anger. "But I wouldn't give him anything else … and I would *never* marry a guy like him."

Peter's stony features melted into contrition. "I had to ask," he said. "Surely you understand."

"Yes, but do you understand now why I want to warn Harrison? The guy's off his nut."

Peter remained silent, one hand stroking his sideburns. "He seemed mean-spirited, but an assassin?" He shrugged his shoulders. "How can you be so sure of his plans?"

"I already told you—where I come from this is history."

"And I told you, there must be another explanation, a logical explanation."

Joey felt the heat in her cheeks. "You don't believe one damn thing I've told you, Peter. Not one."

"Don't swear." Peter said, frowning. "Joanna, I believe many things about you. I believe your husband's death had a traumatic effect on you. I believe you live in Chicago, but your grief prevents you from remembering your address. I believe you have a son, and your inability to locate him causes you great stress."

He put a hand on her shoulder. "You've named only two other people since I met you: Mayor Harrison—whom you wish to protect, and Prendergast—whom you wish to confront." A lifeless chuckle escaped him. "I had planned to locate Prendergast, but our chance meeting today eliminated the need. I do believe he hadn't met you before Tuesday, and that," he sighed, "leads me back to the beginning of your quandary."

His grip on her shoulder tightened, but Joey sensed no threat. He leaned over, close to her ear, and the weary tone of his question washed over her.

"Who are you, and where do you come from?"

She sighed. She couldn't blame him. He had no clue what to make of her. God knows he tried, but it was an impossible story. He was understandably frustrated, the poor guy. She spoke slowly, and repeated her truth because it was all she could do.

"I am Joanna Lawrence Fagan. I was born in Chicago in the year 1963, and someday, Peter, someday I will prove it to you."

Peter started and stepped back. "1863? You're thirty years old?"

"No, 1963, and yes, I'm thirty. Is that a problem?"

"I assumed you were younger." He frowned. "You married late."

Joey burst out laughing. "Not by 20th century standards. I went to college, remember? Many women finish school and start careers before they marry." She faced the shore breeze again. "Man, this feels good. I haven't been near the lake since last Saturday. I didn't realize how much I missed it."

"You're forgetting Tuesday."

"Doesn't count," she said evenly. "That was an experiment."

"A failed experiment."

"An experiment, nevertheless."

Peter threw down an unexpected challenge. "What would you be doing now, had you succeeded?"

Joey eyed him and thought for a moment, missing Michael, hungry for the rhythm of her old routine. "Well, around five I'd leave work and head down to Bright Eyes—that's Michael's preschool—to pick him up. We'd hit the grocery, grab a couple of movies and—"

"Your son is in school? I thought he was only three years old."

"He's nearly three and, yes, he's in preschool. It's not academic; it's more like the daycare center in the Women's Building. The kids sing alphabet songs, finger paint, that kind of thing."

Peter stopped walking. "You should be home with him."

Joey flinched. "I ... what?"

"You should be home with him," he said simply.

"Hello!" she pointed to her chest. "Widow here! As in: single income. As in: providing for him is my responsibility." She crossed her arms to contain her mounting rage. "Come on, Peter. There are plenty of women alive right now who have to work to keep food on the table."

He shrugged. "Your husband was a physician. Surely he left you with some means to survive."

Joey held her breath, fighting for control. "We had insurance, but I had to think of Michael. He comes from a long line of physicians, and everyone expects he'll become one. I can cover living expenses on my salary, but if he follows his father into medicine ...." She raked a hand through her hair.

"Peter, in the future medical school is extremely expensive. My annual college tuition nearly doubled by the time I graduated. God only knows how much a bachelor's degree will cost in fifteen years, let alone a medical degree. I paid off the house with some of the insurance settlement and put the rest away for Michael's education."

"I meant no offense, Joanna. You're wise to think of your son's future. I only meant a child so young ...." He looked past her to William, digging by the water. "A life without a mother is a forlorn existence, and it's difficult to shed the sense of being forsaken. It's a shame you're not able to remain at home with him."

Up to this point, Joey was still bristling, eager to retort, but as Peter spoke, she lost her edge. She closed her eyes and rubbed her temples. More than one motherless child lurked in the shadows of this conversation. Knowing Michael was in league with them, she confessed a loss.

"I stayed home with him for a whole year, and I loved every minute of it, but taking a leave of absence from work came at a cost." Her eyes dropped to the hat she carried. "It was hard to go back."

"You miss them." Her voice grew reed thin, and she lacked the nerve to raise her head. "You miss seeing all the little changes they go through, and it nearly kills you, knowing you'll catch what little you can on evenings and weekends. You constantly ask yourself, 'Should I just abandon my degree and stay home?' But that feels like giving up on who you were and you're not ready to do that, either. So you keep going, thinking you'll find some kind of balance." She rambled on, barely aware of Peter's presence.

"Back at work you're considered a novice again. You don't fit in like you used to. Opportunities that should have been yours aren't now, because your dedication has been called into question. And no matter how hard you work, the demands of your family require that you stop pulling late nights or weekends. Then you're perceived as lacking initiative, letting your career take a backseat to other priorities."

Joey heard the sound of her own bitterness and disliked the sour taste it left at the back of her throat. It was an old fight and she'd fought it many times in her head. She could do nothing but soldier on because there was no end to the argument, and no choice available to her since Martin died. Still, the acid was there and she sought to contain it. "It's difficult," she finished, her voice low.

Joey braved a look at Peter and found him eyeing her critically. Feeling exposed, she swallowed hard, squared her shoulders, and regained her nerve. "But you have to rebuild. You reinvent yourself at work, and you find a way to shore up what's eroded at home. You find a way," she repeated quietly, "because you have to."

Peter stepped up beside her and they resumed their walk.

A weak laugh escaped her. "At first I went back because I wanted both a family and a career. But a year later, after endless debate over the decision, I was still on the fence. Then one day it simply wasn't a choice anymore, you know?"

"I think I do," he said, pointing to a tree-lined path. "The French Pavilion is over there. Did I mention they serve wine?"

"No, you didn't, but I sure could use a glass."

They reached William, pulled him away from his excavation, and made their way up the path.

Never having seen the original, Joey didn't know if the French Pavilion really mirrored Marseilles, but she thought it was beautiful. The restaurant opened onto a veranda and a sculpted garden filled with colorful flowers and ornamental greenery. They arrived early enough to get a garden-side table and the atmosphere offered soothing reparation to the strain of the day. In no time they were sipping wine, examining the rocks and treasures William collected from the shoreline. The crepes arrived and were delectable, as was the Bordeaux Peter selected. By the time they finished eating, the sun was well behind them and dusk had settled in.

Joey leaned back in her chair and raised her glass to salute the garden. William had befriended a boy from another table and they chased each other there, laughing amid the shrubbery.

"This is so different from everything we saw earlier. I understand why people spend more than one day here." She sipped her wine. "You've been before. Have you seen all you wanted?"

"This fair always holds a new surprise. On our last visit, I took William to Buffalo Bill's Wild West Show, playing outside the fair. Miss Annie Oakley shot the ash from her husband's cigar—as he was smoking it." He tipped his glass. "Remarkable."

"You favor wine," he said, pouring the last of the bottle for her. "In the Horticulture Building you can taste wine from all over the world."

Joey started to put her feet on the empty seat beside her, but realized it would be inappropriate. She sat up instead, crossing her legs. She wasn't drunk, but her conflicting shift revealed an unsteady state. She offered Peter a lazy smile. "I think this bottle has served me quite well, thank you."

"Why Miss Fagan!" he returned in mock distress. "Am I to assume you are flushed?"

"If you mean drunk," she said, eyes closed, taking silent stock of her capacity, "then, no, but I will freely admit to feeling quite content."

She giggled at her sense of placid detachment. Placing an elbow on the table, she rested her chin in the palm of her hand, and, without any sense of propriety, began scrutinizing her host.

Peter looked nothing like Martin, but he was an attractive man with genteel features. His nose was straight and not too broad. His cheeks were all but hidden by his sideburns which, she noted with pleasure, had nearly grown into a beard. It looked it better now, scruffy and wild.

She leaned forward, peering into his coffee brown eyes, and remembered the night they met. The circumstances were considerably more relaxed now. Fully content, she gazed unabashedly, ensconced in the warmth of his eyes. At length she realized he beheld her as well, but showed no emotion, as if he too were taking the opportunity to observe her.

She shifted her gaze to his thick hair. Normally combed back, it had been freed by the wind today, and loose curls now graced his head. The evening breeze played at his forelocks, sweeping random strands across his brow. Without thinking, she reached up and brushed one aside. He didn't flinch, but his nervous cough brought her back to their surroundings. She lowered her hand into her lap.

"Ah ... thank you." Peter passed a self-conscious hand along the side of his head. "I suppose I should see a barber soon."

"Mmm ... I disagree."

She knew he was ruffled, but didn't care. Perhaps she was a little flushed. Joey leaned back, giving him the distance she suspected he would prefer. Crossing her arms over her chest she tilted her head, regarding him.

"In fact, I think you should let it grow longer. Your hair looks nice with a little length."

"What about you?" Peter countered with obvious discomfort. "Was your hair ever long?"

"Sure. Growing up I wore it long, but I chopped it off when I went to college."

"Any particular reason?"

She shrugged. "First declaration of independence, I suppose."

"You felt the need for that?" His voice was earnest.

Joey drained her glass. "At some point, doesn't everybody?"

Peter pressed a fist to his lips, considering the question.

Joey smiled. The notion of personal independence probably meant little to a man in this era.

William bounded in from the garden, waving good-bye to his friend, and rejoined their table. "Papa, it's getting dark."

"So it is," Peter said. "We should head back to the Court of Honor."

Lulled by the wine and the setting, Joey was not inclined to rush. She'd seen enough of the exhibits.

"Peter, I'd love to check out the lights, but I'd rather skip the interior of the Manufactures Building. Can we get to the roof without wading through all the ..." She paused, not wanting to seem ungrateful, "... all the excitement?"

"Of course. Access to the roof is right by the lakeside door."

Joey stood. "Then I'm in. Let's go."

Chapter Thirty-four
Car's Theory

Thousands of incandescent lights overpowered the evening sky, transforming the Court of Honor into the White City. With some spirit Joanna said as much. Peter concluded she wasn't in her cups, as Maeve used to say. She was animated, but sound of step and clear in her enunciation. Most important, William took no notice so Peter wasn't overly concerned.

Sousa's band played "After the Ball," and tonight the music lent an air of significance Peter hadn't expected. Understandable, he thought, so close to the end of the Exhibition. He glanced at Joanna and found her profoundly moved, two large tears rolling down her cheeks. He passed her his handkerchief.

"Is everything all right?"

She nodded, accepting the handkerchief. "Pictures don't capture a tenth of this. I mean, I expected to be impressed, but it's so majestic. I can't believe it's going to burn."

"What?"

Peter watched her carefully. Her features shifted several times, giving silent voice to the thoughts in her head, but she managed to regain her composure.

"Forget I said anything. Let's just enjoy the view, okay?"

He caught the weary note in her plea and nodded, though he wondered what part of the brain controlled mental projection or, in Joanna's case, failed to do so? How unfortunate this affliction should befall so lovely a woman. Had she fallen from another dock, her fate would have .... Peter shuddered and, quite without thinking, put his arm around her. Joanna leaned against him and he smiled, enjoying the view.

The Court of Honor was the crowning achievement of the fair. Seven starch-white classical buildings paid homage to history while the contents within saluted innovation. An oblong body of water, the Grand Basin, separated the buildings, lending greater perspective and appreciation to the generally stunned observer.

Their view was above the center of the Grand Basin. The entrance was marked by the sky-scraping Administration Building. Ablaze with lights, it resembled a three-tiered wedding cake, capped by a massive dome that was illuminated by hundreds of Westinghouse light bulbs.

The show of lights continued at the Agricultural Building, directly across the water from them, and the opposing structures mirrored each other in height and design. At the far end was the Peristyle, a regal 48-column colonnade. A grand arch at its center opened to the lake, allowing boat traffic access to the fair. Brilliantly lit, and outlined by the dark water from behind, the sweeping majesty of the Peristyle served as a balance to its domed rival at the opposite end.

William stifled a yawn and Peter checked his pocket watch. "Car will be here soon. We'd best be on our way."

Long before they reached the bridge leading back to the Midway, William's fatigue became evident. Joanna seemed tired as well.

"Whoa!" she said, slowing to a stop. "There's got to be a better way to do this. William needs a break."

Peter looked in vain for one of the personal rental carriages dotting the fairgrounds, but all those visible were occupied. They had over a mile to go, and carrying William through the swelling crowd would be cumbersome. He was about to say so when Joanna spoke.

"Put him on your shoulders, Peter."

He gave her a mildly skeptical look, but agreed. Aside from a kick to Joanna's rib as she helped him up, William reached his new perch easily. Peter had his misgivings, but moving through the crowd proved easier than expected. William, thrilled with his elevated status, regained some energy. "Papa! You're so tall! I can see the whole fair from here."

His enthusiasm was infectious and Peter relaxed, rubbing William's shins as they walked along. "Tell me what you see, son."

"Everything! I'm taller than a camel. And you're faster, Papa! This is fun."

"Glad to oblige." He gave William a little bounce. "Consider it your last ride at the fair."

By the time they reached Car, the walk and the wine had taken its toll. Joanna lagged behind as William had earlier. Peter settled her in the back of the carriage with William and joined Car on the bench. They had gone only a few blocks when he turned to find William fast asleep, snug under the lap robe, his head in Joanna's lap. Joanna lay slumped against the side of the carriage, eyes closed, one hand draped over William. Victoria's hat had slipped to the floor.

"Asleep, are they?" Car asked quietly.

Peter nodded.

"How did Joey take ta the fair? Enjoy herself?"

"She did, and she often surprised me." He paused, recalling her reactions. "Certain aspects of the fair left her in awe, but she found many of the newest inventions merely quaint."

"Well," Car said, "that'll be owin' ta the fact that she comes from the future. Or thinks she does."

Peter drew a quick breath and stared at Car. "You know about that, too?"

"Em … well, she told me on Sunday, while ya were gone. I didn't think much of it, not until Tuesday when she asked me ta take her ta the dock."

"Yes," Peter said, arms over his chest, "Exactly what transpired on Tuesday?"

Car supplied a brief synopsis.

"So, Mrs. Milford actually suggested that Joanna dive into Lake Michigan?"

"Suggested is one way of puttin' it. Seems ta me Mrs. M's a bit harsh with Joey."

"Well," Peter ran a hand over the back of his neck, "Mrs. Milford tends to be cold, especially with strangers."

"You say cold. I say spiteful, and I ought ta know. I've had my share a lashes from her whip. Mrs. M. showed some teeth, callin' her names, tellin' her ta jump back in the lake where she belonged."

"She called her names?" Peter frowned, clasping his hands together. "I'll have to speak to her about this." He leaned back, trying to sort through his thoughts. Mrs. Milford had overstepped her bounds before, and apparently she was at it again. Long ago he had to address her issues with Car. Apparently it was time to speak to her once more.

Thinking of Joanna, he felt … well, he felt many things. He shared more with her today than he had intended, but felt closer to her because of it, as it he'd gained more of her trust.

No, that was not entirely true. It was more than trust. He had an inkling that he was somehow bound to her, and was surprised to realize the notion didn't upset him. Peter shook his head and sat up. Despite what he felt, his purpose was to help her heal. Elements of today's outing might yet prove helpful. Perhaps Car's version of her escapade held some useful information. He turned to his protégé.

"So, once you reached the dock, did Joanna seem impulsive?"

"Not a'tall. She took her time, admitted she had her doubts, but said jumpin' in was the only way ta find out. And she gave me a lot of instructions."

"Such as?"

"Tell everyone goodbye. Thank ya for yer hospitality. Then she said, 'Count to a thousand.' If she didn't come up, it would mean she made it. Ta my way a thinkin' it would mean she drowned, and I told her as much. But y'know Joey, stubborn as a mule." He tilted his head toward the back of the carriage, "Told me she knew how ta swim, which she did, because she came right back up and we headed home."

"What did she say when she failed?"

Car fought a grin. "She ... em ... she used a few choice words."

Peter frowned. "She seems to know a number of choice words."

"Yeah," Car laughed, "but she knows a lot a nice words, too." He nudged Peter with his elbow. "Joey's all right, Doc. She's real easy ta talk to, and it's nice havin' her around. I can't really say where she comes from, but I hope she's with us a while yet."

Peter rubbed his beard, contemplating his houseguest. Car was right. She was easy to talk to and Peter did enjoy her company. Quite a lot. But, she had a child out there somewhere who missed her. He would be sad to see her go, but it was his job to see her safely home. There must be something he had overlooked, something that would lead to a logical explanation. People don't just appear out of nowhere, and they don't pop back and forth in time. A swim in the lake didn't work because it couldn't, despite her dogged insistence. Finding no answer on this train of thought, he decided to seek another opinion.

"So, where do you think she comes from, Car?"

The lanky Irishman shrugged his shoulders. "I don't know, Doc, but em ...." He glanced briefly at the night sky. "Maeve used ta tell me stories about special creatures that live in the sea. Merrows and selkies, she called 'em." Car leaned forward as he spoke, elbows on his knees.

"Merrows are sea maidens, born of the water. They live quite happy there, though they do find the same sort a joy on land when they've a mind to. From time ta time they come ashore, and occasionally one will meet a fella alone among the rocks—or so the stories say." He gave Peter a look of amusement and then his voice softened to a gentle, spellbinding tone.

"Beautiful creatures they are, dark of eye and of hair. And, though they seem like us when on land, there's just somethin' different about em. Somethin' ya can't quite name. Not bad, ya see, just not quite like what a man is used to. Maeve always said that difference was the key ta their enchantment, and it was a wonder for a man ta behold."

Car's voice flowed like warm caramel, moving smoothly into the cool night air. Peter was always charmed by his turn of phrase, but tonight the lilt of his accent and the cadence of his delivery were mesmerizing. For the first time, he was struck by the finesse of the boy's oration. Peter eyed him with new appreciation. Car met his look with a hint of mirth in the lift of his brows. He shifted his gaze to the road and continued.

"Now, it's wicked rare, but should a man lock eyes with a sea maiden in her first hour ashore, while she still holds, close ta her heart, all her secrets a the sea … should their eyes meet in that special hour, why she'll grace him with a look so gentle and yet so penetratin', it's as if she found her home in the depths of his eyes." Car's quiet tone held absolute authority. "And if he's the will within him ta hold her gaze, legend has it he'll see a bit of himself in her eyes. Not a reflection, mind ya, but a part of him he didn't even know was his. And he understands it's safe there, that bit of himself … he's always safe inside her."

He paused, adjusting the reins. "Once they lock eyes, it seals a connection which man and maiden forever share. They say the experience changes a man. Though never havin' been graced with the look m'self, I couldn't tell ya how."

Peter swallowed with difficulty. He and Joanna shared such a moment the night they met. The night William nearly drowned. They had locked eyes as he looked for a pulse, before she revived him. A chill ran the length of his spine, and he shifted in his seat.

"So the lovely creature swims ashore and sheds somethin' of herself—skin or hood, depends on who's tellin' the story—and, upon the shedding of it, she takes on a human form, that of a beautiful woman with skin so milky smooth it calls ta mind the finest pearl. Legend holds that the man who finds her collects her sea skin and takes her inland." He paused in his narrative and Peter waited, thoroughly caught up in the tale.

"Now, in every story the man hides her skin, which prevents the maiden from returnin' ta sea. So, bound ta the land, she gives in without much fuss, because they do like the land, ya know." Car nodded, emphasizing his assertion.

"So she marries the fella, bears his children, keeps his house, brings him joy and finds plenty for herself in the bargain. But by and by, and always quite by accident, the creature eventually finds her skin, and she knows full well it'll take her back ta sea. After mullin' it over, she takes her skin and goes ta the water's edge, fightin' with herself every step of the way, wonderin' should she stay or should she go." Car stopped speaking. The steady clop of the horses seemed to hold the conclusion within the rhythm of their hooves.

Peter cast an eye to Car. "What does she do?"

"She goes, Doc," he said sadly. "She always goes."

Peter bowed his head, the loss cutting him more than he had expected.

"But, it's not all sadness, Doc. The man lives on, happier for havin' met her, for knowin' she keeps that bit of him safe, and for the memory of her in the faces of his children."

Peter nodded toward the back of the carriage. "So, you think our friend is a sea creature? A merrow, you said?"

Car was quiet for a time. "Nah," he answered with conviction. "Selkie. With her short hair, she's most likely a selkie." His accompanying wink left them both laughing.

"I gotta say though. She did come from the water, and she is a bit different, and y've yet ta find a relative on dry land. It calls ta mind the legend, is all."

Peter gave him a pat on the back. "It's an intriguing story, and from your perspective I suppose it does recall the legend. From mine, it simply means I haven't looked hard enough. She has family somewhere, Car. I just have to keep searching for them."

They reached Chapman Lane and in short order William was in Mrs. Milford's arms and on his way to bed. Extracting Joanna was a slightly more cumbersome task, but with Car inside the carriage pulling her to her feet, and Peter standing below ready to take her, they managed well enough. She opened her eyes and relaxed into the curve of his shoulder as Peter walked across the lawn.

"Mmm … we're home?"

"Home and nearly to bed."

"S'nice."

He entered the house, mounted the steps, and reached the top just as Mrs. Milford stepped from William's room. She stiffened considerably at the sight of him.

"I'll see her to bed, Dr. Hastings."

The chill in her tone set him on edge. Mrs. Milford clearly disliked Joanna. He thought it best to keep them apart until he could speak to her privately.

"There's no need for that," he said.

She stepped forward. "You must be tired. Go on about your business. I'll see to her."

At that moment Joanna's eyes fluttered open. One look at Mrs. Milford and she buried her head deeper into Peter's shoulder. He felt the tension in her movement and opened her door.

"And I said there's no need." His tone was firm. "If you wish to be helpful, please set the brandy out by the fire in the parlor. I'll be down shortly. Good night, Mrs. Milford."

Once inside the room he set Joanna down and helped her out of her coat. He retrieved the bed jacket from the armoire and returned to the bed. She lay crumpled against the pillows watching him through heavy-lidded eyes.

"Lean forward so I can unbutton your blouse. I want to check your ribs."

Joanna complied, dropping her forehead onto his chest. Peter pulled one arm from the sleeve of the blouse then slipped it into the sleeve of the bed jacket. He repeated the process on the other side. Joanna began fumbling with the buttons of her skirt. With Peter's help she removed it, but remained in her running tights. Holding her steady, he pulled back the covers and helped her into bed. She lay on her side, eyes closed, left arm behind her head, affording him better visibility of her bruises. His fingers moved carefully along her rib cage. Judging by her reaction, the rib was still tender, but she seemed to be healing well.

"Hey, Peter?" Joanna murmured.

"Yes?"

"Thank you." Her voice was so faint he thought she'd spoken in her sleep, but as he lowered the bed jacket she spoke again. "I haven't had a day that nice in a very long time."

"You're most welcome," he said quietly, slipping the covers up over her shoulder. He was just about to stand when she spoke again, her voice small and thick with fatigue.

"Peter?"

He inclined his head.

"Yes, Joanna."

"What's a merrow?"

He looked down. Her sweet face was unlined and peaceful, her fair skin touched blue by the moonlight. On impulse, he passed his hand through her hair. Leaning forward, he kissed her on the temple, his hand at home in the feathers of her hair, his breath soft upon her ear.

"You are," he whispered.

Chapter Thirty-five
Genealogy and Generosity

October 28, 1893

Eugene Prendergast left Matins after the final hymn. His shift began promptly at six, and he was a punctual man.

He would have applied the same principle to his job as General Counsel, but even after giving one last opportunity to that foul liar of a so-called Mayor, he still had no word of his appointment. Well, tonight the mayor's silence would be answered. After tonight Carter Harrison would be Mayor no more!

Clutching his bible, Prendergast headed for the warehouse, the ribbon marker imbedded in Psalms. The passage played on his memory as Harrison's false promise played on his anger. "Thou lovest evil more than good; and lying rather than to speak righteousness."

Mayor Carter Harrison was an evil liar.

And Eugene Prendergast was a righteous man.

And this wrong would be righted.

Tonight.

"Shall we begin?"

Pen in hand, Peter sat at the parlor desk, and Joanna faced him from the loveseat. Over lunch he outlined Richard's idea for locating her ancestors. He hoped to uncover an immediate family member whose physical presence might snap her back to the present. She seemed intrigued by the idea, even willing to accommodate his request, though she confessed a spotty command of her family history.

"All right." Peter picked up his quill pen. "What is your mother's full name and date of birth?"

"Susan Brown Lawrence. She was born on May 15th, 1945."

"And your father?"

"Theodore Michael Lawrence, born on November 9th, 1939."

"Do they reside in Chicago?"

"No. After my dad retired, they moved out to Arlington Heights."

"Do you remember their original address?" Peter wrote at a steady pace as she answered. "Now, can you give me the names of your grandparents?"

She nodded. "My maternal grandparents are Rebecca and Daniel Brown."

"Do you know where they lived? Are they still living?"

"They had a house on Fairfield, and both died when I was young. Grandpa Dan died in 1970. Beck died when I was thirteen, in 1976."

"You called your grandmother Beck?"

"She insisted. She never wanted to be pigeon-holed by a title. She once told me her involvement in my arrival was minimal, so she didn't feel she'd earned the distinction."

Peter cleared his throat, fighting an urge to reprimand her. "Well, then. Any idea when they were born?"

"Not exactly."

"Age at death?"

"Grandpa Dan was older, seventy or more, but Beck was only in her late fifties, so she was probably born around 1920. Everyone said she lived life to the hilt."

Peter cupped his fingers, ready to hear more. They were getting closer to a current date. "So, this … Beck. Can you tell me anything about her parents?"

"Her maiden name was Hepburn. Rebecca Hepburn. And Grandpa's name was Brown. Daniel Brown."

"Yes, but her parents—your great-grandparents—can you tell me anything about them?"

Joanna shrugged. "I don't know the name of Beck's mother, but I'm pretty sure her dad was named Bill, Bill Hepburn. Mom planned to name me after him had I been a boy. He died when I was a baby." She gave Peter a helpless look. "I know nothing about Grandpa Dan's family. They died before he and Beck even married."

Peter frowned. "Joanna, you are not at all well-versed in your family history."

She shrugged. "We just never talked about it."

Rather than let frustration get the better of him, Peter changed course. "All right. Let's review your paternal history."

"My father's side is even sketchier than my mother's. My dad seldom spoke of his family. I do know they lived near Douglas Park and that they were pretty poor. Well, everyone was poor in the Depression."

"The Depression?"

"Yeah, the Great Depression." She gave him a guarded look. "Do you want to hear about it?"

Peter nodded, pen in hand.

"In 1929 the stock market collapsed. Banks failed. Businesses closed right and left. Jobs were scarce. Everybody suffered. It was a devastating time in America."

Peter set down the pen and crossed his arms, regarding her with interest. She had her dates mixed up, and he'd never heard it referred to as the Great Depression, but she was actually talking about current events. An encouraging sign, he thought.

In the spring of 1893 the stock market *had* collapsed. Three railroad companies failed, and the outlook for others was bleak. Several hundred banks went under, and much of the country struggled as a result. The impact to Chicago had been minor thus far, largely due to the Columbian Exposition. As the industrial center of the nation, jobs were always more plentiful here. Perhaps Joanna wasn't really from Chicago, but from a place hit harder by the financial panic. He thought about her encounter with Scott Joplin.

"Interesting," he mused. "Did they ever live outside Chicago? Perhaps St. Louis?"

She shook her head. "No. I'm pretty sure they were born here."

"Hmm ...." Peter picked up the pen unsure of his next question. This wasn't going as well as he had hoped. They were still at least a generation away from finding a living relative. Was she really so ignorant of her heritage? Or did the fear of confronting whatever led her to the lake effectively block her memory? He decided to try a different angle.

"Tell me, did you ever visit the homes of your grandparents?"

"Sure. I spent a lot of time at Beck's house on Fairfield. Grandfather Lawrence lived on Washington, 36-something Washington Boulevard. I've never been there.

"Well, perhaps one of your grandparents inherited their home. Maybe we can find a great-grandparent by accident. I'll make inquiries and with luck we'll locate a relative." Having street addresses, even partials, boosted Peter's morale. They would visit them on Monday.

"Now, let's review Martin's family history."

Unfortunately this proved to be a much tougher exercise. Joanna claimed Martin's ancestors left Chicago for Milwaukee long before his parents were born. She knew none of his distant relatives, only the names of his parents. Peter took them down hoping they might be found in town. He intended to search for a match to every name she provided. He felt confident this endeavor would bear some sort of fruit. It was nearly two when he suggested they stop.

"I promised Elizabeth we would come early so I can discuss guardianship with her father. If I intend to do so, we should go upstairs and make ourselves ready."

Joanna gasped and raked her fingers through her hair. "Oh man! I never went back to Marshall Field's. You said tonight would be formal." She gave him a desperate look. "Peter, this sounds cliché, but I don't have a thing to wear."

"Hmm, I suppose we forgot about that over the course of the week." Peter leaned back in his chair, considering the matter. "Perhaps a nicer blouse with one of the darker skirts won't be so bad."

"So bad?" The strain in her voice pushed the word higher. "Peter, we've never been to a formal event together, and I already tend to stick out. I don't want to ruin this evening for you."

"Nonsense. You won't ruin anything. Tell you what. You go upstairs and put on the best combination you can find, and I will remain in my day coat. That way our clothes will complement each other."

Her expression lacked any trace of confidence.

"Oh come now, Joanna. Similarly attired, we will attract no notice. Besides, everyone will be so taken by your charm they won't give a thought to your clothing. Elizabeth already adores you. Please, don't give it another thought. Everything's going to be fine."

One hand clutching the collar of her blouse, she stood. "If you say so."

Joey left the room dreading the night ahead. For Elizabeth's sake, as well as Peter's, she wanted to make a good impression. She knew she was bound to say something wrong tonight, but she felt sure she could, at the very least, blend in visually. Now even that was cast into doubt.

She entered the bedroom, head down, and sat on the bed nearly crushing a box perched upon the quilt. It was the size of a small suitcase and neatly tied with a thick black velvet ribbon. Curious, she untied the ribbon, lifted the lid and let out a cry. Wrapped in a layer of muslin gauze she found a stunning evening dress.

It was a subtle design; delicate black lace covered a white satin bodice, creating a graceful, smoky appearance. It was breathtaking, perfect for tonight. Taking great care, she lifted it from the box. Lace met solid black satin at the ribs and hips, which finished out the remainder of the dress. The smoky lace ran in an hourglass shape from the décolleté down the center of the gown. White cap sleeves, accented with delicate black beadwork, adorned the shoulders. It was a perfect choice for a formal evening. As she moved toward the armoire mirror a piece of paper fell to the floor. She laid the dress on the bed and retrieved the note.

Dear Joanna,

I knew you would eventually worry about attire for this evening, so I took the liberty of checking Victoria's trunks and discovered this dress. She purchased it long ago, but never found a reason to wear it. I am certain she would consider a party in the home of her best friend the perfect occasion.

Peter.

Joey sank onto the bed, still holding the note. Several thoughts raced through her head, all fighting for recognition.

She'd come to expect the unexpected from Peter, but this! He had taken the time and trouble to search through his wife's things just to help her. It must have been a painful experience.

In her mind it was absolute chivalry. Joey was touched, even relieved, but, if she was being honest with herself, she was a little freaked out.

Years earlier, just after they began dating, Martin had asked Joey to attend a hospital fundraiser, her first truly adult formal event. She agreed to go, but voiced her concerns about fitting in. Martin laughed and said he knew just the thing to calm her nerves. When she asked him to elaborate he only grinned. 'Call me when you get home,' he told her. 'Then we'll talk.'

After work she found a package on her doorstep, a box from Marshall Fields. In an eerily similar move, Martin had anticipated her needs and bought a dress for her.

Joey let out a slow breath. It wasn't just similar, it was uncanny. The incident revived her thoughts on reincarnation. Few men would do such a thing for a woman. She knew two of them.

Or was it just one?

Could Peter really be an earlier incarnation of Martin? Did she land back here to help him in a way that spared his life in her own time? No, she'd rejected the idea earlier this week. Besides, they were such different men. Peter was only comfortable in an ordered world; Martin was at home in every situation. Peter enjoyed passive pursuits; Martin was physically active. But both men were kind-hearted and had a strong sense of philanthropy, both men fathered sons, and both of them had—oddly enough—assured she was properly attired for an important event.

A knock on the door interrupted her thoughts.

"Might I come in?" The lyrical voice was welcome and familiar.

Joey grinned and opened the door. "Were you in on this?"

Molly Hannafee offered her a warm smile. "The dress was his idea, an' I wanted ta help as a thank-you for ...." Her hand drifted to the back of her head. "An' he wasn't sure about the fit, so I brought this." She held up a sewing basket. "D'ya need a hand, then?"

"And how!" Joey laughed, pulling her into the room.

The dress proved large in a few places, but thanks to Molly's deft needlework, a little pin tucking at the back of the shoulders, a tiny seam along the buttons down the back and it fit perfectly. Molly took an appraising step back, directed Joey to turn around, and nodded once.

"There. It's a grand dress, an' y've the look of an angel."

Joey blushed. "How can I ever thank you? Molly, you saved me."

"Well, we're even," Molly said, grinning, "so there's no need. Tonight will be brilliant, of that I'm sure. Now, I'd best be on m'way. Enjoy yourself."

After Molly departed, Joey made her way downstairs and slipped into the powder room to brush her hair. Staring into the small mirror, she lamented her lack of jewelry. Still, the reflection verified the gown as a masterpiece needing no accompaniment. She left the room feeling self-conscious, but abandoned the thought once she entered the parlor.

Peter stood beside the fireplace handsomely dressed in a black tuxedo with a stark white shirt and a white bow tie.

"Ah," he said casually. "I see you found something suitable after all." His attempt to hide a self-satisfied smile failed completely.

Joey laughed as he walked across the room.

Peter bowed low and offered her his arm. "Shall we?"

Chapter Thirty-six
Guess Who's Coming to Dinner

"So, what can you tell me about Elizabeth's father?" Joey asked, enjoying the charm of the affluent neighborhoods they traversed.

Peter held the reins steady. "Langston McNair is an extremely successful man, yet to this day he considers himself a laborer. He began his career cleaning slaughtering stalls. Eventually he began buying small stockyards at every opportunity. He met with good fortune and ventured into grain speculation. He once told me retirement would be the death of him."

"He sounds like one of Chicago's founding fathers."

Peter thought for a moment, nodding. "His influence pales next to Potter Palmer, but he's certainly left his mark on the city."

"Well, he's no slouch if this neighborhood is any indicator. These homes are gorgeous."

"They're mere cottages compared to the mansions on Prairie Avenue. Ah, here we are."

They stopped before the largest house on the street. Three stories of regal grey stone were rendered castle-like by turreted corners, and the arched entrance promised elegance within. Peter knocked on the door, which was opened by a servant.

They passed through a vestibule that echoed the entrance, its mahogany panels curving overhead. Joey drew a quick breath as she entered the expansive hall. Tiny black diamond tiles flashed ermine-like on a white marble floor. Centered across the room was a regal mahogany staircase, softened by a plush, moss-hued carpet. The staircase rose to a picture-windowed landing that split in two directions, promising access to the finest respite money could buy.

Joey squeezed Peter's arm, fingered her dress, and whispered her gratitude.

"Peter! Joanna! Welcome." Elizabeth floated down the regal staircase.

A distinct southern accent sounded through a closed door. "An early arrival? I'll be right out."

Peter and Joey removed their coats and hats. Holcroft, the McNair's butler, accepted them in professional silence.

"Thank you for coming early," Elizabeth whispered to Peter. "My goodness!" She turned to Joey, hands framing her cheeks. "I was with Victoria when she bought this dress. It's suits you well." Joey's response was overtaken by a genteel southern drawl.

"Ah, Doctor Hastings."

Langston McNair appeared from a doorway on one side of the great hall. He was a portly man with thinning grey hair and he moved slowly. Joey thought he might benefit from a cane, but given the pride in his steel blue eyes she guessed he would never allow himself to depend on one. He wore a black tie and tails, and he looked uncomfortable.

"My, my. His gaze lingered on Joey. "Who is this lovely young lady?"

"Father, this is Joanna Fagan, Peter's cousin. I mentioned she's visiting from California. Joanna, my father, Langston McNair."

"Indeed. So you did, so you did." McNair extended his hand. "Pleased to make your acquaintance, Miss Fagan. Indeed I am."

"The pleasure is mine, Mr. McNair."

"Please," he buried her hand in both of his. "Let me show you to the parlor."

Elizabeth moved with precision. Adopting a bright tone she tugged on Joey's free arm. "Papa, please. I need Joanna's help in selecting a gown." She let out a tired sigh, shaking her blonde curls. "I'm in a fret over the decision, and I'll never manage discourse tonight in such a state."

Joey smiled at Elizabeth and followed her lead. "Gentlemen, if you'll excuse me." She slipped her arm from Mr. McNair's. "Let me help Elizabeth get ready. We'll be downstairs in no time."

McNair cast Peter a knowing glance and turned to indulge his daughter. "We must, by all means, avoid a dither. Please, set yourself to rights."

The women shared a conspiratorial smile as they ascended the stairs. "You saved me, Joanna." Elizabeth cooed. "I have two lovely gowns and I'm just not sure which one ...."

Joey caught sight of McNair as they turned at the landing. Genuine admiration marked his slack-jawed expression.

"Hmm, lovely young ...." He shook himself and reached for Peter. "Well then. Join me in my study, won't you?"

Upstairs, Elizabeth wasted no time, changing into a dark blue velvet gown that boasted a set of immense round sleeves. Draped in cream-colored silk, they floated like balloons above her shoulders. Additional silk accented the dress, dropping from the waist in a triangular pattern. When she moved, the cream revealed itself modestly amid the dark blue folds. Elizabeth embodied feminine grace, but the gown lent her an air of delicacy Joey hadn't noticed before.

"Wow, Elizabeth. You look regal, but fragile."

"Perfect." Bright blue eyes invited Joey into her gentle collusion. "Delicate, fragile. Tonight I must seem like someone in need of guardianship." Elizabeth raised a wrist to her forehead, and spoke with mock distress. "Someone to be protected at all costs."

Joey laughed. "There aren't many girls like you in California. So, who's coming to dinner?"

"I planned a surprise reunion for Peter. Charles Sullivan, his father-in-law lives next door. He'll come with Richard, and Charles Jr. will bring his wife, Martha. Have you ever met Victoria's family?"

Joey shook her head. "Never had the pleasure."

"You're in for a wonderful evening." Elizabeth studied her reflection in a full-length mirror. "They're an affable family, physicians to a man, though Richard specialized in neurology or … what do they call it now? Psychiatry?"

Joey stifled a gasp. *Psychiatry?* Could Richard be the colleague Peter spoke to on Thursday? He must be. How much had Peter told him? Suddenly the evening ahead had the makings of a chess match. "Well," she managed a casual tone. "I guess they have all the bases covered."

"Bases covered?" Elizabeth looked puzzled.

Joey forced a smile. "I just meant the Sullivans are active in all areas of medicine."

"Mm hmm." Elizabeth swayed back and forth, testing the gown. "So it seems." She smoothed the bodice one last time. "Shall we go down?"

"Now," Elizabeth said as they descended the stairs, "Richard, the eldest, is such a card. He lives for his work, he loves to laugh and he's still a bachelor."

Her voice dropped to a whisper. "I suppose I should take a lesson from him."

Joey grinned. "Oh, I'd say you're doing just fine on your own."

"Charles Jr. married right after medical school. He and Martha have three girls, each one a darling beauty. I haven't seen them since Victoria died." She sighed. "They were my dress up dolls. Sweet, simple Martha. She is strict, but she did let me indulge her daughters."

"What's she like?"

Elizabeth laughed. "Nothing like me, that much is certain. Martha belongs to the Women's Christian Temperance Union. She has absolutely no interest in social events." Elizabeth paused and they entered a large parlor. "She's quiet, like Peter, but the Sullivan family has a way of lightening one's view, and I think both she and Peter are more jovial as a result. Martha and I are not close, but we are comfortable with our differences." Fresh voices sounded in the great hall and Elizabeth smiled.

"They're here."

Oh God, here we go.

Joey smoothed her gown as Holcroft announced the arrival of Charles and Richard Sullivan.

With his sparkling blue eyes, snow-white hair and an intricately lined face, Charles Sullivan reminded Joey of Mark Twain. His measured movement suggested advanced age, but she soon learned he was quick-witted and courteous.

"Ah! The McNair garden is in full bloom tonight," he said, entering the room.

Elizabeth greeted him with open arms.

"Charles! You're looking well." She gestured to Joey. "I'd like you to meet Miss Joanna Fagan. She is a distant cousin of Peter's, visiting from San Francisco."

"Why, then you're family. Miss Fagan, through the bonds of our Peter I shall consider you one of my own." He bowed slightly, one hand on his heart.

The warmth of his greeting eased her fear. Joey extended her hand and offered a bright smile. "Pleased to meet you." Dr. Sullivan raised her hand to his lips. The gesture colored her cheeks and she managed an awkward bob, hoping it was an acceptable response.

"Cousin?"

Despite its light tone, the newcomer's voice sounded ominous. Joey's heart raced and suddenly there wasn't time to dwell on decorum. She looked past Charles to the parlor entrance.

"Well, this *is* a surprise." The younger Sullivan stepped up beside his father. Richard took after him. His hair was a lustrous silver that would surely advance to snow, given time. His voice was light and even tempered, and his devilish blue eyes hinted at mischief. Joey knew she should be on her guard, but he exuded such playful joy that she returned the smile despite her concern. Richard grinned and clapped his hands.

"So you're Peter's *cousin*." He extended his hand, emphasizing the last word.

His emphatic greeting convinced Joey that Richard must be the psychiatrist Peter had consulted. She decided the best course of action was to be as honest as possible. She accepted his hand—and the unspoken challenge—with a firm shake.

"When did you arrive, my dear?" Richard asked. "Will you be with us long?"

"The length of my stay is indefinite," Joey countered steadily. "I arrived on Saturday."

Richard raised his brows and flashed a Cheshire grin. Joey wished she had asked Peter more about his exchange with this man. Unsure what to say, she maintained her grip and her smile.

Richard glanced at her hand. "My dear girl, you are far too slight to be considered rough and tumble, but judging by your grasp I'd guess you have a surprising right cross."

Her hand slackened and heat flushed her cheeks, but Joey took the blow without expression.

So he knew about the fight.

"She does," Elizabeth said, "but when she fights she uses far more than her fists. She came to the aid of a girl on Monday, stopping an attack with some well-placed kicks."

"Oh, Elizabeth." Joey waved a dismissive hand. "Now is hardly the time—"

"Au contraire!" Richard interjected, eyes on his hostess. "Now is the perfect time."

Elizabeth accepted his proffered arm and led him away. Adopting what Joey had come to think of as her Sunday voice, Elizabeth began. "We were shopping at Marshalls when Peter's sweet, unassuming little cousin saw a friend of hers ...."

The senior Dr. Sullivan stepped forward and escorted her to the opposite end of the parlor. "Pay him no mind, my dear, he is an insufferable gossip. He lives for intrigue. Come, do you play? I should love to hear some music this evening."

The innocent question only heightened Joey's anxiety. She'd studied piano, but that was eons ago, and the only credible piece she could remember was the old standard, Heart and Soul. She gave Charles Sr. a nervous smile.

"I haven't played in years, but I know one piece you might like."

His gentle smile put her at ease. "One, my dear, is far better than none." They sat together at a mahogany grand piano. "Please, regale me."

After a few stumbles, the song came back to her and she managed to recapture its easy repetition. The old gentleman seemed to enjoy it, nodding in time with the music, smiling as he did so.

"Well, well. What a lively little piece! You're a fine player, my dear."

The corners of her mouth rose and Joey began to relax. If she could stay close to this guy, maybe the evening wouldn't be so difficult.

"There, now. You have a lovely smile." Sullivan patted her arm. "You should smile more often. When you look troubled, you call to mind your cousin." He turned his head toward a nearby window. "Best to avoid unhappy thoughts. Life affords you many. The trick is to find a way past them."

"Good advice," Joey said, thinking of Martin, "but not always so easy to follow." Elizabeth and Richard joined them at the piano.

"Say!" Richard beamed. "That's a cheerful bit of music. What is it?"

By this time, Joey felt like she owned the tune. She smiled at her audience, easily maintaining the rhythm. "Heart and Soul, by Hoagy Carmichael."

Richard's brow furrowed, his eyes darted skyward. "Carmichael ... I don't recognize the name."

"Oh." Joey flashed on her scant knowledge of the composer. Beck had always liked Carmichael, which meant he probably wasn't even born yet. She began backpedaling. "He's, um ... he's young, and ... just making a name for himself in California."

"Well, he's delightful."

Joey dropped her head in newfound concentration. She repeated the phrase, slowing her pace to end the song. "So." She raised her hands from the keys. "Who's next?"

"Elizabeth, you play exquisitely," Richard said. "Would you be so kind? Father loves Beethoven, and I am anxious to spend time with our prize fighter."

Joey's nervous hand relaxed under the gentle touch of the elder Sullivan. "Steady, dear girl. I am of the opinion that Richard chose his vocation to live vicariously through others. He's just an observer, he means no harm."

Grinning broadly, Richard offered her his arm, and Joey rose from the bench bracing herself for what was to come.

Chapter Thirty-seven
A Subtle Chess Match

Peter mentioned a houseguest, but didn't say it was his cousin." Richard failed to keep the excitement from his voice as they settled onto a plush sofa.

Joey decided to go with a bold opening. "Well, no doubt he told you I'm nuts."

The younger Sullivan cast her a genial smile. "No, he told me nothing of you, my dear. He came around seeking advice on an interesting case. A man who … well, I won't go into detail, but he struggled with his revelation, particularly in light of the Judas incident."

"The Judas incident?"

His words were unexpected, as was the gender reference. Joey asked for details, hoping to keep Richard's focus elsewhere.

"You mean he told you nothing of our day together? Oh, it was most exciting …."

Richard was an animated speaker and despite her fears, Joey was taken by his charm. He leaned forward as he spoke, gesticulating throughout the tale. Without warning, his voice dropped dramatically.

"Then the prophet identified Peter as Judas, and things took an incredible turn ...." At length he finished, applauding Peter's resolve through the ordeal.

"Wow," Joey said. "The guy is such a rock."

"A rock? How so?"

"Oh. You know, he's solid, like the um ... the Rock of Gibraltar." She looked carefully at Richard, hoping her words did nothing to confirm any theories he might be forming. "He's just out there in the elements, taking everything nature throws his way. Not one complaint." She trailed off. "I certainly don't have that kind of strength."

Wincing at her last statement, she averted her eyes. If ever there was a lead-in for a shrink that was it. She'd virtually handed it to him on a platter.

Here, take my bishop. He'll match the pawns you already snagged. Way to go, psycho.

Richard surprised her with his answer.

"Nor do I, and I'm glad of it. A rigid approach to life can settle in the bones and impede movement." His grin returned. "I enjoy a much more fluid existence."

She stared at him, puzzled. "Are you saying you're a coward?"

His hearty laughter carried across the room. "Your candor is beguiling, Miss Fagan. I don't quite know what to think of you."

"I didn't mean to offend you, Dr. Sullivan. You're an eloquent speaker." She shrugged. "I just had trouble equating your statement to mine." She paused, summoning the courage to meet his gaze. "I meant to say that *I'm* a coward. You don't strike me as lacking courage."

"Well," he said, "you heard my father; he thinks I'm no more than an observer. But you? A coward? You? Who bested a man with little more than a new pair of shoes? It takes the heart of a lion to manage such a feat."

"Well, it was purely reactionary," she said. "I've never intervened in something like that before, but the sight of a man breaking a bottle over a girl's head …." Her hands curled into fists. "I couldn't just stand there. I had to at least try to help her." She gave Richard a feeble grin. "I suspect that's what drove Peter to visit you on Thursday. I think the whole thing made him extremely uncomfortable."

Richard Sullivan regarded her in silence. Now he understood Peter's insistence on anonymity, but if Joanna was really Peter's time traveler—*well, the whole story was just a great feast, wasn't it?* It smelled of good drama and from his perspective it was simply too savory to leave untouched. He proceeded in a way that might placate his appetite but preserve the standard of his profession.

"No, no. Not at all. As I said, he did come to discuss a baffling case. I'm not at liberty to divulge the details, but you do know neurology is not his primary field of study. He merely wanted advice on treatment for his patient."

To his surprise, Joanna fed him a bite of the very meal he craved.

"You mean his time-traveler?"

Richard beamed and leaned closer. "You're aware of him?"

She shrugged. "Well, he's right there, so it's kind of hard to avoid him … and he certainly frustrates Peter, though I don't think he means to."

"Then you have acquaintance with the fellow? How exciting!" Richard's eyes sparkled at her admission. "Oh, I would love to spend time with him. Imagine, traveling through time! What a fantastic delusion! He must have some amazing stories."

Joanna's voice rose. "Oh. He's … he's colorful, all right."

"What about you, my dear?" Richard knew he shouldn't press, but the steak was on the table and he couldn't resist putting his professional knife to work. "What do *you* think of him?"

She took a breath of obvious hesitation. "Honestly, I think he's just a nice guy who lost his way." She crossed her arms as if protecting herself. "Peter's been sweet to put up with him, and he's very grateful."

Richard decided to risk one more cut. "Do you think he poses a threat to the household?"

"Oh, no!" Joanna shook her head. "He wouldn't hurt a soul. He really likes Car and William." She swallowed. "And he does his best with Mrs. Milford."

Richard laughed. "As do we all, my dear, but tell me this," he took a firm hold of her hand. "Do *you* think he's crazy?"

Joey straightened her back, eyeing a bust of Mr. McNair on a table in the center of the room. It was a tight match, and it was clear to her that they both knew exactly who they were discussing. She was sure her next answer would be given more consideration than anything else she'd already said. She braved a look at Richard.

"That's a tough question," She said, passing a free hand through her hair. "I can understand how others might think so. His story seems far-fetched, but—" She thought of Michael, of Martin, and her parents. "He just wants to go home, and he doesn't know how to get there." She forced herself to maintain eye contact. "So, I guess he seems … mildly crazy."

Joey knew she was playing with fire, but she risked the flame anyway. "Given what you've heard about him, what is your diagnosis, Dr. Sullivan?"

"Ah." Richard's eyes were alight with understanding. "Well, having never met the man," he said, flashing a warm smile, "it would be hard to make a professional assessment. But hearing you and Peter speak of him as you do, I would say …."

Joey held her breath.

"… I am inclined to agree with you. He sounds only … mildly crazy."

She did her best to exhale casually.

Richard held her gaze, but his expression showed no sign of judgment. "Yes," he chuckled, "I suppose it's as fit a description as any, and who among us doesn't go a little crazy when logic, as we know it, fails us?"

For the first time since meeting him, Joey felt she was on safe ground. Her shoulders dropped and her smile spread. The match was a draw. There was nothing more to say—or so she thought.

"And," Richard continued, "I think he and Peter can help each other."

"I don't understand."

"Miss Fagan, I'm of the opinion that Peter spent much of the last year trying to come to terms with something that evades resolution, though he's never raised the subject with me. Grappling with his time-traveler has freed his mind from that battle." Richard smiled. "Peter is a very determined man. I believe he'll see the fellow home, and his success may soften the edge of what he believes is his biggest failure."

Joey understood the reference to Victoria's death, but replied in a neutral tone.

"If you say so."

"Oh I do. After all, it takes only water to smooth a rock, and Peter—your rock—has been wandering the desert for quite some time. I think this case laps at him as Lake Michigan laps at our shore. It has the potential to soothe old scars." Richard's voice softened, revealing a surprising note of concern. "In so occupying him, this case might wear away the rigidity I mentioned and ease his mind. If Peter can resolve a problem as complex as time travel, then perhaps the other issues plaguing him will lose their significance. It would be a welcome change from my perspective." He raised his brows. "Are you all right, my dear?"

Joey worked to close her mouth. "I'm fine. It's just ... touching. You care a great deal for your brother-in-law, don't you?"

"I do, Miss Fagan. Very much."

She was about to advise him to use her first name when Peter and Langston McNair entered the parlor. Peter stiffened considerably when he spied them sitting together. Richard flashed his signature grin and rubbed his hands together.

"Ah, but I do so love playing him." His eyes sparkled with merriment. "And in my orchestra, he is such an easily-plucked instrument."

"Peter!" Richard fairly shouted his greeting as he stood, grinning from ear to ear. "Look who I found!"

"Please," Joey whispered, "go easy on him. He had no clue you would be here tonight and he looks like he's about to have a heart attack."

"Oh, I will say nothing to cause him concern. Peter is such a thorough deliberator, he'll see to that himself. It is evident in his approach."

Peter darted across the room, concern overriding his normally stoic features. He reached the pair and put his arm around Joey. She smiled at his gallantry. Richard extended his hand and clapped Peter on the shoulder.

"It seems you have a full house these days—a houseguest *and* a visiting relative—Mrs. Milford must be at her wit's end."

Joey, her arm around his waist, gave him a reassuring squeeze. She felt him relax against her hand. Cautious cheer laced his reply.

"I think we may have tested her limits this week."

"As you should, my friend." Richard winked at Joey. "The woman leads far too rigid an existence, in my view."

Joey laughed. "This guy is a crack up. Does he know Car? I have a feeling they would get along very well together."

"Oh!" Richard beamed. "Car is one of my favorite people."

Before they could speak further, Holcroft announced the arrival of Dr. and Mrs. Charles Sullivan, Jr., and additional staff entered, bearing trays of champagne. The group rejoined at the center of the parlor, exchanging warm greetings as the party began in earnest.

Chapter Thirty-eight
The Third Time is not a Charm

If the dinner was a reunion for Peter, it was a revelation for Joey. She marveled at the depth of the conversation. The group discussed every topic with thoughtful articulation and listened with deference to opposing views. Even Martha, though quiet as Elizabeth had predicted, was firm in her opinion and deft in defending her point. She held her own in the Sullivan family. Once Peter recovered from his earlier shock, he relaxed. As dessert arrived and conversations split into smaller groups, Joey grew silent, enjoying the banter around her and the light in Peter's eyes.

Elizabeth had done him a tremendous favor tonight. He would never initiate an evening like this on his own. Hosting a dinner was too far outside his comfort zone, but reconnecting with family was exactly what he needed. He'd been stumbling alone since Victoria died. Yet everyone here would have walked with him, if asked.

Joey tried to imagine life with these people, all of them warm and accepting. It frightened her to consider it, but what if this journey was permanent? Would it be so bad, remaining here for the rest of her life? Maybe she didn't land here to stop an assassination, or to help any one person. She cast an eye toward Peter. Maybe she was here to enable broader change.

Despite his frustration with her modernity, her arrival had shaken Peter from his emotional stupor. Surely that counted for something. Joey tried to envision putting her 'modern notions' to work, joining the suffragists to fight for women's rights, or helping Peter with his charitable work. The certainty of any path evaded her.

Again, she considered the possibility that Peter might be Martin. It seemed off the mark somehow—maybe because of the differences between her era and his. But what if he really was Martin? Was she supposed to reunite with him? Embracing that thought was beyond her reach. Joey liked Peter immensely, probably more than she was willing to admit, and, Martin excepted, she was closer to him than any man she'd ever met. But was he really an earlier incarnation of Martin? Was that possible? She smiled to herself and shook her head.

You went back in time, idiot. Anything's possible.

Peter caught her smile and returned it with an almost imperceptible lift of chin and brow. Almost everything about him was familiar, welcoming and comfortable. As long as she remained here, Joey knew she could call his house her home. But was it really the right place for her? What about her own home?

What about Michael?

He'd already lost his father. Must he lose his mother as well? He would turn three tomorrow, and she would miss it. Granted, had she flown to Hawaii she would have missed it anyway. But to miss every birthday? Content though she might be at the moment, she couldn't bear the thought of Michael alone, even knowing her parents would raise him well. As long as she could still draw breath, she must keep searching for a way back. Suddenly, the pull was overwhelming.

It hurt—the thought of missing everything: playing tooth fairy, watching him enter kindergarten, listening to his voice crack and drop, or overhearing his first nervous phone call to some special girl. With every image the pull gained strength.

Michael.

He was her true family, her reason for being. She was put on this earth to love and raise him regardless of her present situation. Silently she berated herself for ever thinking otherwise. Somewhere out there was the door that led her back to him. In that instant, overwhelmed by her feelings for Michael, every fiber of her being—body and soul—ached to find it.

Had it only been a week since she landed here? It seemed like an eternity.

Joey was suddenly tired. Tired of the antiquated technology surrounding her, tired of pretending to embrace a life of feminine subservience she could never really accept, tired of adjusting her speech to fit the times. Again and again this week she had searched within herself, but found no solid reason for her presence here.

She cast another glance at Peter. It warmed her heart to see him so happy. In another situation, another time, she would love to explore this path with him and see where it led. Her feelings for him had grown considerably this week, but whatever he was—an incarnation of Martin, or the ghost of Christmas past—right now she didn't care. Dear as he had become to her, in this instant she knew in her heart that she wasn't meant for this life, his life. It was time to find a way home.

Home to Michael.

The need to be with her son took desperate hold of her. She shivered, terrified she would never return, never see Michael again. The looming certainty of the notion drained the color from her face. Suddenly there was nothing more important than touching him, bearing the weight of his little body as she scooped him into her arms and held him. She yearned to snuggle with him in the early morning and watch him awaken, or to curl up beside him and play dinosaurs in the long stretch of a lazy afternoon.

Then came another rush, a desire for so many other things. She wanted to sleep in her own bed, to wander the house in one of Martin's old shirts, lost in the fading scent of his cologne. She wanted to listen to her own stereo, to run the streets of her own bustling, *modern* Chicago. More than anything she wanted to stretch her limbs, find her stride and let the wind rush past her, to break free from the 19th Century bonds and revel in her own era. She longed to keep pace with her thoughts as she ran along the lake, challenging her ability, and finding joy in her movement. She shuddered at the idea of waiting until her next anniversary to do so.

Anniversary.

Martin's last word.

Her eyes darted to Peter.

I met Peter on our anniversary.

The connection slapped her hard, landing a solid blow to her contemplation. Joey drew a shocked breath, felt an intense chill and then immediate heat. Her head and her heart pounded in an erratic, unbalanced rhythm. She lowered her head and rubbed her temples.

Her anniversary. Did it open the portal to this era? She fell into the lake on the anniversary of the most significant event in her life. No wonder her first attempt had been futile! Tuesday held no personal significance for her, but last Saturday had been—

"As for Harrison, I've had my misgivings about him, but I'll concede he's done well by us regarding the Exposition. Couldn't ask for more from any other man. Earned his place at the Columbian table. Indeed, sir."

Jolted by the name that had haunted her all week, Joey stared at her Elizabeth's father. He gave her a challenging look.

"Please, don't tell me you're another fluttering advocate of our mayor. Are you, Miss Fagan?" McNair said.

She shook her head, uncomprehending. Her fingers lingered at her temple. "Carter Harrison?" she whispered.

Peter stared at Joey. She read concern in his gaze.

"Why yes, young lady, the very same! What the man lacks in ethics, he counters with charisma. Brighter women than you have succumbed to his charm. Indeed, they have!" He turned to Peter. "He intends to marry right here in the neighborhood, his third trip down the aisle, mind you."

"In the neighborhood?" Richard asked.

"Why yes, son! You've been away too long. He lives not two blocks from here, on Ashland Boulevard." McNair turned his attention to Joey.

"Young lady, are you all right?"

The news was a fresh slap to her senses. The mayor of Chicago was probably eating dinner less than a mile away, *and this was the last night of his life!* All other thoughts vanished.

What if her presence here had nothing to do with Peter after all? What if her sole purpose was to save Carter Harrison? Was she here to change the course of Chicago's history? Does fate work that way? Was she meant to play that big a part?

Only two blocks from here? It was too close. If preventing Harrison's murder was truly her purpose, then she had to act now. Feeling the weight of the next century on her shoulders, Joey crumpled in her chair and closed her eyes, hands still at her temples.

Peter leaned close to her. "Joanna, what is it? Your color is gone. "

She looked at him, quelling her sense of urgency, desperately hoping she remained pale. The clock chimed, announcing the half hour. Seven thirty. There couldn't be much time. Joey turned to her host.

"Mr. McNair, I'm so sorry to end this wonderful evening, but I suffer from migraine headaches and one has just begun," she paused, pressing her temples for emphasis. "Such a shame. You're a marvelous man. Elizabeth, dinner was excellent and I so enjoyed meeting everyone."

She wavered, eyes closed, trying to sell the headache, and then feigning great effort she spoke to her host.

"Peter has seen what transpires and I think it best if we go." Normally she would never be grateful for a migraine, but thank God Peter had already seen her suffer one. On his feet and standing behind her chair, he obviously believed her.

"Langston. Elizabeth. Please accept my apologies. It was such a pleasure to see all of you, and I'm so pleased you could meet a finer member of my family. We will speak well of this night for a long time, but, for my dear cousin's sake, it's best we make our way home. Come, Joanna," he said gently. "Let's get your things."

McNair stood. "Of course, man. Quite understood, quite understood." He moved around the table. "Sorry for your trouble, young lady. Terrible thing, just terrible." He gave Peter a knowing look as he offered Joey his arm. "Such a fragile little thing, but frailty has its charm. Indeed so."

Joey bid everyone good night and accepted McNair's arm, trying not to cringe at his last remark. He escorted her to the door, helped her into her coat and pressed her hat into her hands. Peter followed with Elizabeth and thanked her profusely. She smiled and extended her hand. He kissed it briefly, smiling in return.

Elizabeth embraced Joey. "Do let me know when you're feeling better. I need some company at Marshall's next week."

Joey offered her a weak assent as Peter gathered his coat and led her out the door. With great difficulty she forced herself to move slowly. *Was there enough time?* Would she be able to prevent the assassination? She thought it occurred close to eight o'clock.

As they neared the carriage Joey clutched her hat, steeled herself and faced Peter with a gravely determined expression. He registered mild confusion at her change in demeanor. Joey straightened her back looking for courage, but found only a small measure of height. It would have to do. She stepped away from him.

"Didn't we pass Ashland on our way here?" she asked, taking another step. "It's back there, isn't it?"

Peter, who had been busy with his overcoat, froze. His eyes narrowed and his voice rumbled. "Joanna, no! We will not discuss this again. I forbid—"

She took another step back. "Please, Peter ... we're not going to City Hall."

"That's enough!" he muttered. "I will not have you make a fool of yourself over this insane notion of yours!" As he looked back, searching for the sleeve of his overcoat, Joey seized her chance.

"Well," she said, voice shaking. "If you intend to stop me, you'll have to catch me."

Joey bolted.

Gathering her skirt as she picked up speed, she leaned into the cold night air, eyes open for Ashland Boulevard. The rush was intoxicating, but she had a job to do. She knew she had a decent start, but it was nowhere near her best effort. Her new shoes were cumbersome. Thank God she didn't buy the higher heel. *Could she reach Harrison in time?* Willing herself to perform, she shot forward in a fresh burst of energy. She heard Peter breathing hard behind her.

She crossed Wood Street, abandoned the sidewalk and headed for the middle of the road which was better lit and easier to traverse. She knew he wouldn't call after her—that would draw too much attention, the last thing Peter wanted. He was as tall as Martin, but unaccustomed to running and his pace was uneven. He was bound to gain some ground, but her confidence remained. She could outrun him. She *had* to!

Still, she hadn't run in a week, and her body protested. Her legs resisted because she hadn't stretched. Her rib pounded in anger at the deep breath she forced against it, and the cold night air scraped at the back of her throat. As she passed Paulina Street, Joey glanced back. Peter had gained ground, but she still held a slight advantage. She brushed aside her physical limitations and pressed on.

He called to her as she paused at Ashland, unsure which way to go. She ignored him. On the north side of the street were a few large, well-lit homes. Peter was close, and, judging by the sound of his voice, angry. She sprinted through the gates of the first house on the right, raced up the steps, and pounded on the door. A pudgy middle-aged man appeared just as Peter reached the edge of the property.

"Please, sir," she gasped, clutching her tender side. "I'm looking for Mayor Harrison's house. Do you know which—"

"Joanna- don't!" Peter panted, leaning against the railing below.

"Is something amiss here?" The bewildered man nodded to the bottom of the steps. "Are you with this gentleman?"

"Yes," she said, "I am with him, and nothing is amiss. We just need to speak to the Mayor." Eyes locked on Peter, she silently begged him to go along with her.

Peter looked from Joey to the man. With one frustrated exhale he nodded and began to climb the stairs. The man blinked, but said nothing. Just as Joey started to repeat her question a horrible, familiar crack cut through the night air. She jerked her head toward the sound, which shook the man from his stupor.

"There." He pointed at the home directly across the street. As they followed his gesture, two more shots rang out.

"Oh, dear God, no." Joey reached for Peter and everything seemed to happen at once.

Across the street, visible by the light on Harrison's front porch, Eugene Prendergast backed out the door, and then turned, gun in hand, still firing. Somewhere inside the house, a woman screamed.

"Get down!" Peter forced Joey to the ground before his words were out. He landed on top of her, shielding her, his face a flushed, contorted portrait of shock and comprehension.

Their unwitting host remained dumbstruck until a wave of horror passed across his features and he found his voice. "Good God, those were gunshots!" He stumbled down the stairs and hurried across the street.

Servants emerged from the house and ran after Prendergast. As the danger receded, Peter eased his grip. He stared hard at her, mouth ajar, eyes wide, as the magnitude of her prediction finally reached him.

"You ... knew."

Joey couldn't quite grasp his whispered acceptance.

"I tried to tell you." She struggled beneath him, trying to get up. "Maybe we—*you*—can still help him."

They rose together, supporting each other, and descended the steps. In what seemed like slow motion, they crossed the street and entered Harrison's house, lights ablaze in every room. The neighbor was there, kneeling beside the mayor, uselessly reassuring him. A woman held his head, crying, stroking his face. Joey staggered to a nearby wall as Peter moved swiftly into the room. He introduced himself as a physician, removed his coat and rolled up his sleeves.

The rest was a blur, a muted mix of muffled noise and ragged breath, voices urging the dying man to hold on. The scene was too familiar. Joey stopped listening; she'd heard this before. Martin's death came rushing back to her, draining her of all remaining energy. She slid down the wall and sat silently, waiting for Peter, for the end.

Joey lost track of time.

The house became strangely populated. At some point the police arrived. Once it was clear he could do nothing more for Harrison, Peter made his way back to her and spoke for both of them. He told the officer they had been out walking, heard gunshots and tried to be of assistance. The police didn't bother to question her. Her version of events was of no importance. It didn't matter. The mayor died, just as she'd always known he would.

They walked in silence back to the carriage and Peter helped her up onto the bench. He offered her the lap robe, but she didn't take it, as indifferent to its warmth as she was to the cold night air. He set the blanket between them and they made their way home without a word.

She barely noticed when they stopped moving. Car appeared and helped her down. She didn't hear his questions and only caught pieces of Peter's reply, something about her migraine. She left them, wandered upstairs, and collapsed across the bed, defeated.

Some time later, the door opened and she was offered a glass of water. She accepted it, but made no move to drink it. Eventually it was taken from her hand. She felt someone touch her foot, remove her shoes. A blanket covered her, but it held no warmth, no relief. Then Peter was beside her, stroking her hair, speaking softly. She barely heard him. His voice was muted, distant. His touch was faint. For Joey, there was nothing. A man was dead and she was stuck in 1893. There were no more ideas, no more possibilities. She was without hope.

Everything felt black. Eventually everything was....

Chapter Thirty-nine
Newton's Laws Applied

Hours later, when Joey finally stirred, the black had receded, replaced by the cold light of a half-moon standing watch over a clear night sky. She found little comfort in its glow, but felt a pleasant weight about her. It took a moment to understand that it was Peter, fast asleep and cradling her from behind.

She slipped out of the blanket and shifted slowly, conscious of the need to see him. Even asleep, he looked like a man reliving a nightmare. Waves of guilt washed over her. She may have saved William's life last Saturday, but Peter had saved hers every day since. Before she landed here she had been stuck, mired in the aftermath of Martin's violent end. Living here had forced her to take stock of what was most important—her son, and her own survival. But Peter was an important part of her life now, too. He, more than anyone, understood the depth of her loss, yet he carried on every day, despite his own grief. And he took her in without hesitation, offering her everything when she had nothing save the clothes on her back.

In return she gave him only fits of frustration. Given the paralyzing nature of her own loss, it was foolish to think she could help him overcome his. Instead, her presence had only made things worse for him. Touched by the depth of his kindness—and the enormity of her failure—Joey closed her eyes and sobbed, tears falling silent and warm on her skin.

"No."

Peter was awake, his rich, velvet voice offering a solace she didn't deserve.

"Joanna, please. Don't cry. You did everything you possibly could." He caught a tear with the tip of his thumb and brushed it aside.

She stared at him, tears flowing unchecked. He should have nothing left, but here he was, consoling her. Concern filled his tired eyes. She knew the price this night exacted from him. Her vain attempt became his medical emergency. He shepherded Carter Harrison to his end, and now he summoned his reserves to comfort her. The magnitude of his generosity brought a fresh round of tears. He pulled her closer.

"Please, Joanna. The mayor's death ... I should have trusted you. I shoulder the blame for his end."

No.

Peter had staggered under the weight of unnecessary blame ever since Victoria's death. Accepting Harrison's murder as his mistake wasn't his cross to bear. Determined to console him for once—to absolve him of a misperceived sin—she cupped his chin firm in her hand, and forced him to acknowledge her.

"Look at me," she said wiping her cheek. "There's no blame to take, Peter. The mayor's death was destined to happen. Nothing could change it. You already carry so much; don't take this on."

He gave her a skeptical look.

"Think about it. If we hadn't met, then in a few hours you'd be like everyone else in Chicago. You'd wake up, grab the newspaper and have heart failure when you saw the headline." She frowned, thinking. "Well, in your case, Car would tell you first, so the shock of reading it would be secondary."

The doubtful expression eased into a grin.

"That's all, though. You'd be shocked, nothing more. I promise you, what happened tonight was never your burden to bear."

His smile faded, but his eyes stayed with her.

"Peter, in my Chicago, in 1993, what happened tonight is discussed in classrooms, and recorded in countless books." Encouraged by his steady gaze, she continued.

"You know, in trying to justify my being here, I thought maybe I could change the outcome. Change history." She raised her brows with a rueful smile. "How's that for crazy?"

Peter's grin returned, easing the lines on his forehead. "I suppose I can confess it now. I did think you mentally off balance."

"I don't blame you." She pointed to her chest. "Walking enigma here. What do you think now?"

"Do I still question your sanity? No." Peter ran his fingers through her hair as he spoke, and Joey found she enjoyed the sensation. "Now, do I believe you traveled back in time?" He looked beyond her to the moonlit sky. "Well, the whole concept is incredibly difficult to embrace—"

"Tell me about it."

"And yet …."

"Yes?"

"And yet, after tonight it earns serious consideration."

"So it's still only theoretical for you." Joey refused to let her disappointment show. Acknowledging that her story was within the realm of possibility was a big step. She accepted the small victory without emotion. "Would it help to hear more about the future?"

Peter froze. His eyes narrowed and his hand left her hair.

"Joanna, please. I cannot endure another assassination."

"Relax. I'm fresh out of those."

He exhaled in a soft chuckle. "Thank heaven for that." His hand came to rest at her temple and they lay quiet for a time.

"What is it like for you," Peter said, "living in Chicago now versus ... versus one hundred years from now?"

"Oh. Well ...." Joey considered the question carefully, determined not to drag him down.

"Your Chicago is so much prettier. The architecture. I mean, wow!" She grinned. "All these beautiful buildings! And, even though I hate wearing them, the hats really add something unique. Your Chicago is a visual smorgasbord ... but it smells a lot worse."

Peter laughed. "The stockyards do permeate the air."

"But the Columbian Exposition," she continued, "to see all that technology in its infancy; to learn just how much women did for this country. What a huge surprise." Her brows arched. "I met Scott Joplin! And Bertha Lamme. I heard Sousa play his own music. It was an incredible experience. Thank you."

"You're most welcome. What's left of the fair in 1993?"

"Not much, I'm afraid, only one building."

Peter frowned. "Only one building survives? What a pity. The White City is such an achievement. One would think .... Was no effort made to preserve it?"

"Preservation was under debate, but a fire destroyed everything before they could come to an agreement. That's why I cried at the Court of Honor."

"So it's going to burn, then." His voice softened. "How very sad."

Joey could have kicked herself. She meant to boost his spirits, but instead they were courting misery again.

Without thinking, she guided his hand from her temple to her lips. She gave his palm a tender kiss, then nestled her cheek into his palm. She closed her eyes, weary but content. Seconds later she opened them and read conflicting emotion in Peter's expression.

Joey dropped his hand and leaned back.

"Sorry," she said, shifting her weight to one elbow. "No offense intended."

Peter still looked undone. Her gesture sparked something unreadable. She started to apologize again when he spoke.

"None taken," he replied. Raising his eyebrows, he said, "Quite the contrary, actually."

Joey felt heat rise in her cheeks, both pleased and unsettled by his response. She was fully aware she'd crossed a boundary and she studied him in silence, wary of the place they'd reached. She cleared her throat and changed the subject.

"Hey, can I tell you something? Something that might land me back in the crazy category?"

Peter nodded, shifting to the head of the bed. He settled into the pillows, stretched out long, and put his hands behind his head.

"Are you familiar with the concept of reincarnation?"

"I'm aware of it."

"Well, at times I thought you might be …. I mean, in some ways you remind me of …"

"… of Martin," he finished for her.

Joey searched but found no trace of judgment in his face. She nodded. "Yeah. Weird, huh."

Peter sighed. "To be perfectly honest, Joanna, certain things you say and do remind me a great deal of Victoria. You're nothing like her, and yet there's a familiarity about you …." He scanned the room, as if searching for words. "I find it unsettling because it seems so natural."

She smiled and shrugged her shoulders. "At least I'm not the only one getting this vibe."

"*Getting this vibe?*" Peter laughed. "Some of your phrases are so puzzling."

"What can I say? I am a product of my generation." As she considered her statement another thought arose. "Listen, if you had the opportunity to do this, would you travel through time?"

"That depends," he flashed an inviting grin, "upon whom I am visiting."

Joey blushed a second time. "I'm serious. If you could do it, would you visit me? Meet my son? Experience my Chicago?"

Something in her tone checked him. The silence gained length and Peter's grin faded. He studied the ceiling for a long time before answering her.

"Please don't misinterpret this, Joanna. If you lived down the street, I would visit frequently. If you lived in St. Louis, I would board a train to see you, but—" He crossed his arms over his chest.

"You do understand I've just reached a theoretical acceptance of your origin. It is difficult to fathom such an adventure." An errant fist reached his lips. "I'm not a man who takes risks, or goes to extraordinary measures. I'm afraid I lack the fortitude to make such an uncertain journey." His eyes seemed to plead with her as he finished.

"You know your eloquence is really something." Joey fought the quiver in her voice. "It's okay. It was a harder question to answer than to ask. Thanks for being honest." With great effort, she held his gaze. "You know if I ever do get back I'll … well, I'll miss you." Fresh tears rolled slowly down her cheeks.

Peter opened his arms.

"Come here."

Joey joined him, hungry for the comfort of his embrace. She melted against his chest, her head in the crook of his shoulder. He wrapped his arms around her and kissed the top of her head.

"I'm sorry," he whispered. "It's just not in my nature."

"It's okay. I understand." She drew a hitched breath and found herself distracted by the scent of him. He smelled nothing like Martin, but he smelled good. Musky and masculine, like a treasured piece of life that she'd been missing. She sighed, relaxing into the connection. Her hand found its way to his chest, and she traced circles around a button on his shirt. "I can't imagine doing this willfully either. Peter, I'm not a risk taker, just someone who didn't watch where she was going."

It was a night for honesty. Joey decided to tell him everything on her mind.

"Tonight, though, before we left the party, I had something of a revelation, kind of a new theory about how I got here."

"I knew something had unsettled you. You turned white so quickly."

"So many things came to a head all at once. I kind of took advantage of your reaction."

"So you could warn the mayor?"

"Yes, but let's not go there. Okay?"

"Agreed." Peter said. "Please, tell me about your revelation."

Joey eyed the night stand, grateful to look at something other than Peter. Voicing this meant asking a lot of him, and he'd already given so much.

"Well, it occurs to me that I may be pushing the limits of your hospitality."

"Meaning?"

"Meaning that when I went for that run last Saturday, it wasn't just any day, it was my anniversary."

"And?"

"And … okay, bear with me." Joey knew she had to face him. She shifted her weight and sat up.

"Okay. Assuming you really are an earlier incarnation of Martin, and I really did travel through time, I think it was the specific date that made at all possible. I mean, Martin was on my mind the entire run, and it was our anniversary. I think maybe the fluke was falling in the water. In doing so at that particular moment I think I slipped through a—I don't know—a portal or something … and I think maybe my anniversary is the only day I can travel through time. It might be a year before I can go back."

She stared hard at Peter, eager for a response. His expression gave nothing away. Joey held her breath as he stroked his beard, lost in thought.

"I'm not sure I agree with your theory." He offered her a sincere smile. "But, I would be pleased to have your company for the next fifty-one weeks."

Joey sighed her relief as she settled back onto his chest. "Thank you. I can't test my theory until my next anniversary, but if I come up with any new ideas I'll let you know. And if I do, you have to let me jump in the lake again. Agreed?"

Peter laughed. "Absolutely not. Tuesday was the first day I called your sanity into question, and Car's as well. I still struggle with his role in that little incident."

Joey jumped to his defense. "Please, don't blame Car. I put him up to it. He's a good guy, Peter. Things are lighter when he's around. It's like he keeps everyone going, and he thinks the world of you."

Peter drew her back to his chest. "Calm down," he whispered. "I wasn't planning to throw him out on the street."

She let out an anxious breath. "Did you know he's in love?"

"Mm hmm. Molly, isn't it? I think I realized it on Monday, but I had other worries at the time." Peter grew still again, save for a gentle caress on her shoulder. "I knew this would come eventually. Car's very nearly his own man now. It's natural he would want to marry and move on."

Joey sat up again. "No, no! I mean yes! I believe he's in love with her and he may want to marry her, but I don't think he wants to leave."

"What makes you so sure?"

"Well, I'm just guessing, but I think it has something to do with the Dennaheys."

"Conall and Maeve?"

"Yes. I get the impression they were like parents to him. He speaks of them with a tremendous amount of fondness."

Peter pursed his lips. "They were extremely nice people. I suppose I thought of them in the same way when I was a boy. But I fail to see what they have to do—"

Joey laughed. "They have everything to do with his desire to stay."

"How so?"

"Continuation. Peter, at the risk of stepping in it, I think Molly spends a good deal more time with Car than you realize."

Peter leaned forward, frowning. Joey pushed him back against the pillows.

"Ease up. Car's a gentleman. You're jumping to the wrong conclusion. The point I'm trying to make is that Car and Molly spend a lot of time with Will. Do you follow me?

Peter said nothing.

"It's just a theory, but I think in Car's vision of the future he's married to Molly, *but still here*, both of them living here, like Conall and Maeve. I get the sense he would love it if he and Molly could be, to Will, what Conall and Maeve were to him. To some degree, I think they already are.

Peter exhaled long and hard as he leaned back against the pillows.

Joey made a face. "Oh God, I went too far again. I offended you somehow. Talk to me, Peter. What are you thinking?"

Seconds passed and Joey closed her eyes, waiting for a verbal blow.

"I'm thinking." His voice lacked emotion. "Mrs. Milford will not be happy about any of this."

A relieved laugh escaped her. "Are you kidding? The minute she learns I'm staying she's probably going to excuse herself and pack her bags."

Peter suppressed a laugh.

"If she doesn't, maybe I'll ask her to teach me how to cook in this century. That should send her running for the hills."

Peter chuckled. "You're awful, you know."

"I know," she sighed happily, returning to the warmth of his chest. "But I run fast."

Peter hugged her closer. "Yes, you do. I had no idea it would be so hard to catch you."

"Ah, but you never did catch me."

"Not then." He smiled down at her.

Slowly, almost imperceptibly, his demeanor changed. There was a new intensity in his gaze, and Joey was suddenly aware of the power in his arms. His rich tone dropped lower and took on a distinctly seductive tone.

"But now …."

He leaned forward. Joey felt her pulse quicken. Peter gathered her close, locking her in his embrace. It happened so quickly—the conviction in his touch delivered a sharp jolt of electricity, snapping her sense of reason. He leaned to the right, forcing her back, his face inches from hers. Joey gave in to her senses, breathing him in, melting into his energy, her body responding to this sudden obliteration of the boundary line.

"Now what?" she whispered.

"Now this."

Peter eliminated the last remaining boundary, his lips reached hers in a fury. Joey felt every ounce of emotion he'd experienced this week expressed in his kiss, and she matched his fire with a physical declaration of her own. She threw her arms around him, demanding his control, his strength. Peter's hands pressed her shoulders, peeling the sleeves of her dress away from her skin. She matched his effort, nearly tearing the buttons from his shirt, hungry for the source of his amazing scent. They broke the kiss, each struggling to shed their clothing. Peter moved faster, knocking over the water glass as he flung his shirt at the night stand. The crash of shattered glass reignited him. His eager hands tore at her dress, hungry for more of her.

Joey pulled back for an instant, struck by the intimate sight of him. In a flash they reconnected, lips touching lips, hands seeking flesh, hearts pounding their demand. Peter lifted her dress. His hand met her bare calf and traveled upward. Joey shivered, pressing herself into the swell she found between his legs. He uttered a low cry as his hand slid up her thigh. She moaned and thrust against him, urging him on. They parted briefly, eyes locked, panting heavily, desperate to explore the depths of their unique relationship.

Again they came together, like two bolts of lightning lashing at each other—fierce, hungry and alive. Lost in their connection, they missed the rap on the door and the turn of the knob. They remained passionately oblivious until the shrill scream from Mrs. Milford wrenched them apart.

Chapter Forty
The Path Yet Traveled

Peter found Mrs. Milford in the kitchen gripping the rim of the wash basin. She gave him a disgusted look, snatched the tea kettle from the counter and set it on the potbelly stove. Wiry gray hair escaped from her cap, scratching the collar of her night dress as she leaned over, forcing a log into the opening of the cast iron heater.

"That girl is a trollop," she muttered, prodding the wood into place.

"Mrs. Milford, you know nothing about her. She—"

"Don't I?" The old woman banged the fire door shut. "I knew the minute she came truckling into this house she was up to no good, the cloying little sneak. I'm not deaf, you know. I hear more than breaking glass." Placing her hands under her chin, she adopted a coquettish tone, batting her eyelashes for emphasis.

"Oh, Peter, this hat is far too fancy for me. Peter, let me do your filing, anything for you," she said, cooing the last word.

"Mrs. Milford, that's quite enough. What on earth is the matter with you?"

"There's not a thing wrong with me, but you!" She thrust a knobby finger in his face. "You're as blind as a bat where she's concerned, and she's taken full advantage of you." With one hand on her forehead, she resumed her imitation. "Peter, I can't possibly go home, I live in the future. Can't I please stay with you?" She rolled her eyes and shook her head. "The boldest lie ever told, and you believed her."

"I said that's enough."

"I know the likes of her far better than you do." Mrs. Milford charged on, ignoring him. "She appeals to the basest part of a man. It was only a matter of time before that whore offered her flesh in exchange for your finery.

"Enough!" Peter slammed his fist onto the counter and the old woman flinched, square shoulders rising to guard her thick neck. Peter leaned forward, adding weight to his fist to keep it from leaving the counter.

"Mrs. Milford." He spoke in stiff, measured phrases. "Although a kind heart was never a requirement for this position, I always found you sadly lacking in that capacity. You perform your duties well, but you treat everyone with cold efficiency. You once went to great lengths to disparage Car, and you barely tolerate him now. In the last five years, you've warmed only to William."

"And thank God he had me! Ever since *she* died, you've all but ignored him. If it weren't for me he would have no one to mother him. He spends most of his day with that Irish louse who's teaching him God knows what, and now he consorts with that filthy slut—"

With a resounding smack Peter's open palm struck Mrs. Milburn, snapping her head rudely to one side. She grappled for the counter in an effort to remain upright. Eyes cold with fury, she faced him, rubbing her cheek.

"Never!" Peter said. "You will never again malign a member of this household. Now sit down." He pointed to a chair by the stove. She didn't move.

"I said sit down."

The gravity in his tone reached her, and Mrs. Milford edged back toward the chair, wary eyes fixed on Peter. He began to pace the floor, one fist behind his back, the other pounding away at his lips. Every time he ventured a look in her direction he fought the urge to slap her again. She returned his gaze, bold-faced and angry, daring him to do just that.

Turning swiftly on his heel, Peter faced her with equal fire.

"Given your dislike of outsiders, I am not surprised by your feelings for Miss Fagan, but your abhorrence of Car sickens me. It is as nasty as it is groundless." His voice cooled, matching the ice in her stare. "You are obviously no longer pleased with your position here. Well, far be it from me to impede upon your happiness. You have my permission to seek employment elsewhere."

"You mean to throw me out? While that sea-snake remains? Of all the—"

"—I suggest," Peter interjected, "you start packing now. Car will deliver you and your belongings to your sister's house tonight. You will work a final shift tomorrow and receive your severance at the end of the day."

Mrs. Milford stood, hands on hips, glaring at Peter. "I'll do nothing of the kind. If I leave today, then I won't return tomorrow. Pay me now, and fix your own breakfast, you ungrateful—"

Peter leaned close, impressing upon her the full measure of his height. "Listen carefully. You will do exactly as I say or I will have you arrested for the attempted theft of my father's match safe."

Her jaw dropped, confirming his suspicions.

"You put the match safe into Victoria's skirt pocket before delivering it to Joanna last Sunday, didn't you?"

Mrs. Milford made a feeble protest and tried to step away, but her back met the chair and she plopped down, mouth agape.

"Joanna had been here a scant twelve hours. She'd saved William's life. You knew nothing about her, yet you hated her enough to paint her a thief, just to ensure her departure."

Peter stepped back and folded his arms across his chest. "Your cold heart saddens me, and your black opinion disgusts me. But your devious nature defies description. You will accept my terms without another word. In exchange, I will not reveal the true nature of your character. We will tell everyone you are leaving to spend more time with your sister. If you refuse, then I will take you directly to the police and have you charged with attempted robbery. Do we have an agreement?"

Eyes downcast, her capped head bobbed slowly up and down as the tea kettle began to whistle.

"Answer me. Do we have an agreement?"

Mrs. Milford raised her head. Defeat lined her face, but hate filled her eyes. "Yes."

"Now, then," Peter said, attempting a return to civility, "if you're making tea, I'd like a cup in the parlor."

"Just keep *that woman* out of my kitchen," Mrs. Milford grumbled, reaching for the kettle.

Though the sun wasn't yet visible, night was fast receding. Peter leaned against the window by his desk, staring at the predawn sky. Images from the last twenty-four hours flashed through his mind: Joanna, looking perfect and slightly overwhelmed in Victoria's gown; the captivation in McNair's eyes as he greeted them; Joanna's determined expression just before she sprinted away; the blaze of lights inside the mayor's house and the bewildered neighbor at his side; then Mayor Harrison, ashen but brave, accepting death as it came for him. Peter remembered how the ice permeated his veins as he finally, fully grasped the truth of Joanna's story. And the intense heat he felt later, as passion circumvented reason.

In a few short hours, Chicago was in for a harrowing jolt. It was familiar ground for Peter. His week had been fraught with seismic activity, all of it courtesy of Joanna. But that thought only renewed the warmth inside him. Despite the tumult, or more likely because of it, he had never felt more alive.

For the first time since he lost Victoria, Peter realized he was approaching a sense of peace with himself. His enjoyment of the dinner party last night exemplified it. Later, waking beside Joanna and talking into the night marked for him a new beginning. He smiled, enthralled by the memory of their exchange. How refreshing to be around someone so familiar, yet so unlike himself.

Reincarnation wasn't a concept he embraced, so he didn't really think Joanna and Victoria were connected, but he knew he had strong feelings for Joanna, and he wanted her to stay. He hoped her theory was sound, and that they had the coming year together. Only a year, but one he looked forward to. Seeing a clear path ahead for the first time in a very long time, Peter smiled.

His mind touched upon Car. He needed to speak to the young man, understand the depth of his intention toward Molly. Joanna's theory on Car's connection to William made perfect sense. Conall and Maeve had been there for Car when he lost his parents. Wouldn't it be natural for an orphaned Irish boy to want to do the same for a kindred soul?

Thinking back, Peter realized his relationship with Car mirrored Peter's relationship with his father. His feelings for Car were always paternal in nature. It occurred to him that what he felt for Car was a form of love. But, as his father had, Peter kept a polite distance.

Joanna spoke the truth regarding Car's kind nature. His light heart was a beacon, particularly in the dark months following Victoria's death, and he deserved more gratitude than he had ever been given. Perhaps Peter could make amends in the months ahead. As the grain of an idea formed, he smiled again.

And William.

It pained Peter greatly to admit that, although he loved his son more than anyone in the world, he kept him at nearly the same distance as Car. In grasping the error, he understood the importance of giving William a more nurturing influence than he had the emotional capacity to provide. He knew Joanna, Car and Molly would help him in that regard.

Assuming Joanna's intuition was accurate, he would need to speak to Mr. Calder. If a marriage was likely, then eventually Molly would join Peter's house. Perhaps he could convince his neighbor to let her come early and replace Mrs. Milford. Then again, perhaps he should wait.

"Hey."

Peter looked over his shoulder. Joanna, already dressed for the day, leaned against the parlor door, her small frame split between the room and the hallway. She wore a troubled expression. Peter gave her a welcoming smile which she feebly attempted to return. He beckoned her over, but she remained where she was.

"Are you all right?"

She shrugged. "I'm feeling a little awkward."

Facing her, Peter opened his arms. "There's no need for that. Come here."

He drew her close and stood behind her, arms encircling her waist as he kissed the top of her head. "I like holding you. This doesn't feel awkward at all."

Her tension seemed to dissipate, but he sensed a lingering unease. In an effort to dispel her angst Peter hugged her tighter and whispered, "Penny for your thoughts?"

"Wow. Where do I start?" Joanna shivered as if trying to rid herself of something unpleasant. She tilted her head and looked up at him. "How did it go with Mrs. Milford?"

His gaze shifted to the horizon. "She said far more than I expected, but the outcome was not surprising. After tomorrow she will be gone. She insists you stay out of the kitchen until she leaves." Peter felt her shoulders tense. "Don't worry, I'll replace her quickly."

"Well, I'm not familiar with a 19th Century kitchen, but I can cook, so I'd be happy to help."

Peter smiled. "That's a generous offer, but I had someone else in mind."

"Molly?"

"Mm hmm. I need to speak with Car first, and pay a visit to Mr. Calder.

Joanna rubbed her cheek against his shirtsleeve as her hands found his forearms. "Sounds like a good idea."

They watched in silence as the sky grew lighter, revealing the stone path that led to the street, the bench in the corner of the yard, and the color in the few remaining leaves on the sycamore trees. Joanna sighed.

"Is something troubling you?"

She nodded, but said nothing. Peter held her close and waited. She shifted her stance, but remained silent. Eventually he prodded her. "You can tell me anything, you know."

"I know. It's not so much what I want to tell you, but what I want to ask you." Her grip tightened. "Earlier ... what almost happened ...."

Peter held his breath. "I take full responsibility. I blame myself—"

"No!" Joanna stiffened. "If there's any blame involved then we share it because I *wanted* it to happen. And I know this sounds inappropriate, but I still want it to happen." She sighed heavily.

"I guess that's what I'm struggling with. I don't know what's ... *appropriate*. I don't know the rules for dating in this century, especially if you're already living together. I mean, you were pretty worried about your reputation after I jumped that guy on Monday. Hooking up with your *cousin*—" She put her quotes in the air. "—doesn't exactly scream acceptability."

Peter chuckled. "Well, I suppose we need to establish a few rules, and determine how best to introduce ourselves socially, but we'll manage. Anything else?"

"Well," she spoke slowly, her voice low. "I know how *I* feel, and I'm pretty sure I know how *you* feel ... and I guess the word appropriate applies here, too. It doesn't seem right to feel like this just yet. Martin hasn't even been gone a year, and alongside my feelings for you is the nagging sense that it's still too early, like it's disrespectful to his memory."

Peter rested his chin on the top of her head. "I'm sure I'll have a similar reaction in time. But in all honesty, I never expected to feel anything again, so at the moment I'm afraid I'm a bit more accepting of all this than you are. I hope saying so doesn't offend you."

"No." She sighed. "In fact, I'm really glad you feel that way. But the realization that we ... *care* ... about each other leads me to another concern. Is it wise to pursue this knowing it's temporary?" Her shoulders inched higher. "Peter, regardless of my feelings for you, I have a son I want very much to return to." She dropped her head, sagging against him as she did so. "And I really hope admitting it doesn't offend you."

"Nothing you say offends me, and I am counting on your theory to give us ample time to address all your concerns. Now, I need to change clothes. We've a great deal to do today." He cupped her cheeks in his hands and gave her the gentlest of kisses. "Joanna, I understand how you feel, but we'll work everything out. Please don't trouble yourself."

She attempted a smile, but Peter knew she was still mired in conflict. "Something's amiss," he said, running a hand through her hair. "Perhaps you could—as you say—throw me a bone?"

"Peter," she sighed, "I spent the last week reaching for the unattainable. I failed to get home. I failed to warn the mayor. And I'm sure my effort to find the connection between you and Martin will come to the same end. It's frustrating." Joanna paused, staring at the bookcase across the room.

"Coupled with that failure is the idea that I can deal with it, with being here. Over time, it will grow on me. I think I could be happy here, and it scares me. What if things go so well that I don't even try to go back next year? How could I live with myself?

"I've already admitted strong feelings for you. If I give into them in the months ahead, if we ... you know ... then, Michael. I might not," she stammered. "I might never ...."

Peter saw the struggle in her eyes. He reached for the small of her back and drew her close, wrapping her in his embrace.

"I understand. You're conflicted," he said softly. "Please know I would never attempt to coerce you, despite how I feel. I consider myself fortunate to have found you, and to know you as someone special. There is no need to rush beyond that, I promise you."

He felt her give way to his assurances. She dropped her head, put her arms around his waist, and spoke into his chest.

"Wow. Where the hell were you on prom night?"

"Prom night?"

She laughed. "That's my way of saying thanks for understanding."

"You're quite welcome. And, please, don't swear. It's—"

"—unbecoming." She finished with him. "Sorry."

He lifted her chin and smiled. "You're tired."

"I couldn't sleep after …."

"Nor could I. Come with me."

He led her to the fireplace, settled her into one of the plush chairs and covered her with the blanket. "Rest here while I change. We'll have breakfast together and plan our day." He added another log to the fire, kissed her hair, and left the room.

Chapter Forty-one
The Best of Intentions

The clatter of wood upon stone woke her. Car knelt by the fireplace, stacking logs against the hearth. Joey yawned and stretched, unfolding her legs from the armchair.

"What time is it?" she asked.

"Comin' up on eight. Didn't sleep there all night, did ya, Joey?"

"No. I woke up around three, but couldn't sleep so I came downstairs. Are you okay, Car?"

"Not a'tall. It's a black day, Joey. Last night we lost Mayor Harrison. Shot through the heart, so they say, and in his own home, too." His gaze drifted from Joey to the fire. "Death comes callin' for everyone, but I wish he called for someone else. We lost a man who cared."

"He was an amazing guy. He'll be well remembered, Car, I promise you."

Car stared hard at her. "Pardon me for askin', but … em … did ya know this was comin'?"

She dropped her head and nodded.

"No offense, but knowin' like ya did, couldn't y've done somethin' ta prevent it?"

Joey couldn't face him. "I tried, Car, I really did. Remember Tuesday? When I asked you to take me to City Hall?"

He nodded.

"I tried then, but he wasn't in his office. I would have left a note, but I watched the clerk throw away a letter delivered by the person in front of me."

"But, ya still had four more days ta warn him."

"It was hard to find another opportunity."

"Ya could a told me. I'd've helped ya."

She sighed heavily. "Car, when we were at the dock you didn't believe for a second I would get home by jumping in the lake. I'm pretty sure that you thought I was nuts. Would you have believed me if I told you someone was going to die?"

Car shrugged. "Maybe not."

"What do you think Harrison would have thought of me, had I managed to warn him?"

Car slipped into a grin. "Guess he would a figured ya for a nutter, too."

"Trust me, I've been fighting that label all week. But I did try, Car. I even took one more chance." Her voice dropped. "It just wasn't meant to be."

"Ah, don't go kickin' yerself. I was just askin'. And I'm glad ta know ya tried. Come on, Mate. Breakfast is ready."

Joey frowned. "Is everyone at the table?"

"All but Mrs. M. She's pullin' another sour face. Says she won't leave the kitchen."

The news made Joey feel worse. Mrs. Milford was hardly a friend, but the old woman was leaving a good job because of her. Just one more life she had managed to disrupt here.

"It's for the best, Joey. Lately she's been so sour even the crab apples are lookin' sweet. So if stayin' in the kitchen makes her happy, then it's fine by me." He pulled her up. "Come on. I'm starvin!"

Peter and William were sitting at the table, heads bent together as Peter whispered in his ear. His little mouth formed a perfect O. His eyes darted from Car to Joey and back to his father.

"Is everything all right?" Joey asked, seating herself.

"I was just telling William about some changes ahead for us."

Car reached for a platter of pancakes as he sat. "For the better, I hope."

"Some of what's ahead will be a bit of an adjustment, but I think everyone will be happier in the long run." Peter poured syrup onto his pancake. "First, Mrs. Milford will be leaving us."

Car's fork fell to his plate with a clatter, his mouth shaped remarkably like William's.

"Evidently her sister misses her. After debating the matter for quite some time, she decided this morning to move back home. The distance from our house is burdensome, so she has given notice. We are on the hunt for a new cook."

He turned to Car. "I may need your help in finding one. Can we discuss it after breakfast?"

Car nodded, eyes shrouded in vague surprise.

"Although we're losing Mrs. Milford, we're gaining a new member of the house. Joanna will remain with us for at least a year, unless we locate her family sooner."

Both boys broke into huge grins. Car gave Joey a gentle punch on the shoulder and William fairly beamed at her. The mood stayed light for the remainder of the meal. Peter advised Car that he would need to help Mrs. Milford move her belongings. He asked Joey if she could take over William's lessons. She readily agreed.

"To prepare me for real school next year," William assured her.

Peter turned to his son. "After breakfast, please show Joanna what you've already learned."

Joey placed her napkin on the table. "I'm ready if you are."

William bounded from his chair. "Come on, Joey. My things are in the parlor."

She stood with a parting smile as William pulled her away from the table. Once they left the room Peter turned his attention to Car.

"The last twenty-four hours have been devastating." He gestured to the newspaper. "It will take the city some time to heal."

Car glanced at the headline. "Hard to believe, Doc. It's like losin' a father. Not like Conall." He tapped his chest. "But he was a father to all Chicago, so ya feel the loss all the same."

Peter nodded, debating what to say next. So much between them had gone undiscussed for so long that he struggled for a logical starting point. Peter decided that since the nature of this talk was rooted in paternity, it seemed a fitting place to begin.

"A father to all Chicago," he mused. "Good words for Harrison's tombstone. You know, Conall was a great father figure. It's difficult to believe he's been gone so long."

"Three years," Car rejoined, staring at the tablecloth. "Three years since he went home ta Maeve, may the good Lord keep 'em both safe in His arms."

"When I look at you now," Peter said, raising his coffee cup, "I find it hard to believe you were only sixteen when he passed. You've all but grown up, and quite well I might add, all thanks due to Conall. You learned everything from him, and mastered all he taught you." He sipped his coffee. "You're a fine young man, a good influence on William, and a good friend to Joanna. Conall would be proud."

Car blinked. "Thanks, Doc. But, if not for you I'd never have known him a'tall."

"Well, I'm pleased to be good for something around here, and I think ...." Peter hesitated, awkwardly broaching his intended subject. "I think since he's no longer here, I should step into his shoes and offer you some guidance."

"Guidance?" Car stared at Peter. "Did I put off Mrs. M? Is she leavin' on my account?"

"No, of course not, nothing could be further from the truth. I just thought perhaps … moving forward you might ah … need some advice on—" He faltered, eyes drawn to the contents of his cup. "I meant to say … guidance on … on other matters."

"Other matters, Doc?"

Peter found he had trouble meeting Car's eyes. "Matters of the heart," he said quietly.

Car remained mute. The silence forced Peter to face his protégé. Car met his gaze, looking somewhat confused. Peter cleared his throat and fumbled on. "It occurred to me on Monday that the young lady Joanna assisted might be a friend of yours."

Car nodded his acknowledgement. Peter waited, hoping he would speak. An odd silence hung between them. Peter struggled on. "Perhaps a very special friend."

Another nodded affirmation came, but still no words. Peter shrugged, waiting for the boy to find his voice. The silence lengthened and when Peter realized Car had no intention of responding, he cleared his throat and stumbled on toward his point.

"Car, I don't find this easy to discuss, but as your benefactor, I need to ensure your *intentions* toward Miss Hannafee are honorable." He gave his ward a pleading look. "Are you inclined toward matrimony?"

His wide eyes revealed surprise, but Car remained silent.

Peter gave up on drawing him out, and in one great breath he blurted, "Car, do you want to marry this young lady?" He turned away as he finished, exhaling in relief. It was awkwardly stated, but at least the question was on the table. Peter refilled his coffee waiting for a response.

Car wiped the back of his hand slowly across his mouth, sighed mightily and began his own stumbling reply.

"Peter, I've had eyes for Molly since the day we met. And I mean no disrespect in admittin' this, but I never thought about my intentions until Monday, when I saw her lyin' in that alley." He paused to take a sip of his coffee. "When we first got on, it seemed best ta keep it quiet. We didn't want ta go upsettin' anyone." He glanced briefly at Peter, then shifted his gaze to the window. "But after Monday, I s'pose y'could say I took stock of my intentions and I … em … em …." Car swallowed hard and changed course.

"Doc, thanks to you I have so much that others didn't get when they crossed the pond. I've a roof over my head, a full belly, a warm bed, and a couple who raised me as if I was their own. I fared far better than I should have, given how ya found me, and I'm forever grateful to ya. Yer all aces, all the time. But, as for my intentions …."

Peter was confused. He suspected Car would have a good deal to say once he got started, but upon hearing him thus far, he had no clue where the boy might be headed, though it didn't sound like his usual sunny discourse. Still, he was an honorable fellow, not inclined to malign anyone, least of all someone he cared for, so Peter withheld judgment and waited patiently.

"As for my intentions …." Car braved a look at Peter and continued in a rush. "If I could parlay all my feelins' for Molly inta cash I'd be a wealthy man. I'd marry her today and give ta her all that has so generously been given ta me. But my … my … wealth isn't monetary and I'm not—" Car's voice dropped to a whisper. "I'm not a man of means, Doc. What on earth can I offer Molly, beyond my hand?" He slumped forward, his head bent low. "Molly's somethin' special, and she deserves far more than I can provide her."

Peter smiled broadly. This wasn't the concern he had expected, but thanks to Victoria, this wasn't a problem at all. He reached across the table and gave Car's hand a reassuring pat. "I think you vastly underestimate yourself. You have a good deal more than you realize." The young man raised his head.

"Car, do you remember years ago, when I brought Victoria home for the first time? You had just turned nine if I remember correctly."

He nodded.

"Victoria was completely taken by you. She adored you. In fact," Peter suppressed a smile, "were it not for you, I don't think she would have been quite as taken by me, but that's beside the point. Before we even married, she pointed how hard you worked, and how much you did for Conall and Maeve. She felt strongly that your effort shouldn't go unappreciated, and she made a suggestion that I took to heart. Since you were just a child I thought it best to," he paused, "to hold onto my appreciation until you were older."

Car stared at Peter, attentive but confused.

"For years we've been setting aside a monthly allowance for you. In the beginning it was two dollars. Gradually, we raised the amount. Right now I deposit twelve dollars each month to your account. Car, you have nearly one thousand dollars, held at the First National Bank in your name and," he said, breaking into a smile, "it is yours to use as you please."

The boy's mouth formed another perfect O. Peter continued, pleased by his reaction.

"I planned to discuss this with you on your twentieth birthday, and adjust your salary again, but I suppose nineteen is close enough." He pushed his cup to the side of the table. "Does knowing you are a man of some means make it easier to consider your plans with Molly?"

Car shook his head as if it were wet. "Well," he said, his voice showing a hint of sun, "my intentions are easier ta consider, but it's got me stumped on just about everythin' after."

"Everything after?"

"Well, livin' arrangements … and I s'pose there's loads more that'll come ta me later."

"Well, living arrangements needn't change too dramatically." Peter cleared his throat. "Once you're married you and Molly could move into the living quarters off the kitchen. Or, we could modify the garret to suit a young bride." He laughed nervously. "Of course you may have other plans, but I hope you … you might consider staying here. I'd pay both of you, just as I did Conall and Maeve, and we … we'll continue as we always have. What do you think?"

A flash of joy lit Car's face. He leaned back in his chair, adopting a casual air, and, like an honest man with a good poker hand, he eased into a mischievous grin. "Well," he drawled, "I'll have ta check with my missus, see what she thinks of all this."

With a hearty laugh, Peter rejoined, "That, young man, is the beginning of a wonderful union. For now, I think it best to hire someone else, until you two are married. If you know anyone who can cook and keep house, it would certainly help." The last image of an angry Mrs. Milford flashed through his head. "And the sooner we find someone, the better."

Car nodded, still smiling. "Leave that ta Molly and me, Doc. No need ta trouble over it."

"Thank you, Car, and ah," he paused, raising a finger, "one more thing."

Peter retrieved a red velvet pouch from his coat pocket and placed it in the center of the table. "I will speak to Mr. Calder today, but it is not my intention to force you to propose to Molly before you're ready. When you are, perhaps you'll find this helpful. It belonged to Victoria. It was a gift from her father on her 16th birthday."

Car loosened the strings and turned the pouch upside down. A delicate Irish Claddagh ring tumbled into his hand. The band and hands were made of gold, the heart and crown, from diamonds. It was a lovely piece, and Car obviously thought so.

"Like you, Victoria was of Irish descent. I'm sure she would want you to have it."

Car looked from Peter to the ring and back again. "Doc, it's grand, but are ya sure about this? Won't Will be needin' it someday? He's yer son. Shouldn't this go ta him?"

Peter shook his head. "In terms of your paternity, there are your parents, who risked everything to bring you here; then Conall and Maeve, who claimed you as their own. I stand last, filling in the precious few blanks left by the others." He leaned back in his chair. "Car, you've been a member of this family since the day you arrived, and although speaking of it doesn't come naturally to me I ... I think of you as a son, just as Conall did." He nodded to the ring in Car's hand. "As for William, I know he would want his big brother to have it."

Car's broad smile told Peter he need not say more.

Chapter Forty-two
Lessons, Laundry and Light

"Very good, William. Can you spell other words?"

Joey and William were in the parlor, reviewing William's scholastic skills. Joey thought, judging by modern standards, he was well-qualified for 'real' school. He could recite the alphabet, count to one hundred, and was already working on penmanship. With painstaking precision he printed his first name and, as he proudly demonstrated, the names of the horses as well.

"Not yet," he replied

"Hmm ...." Joey surveyed the room. "Hand me your chalkboard and we'll play a game. Close your eyes and don't peek. Okay?"

William complied as she explained the rules. "I'll write a word for something in this room and put the chalkboard by the object. Your job is to find the chalkboard, say the letters out loud and try to sound out the word. So wait here, and keep your eyes closed." She wrote the word 'pen,' set the board beside Peter's quill pen, and moved back to the center of the room.

"Okay, you can begin."

William moved eagerly around the room. He reached the desk and collected the chalkboard, calling out the letters in quick succession. "P. E. N." His eyes lit up. "Oh! Papa's quill pen. P-E-N spells pen. This is fun."

William gave her the board and closed his eyes. She wrote the word 'rug' and placed the chalkboard on the floor. "Okay, the hunt is on."

William gave her a puzzled look. "But you didn't move."

"Maybe I didn't," she said with a wink, "and maybe I did."

He walked past her, glancing around the room. "I didn't hear you walk anywhere so …" he checked the bookshelves and windows. Looking bewildered, he turned back and noticed the board at Joey's feet. He ran over and retrieved the chalkboard.

"R. U. G. Hey, the rug!" William stomped on the carpet for emphasis. "R-U-G spells rug."

"You're doing a great job. Shall we go again?"

The game continued for over an hour moving from the parlor to the front yard, identifying trees, flowers and bugs. William had his eyes shut tight when Car emerged from the house. Joey put a finger to her lips and motioned him to stay where he was.

"Keep your eyes closed, Will. I'm still working on this one." She wrote Car's name and handed the chalkboard to him.

"Okay. You can hunt now."

The boy opened his eyes and smiled. "Hi, Car. We're playing a reading game and Joey … hey! C. A. R. Car. My favorite name."

A door slammed nearby. Mrs. Milford trudged into the back yard, a basket full of wet clothes at her hip.

"Hey, can we call it a day?" Joey asked, collecting the chalkboard. "I need to speak to Mrs. Milford."

Car crouched down, calling to William. "Climb on, man! The kids need their carrots." William scrambled onto his back and waved goodbye.

As they reached the carriage house, Joey started toward the back yard, but after a few steps she hesitated. What was she doing? She'd said barely twenty-five words to this woman since her arrival. Why speak to her at all? Nothing she could say was likely to alleviate the situation. Nevertheless, Joey wanted to know why the woman disliked her so. Curiosity overruled caution and she rounded the corner.

A speckled brown chicken emerged from humble wooden shed at the far end of the backyard, searching the ground for stray specks of grain. Two others sat a few yards away, sunning themselves. Along the back fence, Mrs. Milford pinned laundry to a clothesline strung between two sturdy wooden posts.

With feeble optimism Joey edged closer, hoping for a civil exchange. She thought offering condolences might lead to a discussion. An airing of their differences might ease the woman's mind. She coughed lightly to announce herself.

"Mrs. Milford?"

The housekeeper spoke, hands locked on a wet shirt, back stiff like a shield, broad and unyielding. Her voice was brittle, but clear.

"I told him you were to stay away from me."

Joey stopped on the opposite side of the laundry basket. "Ah ... well, technically, you said to stay out of the kitchen and I will, but I thought ...." She ran a hand through her hair. "Please, Mrs. Milford, I'd like to talk to you."

The old woman pinned the shirt to the clothesline and selected a pair of trousers from the basket. "I have nothing to say to the likes of you."

"What do you mean *the likes of me*?" Joey hitched a bewildered shrug. "You don't even know me. What did I ever do to you?"

"You know exactly what you did to me!"

"I do? Well, I'm drawing a blank. Could you please refresh my memory?"

Mrs. Milford's stubby fists strained white against the dark cloth in her hands. "You took him away from me, just like before. I had everything I wanted here and you swept in like some stray kitten, feigning helplessness but all the while—"

"What do you mean, just like before? I never met you before last Saturday!"

Mrs. Milford spun around and thrust a wooden clothespin in her face. "Oh we've met!" She wagged the pin back and forth. "You invaded my home nine years ago, just like you did here. Arrived wayward and soaking wet, and my husband took you in. Said we should be charitable. Said we should help. I suspected you were no good, but I did as he asked, and what did it get me?"

Joey stood, mouth agape. Mrs. Milford's face had acquired a trancelike stillness, save for a distant fire burning in her eyes, which stoked hotter with every word she spoke.

"What the—" Joey leaned closer to the old woman. "Are you crazy? I never met you before last Saturday, and I have absolutely no clue who your husband is."

Mrs. Milford's hand shot forward, poking Joey hard on the chest with her clothespin. "Crazy? Me? You're the one claiming to be from the future."

Joey flinched, too stunned to respond.

"You came in, claiming to be lost, but we both know better. You found what you wanted, and you took him!" Her hand dropped to her skirt and she brushed at the fabric as if trying to remove a stain. "I was content. It wasn't much, but it was enough. I … didn't like everything, but I did what a wife should. I cooked and cleaned and suffered through my duty. And then …."

Her focus returned to Joey, eyes ablaze at the sight of her.

"Then, you took him. With us barely a month and you snuck away in the night with my husband, my life. Everything I worked for, everything I deserved!" With rekindled rage she advanced on Joey, who took a wary step back.

"Whoa! I think you have me confused with—"

"—And now you're here." She halted a second time and shook her head, her hand still brandishing the clothespin. It was better this time. I wasn't marri… I wasn't expected to—"

Joey clutched her stomach, and listened as disjointed pieces of Mrs. Milford's past and present jumbled grotesquely together in her explanation.

"I even had a son this time, then you arrived and ruined everything. EVERYTHING!"

Mrs. Milford lowered her head and charged like a bull, but Joey sidestepped the old woman, who ran headlong toward the wooden shed. Joey turned to leave. Mrs. Milford had bigger problems than she realized. As best she could tell, Mr. Milford left his wife years ago for another woman, and for some reason Joey reminded her of the whole sad mess. No wonder the housekeeper disliked her.

What a shame.

A sharp sting at her back took her by surprise. Mrs. Milford lunged from behind, hitting Joey below the shoulder with a clothespin. The chalkboard slipped from her hands as she cried out. Both women fell to the grass in a tangle of arms and legs. Joey recovered quickly, pinning the housekeeper to the ground.

"Mrs. Milford, whatever happened to you in the past—I'm sorry for your loss, but I had no part in it." Joey put a shaking hand on the ground. "As for what you saw last night, that was none of your business. I've taken nothing away from you. Not then and not now." Joey released her hold and scrambled to her feet. She bent down to offer her adversary a hand, but received another angry stab from the clothespin for her effort.

"Oh, for the love of Pete!" Joey grabbed Mrs. Milford by the wrist and yanked the feeble weapon from her hand.

Further discussion was pointless. The woman nursed a deep-seated, misdirected hatred of her. Joey could do nothing but walk away. Two steps later a clothespin struck her in the back of the neck. She spun around and another struck her collarbone.

Mrs. Milford sat on the ground, firing clothespins with admirable force and accuracy. Joey raised her hands in defeat and turned away. The barrage continued and Joey withstood each makeshift knife in silence. She kept a slow pace, refusing to give the old woman the satisfaction of a hasty retreat.

"Stop!"

William raced to Joey, screaming as he ran. "You mustn't throw things! You told me so!"

The assault ended. Whether it was because she ran out of clothespins or because of William's voice, Joey didn't know, but she heard muffled cries behind her.

"D- d- did she hurt you, Joey?" His small hand reached for her.

"No, sweetie. Don't cry. Come on, come with me."

They walked to the front yard and Joey led him to the porch. She sat by a column and pulled William onto her lap, murmuring softly as she rocked him back and forth. "Really, Will. She didn't hurt me at all." At length he calmed down, his brown eyes glistening with tears.

"Why would she do such a thing?"

Joey took a deep breath, eyes fixed on the stone walkway. "Evidently I remind her of someone who wasn't very nice to her."

William looked puzzled. "But she shouldn't throw things at you. That's wrong." His dark eyes narrowed in a remarkable imitation of his father. "She was mean to you. I hate her now." His hands curled into small fists. "I hate her!"

Joey hugged him tighter. "No you don't, Will. Sure, you're mad at her, and you may be mad at her for a long time. But, hate? I bet you and Mrs. Milford had a lot of good times together, and hate's a pretty strong word, don't you think?"

His fists went slack, but his eyes remained dark. "Well I am very, very mad at her." He dropped his head onto her chest and she continued to rock him. At length he spoke again.

"Why did she do it?"

"Well, at times, when bad things happen, some people have a hard time letting go of their anger. And I think something very bad happened to Mrs. Milford a long, long time ago—before she ever came to live with you. You were such a nice boy she was able to forget her troubles, but when I arrived last week, something about me reminded her of that bad time in her life, and she got angry again."

"But you would never hurt Mrs. Milford. It doesn't make any sense."

Joey sighed. "Some things in this world make very little sense, William. The longer I live, the more I begin to understand that."

"So you're not mad at her?"

"No, not really. We'll never be friends, and I can't change the way she feels about me, but I'm not mad at her."

"How can you not be mad at her?"

Joey cupped William's face in her hands and pressed her lips to his forehead. She pulled him close, hugging him. "I guess because, in a way, I know how she feels," she said softly. "I know what it's like to see one person and be reminded of another." She held him at arm's length and looked straight into his large brown eyes, thinking of Peter, of Martin, and of Michael.

"Sometimes it's hard to separate the two. For instance, you remind me a little bit of my son."

"I do?"

"Yes, you do." She touched his nose with her forefinger. "You're older than Michael, and you don't look a thing like him, but you're sweet and curious and happy, like he is. I like being around you because of all those things, but also because you remind me of Michael."

"And you haven't seen him?"

"Not since I came here."

"Through the water?"

"That's right, sweetie. The day I fell in the water and found you, I was supposed to take a trip. Michael is staying with my mother while I'm gone."

"What happened?"

"Well," she said, with a rueful smile, "I took a trip all right, but not the one I intended to."

"And now you can't get back."

His words exposed a simple, unalterable truth. Joey felt tears mounting and tried to blink them away. "That's about the size of it. I don't think I'll be able to get back for a year."

"A whole year? That's a long time to be away. Why a whole year?"

Joey leaned against the porch column and turned William so that his back was against her chest. She put her arms around him and kissed the top of his head.

"Well, the day I fell in the water was a very important day, my wedding anniversary. And I think for some reason that particular day made it possible for me to travel through the water to meet you guys. But that day only comes once a year, so I think I have to wait until my next anniversary in order to go home."

"A whole year," he repeated. "Gosh, that's a long time. You must miss him."

Her tears flowed freely, but silently. "Very much," she whispered, "especially today."

Again, his little questions, quite without meaning to, tugged painfully at her heart.

"Why especially today?"

Joey wiped her cheeks with the back of her hand, "Because today is Michael's birthday."

"Oh my."

Joey squeezed him for the sentiment. "You got that right, buddy. Oh my, my, my."

"And you're going to miss it."

"Mm hmm."

"But why, Joey? Why do you have to miss it?"

"Because—" She swallowed hard, trying to keep her patience. "Because, I think I can only get back on my anniversary. That's the day I came, and it was a very important day."

He faced her with an earnest look. "But a birthday is a very important day."

"Yes, it is."

"Well, if you came here on one very important day, maybe you could go back on another."

Joey flinched. "Wait a minute, say that again."

"You came here on one very important day, so it's only fair to go back on another one. And a birthday is a very important day."

His logic was hard to fault. If her wedding had been the most significant day of her life, surely the day of her son's birth was just as important. Michael had been on her mind constantly today, just as Martin had last Saturday. Joey took a great breath with one eye on the sky. It was colder today, but the sun was bright and the air was fresh—an excellent day for a run.

"William?" She rubbed her cheek against the top of his head.

"Yes, Joey."

"You are one smart little boy and you're going to do very well in real school."

He looked up at her and smiled. "Are you going home to Michael today?"

"I'm going to try." She hugged him. "Thanks to you."

"I'll miss you."

"Oh, buddy. I'll miss you, too."

She thought of her conversation with Peter, his jovial refusal over a return to the lake. She didn't want to sneak away, but she wouldn't be prevented from making the attempt. Joey rubbed William's hair. "But, let's keep it between us for now, because it might not work. Can you keep our secret?"

"Even from Car?"

She nodded. "Even from Car."

William looked extremely troubled. Joey thought this might be too much to ask the little guy. "Tell you what. You only have to keep quiet until three o'clock. Then you can tell Car and your father. Okay?"

A relieved smile spread across his cheeks.

"Now, can you tell time? How will you know when it is three?"

William grinned. "Easy. When the clock chimes three times."

"That's perfect. Now, you just need to do one more thing. You need to find Mrs. Milford and talk to her. Despite what she did to me, she loves you very much, and she'll be gone soon. She wouldn't want to leave with you feeling mad at her."

"But I am mad at her."

"I know," she said, patting his back, "But I also know that, deep down, you like her. If you don't talk to her before she leaves, you might feel bad about it later." She gave William one last hug and kissed both his cheeks. He slid from her arms and onto the front steps.

"Remember, not a word until three. Now, off you go. I need to write a note to your father."

Some four hours later William sat in the parlor, watching the clock. After the third chime he ran into his father's office where Peter was slouched in his chair, dozing at his desk.

"Papa! I think I helped Joey today," he said, beaming.

"Well done, William." Pater rubbed his eyes and leaned back in his chair. "What did you do for her, son?"

"I helped her find a way home. Joey's going home today, Papa."

Chapter Forty-three
Return to the Dock

Peter took the stairs two at a time, burst into the guest room and found it empty save for Victoria's skirt and blouse folded at the foot of the bed. A note bearing his name lay on top of them. He flung open the door to the armoire. It held only the clothes she had borrowed. Hands shaking, he retrieved the note.

> Dear Peter,
>
> I know you don't believe the lake will lead me home, but I do. That door opened for me on one landmark day and I believe today, Michael's birthday, is another. I'm on my way to the dock to test my theory. I'm sure you're angry, but I think you'd agree I wouldn't be much of a mother if I didn't act on this of all days.
>
> The thought of leaving without saying goodbye is more painful than I care to admit. Please, meet me at the dock. I'll wait as long as I can. If I

fail you can yell at me all the way home. Just bring along one of those lap robes, because I'll be freezing.

Yours,
Joanna

A sense of dread engulfed him. Peter pinched the bridge of his nose as he stumbled toward the stairs. By the time he reached the front door anger had taken root, fast replacing angst, and he quickened his pace, fury building as he stomped across the front lawn.

"Car!" he bellowed, "Saddle a horse. Now!"

"Trouble, Doc?" Car asked, leaning against the frame of the carriage house door.

"Joanna's gone for another swim in that damned lake."

"Jesus, Mary and Joseph! Was she wearin' her skin? Em … I mean her old clothes?"

Peter nodded and Car sprang into action, sliding the stable door open as Peter strode through. He opened Coco's stall, grabbed a saddle and readied the mare. Peter removed a lap robe from the shelf and mounted.

"Doc, that merrow legend, it's just stories, ya know?" Doubt sapped the energy from his voice. "Bring her back if ya can."

With a silent nod, Peter set the horse in motion.

Fortunately the five-mile trek to the lake was sparsely populated due, Peter thought, to the death of the mayor. Upon reaching a main thoroughfare, he pulled up sharply. People spilled from the shops onto the street, all wearing similar expressions of sorrow. He picked his way through the crowd and turned as soon as he found a quiet cross road. As the afternoon sun began to flirt with the horizon, Peter reached the dock.

He spotted Joanna sitting near the ladder, legs buried beneath the oversized sweater, hugging her knees to her chest, looking no bigger than a mooring post. She turned at the sound of the horse's hooves.

"You came." Relief played upon her features as she stood to greet him.

Peter pulled up a short distance from her and dismounted. The sight of her rekindled his ire. He was vexed by her stubborn insistence on performing this ritual, and her veiled departure insulted him. He advanced on her, eyes clouded with fury.

Her demeanor stood in stark contrast to his. She raced to him, arms outstretched. He stumbled back as she threw herself at him, her arms locked around his waist. He held tight to her in an effort to regain his balance, vaguely surprised that, small as she was, she could unsteady him.

"I knew you'd come!"

"I came to take you home," he said curtly. "I should take you straight to Richard, expose you to true madness, and scare some sense into you." Her laughter surprised him.

"Peter, if this doesn't work I'll go gladly. I'll take my lumps: padded cell, shock treatment, ink blots—whatever you want. Just let me out when you get over it, okay?"

He let out an exasperated groan and loosened his hold. "Joanna, you are the most confounding woman I've ever met. What on earth am I going to do with you?"

She smiled. "Well, first I test this theory—"

"NO!"

She started at the force of his response. "What do you mean *no*?"

"I mean you will not jump from this dock into that lake."

With a vigorous shove, she pushed him away. "I told you last night if I came up with any new theories you'd have to let me test them, even if it means a dip in the lake."

"And I told you," he countered, "absolutely not. I meant it then and I mean it now." He scanned the empty dock. "Enough of this nonsense. Now come with me."

Joanna stepped back, hands on her hips.

"You've got to be kidding! I thought since you reached a *theoretical* acceptance of my theory," she said, taunting him with quotation marks, "you would want to see it tested. Or was that just bedside appeasement on your part?"

Peter said nothing and saw the color rise in her cheeks.

"Ah! And to think I almost … we nearly … Jesus Christ!" She paced about like an agitated cat. "You are a hard man to love sometimes, you know that? You make me so mad. Do this. Don't do that. Wear a hat. Don't swear. I'm not your wife, Peter, and I'm not your ward. Not out here, so back off."

Peter took a tentative step toward her. Joanna dropped to a crouch, fists raised, arms blocking her chest. "I *will* test this theory, Peter. I'm not kidding. One step closer and I'll raise your voice a full octave."

He stepped closer. "That's enough, Joanna. I—"

Her right leg shot forward like a cannon ball. Peter expected no less, given her stated intentions. He caught her foot before it reached his crotch and twisted hard. She groaned and fell to the ground. Peter was on top of her in an instant.

"I already raised my hand against one woman today," he said. "Do not force me to repeat my indiscretion."

"Then don't lie to me." She struggled beneath him. "It's a thousand times worse than swearing."

His hand moved gently down the curve of her arm.

"Don't," she said, flinching. "If everything you said last night was to get—If you really didn't believe—Don't touch me." Her body was rigid, her voice firm with conviction.

Ignoring her command, Peter gathered her into his arms.

"Joanna, you possess an insightful mind, but it always fails you where I'm concerned. It's *because* I believe you that I won't allow it. Because I started my day thinking we had a year together and now we may have only a few minutes." He kissed her temple and whispered, "And, because I'm not ready to say goodbye. Not yet."

Tension gave way and she collapsed against his chest. Peter ran his fingers through her hair, rocking her as he did so.

"Why the tears?"

"You have to ask?"

"I do."

"Because I'm not ready to say goodbye either."

He smiled, touched by her admission. "Then let's go home and come back in a year."

"I can't. You read my note." He began to counter, but her finger on his lips stifled his reply. "And if I don't try today, a year from now I may not want to."

Peter smiled, relieved to know she felt as he did. He lifted her chin, and found her eyes, big and brown and worn from the weight of her conflicted emotions. He asked one question, his voice a down blanket offering her all of his warmth.

"Would it be so bad, staying here with me?"

For a long time she studied him in silence. Her expression promised a painful answer.

"No, but the decision to abort the attempt would eat at me. Eventually I would hate myself for it. Worse, I'd hate you."

Peter struggled to hide his frustration. Her hand reached his brow, smoothing the lines he knew were there.

"Don't be upset. I think we both figured out it's possible to move beyond the loss of a loved one, but I have a son who needs me. He's already lost one parent." Her hand reached his shoulder, her fingers pressed into the cloth of his coat. "If Michael wasn't back there, I probably wouldn't have a decision to make. But he is, and I can't give up on him. Put yourself in my shoes, Peter. If our roles were reversed and William was all alone, you'd be exactly where I am now, and I think I know you well enough to guess what you would do."

A long silence ensued, broken only by the water lapping against the pillars beneath the dock.

"When was he born?"

Joanna stared at him, confused.

"What time was he born? How much time do we have?"

"Oh." She glanced at the sun dipping lower in the sky. "Around four thirty, so not much. Don't … don't look so sad. If this works, I'll be back next year. I mean … if you want my company."

"That's very brave of you, Joanna." Peter looked across the water. "This morning the notion of enjoying your company for a single year seemed like such a short time. Now it sounds unbearably lengthy, waiting a year for your return. And to make matters worse, I'm not at all sure you'll succeed."

"I made it once. Why couldn't I do it again? Peter, I don't know what it is about us." Her words tumbled into his chest. "Reincarnation, some link, maybe just our common grief, but we're connected somehow. Don't you feel it? You're not Martin, and yet—" She tapped her chest. "You're in here. You know what I mean?"

Peter gave her a half-hearted laugh. "Not at all." Her brow narrowed and he raised a hand. "Ah ah. Don't misunderstand me. I feel the same connection, but I fail to see how it can transcend time. It is still," he sighed, "quite beyond my comprehension."

Joey eyed him carefully. The simplicity of his reply tore at her heart. He'd been candid with her from the beginning. He'd taken her claim as far as his logic would allow. But, not having traveled her path—even now, even after the mayor's death—he couldn't really accept the concept. She scanned the dock, hoping for inspiration. There had to be a way to make him understand.

"Fideism," she said firmly. "You're devout in your faith, aren't you? You believe in God."

"Yes."

"Why?"

Peter shrugged. "Calling it into question never occurred to me."

She laughed, hugging him. "My God, you're logical. Well, I'm here, flesh and blood, right? You've seen me, but you still don't quite believe in my origins. As for God, you've never seen him at all, and yet you believe in his existence."

"So ...."

"So, I'm asking you to apply a little less logic and a little more faith to our situation. When I landed here I thought it was a fluke, but maybe there is some kind of faith involved in all this. I mean, my jump today is a leap of faith, pure and simple. I have to believe there's some merit in it, because today is Michael's birthday." The wind picked up, cool and insistent. "Hey, when did you and Victoria get married?"

"December 28th."

Joey shivered, eyes on the lake. "And when was William born?"

"January 5th. What are you thinking?"

She ticked the numbers off on her fingers, silent at first, finding volume toward the end.

"... six, seven, eight. Whoa! Get this. Your wedding date is exactly eight days before William's birthday; so is mine. We married on October 21st and Michael was born on the 29th." She squeezed his arm. "You should try this, Peter. I mean it would be cold, but I'd be at the other end with dry clothes, motor running, heat on full blast. You could do this."

"Are you suggesting I—"

"Take a leap of faith. Yes! What do you say?"

"Joanna, I've told you before, I'm not a man who goes to extremes."

"Asking you to build a time machine—that's going to extremes. Asking you to jump into a lake is merely eccentric, by comparison. If I'm right you'll get to see my Chicago. If I'm wrong, you'll just get cold and wet." Her excitement over the possibility clouded her vision. Completely missing his doubtful expression, she forged ahead.

"You'll have to enlist Car's help." She smiled to herself. "If you succeed, maybe we can find out who we really are to each other." Her expression wilted as she finally read his face.

"What?"

He said nothing.

Joey took a slow breath. Peter would never make the attempt. She understood. It hurt, but she understood.

"Look, don't … don't feel bad. I guess I just got ahead of myself." She pulled away and shifted to her knees, one hand on each of Peter's shoulders, staring directly into his coffee brown eyes. The wind brushed through his hair and she smoothed it back, resting her hand at the base of his neck.

"Don't beat yourself up over this. If I make it home today, I will try to come back next year. I just thought if you didn't want to wait so long you could … you know." She cupped his face in her hands. "I do understand, Peter. It's a lot to ask. I didn't mean to put you on the spot."

Peter watched her, measuring the sincerity in her voice. She did understand. He touched her cheek, probably for the last time. She was as kind as she was beautiful. His feelings for her were strong, but in exactly what way? Was this love? He didn't know, but decided to find out in the few remaining minutes they shared.

She glanced at the reddening sun. "It's getting late. If I'm going to jump, I'd better do it now." She moved to stand, but Peter put his arm around her waist and held fast.

"Come on, Peter. Don't make this any harder than it already is."

"You're not going—" He held up a hand to quiet the protest he knew was coming, "—without a proper goodbye." He kissed her generously, intimately, begging her to stay.

She felt a delicious twist in her stomach and responded with a hunger that surprised her. *All that could be with him.* All the times she'd thought about what he might be to her; she needed to know right now—in this kiss—because there might never be another chance to find out. That sense of finality fueled her passion. Soon she was leaning into him, climbing onto his lap, forcing him down on the dock.

Peter let her overpower him, reveling in the strength her passion unleashed. He wanted her to take what he offered, to understand what she risked losing. Unwilling to break the kiss, he spoke with his hands. In deep velvet tones they slipped under her sweater, and whispered into the small of her back, the ridge of her spine, the silk of her skin. She shuddered at his touch, matching it with her lips, reaching his tongue, his chin, and the small dip at the base of his neck. Peter finally found his voice as she delighted him there.

"Don't go." He rasped his plea. "Please, don't go."

His voice.

His beautiful fathomless voice. So sad now, so desperate.

She stopped. Anything further would only be recalled in pain. The realization sapped her of her strength and she slumped on top of him.

It was time to go. She rolled away, rose to her knees and looked at him. His eyes were closed, familiar fist at his lips, holding back his despair.

"I'll be back, Peter. You can bank on it." She moved his hand and gave him one last, playful kiss. "And, believe me, we're going to finish this little discussion when I return."

She stood and reached for him. "Come on."

He accepted her hand and scrambled to his feet. With a firm grip she tugged, leading him closer to the edge of the dock. He stood behind her and she glanced back, the front of her running shoes peeking out over the water.

"Here goes." She faced the water and moved to step off.

No.

He couldn't release her hand, couldn't bring himself to let her go. His grip tightened as he tried to pull her back from the edge.

She anticipated his move and ducked underneath his arm. Building on the momentum of the swing, she leaned back and continued in a wide arc, throwing her weight out over the water, one foot on the dock, her hand twisting in Peter's grasp. It hurt, but she didn't let the pain stop her. Either he was going to let go or he was coming in the water with her.

The dodge he half-expected, but the arc over the lake surprised him. Because he couldn't bear to see her go—or perhaps because he simply had to see for himself—Peter held on. They tumbled together, headlong into Lake Michigan. He caught her eye as they fell. She seemed surprised, even pleased. He adjusted his grip as, hands clasped, they reached the water.

For Joey it was cold, but expected. She was prepared to sink to the depths of it, but she felt Peter struggling. He fought the water, instinctively seeking air. Within seconds, he started kicking toward the surface. His grip on her hand strong, pulling her up with him.

Peter knew the lake would be cold, but this! This was like a stab wound, only he was the knife, warm and human, and the lake was liquid metal. He plunged, razor sharp, into the body of icy water, slashing through in a vague attempt to keep her. The lake surrounded him in a deadly cold embrace. His first thought was of William, locked in this chilling fluid steel until Joanna had set him free. The image shook him to the core. He needed to escape this frigid wound. With one hand tight on Joanna's he kicked hard toward the surface.

Strangely, Joey didn't fight. She wanted to stay, wanted him. A very distinct part of her was happy. She had tested her theory. She could live with the consequences. Although it would be infinitely harder to do this again, she would come back on her anniversary. Secure in her decision, if she had access to air she would have sighed contentedly.

In seconds the water was clear enough to see her face. After only one tug, Joanna had given in. One look told him she wanted to stay. She accepted her fate. When he reached the air above, Peter would offer a silent prayer to the Almighty and draw a grateful breath of relief.

Their combined weight had taken them reasonably deep. They were still a few feet from the surface when Joey felt her grip begin to alter. Startled by the sudden change she looked at Peter. His expression was vivid, and just as frightened as she. Her grip on his hand deepened, boring into his skin, his muscle, reaching bone, not stopping.

As they rose together Peter glimpsed random images of the year ahead with her. He blinked only once, but when he opened his eyes she was already fading. He saw her fear, felt her hold loosen in the same instant that his hand sank beyond her flesh, past soft tissue, diffusing bone. In an instant she disappeared altogether.

He was fading before her. Too soon he was indistinguishable from the water surrounding them. In a flash her hand closed in on itself. She was alone, close to the surface, and when she broke through she knew she would be home.

Peter burst through the water gasping for air. Desperate to find her, he went under again. He kicked hard, reached out into the dark water, but he knew the search was in vain. Joanna had been right about the mayor. She had been right about everything. As hard as it was to grasp, he had seen it with his own eyes. Joanna had found her way home. Peter broke the surface a second time. Laden with fatigue brought on by defeat, he made his way to the ladder.

Joey broke the surface to a cacophony of modernity. She lingered in the water, yearning to go back down, back to Peter. But somehow she knew that door was closed and it was pointless to try and open it, not until next year. With a heavy heart, she swam to the ladder.

Peter climbed to the top, oblivious to the cold, indifferent to the air he so recently craved. Coco stood a few feet from him. She snorted a greeting as he approached. He rubbed his hand along her flank, pulled the lap robe from the saddle and covered himself. Stepping back to the edge of the dock, he surveyed the lake. He had never asked her about the distance to her home. He hoped it wasn't far. She would be soaking wet. She would be cold.

A few empty cars populated the dock, and a couple of people milled around in the distance. No one had noticed her. Joey slipped out of her sweater, wrapped it around the dock rope and twisted the excess water from it. It wasn't as cold here, but it would be soon if she didn't start moving. Still, she stared out at the lake, considering what might have been, wondering if Peter would dive in on his anniversary.

As the sun cast its last red streaks across the edge of the sky, Peter watched the water turn black, sealing the entry she had stumbled through only days ago. She wanted him to come forward in time. Had he released her hand while on the dock, he never would have considered the idea. But he had gone down with her, felt her melt in his grasp, seen her fade away.

Joey didn't think he would try. She would wish for it in the weeks ahead, will him—if she could—to make the attempt. In her mind she could see him at the edge of the dock, eyes uncertain, a familiar fist at his lips. She shook her head. It wasn't like him to indulge in something so foreign to his beliefs. Still, she had often misjudged his thoughts in the past week.

Peter still considered himself a man who didn't go to extremes, *but did what he'd just experienced constitute an extreme?* It was well outside the bounds of normalcy, but it was, after all, just a dip in the lake. He saw the value in Joanna's perspective, and tried to picture himself breaching the ladder to find her at the top, dressed in some ridiculous, ill-fitting clothing that made her happy. He mounted Coco, gathered the lap robe around him and started home. Sitting straight in the saddle, Peter smiled. He would come back on his anniversary. He knew it.

The wind kicked up and Joey began jogging along the pier. She quickened her pace and smiled. Soon she would be at her mother's, collecting Michael. Just before she turned the corner, Joey looked back at Lake Michigan. She didn't know if Peter would come, but on December 28th she knew she would be here, waiting for him.

A Note to the Reader

First, thanks for taking a crack at this book. I really hope you enjoyed it. Merrow is my first novel. For those of you interested in knowing what becomes of Joey and Peter, there is a sequel in the works. I've included a sneak peek at the end of this book.

Second, I'd like to ask you a favor. I would really appreciate a review on Amazon. I'm not looking for a quick-click five stars; I am asking for your honest opinion of the book. Tell me what you liked about it, and—more importantly—tell me what you didn't like. Both are helpful, but the latter will make me a better writer.

Third, if, by chance, you really loved it, can you mention Merrow on whatever social media you use? I stumble around on Twitter and Facebook—and I'd be happy to friend you or follow you—but I am a timid user at best. So, any mention from tech savvy friends of the novel would be most appreciated.

Thanks again for reading, for reviewing, and for passing on the word.

Best regards,
Claire O. Fahey

Acknowledgments

I'll begin where I started: The Optional Book Club in Austin, Texas. Special thanks to Sam Bond, founder of the club, and a fellow writer who challenged me to keep going. To Tracy Hill, Stephanie Hudnall, and Holly Quinn, who slogged through the first draft: You guys got the worst of it, as did my in-laws, Dick and Betty Fahey. Thanks to all of you.

This book evolved from a passionate mess to a reasonable story thanks to my colleagues at The Next Big Writer (www. thenextbigwriter.com). If you are a fledgling author and in need of critical eyes, this place can help. Special thanks to everyone who managed a chapter or two, and to all who went the distance. They are:

Bisi Adjapon, Sandy Anderson, Dennis Bailey, Maggie Banks, Sara Basrai, Tess Black, Nathan B. Childs, Lucy Crowe, John L. DeBoer, Jeni Decker, Nancy DeMarco, Scott Eberhart, Ann Everett, Matthew Hance, Larry Holcombe, Andrew Hubbard, David Hunter, IMAwriter, Jackson James, C.E. Jones, R.M. Keegan, Doralynn Kennedy, Jim Knight, Linda Lee, Rose Mandan, Phyl Manning, Rebecca Mitchell-Dhillon, Sharon Morgan, Doug Moore, Paul Negri, Pamlajj, Donald Phillips, Odin Roark, Wendy Squire, Susan Stec, Beth Stevens, Linda Ulleseit, Patti Yeager, and last but not least, Ocean and Tracy

Zhang who were the first to review me at TNBW. This book wouldn't be here without your help.

In California I was fortunate to have help fine-tuning the book thanks to the following people: Judy Alexander, Rachel August, Barbara Brooks, Katherine Couture, Pam Day, Carin Elam, Alison Finch, Ivy Franaszek, Dora Futterman, Mary Glenn, LaRene Kidd, Cathy Kupper, Patricia Mah, Denise Monday, Kate O'Connor, Mary Frances O'Connor, Margaret Peterson, Kelsey Peterson, Debbie O'Brien, Alex Riley, Marie Stapleton, Debra Turner, Leslie Wong, and Beth Zoeller.

Last, and most important, you wouldn't be reading this if I didn't have the support of my husband, Kevin, and my children, Brennan and Barrett.

Thanks to all of you.
COF

A sneak peek at
The Skin of a Selkie

Peter Hastings wanted only two things before he died—a breath of air, and one last look at Joanna Fagan. Death awaited him. He knew it the second he hit the water. Submerged and freezing in the icy lake, death seemed inevitable.

Joanna.

He concentrated on the woman who compelled him to this destiny, the woman who, even now, was more mystery than material to him. Only six weeks ago she had begged him to dive into Lake Michigan on his anniversary and follow her into the future. Unwilling to let her go he had jumped in the water with her, and the distinct nature of her departure convinced him that the lake was, indeed, the only route back to her.

He'd been under only a few seconds, but his lungs clamored for air, his mind for a return to normalcy. Movement was nearly impossible. The frigid lake chewed the life from his extremities and stole the heat from his body. If he tried to straighten his fingers he was sure they would snap like dry tinder. The cold water pressed hard against his temples, making them ache, and it felt as if his blood was coagulating in his veins. With more effort than he'd ever expended in his life, Peter forced his legs to move, kicking toward the surface, desperate for breath.

He broke through with a gasp he instantly regretted. The evening air was its own form of ice, and it slashed down his windpipe, saber sharp and unrelenting. Shards of air cut his lungs and remained there, adding weight to his failing resolve. He clutched his chest and stopped kicking. Death could have him. It was certainly preferable to this circle of hell.

"Peter!"

Joanna called from somewhere nearby, her voice low and lovely. He looked up to the dock, hoping to catch sight of her before the lake reclaimed him. He could die happy with her image as a farewell.

Someone grabbed his arm.

"Peter, stay with me! I'm here."

He glanced at the black hand holding him aloft. His eyes traveled up a black arm, reaching a black chest and neck. There was a face. Joanna's? Hard to tell, only a small circle of human flesh protruded from a mound of sleek wet black.

"Peter! It's me. Joey."

"G-g-good God!" He tried to pull from her animal grasp, teeth chattering so hard they threatened to shatter. "You are a m-m-m-merrow!"

"Hang on! We've got to get you out of here."

She dove underwater and slipped something around his waist. He heard a muffled click and found himself facing a thick chain, attached to the device he now wore.

Joanna, encased in what must be her sea skin, emerged. She turned toward the ladder shouting, "Dallas, he's hooked. Pull him up."

"Keep your hands right here." She curled his fingers over each side of the harness. "Hold tight."

Peter heard a mechanical whirring and felt himself rising from the water. Joanna swam to the steps as he was lifted into the air. It was hard to imagine her as anything but a mythical creature, her black limbs scaling the ladder with remarkable agility. She stood on the pier and held him steady as he was lowered to the ground.

"Oh my God, Dallas, he's frozen. Quick, get him to the truck!"

Agile hands unhooked the harness, grabbed him from under the shoulders, and dragged him past an imposing machine. A sign on the side proclaimed COSBY TOWING, MOWING AND MISCELLANEOUS SERVICES.

Another mechanical cart came into view. The next thing Peter knew he was being forced through an opening at one end. A large Negro loomed over him. Insistent black hands tugged at his clothes, and he tried to bat them away.

"Chill, Aquaman, or you gon' die."

"Get his pants Dal." He watched as Joanna used one black hand to peel the sea skin from another. White human hands reached for his shirt. "Peter, don't fight him. We need to get you out of these wet clothes."

She removed her hood and raked blue-white fingers through her wet hair. Despite his frozen state Peter managed a smile, pleased to see her return to her human form.

Man that was freezing—even in a wetsuit! Here let me get that."

Familiar hands reached him and his outer clothes were fast replaced with warm blankets.

"You still want I should drive?"

"Do you mind? Is Nash okay with the tow truck?"

"Gnaw Bone? He was born in that tow truck."

"God, I hate when you call him that. Let's move."

The opening was lowered and latched and Peter felt Joanna hug him through the blankets. From the front he heard the Negro announce, "Okay, now. We gon' vacate. You down, Aquaman?"

Before the words were out, the machine began to move.

"He's good Dal. You were awesome! That towing winch was perfect." Her confident brown eyes returned to him. "The hard part's over, Peter. We're headed home."

"Who … who is that Negro?"

An admonishing finger met his lips.

Sushh. It's African American and his name is Dallas Cosby." Joanna released a triumphant grin. "I met him through Hull House. I help out there now."

About the Author

Claire O'Connor Fahey is a native of southern Indiana, and holds a Bachelor's Degree in English Literature from Indiana University. She currently resides in Northern California, with her husband, Kevin and their two children. This is her first novel.

Discover more information about Claire at:
www.madisonready.com

Resources

Internet:

http://historyrat.wordpress.com/2013/01/13/
    lighting-the-1893-worlds-fair-the-race-to-light-the-world/
http://www.alchemyofbones.com/stories/dunning.htm
http://americanhistory.si.edu/collections/search/object/
    nmah_1341886

Print:

Dedmon, Emmett. *Fabulous Chicago*. New York NY: Random House, 1953.

Kogan, Herman and Wendt, Lloyd. *Give the Lady What She Wants! The Story of Marshall Field & Company*. South Bend IN: Marshall Field & Company, 1952.

Lowe, David. *Lost Chicago*. New York NY: American Legacy Press, 1985.

Miller, Donald. *City of the Century: The Epic of Chicago and the Making of America*. New York NY: Simon & Schuster; Reprint edition, 1997.

Video:

EXPO—Magic of the White City, Inecom Entertainment Company, 2005. DVD.